Reunion
Beach

PATTI CALLAHAN

ELIN HILDERBRAND

ADRIANA TRIGIANI

MARY ALICE MONROE

CASSANDRA KING CONROY

MARY NORRIS

JACQUELINE BOUVIER LEE

GERVAIS HAGERTY

MARJORY WENTWORTH

NATHALIE DUPREE

Reunion Beach

Stories Inspired by

DOROTHEA BENTON FRANK

PREFACE BY CARRIE FERON
FOREWORD BY PETER FRANK
INTRODUCTION BY VICTORIA BENTON FRANK
AFTERWORD BY WILLIAM FRANK

WILLIAM MORROW
An Imprint of HarperCollinsPublishers

This is for the fans of Dorothea Benton Frank.
She loved and appreciated every one of you.

CONTENTS

A Letter from the Editor

Carrie Feron

Dear Readers—

In the summer of 2018, a year prior to her death, Dorothea Benton Frank attended her fifty-year high school reunion in Charleston, South Carolina. The event brought back a lot of her memories of high school—rivalries and cliques, as well as long friendships—and Dottie (as I called her) decided her next book, scheduled for 2020, would center on a similar event. Dottie called the book *Reunion Beach*. The twist was that each of the various characters would resemble a South Carolina bird—most would be raptors, or birds of prey. She was smitten with the idea and could not wait to get started, although at the time she was still working on *Queen Bee*.

Dottie was simultaneously the most professional and most seat-of-the-pants author I ever edited. Though she always knew what she would write, and exactly which bookstores she would visit to meet her fans a year in advance, she never actually finished the manuscripts until late winter/early spring of the year of publication. I spent many February and March weeks in South Carolina, editing pages as she wrote them, and somehow the books came out in May. The fifteen years of editing her books was filled with fun: we would hole up in her house on Sullivan's Island, eat a lot of great South Carolina food at local restaurants, walk the beach, and celebrate Saint Patrick's Day on the main street. Often we would have our hair done for dinner and get manicures and pedicures. Dottie was always elegant. Plus there was usually an adventure at hand when Dottie was around. Did the golf cart once die on the only deserted street on the island? Yes. Did a nanny wreck her employer's minivan by plowing into and totaling Dottie's parked car while we were working on edits in the house? Yes. Did our boat once get stuck in the pluff mud? Of course. Did we once surprise a book club that was reading her book? Yes, indeed. Plus Dottie ended up helping make the appetizers. Did we make major changes to the manuscripts at the very last minute—we did. The year she wrote *All Summer Long* (spoiler alert), the husband originally died at the end of the novel, but I convinced her he was too fine a character to suffer that fate and the ending became a dream sequence. So I guess one year I even saved a Lowcountry life. Every book made its publication date. But most of all we had a lot of fun, and I fell in love with South Carolina.

Editors are usually the cheerleaders and first fans of a novel. But just as favorite books become "friends," authors with whom editors work become friends as well. In the spring of 2019 Dottie went on book tour as always for *Queen Bee,* but was overwhelmed with exhaustion. I believe her favorite thing about writing her books was her May "perspiration tour" of the South and meeting fans, and even though tired she soldiered on. On July 4 she called me with her dire diagnosis, and on September 2, 2019, my friend was gone. Dottie's husband, Peter, was generous enough to let me look through her office computer and memory stick as well as the papers on her desk, but there was no evidence that *Reunion Beach* was anything but a fabulous idea. There were no notes on the story line.

Luckily her creative writer friends were inspired by the title *Reunion Beach* and have joined together with stories, essays, poems, and memories in tribute to Dorothea Benton Frank's love of the Lowcountry and for the books she never had the opportunity to write.

In closing, I will tell you that Dottie loved to give advice, so I thought I should include two of her greatest hits here:

1. If you are choosing between two pairs of shoes, pick the red ones.
2. Remember to sparkle.

Sparkle on, fans of Dorothea Benton Frank. Please enjoy *Reunion Beach*.

> *Carrie Feron,*
> Editor

Peter's Speech at the Celebration of Life for Dottie Frank

Thank you for coming to celebrate the fantastic life of Dottie Frank. She touched millions of people's lives through her bestselling novels. Dottie was larger than life and a force of nature. As we all know, whatever she put her mind to, she made a great success.

From building a women's sportswear company, sitting on educational and art boards, raising money for many causes—some of which many of you were involved in—working on the New Jersey State Council of the Arts, writing twenty *New York Times* bestselling novels to receiving three honorary doctorate degrees.

Dottie had amazing energy, wisdom, and an irreverent wit. She was incredibly generous and brought joy and laughter to everyone she met. Dottie made a difference. The world is a better place for her having been here.

She was beautiful and glamorous. And, man, she sure could throw a party.

Dottie was a wonderful mother, a great friend, and a phenomenal wife and lover.

She made our family's lives fun, exciting, and meaningful, she taught me so much about being selfless and the power of happiness.

We had a wonderful, passionate marriage that I am so thankful for. I would take thirty-nine years with Dottie before I would take one hundred years with anyone else. SP—I will miss you so much.

Let's all toast Dottie!

[To Dottie!]

Introduction

Victoria Benton Frank

Dorothea Benton Frank was Dottie to the world, to her friends, and to her family, but to me she was always Momma. Momma believed in magic. She was the ultimate magician whenever there was none to be found. She wove it through her stories, planted it in her garden, made it in her food, and made the impossible seem possible in any way she could.

We all knew that she was an incredible storyteller, but I would always joke that she was just writing the truth and calling it fiction. My momma had a fantastic life. We all miss her, because, well, it just isn't as much fun without her, but whenever I get sad, I think about what a riot of a life she lived, and how everything she touched was better because she made it so, and even though she is gone, her lessons, which she so carefully taught me, are carrying me through. Not just the fun ones like the "Three F's: food, fashion, and family." Or that pink always makes you look pretty, hair is fifty percent of your looks, or when in doubt buy red over black. I hope one day to plant the seeds of Dot's garden in my own children. Making them also believe in magic.

Birthdays in our life were national holidays. Hers especially. One of Dot's rules was "The three-gift minimum." Something had to smell good, something had to feel good, and something had to sparkle. You were not allowed to give a gift to someone that had a plug attached to it, or something that would benefit yourself. It had to be something the person would never buy for themselves, and bonus points were given if it thrilled them. Momma loved to thrill.

When I was four years old, I was obsessed with *The Little Mermaid.* So naturally, Momma turned herself inside out to turn our sunroom into an underwater escape. She hired local actors to put on a live performance of *The Little Mermaid,* and as goodie bags, she gave everyone a *Little Mermaid*–themed fishbowl with two live goldfish. Meanwhile, most of the fish died within a week, and Dot took a few phone calls from upset parents.

When I was five, it was *The Wizard of Oz.* So she bought a sewing machine and made me an exact copy of Dorothy's dress, and with a hot glue gun pasted bright red sequins all over a pair of Mary Janes, giving her permanent scars all along her arms. The same actors came over and performed, and the sunroom was then transformed into the Emerald City. She got on all fours and hand-sponged a yellow brick road for me on mural paper. Nothing was impossible, and everything was fantastic.

Belonging to my mother wasn't just a privilege for reasons obvious to everyone; what she did that I miss the most is that she made me feel like we were a secret team against the world and the rules didn't apply to us. She never told me to be quiet, instead encouraged me to laugh as hard and loud as possible. She wanted me to question things. She allowed me to read anything I wanted at any age. Movies were limited, but not books. I read *Valley of the Dolls* at twelve years old. She sat me down and gave me the honest answer to all of my questions. I remember asking her why people did drugs, and her response was perfect: "Because they make you feel good, but they will ruin your life." As a result, I never did any drugs.

In high school I transferred my junior year to a public school and didn't have any friends. The mean girls ignored me and so my mom pulled up in her navy blue Mercedes-Benz and picked me up every day and took me to lunch so I didn't have to be alone. I was never sad about those silly girls, I was happy to spend the time with my mom. Once I finally did make friends, we would all go over to my house to have lunch with her anyways. Everyone wanted to be around her.

In college, I never went on any spring break trips with my sorority sisters or friends, I went somewhere with her. Some of my best memories are from those trips. I was so lucky to be her friend and her daughter. I spent the entire two weeks laughing.

As I got older, got married, and had children, our relationship changed. She sat me down and said, "Victoria, you're a writer. I know this in my bones. Stop cooking, stop working in boutiques, write your story, or I will." So I started to write. I would send her what I was working on, hoping she'd lend her expertise, and she would always just say, "Keep going." She encouraged me to be anything I wanted, but she wanted me to see the wonderful world she got to see by being a storyteller.

I was lucky enough to go on a book tour with her twice. We had so much fun we couldn't believe we were getting paid to be together! I got to see her in her groove. Talking to packed theaters, libraries, schools, bookstores where the masses would come to hear her talk. If you have ever seen my mom speak, then you know it was a little like stand-up comedy, but then she would open her heart and read a passage from one of the books she had written, and it was like looking into her soul. She connected with her readers because she wasn't afraid to go deep. She could make you laugh and cry and also give you something to think about. Her stories were sad and heartwarming but they were also funny. Humor, my momma always taught me, is the sharpest tool in one's toolbox. You can say anything, if you make them laugh.

Maybe that's what I miss the most, making her laugh. Every single day we talked . . . usually a few times . . . and emailed, texted, etc. I would try to make her laugh. Whenever I did it was like hearing a love song. Her laughter was approval. She would say, "Oh, Victoria, you're so crazy. I love you girl" and my day would be made.

I MISS MY FRIEND. I miss my soul mate. I miss the moon to my tide. I was lost at first, but then I remembered she gave me everything I needed to dig deeper, to try harder, and to never forget to create magic. She gave me hope, and faith in myself and my ability to go on. I am not lost. I am very grounded. My children will always know her, she will never be forgotten. My wonderful, magical Momma.

Right before she got sick, she attended her high school reunion, and was going to write a book about her memories, her friendships, and the women she knew when they were girls. Instead, now we women, her friends and fellow storytellers, have all come together in a reunion, to write about my momma, and how she created inspirational magic in their lives. I hope you read these memories and stories inspired by the great and wonderful Dorothea Benton Frank. If there was one thing my mom inspired and encouraged it was the power of women coming together, and especially to share stories.

Reunion Beach

Bridesmaids

PATTI CALLAHAN

1

The Answer

Lachlan was waiting for an answer. Beatrice's answer.

And she didn't have one.

The lemon-light of the restaurant's overhead chandeliers fell onto the linen-covered tablecloth in shaded patterns, imitating branches of a naked tree. Beatrice stared at that pattern because she couldn't look Lachlan in the eye, her mind scrambling for the right words.

As if there were right words.

"Beatrice." Lachlan said her name softly, and she finally lifted her gaze to his. "Are you here?"

"I am. I just don't know what to say."

"It's simple," he said.

"And complicated," she said.

They, by all rights, looked exactly like who they were: a middle-aged and quite beautiful couple in love at a fine restaurant—the Olde Pink House on Abercorn in the heart of Savannah, Georgia. Soft music played in the background from a piano player in the far corner by the fireplace. Lachlan, in his fifties, silver at his temple with tortoiseshell glasses reflecting the candles. Beatrice, with her thick chestnut hair tied in a low bun at the nape of her neck, her hands clasped in her lap.

"It's not *that* complicated," he said, his voice tightening. "It's a yes or a no. Really, that's all it is."

She held his gaze; his beautiful gaze she had come to love so much—the green eyes rimmed in blue, almond shaped with thick black eyelashes; usually gentle and teasing at the same time. But now serious.

He was right; it wasn't that complicated.

For the second time within a single minute, he lifted the blue velvet box for her to see. It was open and inside rested a two-carat solitaire round diamond surrounded by sapphires, her birthstone. Lachlan didn't miss a beat. He never had and probably never would. He loved her as deeply as she could dare ask. And she loved him. His shoulders a shelf for her to rest upon; his laugh a symphony, and his voice deep enough to make people turn when he spoke. Yet he wasn't a pushover—this ask, for the second time, was as good as his heart exposed.

But marriage? My God. Not again. The first had lasted fifteen years; years that Beatrice had believed were true and real, but that marriage had been over for ten years now. Why would she do *that* again?

"Will you, Beatrice, marry me? Yes or no."

Other patrons of the candlelit restaurant were beginning to stare, whisper quietly, maybe prepare to clap in an outburst when she assented.

How easy it would be to say yes. But the word stuck in her throat, or somewhere even deeper than her throat for that matter. She leaned across the table and placed her hand over the box, shut it, and held his hand under hers. Annoyance rose like smoke—why did he have to do this in public where it would now shame them both? But she wouldn't show irritation; he was trying to be romantic.

"Lachlan, I don't want to say no. It's the wrong answer. But I can't say yes either. I don't know why. I beg you to understand."

"I think I understand." He stood and his face burned red with embarrassment. She wanted to fix it for him, to say yes and get it over with, to lessen his despair.

He turned and walked out of the restaurant, deliberately, with wide strides, his long legs taking him to the door within seconds. He was a proud man, and there was no way he would sit there in humiliation—he'd left his full champagne glass on the table, yet had taken the velvet box, tucked it in his pocket. The hushed voices around Beatrice rose; they sounded to her like buzzing cicadas on a summer night—if cicadas could be judgmental and appalled, that is.

Beatrice sat still and quiet, trying to catch her breath while the crème brûlée turned soggy where she'd stuck her fork in it right before Lachlan had slipped the box from his coat jacket. She took a long sip of her champagne he'd ordered (that should have been a hint; he only orders wine, and red at that) and sat back to catch her breath.

What the hell was wrong with her?

Why would the word "yes" not rise to her tongue? There were many reasons, she knew. A good marriage gone bad. Or to quote Dorothy Parker, she'd put all her eggs in one bastard, in a marriage she'd thought was good but turned out to be a sham. She'd come to terms with that years ago. She'd wept on a stranger's couch in therapy and had eventually found her way through the pain and the lies and the deceit. It'd been ten years; a decade since her marriage to Tom had ended. He could not be the reason she didn't want to marry again. He couldn't hurt her anymore. She wouldn't allow it.

She'd found her way. She'd built a life handcrafted of her own making. But the truth was this: saying no to Lachlan might mean she would lose him. And she loved him. She loved their life together. He had his house and she had hers only two blocks away in downtown Savannah where the cobblestone streets echoed with their two hundred years, where the gas lanterns flickered at night, and the jeweled emerald park squares with their statues and monuments allowed reprieve. From Lachlan's small roof patio, past the steeple of the Cathedral of St. John the Baptist, they could spy the

Savannah River, its gray and silver body moving toward Tybee Island while they watched the sunset and talked about their day.

She was an artist who painted birds—birds in habitat, birds in flight, birds in their nests, birds in cages—anything she could imagine. And he taught art history at Savannah College of Art and Design, where he was by far the most beloved professor on staff: Dr. Lachlan Harrison was an icon. His distinguished face and sardonic smile adorned the cover of the SCAD magazine's student manual. He emanated comfort, reassurance, and bravado all at the same time, and they used his image.

Beatrice and Lachlan loved Savannah. They loved each other. They loved art. What was the full stop?

She didn't know. Honest to God, she didn't.

It was a dilemma faced all over the world, she also knew. Was marriage even worth the trouble? She wasn't special in the face of these larger questions, but so many others seemed to be able to jump in, to make bold decisions one way or the other.

Beatrice picked up the champagne bottle and didn't bother pouring it into her glass; she was the only one drinking. She sipped from the bottle and sat back, heard the laughter at a nearby table. Yes, she was a joke. But she hadn't paid the bill yet; she couldn't just up and leave like Lachlan had.

The waitress, she'd said her name was Sandy or Candy, arrived with the bill and a look of pity. Or was it disgust for sending away the handsome man? Sandy or Candy dropped the black padded envelope on the table and walked away. Beatrice pulled out a credit card and slipped it into the envelope before partaking of more champagne.

There'd been a day, many days, in fact, when she'd dreamed of marriage proposals. In the late eighties, in college, it had consumed hours of conversations with her roommates. Who would get married when? Who first? Who last? How many bridesmaids?

How ridiculous. As if being chosen as a wife and having a wedding was the epitome of life. As if being proposed to verified one's worth.

Ha!

Beatrice made a noise halfway between a laugh and a choke, and a young man with a very big beard two tables over gave her a look as if she'd just burped. Beatrice smiled at him, and he turned away.

As the piano player set off on his next song about tomato tomahto, potato potahto, Beatrice smiled. It'd been a favorite of her college roommates, a song that celebrated their differences. Her much-loved roommates, who'd eventually been her bridesmaids.

All four of them had been with her the first time: her first wedding, when she'd been so sure, when she'd walked down the aisle in the Cathedral of St. John the Baptist in Savannah wearing all white, head to toe white, flowing about her like meringue. Her bridesmaids had worn blue velvet dresses with a bow at the back. Her wedding dress had shoulder pads as large and sparkly as a character from *Dynasty*, and she'd stood in front of Tom and solemnly said, "Till death do us part."

Well, they'd parted and there hadn't been any death.

Why would she promise the same thing again?

The waitress returned and took the credit card, her mood not improving one iota. The champagne was doing its job and Beatrice sat back and listened to the music, now onto the truly demoralizing "Let's Stay Together"—*Whatever you want to do is alright with me.*

She didn't believe in those kinds of sentiments anymore. Yes, at her first wedding she'd believed in all of it, she'd believed in love and in staying together for good and all. She'd made vows while four other women stood by her side.

Dani.

Rose.

Victoria.

Daisy.

She closed her eyes and could see each of them in their ridiculous blue velvet that she'd made them wear. "It's such a beautiful dress; you can wear it again," she'd told them. They never did. No one ever did. It was, in the end, a common bride mantra that was another sham. So much of what they'd been fed about romance and love, about proposals and marriage, had been a sham. Harry and Sally didn't help. Neither did *Cinderella* or *My Fair Lady*. They'd all believed, though. And waited for Harry or Prince Charming or Henry Higgins.

She laughed and opened her eyes. The patrons were now openly staring at her. The crazy woman drinking straight out of the bottle with a man who had just walked away with a sparkling, most likely custom designed, diamond ring. A great Savannah story for the tourists, she thought, as she took back her credit card, signed the bill, drank the last of the champagne, and headed for the door. She stopped, a bit wobbly, at the piano and smiled at the man with the obvious black toupee playing, and dropped a twenty in his tip jar before she walked out the door and into the hot July evening air.

Gas lanterns flickered above the cobblestone streets, and a cloudy sky muted the moon's soft crescent glow into a smudge of a yellow smile. Beatrice ambled across the street to Reynolds Square, taking a seat on a wooden bench next to a homeless woman eating something greasy from a paper bag, her feet propped on a grocery cart full of coats, bags, and hidden treasures.

Beatrice sat quietly for a while, and when she stood to leave, she felt the champagne moving too quickly through her blood. In a few steps, she realized she was absolutely drunk, and she would pay for it in the morning. But for now, the bubbles dulled the pain of seeing Lachlan walk away. She lifted her cell from her purse and texted him.

Please don't be mad. I love you so.

. . . .

The dots of his return typing . . . and then nothing. Beatrice paced the square and then teetered the few blocks up Drayton Street and left on East Broughton toward home, as the ground of her life shifted beneath her. The best thing to do was go home, go to bed, and face it all in the morning. No good came of drunk texting. That was for damn sure.

Unless of course . . . it was to her flock.

She stopped in her tracks, realizing she'd passed her home. Had she been headed to Lachlan's? Probably, but with an unsteady quick turn that almost sent her to the brick sidewalk, she took the few steps back to her home. She reached her address and lifted her gaze to the front door, a blue door set against gray brick in a much loved one-hundred-fifty-year-old house: a classical Georgian with a hip roof and square façade; four stairs leading to the covered entry-way stoop.

The old and warm house was the only thing she'd wanted from Tom when he'd left her. Fumbling for her key, she climbed the stairs, unlocked the door, and entered the foyer where she'd dropped bags of art supplies that morning, and not yet carried them to her studio at the back of the house. She stepped over the mess and down the limestone-floored hallway to the kitchen, where her laptop sat on the white marble countertop.

She flipped it open and then grabbed a coconut water from the refrigerator, guzzled it before sitting down. Only four of the flock remained: Victoria, Rose, Daisy, and Beatrice. Dani had succumbed to a horrible and quick leukemia that took her life and stole light from their little group. They all missed her, and in an odd habit, her email remained on the group list. Who knows who ever saw it, if anyone. Although it'd been twelve years, not one of them could delete it.

She opened the group list called "The Flock" and wrote.

My birds, I need you. Lachlan asked me for the second time, and again I was as speechless as the time Victoria took that bet and streaked across the quad. I must give him an answer and I need you. You were there the first time I married and . . . Here's my proposal:

Beatrice looked up to the glass-fronted cabinets of her kitchen and then out the window to the dark backyard where an oak tree's uplighting cast shadows on the Spanish moss. The sharp tang of oil paint lingered in the air where she'd left open a tube of paint. She looked back down at the flickering cursor.

A proposal to her from Lachlan.

What was her proposal to the Flock?

It was right there on the front of her fizzing mind.

Could they take a trip together? The others might help Beatrice figure this out. Like in the old days.

She started typing again.

I will rent us a beach house for three days next weekend in South Carolina. My treat. I will buy your plane tickets, rent a house, and provide all the food and wine. Please abandon all responsibilities and commitments and say yes or lose me forever. Pegasus.

If they agreed, Victoria would come from Atlanta, Daisy from Charleston, and Rose from North Carolina. No one lived so far away they couldn't get to Savannah. There were no good excuses, as far as buzzed Beatrice was concerned.

2

The Other Proposal

Morning sun burst through the window like swords of light. Beatrice squeezed her eyes against its glare as the memory of last night rushed in with nausea.

Oh, dear God, the champagne. The walk home. The text to Lachlan that he hadn't answered. She rolled over for a glass of water on her bedside table and found only a pile of books. Guzzling down almost an entire champagne bottle had been a terrible mistake. She cursed her choices as she shuffled to the kitchen and made the coffee, gulped water, and downed two Advils.

Surely Lachlan had answered her by now. He'd never ignored her completely. Not once. Their disagreements came with quiet words and long talks; their hurt feelings dealt with head-on and kindly. Sure, there had been times when they'd both needed a breather: when her girls met him and acted rude; when his son inferred that she would never add up to his dead mother; when the art show took her on the road and she stayed longer than she'd said because Tucson was so beautiful. And more. But nothing that ever had him ignoring her; nothing that felt like this, like her heart was twisted in knots.

The first proposal had been casual, not even a proposal at all if you wanted to diminish it, which she did. Two years before, while they cooked Sunday brunch at his place, he'd said, "I think it's time to get married, combine our lives. Your daughters are off and my son is happy and . . ."

She'd looked at him with a confused expression. Yes, she loved him. Yes, she'd thought about marriage—who doesn't? But, no, she didn't want a logical ask. This kind of proposal that assumed that life circumstances and not the heart determined marriage? That's not what she wanted. Not at all. And that's what she'd told him.

"Okay. That's fair," he'd said. And then he'd dropped to one knee, using a kitchen chair to help him as his battered knees from an old marathon-running habit kept him from being limber. "I love you with all my heart and soul, Beatrice McLain. Let's get married. Please." He'd grinned up at her.

She'd held out her hand. "Lachlan, get up."

He stood. "Well?"

"We aren't ready," she'd told him, her heart pounding against her ribs like a ten-pound hammer.

"You aren't ready," he'd said and turned back to the eggs he'd been casually whisking only moments before.

They'd talked about it all morning—why she wasn't ready (she wasn't sure); how her reticence had nothing to do with how much she loved him; how their life was just as beautiful as any she'd dreamed of, so why change it? They were more of a couple than any married couple they knew.

In the end, every last bite of their breakfast gone, and the dishes done, he'd told her. "When I ask again . . . if I ask again . . . I won't ask a third time." The words weren't said cruelly, but with a soft kiss and the truth.

She'd be ready next time; she was quite sure.

She'd nodded in agreement and stood, walked over and slipped onto his lap, kissed him. "I love you. I hear you." His kiss tasted like cheese and croissant, soft and buttery. They barely made it to his bed to make love, stumbling down the hallway and sloughing off their lounging Sunday sweatpants and T-shirts. They didn't leave that bed until late afternoon and only for a long walk to the river.

Beatrice now stood in her kitchen and remembered it all with a flush of love. He would not ask again. That was clear.

So she would ask him. That's what she'd do.

She searched the kitchen for her reading glasses, found them by the computer, and picked up her phone.

Nothing. He hadn't answered.

She'd really done it this time. There she stood: hungover and ridiculous in her too-sunny unrelentingly cheery kitchen because the word "yes" wouldn't fall out of her mouth.

She would seek him out today and tell him yes. Fear or no fear, this was absurd. She loved him. Her reluctance to marry had nothing to do with him, and everything to do with the past, like echoes that wouldn't end.

It was almost inconceivable that he hadn't answered: to be ignored was an insult worse than rudeness. To be ignored—she'd felt it before: the memory of Tom's abandonment that crawled across her skin in a cold sweat.

She poured her coffee and sat at the kitchen counter, and noticed she'd kept her laptop open to email where there blinked messages from the flock. She wondered, briefly, if something was wrong. Her heart hammered—the last time there were that many messages in a string had been twelve years ago when they'd lost their beloved Dani, their oystercatcher, their fragile and beautiful friend.

Her heart picked up a pace and she opened the string to make sure nothing was wrong.

I can do it!, wrote Rose.

I'm in. Booking flights now, wrote Victoria.

Absolutely. See you in four days in Savannah. Details?, wrote Daisy.

Then a barrage of questions—what time should they fly in?

Daisy would drive—she was only two hours away. Had a house been found and booked?

It took Beatrice longer than it should have to stare at these messages, to wonder where they were all going and why.

Then the memory of her own proposal came rushing back. She'd invited and promised her "birds" a beach reunion, a house where they'd all meet; an all-expenses paid trip to help her decide whether to marry Lachlan.

What had she been thinking? Or more rightly, what had the champagne been thinking?

She didn't need them to help her decide. She would go tell Lachlan "yes" today, and this trip would be null and void. She didn't have that kind of cash and that kind of time. She didn't . . . and yet it seemed she did.

Beatrice ran her hands through her hair and groaned. She'd done it this time. To back out would not only be embarrassing but also rude, and with Rose now alone in what had once been a very full nest, she had been the first to say yes. And Victoria booked her flights?

After pacing the house, putting away the art supplies in the hallway, and eating a plate full of scrambled eggs, Beatrice called Lachlan. This was fixable with a single call to him. She could reimburse Victoria her ticket, and they'd all laugh about her drunken night wandering Savannah. She'd tell Lachlan about it, too, about her drunk emailing with the flock.

He'd laugh softly and kiss her.

But he didn't laugh. He didn't even answer the phone.

She knew he wasn't teaching on Wednesdays and there was no reason to ignore her phone call, except to ignore her.

What the hell now? Okay, play a bit of the ridiculous hard-to-catch and then make it up to him? Send a gift? Show up? She had no idea what to do next. She paced; she checked her phone; she cleaned up the kitchen, and then she decided.

She would go to him. She would show up on his doorstep only a few blocks away and he would never turn her away. Even the thought of him turning her away made her dizzy. She pressed her hand over her stomach and waited for it to calm. She'd felt this blooming panic and fear before—when?

Ah, when after fifteen years of marriage Tom had told her he didn't love her anymore. When Tom had told her and their two—then twelve- and fourteen-year-old—daughters, Paige and Emma, he needed to find his way in a new world. When she'd stood on the front steps of a shambled life and couldn't catch her breath. When Tom had packed his suitcases and emptied half the bank account. That's when.

That was the last time Beatrice had felt this way. But this time it was her fault. She had no one else to blame, and she would fix it. She rushed to the shower, thinking of Harry's line to Sally: "When you realize you want to spend the rest of your life with somebody, you want the rest of your life to start as soon as possible."

After Beatrice uttered her own version of that line on Lachlan's doorstep, then it would be off to bed to make love. They would, for the rest of their lives, talk about that moment.

She turned on the water and held her hand under the spray while waiting for it to heat up. An hour later, spruced up, she surveyed her image with care: yes, all was a bit haggard but okay. Her dark hair had been blown to its smooth shoulder-length swing, the blotches from a sleepless night covered with makeup and her blue eyes slightly less cloudy with the addition of coffee. She wasn't the hottest fifty-five-year-old in the city, but that was never her goal. Hot had never been in her bag of tricks; classy and artsy yes, smokin' no.

The hangover a dull memory that lived on as an ache behind her eyes, and as cotton padding around her thoughts, she picked up her cell to see that Lachlan had left a voicemail.

She smiled. Not so bad, after all. Really. She'd made the entire situation worse in her mind.

She clicked on the voicemail, putting it on speaker to listen while she brushed her eyelashes with mascara.

"Bea." He paused. Beatrice smiled at herself in the mirror, at his soft voice using her nickname.

"I think we need to be apart for a while, take a breath. I don't know what that means, really, but do not call or come over right now. Thank you."

Silence.

My God. He had never before used that tone of voice. That kind of finality.

Beatrice's stomach lurched and she bent over, heaving her breakfast, her hangover, and her heartache into the sink of her immaculate white bathroom.

"No!" she said out loud, and it came out more like a moan than a word. A breath or two as she leaned over her sink, and the nausea passed. She grabbed her toothbrush and squirted double the amount of toothpaste as it ran over the side of the brush; she scrubbed the taste of bile from her mouth and then set to cleaning her mess.

Respect his request? What the hell did that mean?

When the bathroom looked as pristine as it had before her emotions took over, and the towels had been dropped into the washing machine, Beatrice rushed to the kitchen and did the only thing her fizzled mind allowed her to do—finish what she'd started with her birds. This group of women who'd started as college roommates, become bridesmaids, and continued to be her dearest friends had once chosen a bird to represent each one of them. From that moment forward they'd become "the flock." Now they would gather and reconnect—it had been too long, almost two years—chat about the old days and help Beatrice figure out her new days. She would draw birds, reconnect with her flock. Yes. This was a very good plan.

She'd take a big breath before making another huge decision that might upend her life.

3

The House

Mid-afternoon sun heated the July air to its steaming point as Beatrice stepped off the small motorboat to gaze up at the cedar-shake one-story cottage that sat on the edge of the coastal river, or if Beatrice was completely honest, almost *in* the water. The waves would lap the house right up within the next generation. But she didn't need the house to last longer than the weekend, so it wasn't her concern.

The Lowcountry island called Oak Island was deserted save for this one house; the instructions on the rental site had been clear and easy: bring everything you need. No stores. No grocery. A getaway on a spit of land just off Savannah with its own beach, dock, and four bedrooms. Cushioned on the east side by the ocean and the west side by the coastal river, it was both safe and comfortable for a weekend getaway.

Perfect, right?

Beatrice stood by herself at the end of the splintered and sun-washed dock and looked around, cataloging her surroundings. Not fancy. Rose would love it; Victoria would complain about the lack of spa and services; Daisy would find the good in it and immediately start the party. Or these were Beatrice's best guesses, based on decades of friendship.

So far, it seemed everything Beatrice had imagined when she

read "getaway" under the house photo posted online. From Savannah, it was only a ten-minute boat ride (very bumpy, very wet boat ride with a kind man about her age if she had to guess, with a baseball cap covering curly hair) to the flat low island a mile wide, a mile long. Making the journey ahead of the rest of the flock, she now observed the overgrown island's scrubby palmetto trees, Spanish moss hanging like the hair of some giant, and a crescent moon–shaped beach just the right size for four women and a cooler.

The squeaky call of what Beatrice identified as the brown-headed nuthatch and the musical trill of a sparrow combined in symphony with the *slap-slap* of water on the wobbly dock. The pure sounds were enough to slightly soothe her aching heart. Wait, that wasn't right. Beatrice realized it wasn't just her heart that ached—all of her from ego to pride hurt like hell. But her birds would make it right; she was quite sure.

The boat's captain carried all of Beatrice's food and drink supplies, along with her overnight bag that held nothing but sundresses, hats, and bathing suits. And then there were two bags with enough chips and salsa to kill them all if they chose to die that way.

Beatrice approached the house when the screen door slammed and the man's flip-flops hit the earth as he jumped from the top step, denting the soft sandy ground, and held out his hand. "Guess it's near time for a proper introduction. I'm Red." He removed his sunglasses, and there were soft brown eyes with a rim of green. His smile reached his ears and folded his sun-crinkled skin to his eyes; his chin bore an *S*-shaped scar and half of his thick left eyebrow was missing.

"Beatrice." She took a few steps toward him onto the soft grass and held out her hand and shook his calloused one. "Nice to formally meet you." She spread her hands out. "This is a downright wonderful place for our secluded weekend. Please tell the owner thank you for renting it to us."

"You just thanked him." Red's smile teased.

"Oh." Beatrice paused. "I thought his name was Ned Blackstone. I sent the money to—"

"Well," Red said in a Southern accent so melodic it sounded false. "That's my first name. Red's the second, given to me by my little brother, and the one that stuck."

"Well, Red and Ned, thank you. The other women will be at the dock in—" Beatrice yanked her cell phone from her sundress pocket and noticed there were zero bars. No service. None. But the clock worked. "—an hour."

"I'll be there to ferry them over," he said. "Would you like some help unpacking and getting settled?"

"I think I've got it. And it's awkward—you know, me unpacking in your house while you're here. I think maybe—"

He nodded. "I get it. I'll make myself scarce while you do what needs gettin' done."

Beatrice stared at him for a moment. Everything he did was so slow, not in an unintelligent way, but how a man moves when he knows the entire world is at his fingertips and things will just be fine, totally fine. Meanwhile, Beatrice was switching from one foot to the next, bounding around like she had somewhere to be and something to do, like save the world from the next nuclear bomb.

"Is there . . . I guess I should have asked before I rented it . . . is there internet or a way to get cell service out here?" She held up her phone as proof of nothing.

"Depends which provider you've got. Some can get service at the very tip of the island if they hold the phone tilted toward Savannah. Seems there's a black spot here. Not that I mind so much."

"But how do you run a business if you don't have . . . ?"

He smiled and walked away, heading toward the back of the house, doing what he called making himself scarce, she assumed. Well, that would explain the day or two it had taken him to answer her first email.

Once inside, she glanced around. It didn't look much like the photos, or more precisely it looked like the photos but sparser and more decrepit.

A man lived here. Alone. That much was obvious. The kitchen, spartan and small, had a two-burner electric stove. The kitchen counters were a 1970s green linoleum, and cracked at that. Okay, so she'd gotten what she paid for. The kitchen was open to the living room, or really one room to be precise, with a stone fireplace that was piled high with burned logs and ash, in the middle of summer.

Beatrice took a few steps toward the back hallway to find the four bedrooms spread out like they'd been added one at a time. She opened each bedroom door and chose what appeared to be Red's with the king-size bed. She shivered. This was weird; sleeping in a stranger's bed. What had she been thinking? The room was simple: a king iron bed; a dresser; and one end table made of a log stump. A clock on the wall and a small bookshelf completely crammed with paperbacks that tumbled and spilled onto the floor. They were stacked three, six, and ten deep.

She lifted her phone to check her texts and emails, only to be reminded that there was no service. It was like flipping a light switch when you knew the electricity was out. What if Lachlan texted? What if he changed his mind and came for her and thought she was ignoring him? What if one of her daughters had an emergency? What if . . .

She sank to the bed and dropped her head in her hands.

Keep moving.

Do not cry.

All is well.

These mantras did no good for her heart but kept her mind in some kind of civilized order.

Beatrice stood from the bed and made her way back to the kitchen, pulled her hair into a ponytail, and began unpacking the groceries. By the time she'd organized everything, her mind racing to the ends of her life and back, Red still hadn't returned with the others.

She unpacked her art folio and slipped out the sketchpad and pastels, placing them on the top of the crammed bookshelf. She removed the drawings she'd made for each friend, wrapped in plastic casing with a white silk bow wrapped around each, their name and bird in calligraphy. This was how she'd spent her time between Lachlan's rebuttal and the day she left for this island—drawing her friends their totem birds.

She walked to the first bedroom and placed the swan for Daisy on a single bed in a small bedroom one door down, and Beatrice's thoughts meandered back to the day when they'd each chosen a bird, their own bird that represented their personality and choices. It had been a game back then, a playful amusement at Beatrice's graduation art show thirty years ago. With over fifty paintings of her bird paintings hanging on the white walls of the SCAD student center, gooseneck lamps illuminating each bird she'd painted, they had stood shoulder to shoulder and picked their favorites.

Dani, both adorable and fragile in a flowered yellow dress, a fashion major wearing one of her own fantastic creations, chose the oystercatcher with its distinctive red beak.

Beatrice had told her, "It's a little shorebird who always needs to be in large groups, so that works quite well for you."

Dani had smiled. "I don't care about all that. I just think it's cute."

Now Beatrice looked for oystercatchers wherever she went, and because of that she often found them and smiled thinking of her friend who had passed twelve years ago.

Victoria, on the other hand, had chosen the brightest and most beautiful of the paintings. Victoria, with her blond chignon and looking like she'd stepped out of a 1940s poster, had lit a menthol cigarette and leaned toward Beatrice, who took the cig from her and took a long draw. Victoria had pointed, "I want this one!" She'd pointed at a bird in flight, its blue feathers intricate and vibrant.

"A Blue Bird of Paradise." Beatrice's words had laughter hidden in them. "Of course you would pick that. They are the most extravagantly beautiful birds in the world. And polygamous to boot."

The roommates had laughed, and Victoria, who now ran her own art gallery in Atlanta, had grinned like she'd just won the bird-choosing contest.

Then Daisy had stepped forward and said, "This is so fun, like pulling a Tarot card."

Daisy, the most ethereal of them, who'd been at SCAD on an equestrian scholarship and whose study of architecture kept her wandering the streets of Savannah day and night, sketching and dissecting the preserved buildings. She'd stood in front of Beatrice in bell bottom jeans and a five-year-old Billy Joel concert T-shirt and said, "I want one of those." She'd pointed at a murmur of starlings.

"Those are starlings," Beatrice had told her. "They're known for speed, agility, and staying in groups, called murmurs, for keeping each other safe."

"Exactly then." Daisy had smiled. "That's my bird."

"You merely want to be safe?" Victoria had asked, stepping next to her, smoke curling from her nostrils. "Please tell me you want more than that."

"Oh, way more," Daisy had said. "But I like how they stick together. You know, like we do. We're a murmur. And the speed and agility. I like that a lot."

"Yes." Beatrice had hugged her friend and turned to Rose. "Your turn."

"So much pressure." Rose had grinned and bit the end of her thumbnail just as she always did when she felt pressure but wanted to pretend she didn't.

"The swan." She'd pointed at a painting of two swans sitting serenely on the water of a pond. "They mate for life just like Chip and I are about to do. And they are so serene and beautiful and peaceful."

Victoria had groaned. "Oh God, here we go. Chip. Chip. Chip. Enough of the Chip. Can't you even choose a bird about *you* without it being about *him*?"

The roommates had tried to stifle their laughter, but it was impossible. Victoria could not have been more right: enough of Chip. He was Rose's childhood sweetheart, and she was going to marry him come hell or highwater. She didn't date. She didn't flirt. She phoned Chip, off at college in North Carolina, every day.

"You think he's waiting for you?" Victoria had scoffed. "He's at Duke, where the sorority and the—"

Rose had stepped up and placed her hands on her hips. "Just because you don't know how to love just one person doesn't mean—"

Beatrice had held up her hands. "Victoria. This is my art show. Let it go, please!"

Victoria had rolled her eyes and turned to Beatrice. "Okay, you choose now."

"Well honestly, they're all mine," she'd told them.

"Pick one." Victoria would not let it go.

"This." Beatrice had walked up to stand in front of the premier painting in the show, one so recently done that the stinging aroma of oil paint could be detected still. Pegasus rose from a forest floor, a black horse with wings wide and in motion.

"But that's not a real bird," Dani, always so logical, as if life were one of her dress patterns and they could sew it together with the right directions, had said.

"It has wings," Beatrice had said. "That's good enough."

Dani had shaken her head, curls bouncing. "But Pegasus flew too high. Right into the sun so her wings melted."

Rose, their resident expert on all things mythic (which, now and then, could get annoying, to be honest), had laughed. "No! That was

Icarus who flew too close to the sun. Pegasus is divine, and the child of the sea god Poseidon, so Beatrice as Pegasus makes sense, right? Here in Savannah at the edge of the water and . . ." She paused for dramatic effect. "And then she became a constellation. Pegasus represents inspiration. Our Beatrice is a winged divine creature, an inspiration, and a constellation. It fits perfectly."

Beatrice had laughed and taken a bow. "Thank you very much!"

Victoria had spread her arms out as if she would take flight. "So the rest of us get to be mortal birds?"

And with that they had each walked into the night with their totems, ones they had carried with them ever since.

Now back in the kitchen, Beatrice smiled at the thought of her friends each finding their bird on their bed.

Daisy the starling who had gone off and built her own murmur: a family of four now dwindled to three with the death of her husband.

Victoria the Blue Bird of Paradise who'd never married but loved her art studio like a spouse.

Rose the swan who did marry Chip Chip Chip and have four children to burrow in their nest.

They could not, Beatrice had thought more than a hundred times, chosen better birds than they did. True totems.

And she, their Pegasus, still and always trying to find a way to fly with every bird she painted.

Waiting impatiently now, Beatrice ambled outside and took a leisurely lap around the edges of the scrubby island, just enough to get her bearings. It was otherworldly: the birdsong, the sunlight falling through thick Spanish moss and landing on the ground in abstract patterns, a silence she was so unaccustomed to that she almost checked to see if she had her noise-canceling headphones in her ears. She spied a gray heron standing as still as time on the edge of the marsh; a painted bunting making a dive for the pine branch, and a sandpiper that skittered across the sandy shore poking the ground in manic thrusts of its little beak. She scanned for an oyster-catcher, her sign that Dani was near in spirit, but not yet . . .

Just the thought of her friends brought her closer to calm. She gazed up at the live oak branches, which were gnarled and twisted by time and wind, at the driftwood piled like bleached bones on the sand at water's edge. She imagined that this was what the land was like a hundred years ago. It had changed all the while with tides and storms, yet at the same time it remained itself.

At the edge of the oyster-crusted east side of the island, she sat on a fallen log. She knew better than to walk over oyster beds; it was the exact right way to slice her feet to smithereens with the shell's edges sharp as razors. She thought about Red living here and what a stupid damn name Red was when Ned was perfectly fine.

What would the flock do for the next forty-eight hours? No spa. No shopping. No internet. No TV. Good Lord. Beatrice was accustomed to a day so full that she never, not once, finished anything on the to-do list that she scribbled every morning on her beautiful stationery. Looking about, she was thrilled that at the last minute she'd packed her sketchpad and pastels. She'd try and capture this mystical place, which was a lot better than doing what she had been doing the past four days: obsessing, ruminating, and crying.

A motorboat's hum interrupted her thoughts and she went jogging, her flip-flops slapping her heels, toward the dock, the dock that looked as if it might blow away in the next storm, to see Red arriving with her three best friends, their overnight bags piled like a stone cairn. They each held a hand over their hat. Victoria's voice rose above the rest; Beatrice would know it anywhere.

The women stepped out of the boat and onto the dock, laughter following, their exclamations overlapping. Beatrice's heart rose to each woman.

Rose, their swan, in her pink and green Lilly Pulitzer sundress and matching hat, her still-blond hair pulled behind in a low knot;

she was first off the boat and she ran toward Beatrice, almost trip-
ping in her strappy sandals. "This is so charming. So adorable. I'm
so happy to see you." She threw her arms around Beatrice and left a
hot pink lipstick mark on her cheek.

Victoria, in full makeup, a blue dress flapping behind her just
like the wild Blue Bird of Paradise she had once chosen, made her
way toward Beatrice with a sway of her hips. "Dear God Almighty.
This looks dreamy." Her smile was huge, not wrinkling her face
and cheeks. Just enough plastic surgery to smooth the edges, not
enough to look done. That was always Victoria's goal. She kissed
Beatrice and then slipped her arm through Rose's as Daisy was still
gathering her bags.

Daisy, their little starling, stood at the end of the dock a few
yards away, slinging her backpack over her shoulder and taking in
the group of friends. She waved and hollered. "This is the absolute
best. Look at us, we'll live like the Swiss Family Robinson."

Red, behind her, laughed and picked up as many bags as he
could and followed Daisy down the dock. Daisy wore a bright red
sundress and feather earrings that brushed her shoulders. Her
red hair, now mostly silver and shoulder length, caught the breeze
and flew into her eyes just as she threw her arms around Beatrice.

"This is the most perfect thing in the world. All of us together
on a deserted island. The only thing missing is Dani."

They all nodded and stayed silent for a moment, thoughts of
Dani blowing past. Victoria wiped at her forehead. "So. The first
thing I need is a drink and to see what our Pegasus has gotten us
into now. What's inside? One can only guess by the absolute decrepit outside."

Beatrice laughed and shook her head. "Victoria, have you met
Red?" She nodded her head toward him and he nodded back.

"Of course."

"This is his house."

Victoria bit her bottom lip. "Sorry. Sometimes when I try to be funny, I'm an idiot. As the girls will well attest, I mean no harm."

Red smiled and carried the bags inside, saying not a word.

• • •

An hour later, each woman had chosen their room and reconvened in the kitchen. Red stood at the far end of the living room as quiet and still as a coatrack until he asked. "Anything else you ladies need?"

"No." Beatrice looked to her friends. "Anything ya'll need before he takes off?"

"Not that I can think of just now," Victoria said with a coy flirt that made the other women groan.

"How will we get ahold of you if we need anything?" Beatrice asked. "No service."

"I'll be right outside."

"Excuse me?" Beatrice's eyebrows raised in a question.

"The shelter a hundred yards away." He waved his hand east. "There . . . I'll be there."

Beatrice took a step toward this tall man and then back toward the safety of her friends. "I don't understand. You rented us the island . . . and . . ."

"I rented you the house. You won't even know I'm here unless you come calling. I can promise you that. If you need anything, I'm here. If not, I'm as invisible as air." With those words, he exited the house and the screen door slammed back on its hinges with a pop.

"He's staying here?" Rose asked. "I can't tell Chip. He'd lose his mind if he thought I was on a desert island with a man."

Victoria rolled her long-eyelashed eyes and made a snorting sound. "It is good to know not much has changed. You can't go more than ten minutes without saying his name. Chip. Chip. Chip. God help us."

Beatrice popped Victoria's shoulder. "Let's play nice and stay focused. This weekend is about my drama."

Great smiles rose on their faces, and the sound of the wind breezing through the palmetto leaves whispered through the screen door.

Daisy, so quiet until now, broke into the conversation. "I like that Red is here. Makes me feel . . . safer."

"Our little starling, the more people, the better for you." Victoria hugged Daisy with one arm and drew her close.

Daisy smiled with the truth and looked to Beatrice. "Okay, Pegasus, tell us what we can do to help?"

Almost as one they moved the few steps toward the living room and plopped down on the couches and chairs to sit in a circle. A fresh breeze that smelled of burned firewood and dark mud wafted through. The far-off hum of a boat joined in the chorus.

"This is really nice," Victoria said and snuggled further into the plaid couch. "It feels like we are a million miles away instead of a ten-minute boat ride across the water. Now tell us what happened."

Beatrice took a breath and started from the beginning, taking sips of white wine in between breaths, staying her tears, keeping her mind occupied with telling the story in a linear way so they would understand, so they would help her know what to do.

"So now. I don't know what to do . . . or nothing I do will matter."

Rose chimed in first. "Do you love him? Like Swan-mate-for-life love him?"

Victoria coughed out a laugh, her vodka and lemonade drink almost snorting from her nose. "I don't know what that even means. What are you talking about swan-love? For God's sake, Rose. Not everyone is Chip Chip Chip."

"I didn't even say his name," Rose protested. "You did. I just meant to ask if Beatrice loves Lachlan in a way that makes her want to stay with him for the rest of her life?"

Daisy, whose husband had unexpectantly died of an aneurysm

six years ago, was trying to navigate the dating scene now that her two girls were off at college, piped up. "Rose just means," she turned to Beatrice. "Do you love him *enough*?"

"That's the thing," Beatrice said leaning forward into her knees and into the question. "What's enough? When we were in college, all we imagined was finding the *right one*. The fairy tales, the movies, the plays, the books: everyone found their soul mate. For God's sake, we even went to a psychic to see who would find their star-twin first." Beatrice looked about the room at her friends. "Who was it?"

"Me," Victoria said with a laugh. "The one who never married; the one whose star-twin must have been confused and ended up in another galaxy."

Beatrice lifted her glass before taking another sip. "Exactly. Who is to know? So, there's no *real* way to know." She stood, began to pace the room. "Not a real way at all. I mean, I *knew* with Tom. I loved him so. Or thought I did. But now I know that I just wanted Tom to choose me. I wanted him. I wanted that life. I wanted to be safe and live in a nice house and have beautiful children, and damn, he was beautiful." She paused and her forehead wrinkled with the thought. "I think I loved him."

Victoria shook her head. "You can't *think* you love someone. That's not how it works."

"And you know because?" asked Rose, still smarting from the Chip-teasing.

Victoria stood, her blue caftan billowing out. "What the hell is that supposed to mean?"

"You've never . . . settled down. How do you know?"

"And that means I haven't loved?" She leaned closer to Rose. "You know what else a swan represents?"

"Just everlasting love."

"The swan maiden. Have you heard of that story? That myth? You're the writer. Don't you know?"

Rose shook her head, tears threatening in her eyes but her voice steady. "I'm the writer who doesn't write. And you're being mean. I forgot about that, how you can be mean."

"No, I'm not." Victoria sank again into the couch seats. "We're here for Beatrice, not for you to poke at the fact that I never got married. Maybe—in case you ever wondered about my life—maybe it's because the person I loved didn't love me. Or because I fell in love with the wrong person or . . . do you think I'm incapable of love? You and your adorable husband and four kids and suburban house. How could you know?"

Beatrice cleared her throat. "Birds. Seriously? This is about love. Not about comparing love."

"Comparing?" Daisy asked, laughter hidden in her voice. "*We've* never compared ourselves to each other, have we?"

Great laughter erupted.

Daisy exhaled. "Try dating with two college daughters visiting back and forth, and a dead husband whose pictures and ghost watch over everything you do."

"I wouldn't even try," Victoria said.

"Exactly. But I *am* trying."

Beatrice walked the few steps to the kitchen and opened a bag of chips, poured out the homemade salsa she'd bought at the farmer's market just yesterday into a bowl, and brought it to Red's coffee table covered in hunting and fishing magazines.

Victoria slipped her hand into her huge flowered bag and pulled out a small round speaker. She set it on the table and then used her phone to start some music—Van Morrison—softly singing about falling into the mystic. She turned it low while Rose leaned forward.

"Victoria, I want you to tell me the story of the swan maiden."

Victoria picked up a chip. "I don't think now is the best time." She paused and held her chip aloft, turning to Beatrice. "How did you feel when you met him? Let's start there."

Beatrice closed her eyes and fell backward into time. "We met at the art museum." She opened her eyes. "Of course it was the art museum. My paintings were part of an 'art and nature' exhibit. He was standing there in his faded jeans and gray sweater, his glasses on the edge of his nose, teaching a class. He was pointing at a Cézanne, the *Jas de Bouffan*—the study of trees—on loan from a museum in Paris, and talking in that deep voice about the history of impressionism and nature and . . ." Beatrice stopped, almost breathless and then, "I could not take my eyes off him, and when he turned to me and smiled, I felt as if I should hug him, as if I'd known him forever."

"My God," Rose said. "Are you making that up?"

"What?" Beatrice asked with an incredulous tone. "Make it up?"

"It's almost too romantic to be real."

Beatrice smiled, and in that smile hid the memory of the entire afternoon they'd spent together immediately after he let his class go early.

"It's real," she said.

"And after?"

"It has stayed just as real."

Victoria sighed. "So, if that's how it started—what's the last thing Lachlan said to you?"

"To not contact him. To give him space. To . . . I don't know really. I've listened to his message ten times. Twenty. And even his voice is different."

"Do you believe him?" Victoria bit into her chip.

"I don't really know." Beatrice glanced at her best friends. "That's the thing with heartbreak. You can't think straight. Or sleep straight. Or eat straight. I feel so upside down and inside out. What's true? What's false?" Beatrice paced the room, wandering from window to window as the light slowly turned from bright yellow to soft twilight. "I've loved Lachlan for so long, and we have such an amazing life together. I just didn't want anything to shift at all. I didn't want to topple things over. I didn't want to . . . change anything. We were happy."

"When did things change with Tom?" Rose asked quietly. "Maybe that's what you're afraid of."

"I never knew things changed with Tom until he announced things had changed. I never saw it coming."

Rose shook her head. "Are you sure? Or did you not *want* to see the changes?"

"What are you asking?" Setting her hand over her heart, Beatrice continued staring out the window.

Rose plowed ahead. "I'm wondering if change is what frightens you—not marrying Lachlan, not shifting things up because the last time things changed . . . they ended. That's all."

Beatrice set her forehead on the glass window, watching clouds move quickly across the sky as they headed toward night with the rest of the day. A flock of white ibis flew by and settled in an oak tree to the right of the window. What Rose had just said—Beatrice had thought about it a million times. Was there a moment when things had changed with Tom and she'd been too busy to notice?

She'd been shuttling carpool with her daughters from school to dance to softball; she'd been shuttling herself from the studio to art shows to social engagements. She'd thought of her family as a team. But it'd ended up being more like a company with a CEO and a secretary who could be easily fired and replaced. But had there been a singular moment when Beatrice had known it was coming off the tracks? No, she couldn't find it.

She turned back to her friends, who sat quietly eating the chips and salsa and watching her carefully, allowing space for her to answer. Her gaze passed over each and rested on Daisy, her starling, whose eyes wouldn't catch hers. "What is it, Daisy?"

Beatrice knew her friends better than she sometimes knew herself, and Daisy had something to say. "What do you mean?" Daisy looked up and tried to smile.

"You know what a starling group is called?" Beatrice asked.

"Yes," Daisy said. "Of course. A murmur."

"Which sounds to me like a secret. Spill it."

Daisy laughed, but the sound was more like a cough than a laugh and she again looked away. "I was just thinking that you might have noticed things were changing at Dani's memorial."

"Why would you say that?"

"Because Tom was so drunk and . . . distant at the event. And he flirted with everyone there like he was still in college and . . ."

Beatrice saw it in her mind's eye: a flash of the memorial at Dani's parents' house after the funeral. It had been a gathering of hundreds of people who had loved their fragile oystercatcher. She tried to remember Tom being there. After a heartbeat or two she recalled him in the far corner of the crowded living room talking to Daisy, his head bent low.

"Holy shit." Beatrice took a step toward Daisy. "He hit on you."

Daisy looked up, her face flaming. "Yes."

Victoria and Rose caught their breath in a quick inhale, and Beatrice drew closer. "You never told me."

"No. Because he was drunk, and I didn't think it was a big deal, and I told him to get lost and—"

The other two women made guttural noises and Rose shot up from the couch. "By hit on, what exactly do you mean?"

"He kissed me." Daisy cringed. "Or tried to anyway. And I pushed him away and told him to f off. Except I said the word." Again she tried to laugh and again nothing came out.

Beatrice felt outrage—not at Daisy but at Tom—pulsing through her body. "I hate to repeat myself—but you never told me?"

"There was no reason to tell you," said Daisy. "Things seemed fine and you were happy, and he was drunk."

"But see? That's the thing!" Beatrice clapped her hands together. "We weren't fine. And I wasn't happy. And he was about to leave me. Maybe if someone had told me, maybe it wouldn't have been such a shock."

"Yes, it would have been." Rose walked to Beatrice. "It would have been a shock whether Daisy told you about his drunken attempted kiss or not."

Victoria fluffed her bluebird caftan and spread out on the couch. "I think we might have nailed it here, Beatrice. I think you're scared of being blindsided. But if you've kept your eyes open with Lachlan, you won't be blindsided. There are never guarantees; sometimes you have to take a chance, but you kept your eyes shut with Tom, or at least you looked away. You didn't *want* to know."

Beatrice let that idea sink in. Maybe Victoria was right. "But I still don't understand the logic behind this. The fear is illogical. It grabs me exactly when I want to say yes. It sends my mind to static. But when I'm not with Lachlan, or think I've lost us, I miss him so badly I feel almost ill."

Rose made a small noise in the back of her throat. "I know that feeling."

"Even all these years later, you miss Chip like that?" Victoria asked.

Rose whirled her wine in her glass. "I don't know if that's it. It's more like . . . fear. Like if I'm not with him, it will all fall apart."

"Well, that's screwed up," Victoria said with a laugh. "Like you have to be there to keep it together?"

"Sort of . . . I don't know." Rose sat back. "This isn't about me. This is about Beatrice."

Daisy stood up and joined Beatrice at the window. "If you want my opinion. Which might not be worth a damn. I think that it's Sam, Jonah, and Annie's fault that we're all screwed up." She paused. "You know, *Sleepless in Seattle*."

"We know," the women chimed in unison.

Rose held up her hand. "Whoa! I'm not one bit screwed up."

The other three women laughed.

"What? You think I'm screwed up?" Rose pouted.

"We all are. Don't worry," Daisy said. "It's not just movies like *You've Got Mail*. And *My Fair Lady* and the movie with the guy playing the radio outside her window. It's *Cinderella* and it's *Snow White*. It's all the stories that show us that the man will save us and then life is grand, for good and all. Not one of those stories—not a one—showed what happens after Richard Gere marries Julia Roberts. Not one clued us in about what happens when the kids get the flu and the money is low and the husband asks the wife not to pursue her dreams or the best friend's husband tries to kiss you or the husband dies and leaves unpaid bills. Did they show us that? Oh, hell, no."

Her words seemed to have come in one long breath, in a single sentence, and the other women just stared at their quiet starling until she rubbed at her face. "Sorry 'bout that."

"Don't be sorry," Rose said. "It's true. Let's add *Jerry McGuire* where Tom Cruise says 'You complete me.' It goes on and on. Every Hallmark movie. Every romance novel. Life is so much different than that; it was always meant to be different than the stories and books, but we got confused. We thought our love stories were supposed to be just like the fairy tale."

Rose nodded. "As a creative writing major, every story I told was a love story. Everything . . . is a love story. It just depends how we want to tell it. I still believe that."

"Or we want to believe it," Victoria said.

"Whoa." Beatrice lifted her hands. "Can we back up about ten sentences? What do you mean the husband who didn't pay the bills?"

"Forget it." Daisy waved her hand and wine sloshed over the edges of the glass and onto Red's pine floors; she didn't notice.

"Oh, hell no," said Victoria. "We will not forget it. What . . ." and she paused, looked at each of the best friends as if they were huddled at two in the morning in the living room of their decrepit house at college, the ragged furniture covered in shared clothes and CDs and schoolbooks. "What happened?"

Daisy exhaled and slumped in on herself, her head bowed before she looked up and told them the truth. "It's been five years. I've paid them off. But yes, he left loads of debt. I went back to work teaching, and the girls went to in-state colleges and we've dug our way out. But I just meant . . . the happily ever after is rarely ever after. It's happy for the moment. Then life. Then some more happiness and then . . . you know . . . life. But that doesn't mean it was a bad marriage or I didn't love him. It's just never a storybook."

"Yes." Beatrice looked up to see that twilight had turned to dark; night had fallen on their conversation. Nature's sounds had changed from birdsong to frogs; the hum of boats rushing by had turned to the slap of water against the dock and the tinkle of oyster shells disturbed by the tide.

Beatrice looked to each woman. "I am so glad you're all here. I don't mean for this to turn into a love inquest. I just want to understand why I resisted Lachlan for so long. I mean, that has had serious consequences, and I don't get it. You three know me better than anyone in the world. Sometimes it takes someone else to show us who we are."

4

The Moon

The moon spread a wide swath of light across the water, a pathway so vivid it looked as if they could walk across it, find themselves on the far side of the earth on moonlight. Dinner of tomato soup and Beatrice's toasted homemade sourdough bread was over, and they'd made their way outside to the beach. A pale slip of sand was sandwiched between the wild grasses and the estuary's waves. The gray-brown sand of the Lowcountry with its rough feel beneath their bare feet was as familiar and comforting as their best memory. Victoria spread a striped blanket and they sat; the four of them sat side by side in silence as a sweet acrid smell floated by on a breeze, an aroma coming from the shack where Red resided.

Could he hear them?

Victoria lifted her face. "I know that smell."

Beatrice smiled. "If you lived anywhere near our house in 1986, you would know that aroma."

Daisy laughed and lay flat on the blanket, stared up at the dark sky. "Victoria, go get us some of that. I think we could all use a little—"

"Daisy!" Beatrice elbowed her friend. "I don't think getting pot from the landlord was in the contract, and honestly, I am horrified he's even here."

But Victoria was gone before they could blink another eye,

before another wave could crash onshore. "Be right back," she called over her shoulder.

They looked at each other in the moonlight and laughed, fell back on the blanket. "Our Bird of Paradise," Beatrice said. "God, I love her."

Daisy settled on her side, propping her cheek on her hand to face Beatrice. "And I love all of you. How lucky we are."

Silence spread across the night until, minutes later, Victoria came bounding back with a thin rolled joint in her hand. Each sat without a word and Daisy lit it, took a puff, and passed it down the row. Beatrice inhaled and held in the acrid smoke, feeling that old 1980s feeling of falling past her own anxiety and into a place that, for a moment, felt padded and soft. She handed the thin joint back down the line. "Even the taste of it brings back memories."

"Sure does." Rose took a long breath of fresh air. "Now, Victoria, tell me the swan maiden story. No more excuses."

Victoria shook her head. "No. Not now."

"When's better than now?"

"Well, you asked." Victoria stood and with the breeze her kimono flew open like wings. She stood beneath the full moon, hair wild about her, looking very much like the bewitched storyteller she was hoping to be. "In a time long ago, but not far away." She stopped and smiled at her friends. "There was a mythical creature called the swan maiden who could shapeshift from human to swan form when and how she pleased. But to be seen as human, she had to shed her swan feather skin and lay it aside. One night while swimming in the lake a man saw her: a beautiful swan maiden swimming naked in the water. He fell instantly and hopelessly in love. How could he possibly convince such a perfect creature to be his own? He came every night for many nights to watch her until finally he devised a plan. While she swam, he grabbed her feather skin, took it for his very own. When the maiden realized her feathers were gone, she begged him for them back, and he promised to give them back to her if she would marry him for a while, for just a little while, he told her. Bear him children and let him love her, and then she could have her feather skin back."

Rose let out a sound so close to a whimper that Beatrice moved closer to her. "You okay?"

"I am. Go on, Victoria. Go on. What happened next?"

Victoria turned to the moon. "The woman gave the man everything he wanted: a house, a home, love, and children. When the time came that the children were safe and on their own, she asked for her feather skin back. She was desperate to return to the lake, to the waterfalls and rivers of her true self. She wanted her swan skin and her feathers. But he refused. He broke his promise and she was forced to stay on land. She mourned her feathers for the rest of her remaining days—"

"Oh my God, Victoria," Daisy cried out. "Give it a better ending than that."

"*You* give it a better ending." Victoria turned around and shrugged. "That's the legend I know."

Rose stood up next to Victoria. "Here's how it should go: One day the swan maiden discovered her feather skin, hidden in a trunk in the attic. She slipped it on and ran to the river, dove into the waters, and was never seen again. Restored to her true self, she swam as far and as deep as she wanted. The End."

Victoria threw her arm over Rose's shoulder. "Yes. Infinitely better."

Beatrice sighed. "Yes, much better. You know, Lachlan has never, not once, asked me to be anyone other than who I am. He loves me. He sees me. I have never loved so much or felt so loved. It's like . . . being with all of you. He's never tried to take my feathers."

Victoria dropped her arm from Rose, took a few steps onto

shore before she sloughed off her kimono. Her bra and panties fell like dark shadows to the sand, and she walked into the water, slipping into the waves and floating on her back to stare at the starry sky. "Come in!" she called.

And they did, one after the other, slipping from their clothes into the warm water at ebb tide to float on their back and watch the stars get brighter and brighter, their fire burning holes through the dark sky.

5

The Next Day

When they awoke the next morning, gathered in the kitchen in their pjs over the coffeepot and sizzling eggs on Red's black cast-iron pan, the friends came out one by one holding their pastel-colored drawings. With hugs and exclamations about how beautiful each of their birds had turned out, they filled their coffee mugs and woke slowly.

"When did you start using pastels?" Daisy held her starling to the light. "It's extraordinary."

"Lachlan talked me into it about two years ago when I wanted to try a few new mediums . . . I've also been painting oil on wood. It's been fun to play with new ways to do things." Beatrice glanced about. "Where's Victoria?"

Daisy motioned down the hallway. "I'll go wake her. Sleepy-head is used to living on her own time and schedule." Daisy walked off and returned in seconds. "She's not there. Her bed hasn't even been slept in."

An alarm raced through Beatrice's heart; a reminder of the days when her daughters were in high school and she would check their beds in the morning, when she couldn't remember hearing the chime of the bell that signaled an opening door in the middle of the night, letting her know they'd come home.

Rose set her coffee mug on the counter. "Oh my God. Is she

okay? Should we call someone? Go search? What if she tried to
swim or . . . ?" Rose got up and went out the door.

"She's fine," Beatrice said. "I'd bet a million dollars she's with
Red."

"No way." Daisy shook her head. "Why do think that?"

"Because every time I was worried about my teenagers' empty
beds, believing they were dead, they had crashed at a friend's house
and . . . she's Victoria."

As if on signal, the screen door opened and Victoria in her
caftan swooped into the cabin. "Good morning, Sunshines," she
said, flouncing past them to the back of the house. "I'll be out soon.
Beach day, right?"

"Right," Beatrice called after her. "Beach day."

The hours passed with swims and naps and paperbacks held
up against the beating sun, and with laughter when someone shot
out an old memory or joke. Victoria disappeared for a few hours,
and no one worried. The day felt beautiful, hazy and slow. Beatrice
thought of Lachlan, but the pain had lessened since she'd arrived
here. That sword of loss would return, she knew. But for now, she
was so cotton padded with love that it would wait. They caught
up on their kids and their lives, on their jobs and the small talk of
facts. They laughed about taking pot from their landlord. Then chat
would fade, books would open, and soft sounds of sleep would arise.

After lunch, they sat around the pine picnic table, pine needles
stuck between the slats of the table and bench. "Sometimes," Rose
said, "when I look at my skin, or my arms, or catch myself in the
mirror I can't believe it's me. Inside I am not fifty-five. Inside I am
the same as I ever was, but outside . . ."

"All of us," said Daisy, who'd made her famous chicken salad
and sangria for lunch. "I'm stunned over and over. When one of
Sara's kids calls me Grandma. When I get the AARP card in the
mail, I am shocked again."

Victoria had just returned, and she twisted her fork in the salad, pushing it around more than eating it. "Beatrice, ten minutes ago we were at your senior project show, admiring your fantastic birds. We were headed into our lives."

"And now," said Beatrice, "already passing the middle of our lives, are we making any better decisions than we did then?"

"I hope so." Rose shrugged and settled back. "But how to know? Daisy, tell us all about the guy you've been . . . seeing? Is that the right word these days?"

"It's weird to date now. Hard to . . . give a word to. I mean, we aren't dating. But we are."

"So it's a booty call?" asked Victoria.

The rest of them ignored the question.

Beatrice propped her elbows on the picnic table. "Tell us about him."

"Well, it started oddly. On a bet really. During that totally surreal social isolation during the coronavirus last year, both my college girls were home with me and without my permission they made me a Bumble account as a widow."

"Bumble. What's that?" Rose asked with raised eyebrows. "Sounds like a society for beekeepers."

"No. It's a dating app but the women are in charge. Women make the first move. So Sara set up a profile for me and the first match was this guy who loved Chopin, the architecture of Frank Lloyd Wright, and the poetry of David Whyte. We started talking—well, texting—and two months later we met for coffee. He doesn't live in Charleston; he lives in Atlanta, so I only see him when he comes to town. He's a magazine writer—a nature writer, so he travels. Anyway, I'm enamored but definitely not in love. He'd like to be more serious but," Daisy shrugged. "I am nowhere near ready. But it's fun."

During Daisy's telling, Victoria drew closer to her along the picnic bench. "He sounds lovely. And . . ." She looked around the table. "Familiar."

"What does that mean?" Daisy pulled her hat's brim up to gaze at Victoria.

"What's his name?" Victoria asked.

"Charlie."

"Holy shit." Victoria stood up and laughed, her neck hinged backward as she lifted her face to the sky. "Are you kidding me?"

"No, why?"

"What's his last name? Please God, don't say Rogers."

Daisy removed her sunglasses and stared at Victoria. "Yes. Rogers. How the hell do you know that? Have you been in my phone?"

"No, I haven't been in your phone, but I have been in his bed. I've been sleeping with him."

"What the hell." Daisy flipped her hair behind her shoulders.

Beatrice pressed her lips together and then said, "This can't be true. You can't both be dating the same guy, right? It has to be two different people."

Victoria threw her hands in the air. "Nope. Same guy."

Daisy stood and then sank again. "Oh my God. I'm such an idiot." She looked up to Victoria. "How the hell am I supposed to compete with the likes of you?" She covered her face.

"Compete?" Victoria sat down and put her arm around Daisy. "Are you kidding? This guy is an obvious scumbag. He's been dating us both and telling us both he wants to get more serious. What is that about? If it's the both of us I guaran-damn-tee there's more."

Daisy looked up. "How did *you* meet him?"

"Same. Bumble."

"He's a Bumble stalker," Rose said. "And I don't even know what Bumble is. It sounds like a thing you drop in your bath or use to clean the toilet."

At that, the women dissolved into laughter, finally even Daisy. "I can't believe this. I believed him. He said he—"

Victoria interrupted. "Loved you to the depths of the sea and back."

"Exactly. Aghhhghg!" Daisy stood, picked up a rock, and threw it into a tree. "What an ass." She looked to Victoria. "Did you tell him you loved him back?"

Victoria shook her head. "No! I barely know him anywhere but the bed."

The friends laughed but then stifled it as Daisy's face fell with disappointment, biting her bottom lip. "I didn't either, so I guess there's some saving grace. But . . ." She shuddered. "We have been sleeping with the same man. I am horrified."

Beatrice took a long swig of her sangria and shook her head. "Maybe we should get together more often. Who knows what else we'd find out."

Victoria walked over to Daisy and lifted her cell phone. "A selfie of the two of us. We'll send it to him, and I don't think anything else will need to be said."

Daisy leaned into Victoria's shoulder, and Victoria snapped the photo. "When I have service, I'll send this beauty right off."

Daisy shook her head. "I think I need a little walk."

Rose nodded toward the shoreline. "There's not very far you can go. Walk in a circle?"

"True, but . . ." And off she went, disappearing around the corner only to appear less than thirty minutes later when they had all returned to their blanket and their books, to their quiet afternoon.

Daisy plopped down and Beatrice set down her sketchpad where she'd been drawing the horizon of scrubby brush across the water. "I'm sorry, friend."

"Well, that's what I get for falling for a guy whose life I know nothing about while I pretend we know each other because we texted for months and months. It's gross. I'm embarrassed of myself, but I get . . . lonely."

"We all do." Beatrice fell back on the blanket. "It's part of it, isn't it? Finding our way while finding if we can ever love again."

"Doesn't seem so worth it to me right now," Daisy said.

"It's worth it. It's always worth it," Beatrice said. "We try anyway. The odds are always against it working out, but there we go—"

"Coming from a woman who loves a good man." Daisy smiled sadly. "You're answering your own questions."

Beatrice wasn't quite so sure.

6

The Last Night

Their last night fell quiet with the thick aroma of pluff mud as they reconvened once more at the water's edge.

Victoria broke open an aloe leaf from a nearby shrub and rubbed the gooey insides on Daisy's sunburned shoulders while speaking to Beatrice. "What's most important for this gathering, for now, is this: Did we help you figure anything out, Bea? Our grand Pegasus, do you know how high you can fly?"

Beatrice dug her toes into the sand. "I know this love between all of us sustains me. Sometimes we have to be surrounded by something to be reminded of what it really truly is—love, I mean. I love Lachlan. He loves me. It's beautiful. That's all I know for now. When I get home, I will go to him and if he'll listen, I'll tell him I love him. I have and I will. Marriage, if it's important to him, is important to me. I've been selfish . . . and scared. But my fears have nothing to do with him and everything to do with the past. We carry these things, these burdens from the past, forward and hurt those who had nothing to do with it."

"Will he listen?" Daisy asked.

Beatrice allowed the question to sink in. "I don't know. He might be done with me and that would hurt. But I am still who I am. There's something inside I want to show to the world, and I was afraid that getting married again would keep me from finding it," Beatrice said. "Like your swan maiden, Victoria."

"Did Tom keep you from it when you were married?"

"Yes."

"Has Lachlan ever?"

"Not even once." Beatrice held up her hands as if in surrender. "Not even close. You know, when I chose Pegasus, I thought it was because she could fly, but it's because she's unafraid, she lifts herself up even as the world tells her to stay on the ground. Now . . . I know."

Daisy's voice came choked with emotion. "And the starling, me, always needing to be in a crowd, always needing approval, always needing someone around. I thought that the best thing in the world was having more and more people around, but it's kept me from flying, literally and figuratively. That murmur has kept me in a safe place. I don't know what that means yet, but I don't need to know. I fell for that idiot Bumble guy under the pretense that I need constant companionship." She turned to Victoria. "And you, our beautiful Bird of Paradise . . . where were you last night and parts of today? Flying on those fancy feathers?"

"The opposite." Victoria sat quietly, now wearing a simple shift of dark blue, her hair in a ponytail and her face free of makeup. "I've been talking to Red. I know you don't believe me—and I wouldn't either—but we've just been talking. It's true. He's been living out here and telling me about it, and I've been just listening. A simpler life . . ."

Rose laughed. "Right, Victoria."

Victoria shrugged, sat back on the towel. "I'm telling you the straight up truth, with a splash of vodka." She lifted her drink. "But still the truth."

Daisy sighed. "Why did we ever think men were the answer?"

Rose was quiet before she said, "Because sometimes they are?" But this time Beatrice heard it in her voice—she wasn't so sure anymore.

"No," Beatrice said. "They are never actually *the* answer, but they can be part of something greater in our life." Beatrice spoke slowly and quietly, wanting to find the truth that was slowly arriving in lessons from their bird icons. "Those movies—they were right in some ways: love is worth the chance. But after that—it's up to us. We have to keep our eyes open. We have to pursue our own true self. Sometimes love isn't what we thought. Sometimes it doesn't work out. Sometimes it shatters our hearts. But it is always worth the chance with a good man."

"Yes!" Rose stood up. "I have to tell you a story. All of you." She stood to face them, backlit by a moon more subtle than the night before, hidden behind the clouds. Only a week ago it had been half waning, when Lachlan had walked away from her, and now it sat bloated and full over them. "Victoria, when you told me about the swan maiden myth, I knew the truth. I chose that bird because of one reason, and that same bird has come to show me another truth. I chose a swan because it meant lifelong union, but in truth, I have given all my feathers to a man who does not deserve them. To a man who has wanted to take those feathers to stuff his own pillows and bed and comfort." She slammed her foot into the sand, then dug her toes below. She was quietly crying now. She coughed and spoke with firmness. "We have to get out of our own way, know what keeps us back, what our wishes are that we are putting onto them, or our fears that we place onto them. In college, we picked someone and then placed all our dreams on top of them, used our dreams to give these guys a Superman cape, never looking closely enough to see who they really were."

Daisy tilted her head toward Rose. "Is Chip . . . not . . . ?"

Rose shook her head. "He moved out two months ago claiming he had fallen in love with some woman he met on an airplane. An airplane! But he's come back, begging, telling me he was a fool and it was a huge mistake and he loves only me, forever. I believe him but . . . I don't."

"Oh, sweetie, and you didn't tell us because—"

"Because I was the one who put that Superman cape on him, and I didn't want any of you to know that my swan was an ugly duckling."

The four women huddled around each other, their heads bent and touching foreheads in a circle. The night settled upon Rose's words and they knew, each of them, that they had chosen the bird all those years ago that spoke to them even now in a way they'd never expected.

. . .

When they told the story later, the story about their last morning on the island, they couldn't agree on whose idea it had been to take the kayaks out on the coastal river side of the island. Victoria? She swears it wasn't. But Daisy and Rose swear it was. Beatrice believes it was Daisy, but either way, Daisy and Rose were in a double kayak, an orange one so battered it looked like it had been chewed up and spit out, while Beatrice and Victoria rowed in single blue kayaks that Red had dragged from under the house.

"Be careful," he'd hollered out before they left.

The first half hour had been dreamy as they rowed across the river smooth as a lake, clouds reflected like a world existed below the water, the sun beating down and the breeze cooling them off. For a while they bobbed side by side holding on to each other's kayaks so they could float.

"What will you do when you get home?" Victoria quietly asked Rose. "I mean . . . will you let Chip come home?"

"That's the first time you haven't said his name three in a row." Rose smiled at Victoria. "That was nice." She trailed her fingers in the water and then looked up. "I don't know. There's so much I haven't done because he asked me not to do them—and I still, since the day I graduated, want to write a book. Write something other than a grocery list. I've been doing it quietly late at night for a few years, but nothing has come of it. It's all garbled words that never turn into anything."

"Well," Victoria said taking off her sunhat and gazing directly at her friend. "Now you go on and don those swan feathers and . . ."

"If I can find them."

They all paused simultaneously, as if something beneath them had been turned on full blast; their kayaks began to move rapidly on their own, heading for the sea.

"Whoa!" Beatrice grabbed her paddle.

"Shit." Victoria pulled her sunhat on quickly. "The tide. It's going out."

And with that, they began to row like crazy, separating and pushing hard toward the shore. Hollering at each other in half sentences, zipping the life vests they'd thought unnecessary but took anyway at Red's insistence.

Rowing so hard her shoulders burned, Beatrice called out. "You think he coulda' warned us, or something!"

"Whose stupid idea was this?" Victoria hollered as a wave washed over the side of her kayak.

Then they went silent as they each rowed as hard and fast as they could without barely moving an inch. Slowly, and sometimes cursing, they reached the edge of the sandy beach one by one. Almost to shore, Victoria's kayak flipped over and spilled her into the shallows. Sputtering and laughing, she rose from the water like a sea creature, her long hair hanging in threads and her bathing suit pulled sideways so that one breast, white and pendulous, was exposed. She didn't even notice as she stumbled to the shore.

"Oh my God, that was thrilling!" She laughed as she fell to the sand. "What a ride." She reached up and pulled at what was now obviously a hair extension and threw it into the water. Then another.

The other friends looked at each other, and Beatrice spoke for them all. "Who are you and what have you done with our friend who can't stand to have her hair messed up and her manicure chipped?"

Victoria lay flat, gazing up at the sky. "I have no idea. A Bird of Paradise who is discovering an island life?"

They laughed and then Beatrice spoke slowly, as if finding her words with every step she took. "I'm going to propose to him," she said, sliding the kayak up to the soft grassy area littered with pinecones and fallen palmetto leaves.

Daisy sat in the sand, catching her breath. "And how is that? It doesn't seem to go with our romantic narrative, does it? I mean . . ." she grinned. "It wasn't Eliza Doolittle who wooed Henry Higgins back with a song about growing accustomed to his face. It was the other way around."

Beatrice thought about this for a long silent moment, about the end of all the romantic narratives strung through their lives, about women having their own agency and choosing what was right for them instead of taking the best of what is offered. She thought about the men she never called because it wasn't proper or the suggestions she never gave because she just needed to wait her turn.

She dropped the kayak and turned to her friends, her face aflame with something more than heat and hard rowing. "Eliza Doolittle. You know she didn't stay, right? In the real version; in the book *Pygmalion*, she left. She found her worth and she left."

"Well," Daisy said and then took a breath, "what kind of messed-up story is it that they fed us the other version—the one where she stays because he sings her a little song about being accustomed to her."

"Exactly!" Beatrice felt the truth moving closer. "What kind of story did they feed us, showing us that being accustomed and safe was enough?"

As Daisy and Beatrice batted these thoughts back and forth

between them, Victoria and Rose watched as if at a tennis match, sitting not in bleachers but on their kayak flipped upside down.

Victoria picked up the ball. "So what does that mean for you? Lachlan has never just said he's accustomed to you."

"But that's the thing, isn't it?" Beatrice said. "He's never treated me poorly and then come back with some sob story about how he misses me and loves me and now knows how much he really loves me. That's the old story. Lachlan is the new story, and I just kept looking for the old story, the one where there needs to be drama and breakup and diminishing worth so the guy can swoop in and save me." She slams her hand onto the side of a tree, the bark breaking the skin where blood seeps.

Victoria stood up and walked to Beatrice, took her hand, and stared at the blood and then into Beatrice's bluest eyes. "You know, you never really needed us. You had the answers all along."

Beatrice shook her head. "Oh, that's not even remotely true. Sometimes, or maybe all the time, we see the truth with those we love most."

"What will you say?" Rose piped up, sitting quietly on the kayak. "How will you ask?"

"I don't know," Beatrice said. "I haven't gotten that far in this whole scenario. Any ideas?"

They glanced one to the other until Rose said, "You'll think of something. You always do."

And with that, they pulled the kayaks up to the soft sandy yard as Red came outside to inform them he was ready to take them across the water and toward home.

Victoria stood, tucked her breast back into her bathing suit, and slipped on a T-shirt. "Can you take me last? I want just a bit more time."

"Of course. I can only take three at the most anyway." He glanced around at the kayaks spread about like tossed shells. "Did you enjoy your rides?"

The friends looked at each other and burst into simultaneous laughter. Damn, it was good to be together, Beatrice thought. Even if nothing had been fixed in their lives, or problems solved, even if the tide had almost taken them to sea, even if Lachlan never answered her call, it was good to know that love and stories and art remained with her birds.

EPILOGUE

What Happens Next

Six Months Later

After Beatrice's weekend on the island, it had taken a few tortuous weeks for her to figure out how to answer Lachlan's proposal: with her own. She'd taken those quiet weeks and written down their love story; from the day they met in the art museum to the day she showed up at his door carrying the pages like a diamond ring in a blue velvet box. She'd written the story by hand, every word in careful cursive, and bound it by hand at the Art School's bindery. She'd hand-sewn every stitch and she'd painted the wooden cover with two doves—birds she hadn't yet painted, this time a first—curled tightly in a nest.

When she'd taken the book to his house, he hadn't answered the door. She knew he was home; she felt his presence shuffling behind the closed door of his house and his heart. She'd left the package on his brick stoop wrapped in thick brown paper, simple string tying it together with the tag: For Lachlan. The last line, on the last page didn't state "The End," instead she'd typed, "I wonder what happens next."

She could give him no more than this—their story, her heart, and the truth. And she waited.

For three days she waited.

For eternity she waited.

She checked her email and her phone and her texts and her mailbox. She began to arrive at the truth that he hadn't only changed his mind, but also his heart. And there was nothing she could do to change it. That was the very thing with hearts—you can love them but you can't make them love back. You can adore them, but you can't convince with logic; you can't, absolutely can't, talk a heart into any-damn-thing.

Logic was never the answer, not in love or art.

So she'd thought a story would have to suffice, and if it didn't, it didn't.

On the third day, near midnight, when despair had turned to resignation and sorrow, a knock came to her door. She'd opened the door, and before she flicked on the porch light, he said only one word.

"Beatrice."

Her name. And who doesn't want to hear their name, just the simplicity of it, said by the person they love the most while in the midst of the darkest night.

• • •

Beatrice's Savannah backyard shimmered with the sudden outburst of rain that had swept through and wreaked havoc and destruction upon the wedding decorations. The silver balloons hung limply, and the white tent slumped sideways. The string quartet huddled on the covered back porch with the rest of the guests, who were trying to decide whether to laugh or cry at the destruction of the beautiful setup.

Beatrice stood with Lachlan, holding his hand, her pale blush-colored dress wet and clinging to her legs. The storm had come just as the last (and late) guest Victoria had arrived with Red on her arm, her hair down and a pale blue dress swirling about her like its own storm. They'd both drawn every eye to them as they sidled to the front and took two seats, cuddled together like nesting birds.

With one loud crack of thunder and a wind that blew sideways, a dark cloud had dumped rain as everyone ran for shelter. The pop-up storm left as quickly as it had arrived, and now they all stared at the mess from Beatrice's covered back porch.

Beatrice glanced down to her brick-walled yard. The caterers in their white aprons were trying to right the small tent; a tall man with windswept hair from the rental company was fixing chairs right, and picking up tossed flowers: the roses and ranunculus that Beatrice had grown in her own garden, the peonies she'd had imported, and the palmetto leaves she'd gathered with Lachlan from his yard. All sent asunder.

A server in a black suit climbed up the back stairs balancing a tray of champagne. He stepped onto the porch and handed them out. While Lachlan and Beatrice decided what to do next, at least their thirty guests could have something to drink.

Rose, stunning in her simple green dress, and alone, was the first to make her way to Beatrice. "They say that rain is a blessing at a wedding."

Beatrice smiled at her friend, now living only a few blocks away. "Will this go in your novel?"

Rose laughed and winked. "Everything goes in the novel."

Daisy, standing next to Rose in a pink off-the-shoulder gown, smiled coyly. "I'll sue you for defamation. Or slander. Or something, unless I'm the heroine who rights all wrongs and—"

"You're always the heroine." Rose linked her arm through Daisy's just as Victoria and Red arrived, gently pushing aside guests to stand on the other side of Lachlan.

"What novel? What are you talking about?" Victoria's low voice had them all turning to her.

Red reached up to remove a leaf that had blown and lodged itself in her waves.

Daisy raised her eyebrows. "You don't know about this?"

"No." Victoria made a pouty face and took Red's hand. "What are you talking about?"

"Well," Beatrice reached out and touched Victoria's arm. "If you weren't always hidden away on some island . . ."

Red and Victoria looked to each other and smiled. "Tell me anyway."

"Rose, our beloved swan, has slipped back into her feathers."

Victoria looked to Rose. "This is true? Tell me."

"I left Chip." She grinned. "Chip. Chip. Chip." She paused for their smiles. "Anyway, it's not final or anything, but I told him I needed to go, after what he did, that this is what I needed. So I've rented a house here in Savannah, only a few blocks from our Pegasus and near the library. I started a novel. It's called . . . The Roommates."

"Oh wow!" Victoria disengaged from Red. "Do you tell all our stories?"

"It's a cross between Sibley's bird guides and *Lord of the Flies*." She grinned with a mischievous glint in her eye. "A story about how one day, a long time ago, roommates chose a bird icon and then flew off to their own worlds, to then come together years later and change each other's lives for good."

Daisy threw back her head and laughed. "So total fiction."

"Totally." Rose smiled.

Victoria smiled. "That is brilliant. Absolutely brilliant."

Lachlan, so handsome in his tuxedo and trimmed silver beard, looking like he should be on top of a cake, looked back and forth between the women and then held up his hand. "Ladies. Ladies. This is about a wedding. Not your old college days." His grin belied his admonishing words as he kissed Beatrice on the lips.

The preacher, their friend Harold Morris, his clerical collar whipped sideways from the wind, and his coat unbuttoned, edged up and interrupted in full fix-it mode. "Okay, I can clear the aisle by dragging out the palm leaves. The band can set up again and . . . I'll check with the caterer how much of the food was destroyed." He pointed down where two men in white chef coats were struggling to lift the left end of the tent.

Beatrice glanced around. There were only thirty people in total at the wedding and they all fit on her porch, disheveled and wet for their wedding. It was surreal to her how they'd come to this.

He'd not hesitated and now she wouldn't either. On that rain-soaked porch Beatrice threw her arms around Lachlan and dropped her forehead to his, kissed him. "Let's just get married right here on the porch with our dearest friends, our soaked clothes, and our vows. Right now."

"Let's," he said. "I never wanted anything fancy. I only wanted you for my wife."

"We don't need anything cleaned up or fixed up. We took a chance with an outdoor wedding and, well . . ."

He touched her cheek. "I will always take whatever chances you want. I love you so, Beatrice."

"I love you, too, Lachlan. So much. And you will always be the man I take the chance with. Every. Single. Day."

And those were the vows Beatrice uttered: that she would take a chance on love with Lachlan every single day. By her side, on a soaked porch with the people she loved most, Beatrice said, "I do."

About Patti Callahan

Patti Callahan is the *USA Today* bestselling author of fifteen novels including the historical fiction *Becoming Mrs. Lewis: The Improbable Love Story of Joy Davidman and C.S. Lewis* and *Surviving Savannah*. In addition, she is the recipient of the Harper Lee Distinguished Writer of the Year for 2020 and the Alabama Library Association Book of the Year for 2019 and the Christy Award—a 2019 Winner "Book of the Year." The author is also the host of the popular seven-part original "Behind the Scenes of Becoming Mrs. Lewis Podcast Series." Patti is also the co-creator and co-host of the weekly web show and podcast Friends & Fiction.

Patti and Dottie met when Patti's first book was released in 2004 at a SIBA conference, where the friendship was instant and long lasting.

ALSO BY PATTI CALLAHAN

Historical Novels

Surviving Savannah

Becoming Mrs. Lewis

Audible Original

Wild Swan: A Story of Florence Nightingale

Stand-Alone Novels

The Perfect Love Song

The Favorite Daughter

The Bookshop at Water's End

The Idea of Love

The Stories We Tell

And Then I Found You

Coming Up for Air

The Art of Keeping Secrets

Driftwood Summer

Between the Tides

Where the River Runs

When the Light Breaks

Losing the Moon

Summer of '79

ELIN HILDERBRAND

1

Hot Child in the City

Jessie Levin ("rhymes with heaven") is drinking an ice cold can of Tab on the northwest corner of Washington Square Park when her sister, Kirby, pulls up in her butterscotch-colored Ford LTD with the sunroof open, strains of Lou Reed floating out like a haze.

Hey, babe, take a walk on the wild side.

Reed must have been talking about Washington Square Park in this song, Jessie thinks. She has done a fair amount of studying in the park while she's been in law school and she's seen it all: punk rockers with purple hair and pierced lips walking their dachshunds, drag queens eating knishes, a couple painted gold who set a boom-box on the lip of the fountain and discoed to Chopin's *Polonaise* in A-flat.

"Get in!" Kirby shouts. "Just throw your suitcase in the back-seat."

Jessie does as she's told—Kirby's backseat is as big as Grand Central Terminal—but even so, the cars lining up behind the LTD start honking and someone yells, "Move your tush, sweetheart!"

Kirby pulls away from the curb before Jessie even has her door closed. Jessie sets her macramé pocketbook on the front seat next to a tray of hotdogs from Gray's Papaya. She kicks off her Dr. Scholl's and puts her feet on the dash.

"I know I shouldn't feel happy," she says. "But I do. I took my last exam this morning, I have a full week off before I start my internship, and we're going to Nantucket."

"I'm happy, too," Kirby says. "Or I would be if I weren't so hungover." She pulls a cigarette out of a pack of Virginia Slims with her lips and leans over to Jessie, who rummages through her pocketbook for matches. She finds a pack from McSorley's. Jessie's exboyfriend, Theo, basically lives there.

Jessie lights Kirby's cigarette and fights the urge to throw the matches out the open window—the city is so dirty, what difference would it make?—because she has taken great pains to rid her tiny studio apartment and her carrel at Bobst Library of everything Theo-related.

"I need to get out of this city," Jessie says at the same time that Kirby says, "I need to get out of this city."

"Jinx," Kirby says. "You owe me a Coke." She blows smoke out the window without taking the cigarette from her mouth.

"Why do *you* need to get out of the city?" Jessie asks. Kirby's life in New York is glossy and fabulous. She's the Sex & Relationships editor at *Cosmopolitan*. She lives rent-free in a loft down on Broome Street where she babysits the paintings and sculptures of the artist Willie Eight while Willie travels the world. He's in New York only one week per month and it's during those weeks that Kirby's life gets even more enviable. Kirby and Willie and Willie's boyfriend, Tornado Jack, have long lavish dinners at Mr. Chow's and the Quilted Giraffe—and then they go to Studio 54. Through Willie, Kirby has met Baryshnikov, Farrah Fawcett, Richard Pryor! It seems outlandish that Kirby, Jessie's own sister, has rubbed elbows with such celebrities, though as Kirby says with her usual worldweariness, "They're just people, Jess."

In Kirby's own pocketbook—a tan suede fringed hobo—she keeps a Polaroid picture in an envelope. The picture is of Kirby linking arms with Willie and Tornado Jack. Sitting in front of them with his signature platinum mop and clear horn-rimmed glasses is . . . yeah.

Andy Warhol. Kirby has met Andy Warhol.

Kirby sighs. "I've been burning the joint at both ends."

Well, yes, so has Jessie. But whereas Jessie goes to Torts and Contracts during the day and studies at night, Kirby strolls into the Hearst offices at the crack of ten-fifteen with her sunglasses still on and receives congratulations for it. Kirby reports directly to Helen Gurley Brown, who has assigned Kirby the task of writing about the after-hours lives of young urban women—which means spending night after night out on the town.

Jessie isn't naïve. Kirby said "joint," but Jessie knows she's drinking every night—tequila sunrises that become more tequila and less sunrise as the hour grows later—and also, she snorts cocaine. Probably a lot of cocaine. Kirby may even be a cocaine addict; the edges of her nose are pink like a rabbit's and she keeps sniffing. Jessie wonders if she should express her concern, maybe tell Kirby the story of poor Cesar Coehlo, her fellow second-year law student, who also liked to frequent Limelight and Studio 54. A few weeks earlier, Cesar overdosed and died. The next day in Jessie's Property Law class, a girl said she'd heard the cocaine made Cesar's heart "pop like a balloon."

The song changes to Player. "Baby Come Back."

Any kind of fool can see!

There won't be any cocaine on Nantucket, Jessie thinks, though there will be drinking, starting first thing in the morning with mimosas. Jessie has vivid memories of her grandmother, Exalta, sucking down two or three mimosas on the patio of the Field & Oar Club while Jessie took her tennis lessons.

Despite the ungodly heat of this sweltering June day, Jessie gets a chill.

Exalta is dead.

She died in her sleep two days earlier in the house on Fair Street, while Mr. Crimmins, their former caretaker, slept beside her. Jessie and Kirby are heading up to Nantucket for the funeral tomorrow, which will be followed by a reception at the Field & Oar Club, which will be followed by a bonfire on Ram Pasture beach. The bonfire is Kirby's brainchild. She's calling it "Midnight at the Oasis," and it's for family and close friends only, although Kirby pointedly has not invited their parents, saying, "They won't want to come, anyway."

JESSIE AND KIRBY SIT in traffic on the Cross Bronx Expressway for what feels like days—Jessie drifts off for a second and she thinks maybe Kirby does as well—but then I-95 clears. Kirby puts the pedal to the metal and the LTD goes sailing right up alongside a tractor-trailer. Jessie yanks her elbow down once, twice, three times, and the trucker honks his horn, which gives Jessie a silly thrill. She feels like a character from *Smokey & the Bandit*.

"Flash him!" Kirby says.

Jessie considers it for a second, then remembers that her older sister is a terrible influence.

They have more fun on the drive up to Hyannis than they should under the circumstances. They devour the hotdogs—Kirby doctored them with just the right amount of mustard, relish, onions, and sauerkraut—and the radio gods are with them because they hear one great song after another.

"Lonesome Loser." *Beaten by the Queen of Hearts every time!*

"One Way or Another." *I'm gonna getcha getcha getcha getcha!*

"Knock on Wood." *Thunder, lightning! The way I love you is frightening!*

After they finish singing at the tops of their lungs with Bonnie Tyler to "It's a Heartache"—*Nothing but a heartache!*—Kirby turns down the radio and says, "So what happened with you and Theo, anyway?"

Jessie doesn't want to talk about Theo but she needs to come up with some kind of answer for her family.

Jessie met Theo her first week at NYU. She'd done her undergraduate work at Mount Holyoke, and so New York City—and men—were a dramatic change. Theo Feigenbaum had thick dark hair, green eyes, and remarkably long dark lashes. He sat next to Jessie in their lawyering seminar and asked her to borrow a pencil and a piece of loose-leaf, which Jessie gave him while wondering what kind of bozo showed up to the first day of class unprepared. But when he raised his hand to offer an example of jurisprudence, Jessie fell in love.

They dated the entire first year, then through the summer, then into autumn of their second year, when they basically cohabitated. But the second year of law school was more difficult than the first, just like the second year of a relationship. The things that had been fun, even blissful—studying together in the park, getting pizza on St. Mark's Place, splurging on a foreign film at the Angelika, or sneaking into the Metropolitan Museum of Art (it was easy enough to find a discarded metal button on the steps and attach it to their collars)—lost their luster. And there was no time, anyway. Besides which, Theo grew increasingly jealous of how well Jessie was doing in class and how easily she had landed a summer associate's job at Cadwalader. He started to turn mean and surly, he put Jessie down in public—at McSorley's, for example, in front of their mutual friends—and argued with every single point she made in class.

Jessie would be embarrassed to admit to Kirby how she backed down, how she *apologized*, how her main objective became to placate Theo and defuse his growing anger, how she intentionally turned in a sloppy opinion so that he would get a better grade. Jessie watched herself make concession after concession even as she yearned to be strong and stand up for herself like a proper women's libber. But she had wanted Theo to be happy. She had wanted him to love her. And so she yielded, she flattered him, she diminished herself to make him appear bigger.

And what had this gotten her? It had gotten her a kick to the gut, a fat smack to her pride. One night when Jessie had spent the last dollars of her monthly stipend on Reuben sandwiches from the Carnegie Deli, Theo stood her up. The sandwiches, which Jessie had transported back downtown on the subway as carefully as she would have her own newborn baby, grew cold and greasy. Jessie left them in the white paper bag and stormed down to McSorley's, where she found Theo at a back table with a girl named Ingrid Wu, a first-year. They were all over each other.

"He cheated on me," Jessie tells Kirby. "So I threw him out."

Kirby is smoking again in a more relaxed way, with her elbow hanging out the window. "Good for you," she says. "You deserve better."

Jessie rummages through her macramé pocketbook for her sunglasses because suddenly she feels like she might cry. She'd wanted to call Theo when Exalta died but she hadn't because she was afraid it would sound like a plea for attention. A dead grandmother, how unoriginal. And yet, Exalta *is* dead and it hurts. Jessie and Exalta hadn't been *close* exactly, but there had been something—a mutual respect and admiration that was, in a way, more meaningful to Jessie than the more typical variety of grandmotherly love. Exalta was proud of Jessie's accomplishments—her impeccable grades at Brookline High and Mount Holyoke, her high LSAT score, her admission into NYU law. Exalta could be stingy with praise, but she had, more than once, said that Jessie was a young woman with a good head on her shoulders who had a very bright future.

Along with her cut-offs and her crocheted tank, Jessie is wearing the gold knot and diamond necklace that Exalta gave her for her thirteenth birthday. Jessie lost the necklace the very first time she wore it and she'd spent one fraught week of her thirteenth summer in a state of agitated panic. Mr. Crimmins found the necklace—

thank God!—and Exalta kept it in her custody until Jessie turned sixteen. At that point, Jessie put it on—and she has never taken it off. It has been witness to every second of the past seven years. It's a talisman and a reminder of Exalta's belief in her. Good head on shoulders. Very bright future.

Theo Feigelbaum be damned.

"You're right," Jessie says, thinking maybe her sister isn't such a terrible influence after all. "I do deserve better."

2

Baby, What a Big Surprise

Over her mother's protests, Blair tells her nine-year-old twins, George and Gennie, to climb into the once-red-now-nearly-pink International Harvester Scout, their family beach vehicle that refuses to die. Blair is taking the twins into town for hot fudge sundaes at the Sweet Shoppe. They arrived on Nantucket an hour earlier and ice cream sundaes are their first-afternoon-on-island tradition.

"Your grandmother's body isn't even cold yet," Kate says, before Blair heads out the door after the twins. "What are people going to say when they see you and the children with whipped cream all over your faces?"

"They'll think we're trying to cheer ourselves up," Blair says. She gives Kate a pointed look. "The kids have been through a lot recently."

"Well," Kate says, and she meets Blair's gaze. "Whose fault is that."

"Mmmmm," Blair says. She has been waiting for this exact confrontation, the one where Kate blames Blair for her divorce from Angus, even though their split was hardly Blair's fault. Angus dragged Blair and the children down to Houston for the most miserable year of their lives so he could work at NASA on the Viking mission to Mars. The children despised their new school—the other kids made fun of their "accents"—and Blair felt adrift in the astronaut-wives society. It was as though she had stepped back in time rather than forward. The astronaut wives didn't have careers. They spent their days getting manicures and planning fondue parties. When Blair mentioned—at the one "garden lunch" she attended, which was held looking at the garden through a plate-glass window because it was too beastly hot to eat on the patio—that she resented having to give up her adjunct professor job at Radcliffe, everyone at the table had stared at her, forks suspended over their cottage cheese as though Blair was speaking in tongues.

Blair hadn't made a single friend and neither had the children. Even a swimming pool in their backyard didn't cheer them. The kids sat in front of the color television and started speaking to each other in a new language they called "Brady," saying things like, "George . . . Glass," and "Marcia, Marcia, Marcia!" in a way that seemed to have a secret meaning.

Angus was, of course, never around. He had a cot at NASA and spent the night there.

In a moment of desperation, Blair had bought the children a dog, thinking this might help. And it had, initially. They went to the SPCA and picked out a mutt, some kind of spaniel-terrier mix. The children named him Happy, which made Blair melt a little— her twins were remaining optimistic!—but Happy was not happy once they brought him home. He was lethargic; he slept twenty-two hours a day, rising only to limp over to his bowl of chow.

A trip to the vet revealed that Happy was a very sick dog. He had tumors all down his spine—in the X-ray, Blair could see them, evenly spaced like pearls on a string. The vet said the kind thing would be to put the dog to sleep.

The death of the dog brought Blair to the end of her rope. She surprised Angus at his office and begged him to return to his job at MIT in Boston. Angus was his usual opaque and uncompromising self. He had a project here in Houston. The Viking mission. Mars.

"Then the children and I will go back alone," Blair said.

She hadn't necessarily meant to ask for a divorce. She had imagined they could work out some kind of long-distance commute. But Angus said he planned on staying in Houston. In addition to the Viking mission, he was in on the ground floor of the Space Shuttle program. His future was at NASA and if Blair and the children refused to support him, well then, he supposed that constituted irreconcilable differences.

"There's no reason we can't work out a civil arrangement," Angus said. "You and the children will be well cared for."

And they have been, financially. Blair took sole ownership of their home in Chestnut Hill; the children are enrolled back at Buckingham, Browne & Nichols. Blair will return to Radcliffe in the fall. Their life is remarkably similar to the way it was before they left. The interlude in Houston was like the pain of childbirth: as soon as it was over, Blair forgot about it.

This is not to say all was hunky-dory. Angus hasn't flown up to see the children even once since they left. They have a Sunday-evening call scheduled. This consists of Angus asking how the children are doing ("Fine"), then how things are going in school ("Fine"). Are they getting good marks? ("Yes.") Then he tells them, "Be good for your mother." ("We will.") And then, with what seems like enormous relief, one or the other of them will hand the phone back to Blair, who will listen to Angus say, "This month's check is in the mail. We'll talk next week."

BEING A DIVORCÉE AT Radcliffe is no big deal. Cambridge is filled with "Free to Be, You and Me" families—divorced mothers and fathers, unmarried couples with children, gay and lesbian couples, biracial couples, married couples with adopted children. Blair's best friend from her Wellesley days, Sallie, has given up on ever finding a suitable man and is now a "single mother by choice." She used a sperm donor—a six-foot-two engineer with dark hair and dark eyes—and she now has a four-year-old son, Michael.

Chestnut Hill, the affluent Boston suburb where Blair lives, is another story, however, as is the community at the children's school. Everyone is married, everyone drives a woody wagon with the backseat and the backety-back crowded with kids and at least one dog, a golden retriever or Irish setter. Blair has a circle of lovely, well-meaning friends who were thrilled when Blair and the kids moved back. But once Blair admitted that Angus wouldn't follow in six months or a year—he was staying in Houston permanently, they were getting a divorce—she sensed everyone pulling back a few inches so they could better judge her. They were "sad" for her, they said, even though she herself was much happier. The truth, Blair knows, is that her so-called friends see divorce as a virus, and if they get too close, they might catch it.

Tom Murray from three houses down offered to mow Blair's lawn, which was very kind, but Blair felt she had to say no. The last thing she wanted everyone to see was another person's husband mowing her lawn or shoveling her snow.

She hired a caretaker, a twenty-four-year-old Puerto Rican named Jefé. He was handsome and friendly and the kids loved him, especially George once Jefé admitted that he had been a baseball star back in Poncé. Blair had once looked out the window to see George and Jefé playing catch in the front yard and, in a moment she regretted perhaps more than any other in her life, she told Jefé that she wasn't paying him to play games and that he should leave immediately. Jefé had been hurt, George had stormed off in a sullen rage, and Blair ran up to her bedroom to cry. She knew that George needed a man around, but she couldn't bear to have the neighborhood whispering about exactly what role Jefé the caretaker was filling over at the Whalen house.

Being divorced is a social stigma; there's no denying it. Blair thinks about dating again, but how to go about it? Back in April, she let Sallie talk her into an outing with Parents Without Partners, which Sallie called "PWP." Blair and the twins and Sallie and little Michael had joined the other single mothers and fathers and their children at Fenway Park to see the Red Sox play the Philadelphia Phillies. It was meant to be fun, Blair knew, like a grown-up version of a mixer in college. The weather cooperated: it was sunny and warm enough to sit in the bleachers without a jacket or sweater. But Blair found herself preoccupied with what was wrong rather than what was right. On the one hand, Sallie chose well. Because it was a baseball game, most of the other participating parents were men. However, Blair couldn't find a single candidate she would consider dating. Some men were fat and sloppy, some had stringy combovers, some had facial hair that reminded Blair of Charles Manson. But it wasn't only appearances that put Blair off—after all, Angus had looked like a central-casting Poindexter. The problem was that the PWP fathers carried the stench of desperation. Most of them slouched, and those who did stand up straight seemed angry at the world.

The gentleman closest to Blair—he introduced himself as Al Sparks and looked straight at her chest—wasn't bad-looking, but he jumped out of his seat after nearly every pitch and cursed at the umpires. He swore in front of his two sons, though they didn't notice because they were too busy tussling over the bucket of popcorn he'd bought for them to share until the older son pulled a little too hard and the bucket upended all over the seat in front of them, which was occupied by a toddler who had fallen asleep with his head cocked at an unnatural angle while his oblivious father kept track of the stats in a spiral-bound notebook.

The children at this outing seemed like ragamuffins. Blair didn't like to be ungenerous, but she couldn't help noticing a little girl with tangled hair and a boy, nearly obese, whose father had stuffed him like a sausage into a Yastrzemski jersey. The children looked . . .

motherless, and this made Blair suspect that, while she was here looking for someone who would trim the hedges and take the car for an oil change, the gentlemen were looking for a woman who knew how to French braid and who might be willing to cook a hot breakfast every morning.

If Blair were to date or, God forbid, *marry* one of the men in PWP, she would become . . . a stepmother. This wasn't something she had considered.

Of course Blair had been raised by a stepfather—David Levin, who had been perfect in nearly every way. But that felt different somehow. Kate had been tragically widowed; David had swooped in to save the day. It hadn't been two broken families awkwardly trying to fit themselves together.

Blair is too much of a feminist to admit that she's now looking for a David—a single man without children who will love Blair, George, and Gennie unconditionally—but secretly, she fears she is.

The Red Sox game was Blair's one and only foray with PWP. Sallie, meanwhile, dated angry Al Sparks for six weeks before declaring him an "absolute psychopath," when he got drunk at a Memorial Day picnic and lost his temper over a Frisbee that landed on the grill.

BLAIR IS IRRITATED WITH her mother's comments about the propriety of her taking the children to the Sweet Shoppe, although as she parks the car on Main Street in front of Bosun's Locker, she does in fact worry that she will bump into someone she knows who will want to express his or her condolences about Exalta—and how will Blair explain that they're on their way out for sundaes?

"Let's hurry along," Blair says. The twins are in the backseat, completely oblivious to their surroundings, despite the rumbling of the Scout over the cobblestones. Gennie is immersed in her book of science experiments and George is doing the crossword puzzle from the *Boston Herald*.

They are, Blair thinks somewhat mournfully, *Angus's* children—obsessed with the world of the mind.

But then she brightens, because at least the twins *look* like Blair. They're both blond, pink-cheeked, nicely proportioned, and they have straight white teeth. Gennie is an inch or two taller than George, but that will soon change. Next month, they'll be ten. How did that happen?

"You know," Blair says. "I went into labor with the two of you on this very street."

"We know," they say in unison.

Of course they know, it's part of Foley-Levin-Whalen family lore. In the summer of 1969, while Angus was in Houston working on the Apollo 11 mission to the moon, Blair went into labor right in the middle of Buttner's department store. She had taken Jessie in to be fitted for her first bra when her water broke. Blair had waddled up Main Street, leaking amniotic fluid all over the brick sidewalk, while Jessie ran ahead to get Kate, who appeared moments later in the Scout. Because Blair couldn't possibly endure a trip over the cobblestones, Kate had driven down one-way Fair Street in reverse. The twins had been born the next morning, a scant hour before the moon launch.

Blair climbs out of the car and has to snap her fingers through the open back window to get the twins to move.

"Let's go," she says. "Hot fudge."

"BLAIR?" A VOICE SAYS. "Blair Foley?"

Blair has been inside the Sweet Shoppe for ten seconds, just long enough to shepherd the twins to the end of the line. The Sweet Shoppe never changes. It's still deliciously cool and smells like vanilla waffle cones.

Blair turns. A man is standing at the cash register holding a double scoop of rocky road in a sugar cone. He accepts a quarter in change, grabs a napkin from the dispenser, and heads right for Blair with a sly smile on his face.

Blair tries to prepare herself. Who is this? The man is her age. He's wearing a powder blue leisure suit and blue gradient-lensed glasses; his reddish hair is long and feathered. Surely this isn't someone she knows?

"It's Larry," he says. "Larry Winter."

Larry Winter! Blair dated Larry Winter for three consecutive summers when she was a teenager. In those days, Blair, Kirby, and Tiger lived in the guest cottage of Exalta's house, called Little Fair. Larry Winter would ride over from Walsh Street on his Schwinn, throw a pebble at Blair's bedroom window, and the two of them would neck—Larry perched on the top rail of the fence, Blair tucked between his legs. To this day, it was some of the loveliest kissing Blair can remember, and some of the purest desire. They had been caught once by Mr. Crimmins, the caretaker, who had passed down the side street, Plumb Lane, late at night on his way home from somewhere, probably Bosun's Locker. He'd stepped out of the darkness, startling them both, and said, "Time to call it a night, kids." Then he continued on his way in the direction of Pine Street, where he lived in an efficiency. Blair remembers wanting to chase after him to beg him not to tell her mother or—horrors!—her grandmother. But Blair needn't have worried; Mr. Crimmins kept her secret.

"Larry!" Blair says. "What a surprise! I thought you were a Floridian these days."

She hopes she has this right. Larry Winter went to Georgetown to study political science but somehow he'd ended up as the food and beverage manager at a private club in Vero Beach. He'd risen to general manager and then had started a venture of his own somewhere else in Florida. The Everglades, maybe?

"I'm up for a couple of weeks," Larry says. "The heat in Florida this time of year, even in the Keys . . ."

Key Largo, Blair thinks with a mental snap of the fingers. He owns a nightclub in Key Largo.

". . . plus, Mom isn't getting any younger . . ." Larry stops himself. "Which reminds me. I heard about Exalta passing. I'm so sorry."

Blair feels tears burn her eyes. The Sweet Shoppe is only a few blocks away from Exalta's house on Fair Street and it's inconceivable that, should Blair and the twins venture up there after their sundaes, the only person they would find would be Mr. Crimmins, who had become Exalta's devoted companion.

Unlike Blair, Exalta hadn't given one whit what people thought about her shacking up with the caretaker. She and Bill Crimmins had fallen in love. For the past ten years, Exalta had been a different woman. Gone was the stern, judgmental blue-blood and in her place they'd enjoyed a fun-loving old lady who listened and laughed.

When Blair last visited Exalta, she had meant to tell her grandmother that she and Angus had divorced. But Exalta was so sick and frail at the time, swimming in and out of lucidity, that Blair couldn't bear to deliver the news. Exalta had adored Angus. Why burden her with news that would only make her sad and disappointed?

At that point, Exalta had still been living in her house in Boston, on Mount Vernon Street in Beacon Hill, but a few days after Blair's visit, Exalta sat bolt upright in bed and clearly announced that she wanted to spend her final days in the house on Nantucket. And so, Bill Crimmins arranged for a door-to-door ambulance transfer—the ambulance even went over on the ferry—and they installed Exalta comfortably in the house on Fair Street where she died two days ago none the wiser about Blair and Angus.

Blair leaves the twins in line and steps away a bit so she can talk to Larry more privately. "As I'm sure you've heard," she says, "I got divorced."

Larry turns his head so he's looking at her with only one eye; this, she recalls, is a gesture of his. "I had *not* heard that, actually."

Ah, right. Larry lives in Florida. The only person who would have told him is his mother, Mrs. Winter, and she would only have heard it from Exalta. Even so, Blair is glad she came out with it before Larry had a chance to ask about Angus.

Blair shrugs. "Didn't work out, but the kids and I are fine. We live outside of Boston. Everyone's happy." She flashes Larry a smile that she hopes indicates "happy," or appropriately happy, considering they're on island to attend a funeral. "How about you? Married? Kids?"

Larry stares at the ice cream cone that is slowly melting in his hand. "Not married, no kids," he says. "Haven't met the right woman."

Blair feels herself flush. "Oh. Well, I'm sure it's only a matter of time."

Larry stares at his cone for a second; he must be finding this run-in as surreal as she is. "So, listen, I'm planning on coming to the funeral and the reception. Escorting my mother."

"Of course," Blair says. "You belong there. And Kirby has planned a bonfire tomorrow night at Ram Pasture. Young people only."

Larry laughs. "That leaves me out."

"And me," Blair says. "I'm thirty-four. Twice as old as the summer we last dated."

"I've got you by a year, don't forget. And you, Blair Foley, are far more gorgeous now than you were at seventeen."

Flush turns to blush. He's lying, though Blair *has* lost a lot of weight since the divorce and now might be nearly as slender as she was in high school. "Thank you, Larry. I needed to hear that."

"I'll see you tomorrow," Larry says. "Enjoy your ice cream."

BLAIR IS AS PREOCCUPIED as the twins as they sit and eat their sundaes. Blair made George and Gennie leave their projects in the car and so they've moved on to their second favorite pastime—dissecting a special trilogy-episode of *The Brady Bunch*. The Bradys go to Hawaii, they find a tiki that appears to be cursed—Greg Brady has a surfing accident, a tarantula crawls on one of the other brothers—and then Blair loses the plot when they start talking about a cave and someone (or something?) named Oliver. Doesn't matter. Blair is doing her own dissecting. Larry Winter, of all people! Single and without children, telling Blair she looked more "gorgeous" than she had at seventeen. And she'll see him tomorrow—at the funeral, the reception, and the bonfire.

"Time to go," Blair says, though she has barely touched her sundae at all.

BLAIR DRIVES BACK TO her mother and David's sprawling beachfront compound on Red Barn Road, listing Larry Winter's pros and cons. The only con she can come up with is that he lives in Florida and owns a nightclub, which might explain why he looks like one of the Bee Gees. Well, another con is that Blair felt no particular emotion when she saw him, other than a fondness when remembering the kissing. And she'd liked being complimented, of course, because who didn't? But there was definitely something missing—a zing, a ping, a tingle. They had broken up so long ago, Blair remembers, because she had grown tired of him.

The pros are that he's single and without children. But surely she's entitled to ask for more than just that?

Blair wonders if the divorce has turned her heart to ice. Look at how she spoke to poor Jefé. Maybe she'll feel differently about Larry tomorrow night at the bonfire, once she's had a few drinks. Maybe her run-in with Larry was meant to be, orchestrated by Exalta, who is watching out for Blair from above.

The driveway of Kate and David's compound is crowded with cars. Blair sees the Trans Am that Tiger drives; he'll have to give that thing up once he and Magee finally have children. She sees Kirby's LTD and Mr. Crimmins's pickup truck. And she sees a turquoise Porsche 911 with the top down.

Blair freezes. Only one person she knows would drive a car like that.

"Looks like we have company," Blair says.

KATE AND DAVID BOUGHT the sprawling old house on Red Barn Road ten years earlier, right after the twins were born, back when Tiger was still over in Vietnam. They lived in it for five years without making a single change. Then, once Jessie left for Mount Holyoke and Kate no longer had children at home, she and David sold the big house in Brookline, rented an apartment in Charles River Park, and poured their time, energy, and resources into the Nantucket property. The main house got a complete facelift—a new roof, new doors and windows, new wood floors throughout, except for the family room which they carpeted, paint for all the bedrooms, an updated kitchen with avocado green appliances and bright pink and orange wallpaper so that when you were at the counter making a sandwich, you felt like you were standing in the middle of fruit ambrosia. (Only Exalta was brave enough to say to Kate, "You might have chosen something more classic, darling.") But Kate wanted a happy, modern house as a counterpoint to the staid, history-laden confines of All's Fair. She and David built a guest cottage on the back edge of the property—two bedrooms, one bath; this was where Blair and Angus had always stayed with the children, now just Blair and the children—and between the guest cottage and the main house, they built a clay tennis court and a turquoise lozenge of an in-ground pool that had a curved fiberglass slide at one end. There was a concrete patio for barbecuing and even a portable tiki bar that David hauled out of the shed every Memorial Day for the summer. Kate had newly discovered frozen blender drinks—strawberry daiquiris and margaritas—which she served in obscenely large glasses that she got on sale at Kmart.

If the whole thing sounded out of character for Kate, well, it was a bit—but Kate made no secret that she wanted the compound filled with grandchildren someday.

On that front, Blair had done her part. The onus now fell to her other three siblings.

KIRBY, TIGER, AND JESSIE are all out on the back patio, sitting under the awning by the pool. Mr. Crimmins and Kate and David are there as well, and Magee, Tiger's wife, who quit her dental hygienist's job to care for Exalta when she first fell sick. (Kate had been relieved, Blair knows. She was certain the reason Tiger and Magee didn't have children was that Magee worked too hard.)

The blender isn't purring, the grill isn't smoking; there isn't a drink in sight, not even iced tea. Kate is holding tight to her principles. They are a family in mourning; no one will enjoy himself. Blair's not sure how she'll explain that she and the children have just been to the Sweet Shoppe, though perhaps Kate has already announced this. Perhaps everyone has been discussing Blair's blasphemy, her loosened morals since getting divorced.

Tiger moves to the edge of the patio to light a cigarette and he's joined by a dark-haired gentleman wearing a white polo, madras shorts, and Wayfarer sunglasses.

Blair's heart isn't frozen after all because suddenly, it revs like a race car engine. She will be taking a ride in that Porsche later, her face raised to the night sky, her hair streaming out behind her.

It's Joey Whalen, Angus's little brother, who was Blair's boyfriend before (and after) she met Angus.

"How about that, my darlings," Blair says. "Your uncle is here."

3

Sad Eyes

Magee hasn't stopped crying since Exalta died and finally, on the morning of the funeral, Tiger realizes he can't ignore it any longer. This isn't normal, run-of-the-mill grief. Something else is going on with his wife.

They're in their summer bedroom, getting dressed. Kate has okayed navy blazers instead of suits for men. Tiger is still in just khaki pants and an undershirt. Magee is in her slip, her hair in the pink spongy rollers she sleeps in when she wants waves. She's sobbing into Tiger's pajama top, presumably so no one else in the house will hear her.

"Mags," he says, sitting next to her on the end of the bed. "What's wrong?"

She raises her face and her sweet, soft pink bottom lip quivers. "I can't believe you have to ask that. Your. Grandmother. Is. Dead."

Tiger is careful how he proceeds. Yes, Exalta is dead. Exalta was sick for months, her internal organs shutting down one after another, like someone shutting the lights off in a house before bed. It wasn't a violent death or even gruesome and it wasn't a surprise. Exalta was eighty-two years old. Tiger watched men die nearly every day in Vietnam, some of these "men" only eighteen years old, some still virgins. Exalta lived a full and privileged life. She had known love not only with Tiger's grandfather, Pennington Nichols, but also with Mr. Crimmins. She had one child, four grandchildren, two great-grandchildren—with more, presumably, on the way.

This, Tiger knows, is the real reason Magee is crying. She and Tiger have been married for nine years next month and although they've been trying since day one, they haven't been able to conceive a child.

At first, they were too busy to notice. When Tiger got home from his tour, he was eligible to inherit his trust from Exalta. The first thing he did was to buy a house in Holliston, thirty miles southwest of Boston. The house had been built in the 1840s. It was three stories and had plenty of charm—five bedrooms and a finished playroom in the attic. (In retrospect, Tiger wonders if buying such a big house wasn't what jinxed them.)

The second thing Tiger did was to open a bowling alley on the Holliston-Sherborn line called Tiger Lanes. Tiger had spent countless hours in-country, dreaming about the perfect bowling alley. He would have twelve state-of-the-art lanes on one side of the building and a pinball arcade on the other, with a soda fountain and snack bar in the middle. There would be music and party lights. It would be a hangout for teenagers and adults alike, a place to bridge the widening generation gap. He would start a Tiger Lanes bowling league for veterans.

Tiger is aware that he was lucky to come home not only in one piece physically, but one piece mentally. Lots of veterans found themselves at loose ends. They were traumatized, they'd become drug addicts, they'd become *adrenaline* addicts, in search of the high that was part of being on the front lines. When every day was a struggle to stay alive, coming home to conveniences like ten kinds of bread at the supermarket and Johnny Carson every night at eleven-thirty felt like trying to sleep in a bed that was too soft. Where was the action, the danger, the purpose? Some soldiers came home from thirteen hellish months of defending the ideals of American democracy only to be spit upon, harassed, and called "baby killers."

None of this happened to Tiger, but that didn't mean he was unaffected by the war. He'd watched his best friends, Puppy and Frog, get blown to bits. They didn't have a chance to make something of their lives, but Tiger did and he'd be damned if he was going to waste it. He would be enough of a success and make enough positive change in the world for all of them—Puppy, Frog, and every other American serviceman and -woman who died in Vietnam.

Tiger bought a defunct shoe factory and transformed it into the first Tiger Lanes. It was such a surprising success that Tiger opened a second location in Franklin the following year—followed by one in Needham and one in Mansfield. He then opened the grandest of them all, a flagship with twenty lanes, a disco floor, and a full bar in Newton-Wellesley. At that point, Tiger sold the five-bedroom in Holliston and bought a brick center-entrance colonial in Wellesley that had four bedrooms and a finished basement rec room with shag carpeting and a wet bar. The house also had a detached two-car garage where Tiger kept his Trans Am and Magee's hotrod, a Datsun 240Z.

Magee still worked as a dental hygienist for Dr. Brezza in Waltham. She'd been working there since Tiger met her, and she told Tiger she would only leave once she got pregnant.

There had been some tense discussions—spurned by visits to Tiger's parents—about Magee's job being the reason why they didn't yet have a baby. Kate Levin felt that Magee should stay home and develop a nurturing side. She should do the things that mothers did—go to the salon, volunteer, redecorate, take a pottery class at the community center. Kate privately asked Tiger if it wasn't difficult for poor Magee to clean the teeth of sixteen children per day, none of whom were her own? And how did she handle the busybody mothers, who must be wondering when Magee would have good news to share?

Magee held up surprisingly well to Kate. She loved her job, loved her patients, loved Dr. Brezza. There had been one agonizing moment when Tiger wondered if maybe Magee actually *loved* Dr. Brezza—maybe they were having an affair and Magee was secretly on the Pill so as not to become pregnant with Dr. Brezza's baby. When Tiger came home (after a few too many beers following the Vietnam Veterans Bowling League championship) and asked Magee if this were the case, she crumpled.

She wasn't having an affair with Dr. Brezza or anyone else. She loved Tiger, and she wanted a baby with Tiger more than she wanted to breathe. She didn't know what was wrong. She didn't drink, didn't smoke, and didn't take Quaaludes like so many other Wellesley women did.

Magee quit her job and gave Kate's method a try. She joined the Ladies' Auxiliary, audited an anatomy class at Pine Manor, learned to roller skate because she heard it was good physical fitness.

When there was still no sign of a baby, Magee agreed to see a doctor. Magee's own mother had a theory that radiation from all of the mouth X-rays that Magee administered had somehow fried her insides. Magee knew this wasn't the case but she submitted herself to a complete physical exam at the Brigham nonetheless, which involved a lot of poking and prodding both of Magee's body and her psyche. Magee waited three days for the results of the exam—all she could think of was Jennifer Cavalleri in *Love Story* learning that she had leukemia—but when the call finally came, it was with the news that she was in perfect working condition.

Then, it was Tiger's turn. He'd been at war. He could have been exposed to chemicals or gases that affected his sperm count or motility. And so he went to the Brigham as well and gave the doctor a specimen (that was weird) but his sperm count was high, his swimmers veritable Olympians.

The problem then became that there was no problem. The problem was lack of patience and high expectations. The problem was that sex stopped feeling like a natural manifestation of Tiger's love for his wife and more like a test he was failing. Magee started going to the public library to research fertility issues. There were options—medical procedures, drugs—that could be pursued right there in Boston, right at the Brigham! The science, Magee said, was remarkable. A baby had been conceived *in a test tube*!

Tiger didn't want his child conceived in a laboratory. Call him old-fashioned, call him stodgy, but he'd rather adopt one of the millions of children orphaned in Vietnam than be subjected to "drugs," and "procedures."

Before Magee could get too carried away, life intervened. Exalta got a head cold that turned into pneumonia. Then she suffered a minor stroke and became bedridden. Bill Crimmins was good for hand-holding, but not much else. Kate was alternately too worried and too impatient to be helpful and so she looked into hiring private nurses, but it was very expensive for round-the-clock care. Magee saw a chance to put to use all the love and attention she had been storing up for their future children. She spent countless hours caring for Exalta. She fed her soft foods, made sure she took her pills, read to her, plumped her pillows, sat with her through endless episodes of *The Flying Nun*, consulted with Exalta's doctor over the phone and with the night nurse each morning.

Now that Exalta is gone, so is Magee's newfound purpose. And what's left is not only Exalta's absence, but the absence of a baby as well. Tiger gets it.

HE HASN'T BEEN INSIDE a church in over ten years. Even when he and Magee got married, it was outside on the front lawn of his parents' Nantucket home. He can't quite explain why he's avoided it. He certainly has a lot to be grateful for—his success in business; his beautiful, devoted wife; hell, the mere fact that he's alive. A lot of guys Tiger knew in the war became either atheists or Born-Again Christians. If it's one thing Tiger learned, it's that God doesn't live in a church. For Tiger, God lives in the shaking hands of a US Air Force fighter pilot who needs Tiger to tie his bowling shoes but who can, somehow, send a ten-pound ball down the boards for a strike. God is in the illuminated windows of Tiger's neighborhood, homes occupied by Americans who are safe and sound inside, enjoying pot roast and *Donny & Marie*. God is in the Firestone tires of Tiger's Trans Am, in the gravelly voice of Wolfman Jack on the radio, in four-year-old Joey Bell from down the street who saluted when Tiger marched past in the Memorial Day parade. God is in the glove of Carlton Fisk. God is in the ocean as seen from the windows of their summer bedroom.

God is all these places, so why would Tiger—or anyone—need to go to church?

Well, today he needs to go so his mother doesn't wallop him. She spies him smoking outside the front door of St. Paul's Episcopal and, perhaps, suspects that he'd like to skip the service altogether because she plucks the cigarette from his mouth and grinds it out beneath the sole of her black slingback heel.

"Get inside," she says, "and pray for your grandmother."

"Too late now," Tiger deadpans. Then, he grins. Will his mother find this funny?

Kate shakes her head before letting a fraction of a smile slip. "Pray for yourself, then. And your sainted wife."

Maybe he should go inside and pray for a baby, he thinks. It couldn't hurt.

4

Heart of Glass

With Exalta's death, Kate is now the matriarch of the family. Alongside her deep sorrow, she feels a rush of power, of agency. There's no one left to please, no one left to placate, no one left to impress.

There is no one left to judge her.

She's free.

"Is it horrible to feel this way?" Kate whispers to David in the car. "I loved her . . ."

"You worshipped her," David says.

"I respected her . . ."

"You revered her . . ."

"I even liked her at times."

"She *was* a great deal easier to deal with once we bought our own house," David says. "And once she and Bill got together."

Bill Crimmins, yes. Kate owes a tremendous debt to Bill—not only for four decades of service to their family and the house but for the past ten years as Exalta's companion. In her will, Exalta granted Bill lifetime rights to All's Fair and Little Fair. Only when Bill dies will Exalta's Nantucket home pass to Kate. This was an appropriate gesture, and yet Kate can't help but worry that Bill will mend his relationship with his daughter, Lorraine, who is responsible for every bit of heartbreak Kate has known in her life, and Lorraine Crimmins will end up spending time, maybe even entire summers, in All's Fair.

Bill Crimmins wouldn't encourage this, certainly. However, if Lorraine is to discover—from one of her former chums at Bosun's Locker, let's say—that Exalta has died and Bill has been granted residency, and Lorraine decided to simply show up, would Bill have the willpower to turn her away?

Kate fears the answer is no. So many of us are powerless when it comes to our own children.

KATE TRIES TO PUSH all unpleasant thoughts from her mind in order to be properly attentive during the service. She, David, and Mr. Crimmins sit with the twins in the first pew, while Kate's four children and Magee sit behind them.

Exalta wanted zero frills. Straightforward service, no poetry, no eulogizing, no dreadful receiving line where Kate and the children would have to, in Exalta's words, "listen to everyone lie about what a wonderful woman I was."

Reverend Meeker conducts a proper mass (without communion, also Exalta's choice) and during his rather bland homily, Kate's mind wanders. Exalta built an extraordinary family, although really, it was Kate, Exalta's only child, who built it. She had her first three children with Lt. Wilder Foley and then, once Wilder confessed to an affair with Lorraine Crimmins, got Lorraine pregnant, and shot himself, Kate married David Levin and had Jessie.

Each of her four children have something that sets them apart. Blair has the twins, Kirby the glamour, Tiger the money, and Jessie the smarts.

They also each have problems. Blair is divorced, Kirby wild. Tiger and Magee can't seem to conceive. And Jessie—well, Jessie is a long way, still, from being settled.

REVEREND MEEKER LIFTS HIS palms to the sky, they stand for the creed, segue into prayers, and sing the final hymn—"I Am the Bread of

Life"—then await the benediction. Exalta's casket is so close to Kate, she can reach out and touch it, but Kate doesn't feel even the faintest vestiges of her mother's spirit hovering. To haunt one's own funeral, Exalta might say, just isn't done. Better to make a complete and graceful exit. Think of me fondly, but for heaven's sake, don't cry.

Kate doesn't cry. Exalta raised her sensibly. However, Kate does notice Mr. Crimmins pull a handkerchief from his pocket and dab at his eyes, which is sweet. Magee's muffled sobs are less so, though understandable considering how much time she spent with Exalta at the end. One of Exalta's last clear-minded quips to Kate was a *sotto voce* comment after Magee left Exalta's bedside to go fetch Exalta some tapioca pudding.

I see I have a new best friend, Exalta said.

All in all, Kate is relieved when the service is over—and even more relieved once the casket is lowered into the ground in the cemetery on Hummock Pond Road and the rich, fresh dirt smoothed over the top. Gennie squeezes Kate's hand so tightly she nearly fuses Kate's fingers. Cemeteries are scary for children; nobody likes to think about being put in a box and buried for all eternity. Kate nearly says, "We can come visit Grand-Nonny here whenever you want," but she doesn't want Gennie to think for one second that Exalta is actually *here*—and so she says nothing at all.

Kate can't get to the Field & Oar Club fast enough. She's in desperate need of a drink.

SHE SUCKS DOWN A Mount Gay and tonic—this has been the favorite cocktail at the club in recent years—and makes sure that all four of her children are present and accounted for on the lawn between the clubhouse and the waterfront before she begins the odious business of socializing. It's a brilliant day with deep blue skies and a tennis wind—enough to be refreshing but not so strong that you wished you were out sailing. There seem to be more people at the reception than were at the church, and isn't that just typical of their set—skip church, how dull, and choose instead to pay respects over cocktails and the lunch buffet on someone else's chit.

Kate sees Bitsy Dunscombe step onto the brick patio with her second husband, Arturo; her identical twins, Heather and Helen; and their husbands. Heather and Helen are Jessie's age, twenty-three, they both went to Briarcliff and are both new housewives of just under a year. Bitsy and her loathsome first husband, Ward Dunscombe, threw the twins a double wedding here at the club last July. Kate and David had attended, mainly because Bitsy declared it would be the "wedding of the decade," and Kate had wanted to see what that looked like. For Kate the best part of the wedding wasn't the girls in matching dresses—they looked lovely, though the double vision came across as something of a sideshow spectacle—but rather when Bitsy's first husband and second husband had a fistfight in the parking lot. By all accounts, it was Ward who threw the first punch (he was a notoriously nasty drunk), but, alas, it was Arturo who had gotten posted. Ward was the sixth wealthiest man on Nantucket and was a lifelong member of the Field & Oar, whereas Arturo was a Panamanian national who came to the island to work as a waiter at the Opera House restaurant.

Technically, Arturo isn't allowed to set foot in the club, but Kate won't say a word. It's a funeral.

"Kate," Bitsy says, her arms open in a *V*, and her head cocked back. "I'm so sorry for your loss. Exalta was one of a kind."

These are probably the nicest words Bitsy could say about Exalta without lying, because for seventy-one of her eighty-two years, Exalta was imperious, judgmental, and cold. That she had thawed so late in life was the only thing that kept today from being a celebration. *Ding-dong, the witch is dead.*

Out of the corner of her eye, Kate sees Bill Crimmins standing out on the dock, hands crammed into his pockets, gazing at the water. He might feel more uncomfortable here at the Field & Oar than even Arturo. Kate should go over and bring Bill into the fold, but she can't dismiss Bitsy quite so fast.

"Thank you for coming, Bitsy," she says. "Of course Mother adored you." This isn't true, but Kate treads lightly where Bitsy is concerned. Ten years earlier, Kate and Bitsy had a fight in the middle of dinner at the Opera House—the night Bitsy revealed that she was sleeping with Arturo—because Bitsy accused Jessie of stealing from her daughter Helen. Kate had stormed out, indignant, only to later find out that it had been true. Jessie had stolen five dollars and a lip gloss from Helen Dunscombe's Bermuda bag.

That had been a tumultuous summer for them all—1969. Kate wouldn't relive that summer for all the tea in China.

Kate had never apologized to Bitsy the way she should have but by the following summer, Ward had found out about Arturo, and a messy divorce followed. Kate made amends by supporting Bitsy and inviting her and Arturo to their new house on Red Barn Road for cocktails. Bitsy had loved the house and intimated that she, too, might leave the socially suffocating cobblestone streets of downtown and move to a place that was secluded and private, where "not everyone knows what you had for breakfast."

In the intervening years, Kate and Bitsy have handled their relationship like some kind of fragile family heirloom that will shatter if they aren't careful.

"I'm sorry we didn't make it to the church," Bitsy says. "Robert had a call with his law firm that ran longer than we expected." Robert was one of the husbands, the lawyer, and the other husband was a doctor. Both twins now lived in Westchester County—one in Rye, one in Ardsley. "But I knew you wouldn't mind. Exalta wasn't particularly *religious*, was she? She used St. Paul's like the rest of us. For networking."

Networking? Kate thinks. What a bizarre thing to say! Their family attended St. Paul's for one reason only—because they were Episcopalian.

"Mother loved the music," Kate says.

"Speaking of," Bitsy says. "The girls tell me there's to be a bonfire at Ram Pasture tonight in Exalta's honor. For the young people?"

"Bonfire?" Kate says. "Ram Pasture? I think you must be mistaken. I've heard nothing about this."

"Helen?" Bitsy says, calling over one perfectly coiffed twin, who's wearing a Lilly Pulitzer patio dress printed with turquoise giraffes. "Didn't you tell me there was a bonfire tonight at Ram Pasture?"

"Yes," Helen says. "Midnight at the Oasis, Kirby is calling it. Heather and I have been discussing what to wear. It sounds vaguely Moroccan so we were thinking caftans." When Helen brings her Mount Gay and tonic to her lips, Kate can't help noticing the enormous diamond on her left hand, resting over a simple gold wedding band. She fights the jealousy she feels that Bitsy has two married daughters and Kate has zero. Zero married daughters out of *three*! "Kirby is so clever. So . . . sophisticated."

"Yes," Kate says. "Isn't she just."

KATE FINDS KIRBY LOOKING deceptively wholesome in a sleeveless navy silk sheath with one of Exalta's brooches at the neck, eating finger sandwiches and chatting with Reverend Meeker. Kate wonders what Kirby and the reverend could possibly be talking about; they have exactly nothing in common. Kirby's life in New York, as Kate understands it, includes a lot of expense-account lunches with that dreadful Gurley Brown woman and then it's off to the disco every night, wearing gold lamé jumpsuits. Kirby sleeps with men but doesn't date them; she flits from one to the next like a child who grows bored with her toys. This is her excuse for not settling down: she can't find anyone who holds her attention. She thinks marriage should be one episode of *Laugh-In* after another, which it most decidedly is not.

"Reverend," Kate says. "I need to borrow Katharine for a moment."

"Uh oh," Kirby says. "If she's calling me 'Katharine,' I'm in trouble. Pray for me, Reverend."

Kate leads Kirby into the snack bar where it's shaded and quiet and smells like French fries.

"Did you plan a bonfire for tonight?" Kate asks. "At Ram Pasture? In your grandmother's honor? Did you do this and not . . . *inform* me? Did you not . . . *invite* me?"

"Mom," Kirby says.

5

Night Fever

They drive the Scout right onto the sand, near the spot where Tiger dug the giant hole and filled it with stacked wooden pallets that he took from the back alley behind Charlie's Market. Jessie and Kirby set out thin kilim rugs that Kirby transported from New York in the back of the LTD. There was a place downtown that practically gave them away, she said. They cover Kate's long folding table with a tapestry and arrange a row of votive candles down the center. They set out the refreshments: whole salted almonds, dates, dried apricots, an assortment of olives, goat cheese sprinkled with pista-chios, melba toast, hummus, and lots and lots of grapes. Jessie had suggested they also get fixings for S'mores but Kirby shot that idea down. They were strictly adhering to the theme.

Well, there were no kegs of Schlitz in northern Africa, Jessie thinks, and yet that's what they're drinking at this oasis. The keg is in the back of Mr. Crimmins's pickup, which he's letting them borrow, though Mr. Crimmins isn't coming to the bonfire.

"You young people have fun," he said. "And tomorrow, come over to the house. Your grandmother left a list of things she wanted you to have."

Things she wanted you to have: Exalta's considerable collection of whirligigs and whimmy-diddles will be divided up between the four grandchildren. Exalta's jewelry—the rings she kept in exquisite porcelain boxes, and bracelets and necklaces that lived in a locked case—will be passed to Kate, Jessie, Blair, Kirby, and Magee. Even one-quarter or one-sixth of these possessions will be worth quite a lot, Jessie knows, but only if she sells them. She may, in fact, sell some of the jewelry to ease her third year of law school—maybe buy a new desk lamp or an interview suit—but the whirligigs and whimmy-diddles are so inexorably *Exalta* that Jessie could never let them go. She will be their steward until she dies and every time she sets eyes on them, she will think of her grandmother.

PEOPLE START ARRIVING THE second it gets dark. Blair has left the twins back at the house; she hitches a ride to the beach with Tiger and Magee. The Dunscombe twins show up with their new husbands. Joey Whalen pulls up in his Porsche and Larry Winter is driving his grandmother's ancient Jeep Cherokee. There are a bunch of friends of Kirby's from her Madequecham days, as well as people that Blair, Kirby, and Tiger knew from sailing at the Field & Oar.

Kirby has a boombox and Tiger brought serious speakers. As soon as the fire is lit, there's music: Led Zeppelin's "Kashmir" sets the mood, followed by Earth, Wind & Fire, the Doobie Brothers, Bob Seger, Rod Stewart. Jessie stands at the food table and tries an olive, though she isn't hungry. She's not sure who to hang out with. Kirby is surrounded by her old friends, smoking clove cigarettes. Tiger and Magee are talking to the Dunscombe twins about whatever it is that's important to married people—mortgages? casseroles?—and Blair is the bologna in a Larry-Winter-and-Joey-Whalen sandwich.

Blair tries to lasso Jessie. "You remember Larry Winter, don't you, Jessie? He lives in Florida now."

Blair obviously wants to do the sorority bump-and-roll, passing off Larry to Jessie, but nope, sorry, Jessie isn't *that* desperate for company. Larry Winter is a hundred years old, or thirty-five, and he has a mustache like Rollie Fingers.

"Hitting the keg," Jessie says.

She does hit the keg, filling two plastic cups with cold Schlitz, then she strolls past the fire pit to the water's edge. She feels like a stranger in her own family, but there's nothing new about that. She fingers the gold knot at her neck and runs it along the chain. The necklace was originally a gift to Exalta from Jessie's grandfather on the occasion of their first wedding anniversary. It's priceless, and Exalta chose to give it to Jessie.

Jessie guzzles down one beer, feels a little better, tries to remind herself that, as soon as she wants to, she can rejoin the party and talk to Heather and Helen Dunscombe. They went through the predictable trajectory of being friends, then hating each other, then being friends again after it turned out that both Jessie and Helen Dunscombe had been molested by their tennis instructor, Garrison. But Jessie's afraid they'll have nothing in common now. Jessie is in law school and lives in Greenwich Village. She's single. The twins are married and live in the suburbs. Jessie takes the subway; the twins drive station wagons. This time next year, Jessie will be studying for the bar exam. This time next year, one or both of the Dunscombe twins will be pregnant.

Will Jessie still be single this time next year? She can't believe it's 1979 and the first thing a person wants to know about a woman is if she has managed to catch a man. The song changes to Donna Summer, "Heaven Knows." *Heaven knows, it's not the way it should be!* Do people care if Donna Summer is married or single? They do not; she is fabulous either way. So there's hope.

Jessie has nearly finished her second beer when someone plops in the sand next to her.

"Jessie Levin," a voice says. "Surprise."

Jessie turns. Male person, her age, or maybe a little older. Shorn head, so what Jessie first thinks is that Tiger saw her sitting by herself, felt sorry for her, and sent over one of his army buddies.

"Surprise?" she says.

"It's me," he says. "Pick."

6

Paradise by the Dashboard Light

Blair is desperate to get rid of Larry Winters. How had she entertained even for a second that there might still be something between them? He came to the church in a tan leisure suit with a wide-collared paisley shirt underneath, and although he was kind and solicitous with his mother, Blair had to close her eyes against the sight of him. Then, at the reception, he'd been stuck to her like flypaper. She was unable to talk to anyone else—meaning she couldn't have a proper, private conversation with Joey Whalen.

Well, that's not exactly true, is it? There were the stolen moments the night before.

After the twins went to the guest cottage to watch *Mork & Mindy* before bed, Blair slipped out to Joey's Porsche under the auspices of saying good night.

"I can't believe you came," Blair said.

"Family," Joey said.

"Yes, well," Blair said, meaning: your brother didn't think it was worth flying up from Houston for. But Angus must have called Joey—because how else would he have heard about Exalta? Maybe Angus suggested Joey appear on Nantucket in his place. Maybe—is Blair reaching here?—Angus realizes that long ago, he thwarted the romance between Blair and Joey. Because Blair and Joey had been a couple first! "I'm grateful you're here. And the kids . . ." The kids had been ecstatic when they saw their uncle, all thoughts of experiments and puzzles abandoned. They had launched themselves into Joey's arms like little rockets. Joey was God, Santa Claus, and Jim Rice rolled into one.

"I love those kids like they're my own," Joey said.

And me? Blair wanted to ask. *Do you love me like I'm your own?* Joey is still a bachelor, still working in advertising. He's the head of the national campaign for Stouffer's, so he travels the country and eats a lot of French bread pizza. The pay is good and he has no one to support but himself—hence, the Porsche, and a summer place in Newport.

"Well, Blair," Joey said, sliding down into the leather bucket seat of the Porsche. "I guess I'll see you tomorrow."

Tomorrow meant church, family, obligation. It seemed like Joey was going to leave without so much as a good-night kiss. Was Blair going to let that happen?

Blair ran a finger along the racing stripe. "This car is foxy," she said. "How fast does it go?"

Joey hadn't hesitated, even for a second. "Get in," he said. "I'll show you."

They'd ended up zipping down the Madaket Road then careening along Cliff before they stopped to make out at the end of Hinckley Lane. It might have gone even further, Blair might have let Joey have her across the hood or she might have followed him back to his room at the Jared Coffin House, but at the last minute, she suffered a crisis of conscience and stopped him.

"My brother wins again, I see," Joey said.

"Just think how it will *look*!" Blair says. "It'll look scandalous . . . *incestuous*, even."

This made Joey laugh. "*We* aren't related," he said.

"I know . . ."

"But you care what people think," Joey said. "Because you're just like your mother and your grandmother."

"I am not," Blair insisted. "I'm my own woman."

"If you want to know how it will look, I'll tell you," Joey said. "It'll look like I've been crazy for you since the day I met you. It'll *look* like I've been biding my time until the inevitable happened and you and Angus split. And even then, I've let a proper amount of time pass. But now I'm here and I want to make this work."

Wasn't that what Blair wanted, too? She had thought of Joey every day since returning to Boston, but she'd been too timid—and yes, too conventional—to consider calling him. Plus, he was impossible to pin down; the only person she could have asked about his whereabouts was . . . Angus. So his appearing on Nantucket was both a surprise and an answer to a longing that Blair was hesitant to admit she'd been holding in her heart.

"Drive me home, please," Blair said. "I need to think about it."

NOW, HERE IT IS, a full twenty-four hours later, and Blair has reached a decision. She wants to be with Joey Whalen. Maybe it's outrageous—dating her ex-husband's brother—or maybe it happens all the time. Angus won't be at all surprised and neither will Blair's family. The children, though—how will Gennie and George feel about their mother dating their *uncle*—and their uncle, possibly, becoming their stepfather?

Well, they'll either be thrilled or disgusted. Or, more likely, thrilled one day and disgusted the next. But Blair won't sacrifice her own happiness for the sake of the children. She reasons that if she's happy, the children will be happy. This is a modern attitude—her neighbors will say she's been reading too much *Redbook*—but come on, it's 1979, and in six months, it will be 1980!

Blair is going to tell Joey Whalen, yes. Yes, she wants to be with him. She doesn't care that he lives out of a suitcase. He can spend time at her house in Chestnut Hill; she can take the twins to New-port. It'll be exciting. Blair will have a family situation that is just as wacky as everyone else at Radcliffe.

Her only problem now is a small one. She has to get rid of Larry. But how? He can't take a hint!

Kirby approaches out of the darkness. "Anyone here want to smoke some weed?"

Blair says, "I bet Larry does."

Both Joey and Larry laugh, then Larry clears his throat. "Actually, I'd love to."

"Dynamite," Kirby says. She's wearing an ivory caftan, which in that moment makes her seem like an angel of mercy. "Come on, Larry. Let's go for a walk."

Kirby links her arm through Larry's and they wander away. Blair reaches for Joey's hand.

"Drive?" he says.

"You must read minds," she says. "Let's go."

7

Life in the Fast Lane

The weed is schwag—Kirby got it from her Spring Street dealer, Pope, whose product is inconsistent—but it hardly matters because Kirby is with Larry Winter! Kirby stole him right out from under Blair's nose!

It's a triumph worthy of its own *Cosmo* column. WHEN DREAMS COME TRUE: HOOKING UP WITH YOUR TEENAGE CRUSH AS A GROWN WOMAN.

Seventeen years earlier, 1962, back when *Kennedy* was president, Kirby harbored an excruciating crush on Larry Winter, but he had been in love with Blair. Kirby used to babysit Larry's pain-in-the-ass little sisters and Larry would be saddled with the task of driving Kirby home at the end of the afternoon. Kirby was only fourteen, she wore braces and had acne across her forehead and was every bit the Ugly Duckling. Larry, meanwhile, was a man—seventeen, eighteen—headed to Georgetown to major in political science. He wanted to run for president.

Reports from Mrs. Winter that were relayed to Kirby through Exalta pointed in a different direction. After college, Larry worked as the food and beverage manager at a private club in Vero Beach, Florida.

Kirby won't lie: it was disappointing to hear this.

But then, recently, Exalta made a point of mentioning that one of the wealthy members of the Vero Beach Club had given Larry seed money and he was opening a nightclub in Key Largo.

A nightclub! That was something Kirby could get behind.

She isn't at all surprised that Larry accepted her offer of a toke because everyone in the nightclub world partook in a little something, and usually more than a little and occasionally more than one thing. She also isn't surprised when Larry exhales, winces, and says as he passes the joint back to Kirby, "This shit is terrible."

"I know," Kirby says. "Sorry. I do have some powder if you want to snort a line."

"What?" Larry says. "You mean . . . *cocaine*?" He sounds completely scandalized and Kirby rolls her eyes, but it's dark so he doesn't see. You own a *nightclub*? She thinks. In the Florida *Keys*? Just south of *Miami*, which might as well be renamed Cocaine *City*?

"Yes," Kirby says. "I mean cocaine." She has a glass vial hanging from a chain around her neck, which she pulls over her head. She taps out a tiny amount onto the back of her thumb and snorts it up. "Want a line?"

"No, I don't want a *line*!" Larry says. "You should be ashamed of yourself. You just did cocaine right in front of me."

"Are you stuck in the Stone Age?" Kirby asks. "Because you sound like Fred Flintstone. I wouldn't have pegged you as being so . . . square."

Even in the dark, she can see Larry grin. His teeth are so white, she wonders if they're fake. "I'm not square," he says. "I was putting you on. Of course I want a line."

Ha! Oh boy, Kirby is relieved. She had a vision of Larry tattling on her to Mrs. Winter or, worse, Kate, and then it would be straight to rehab for Kirby. She had thought twice about bringing the cocaine to Nantucket because no one on the island partied this way, but now her gamble has paid off. She is going to fly high with her teenage crush, Larry Winter.

She taps out a bump for Larry and he hoovers it right up, then sniffs, waiting for the rush to hit.

"God-*damn*!" he cries out at the ocean. He turns back to Kirby, who has capped the vial and tucked it back down her dress. "Is it all right if I kiss you?"

Hell, *yes*! Kirby thinks—and a second later, she and Larry Winter are making out. But something is wrong. Larry's mouth is open too wide; it feels like he's trying to swallow her. Maybe it's the drugs, or maybe he's just completely inept. They clash teeth, which makes a plasticky sound, and Kirby thinks, *Definitely false teeth*.

She pulls away. "Easy there, Cowboy." She can feel Larry's erection through his tight polyester pants. The *Cosmo* girl in her is mildly intrigued, it's bigger than she imagined—but Kirby can't decide how far she wants this to go. She finds herself in this position all the time when she's out. She'll be dancing with some guy and he'll want more and if he's cute, or ugly but confident, she'll lead him to her secret alcove and kiss him. But she always remains in control of the situation. Occasionally this leads to sex in Kirby's loft—she never goes home with anyone and she never, ever has sex in the club. Part of being a liberated woman, she tells the girls at the magazine—they hang on Kirby's every word—is remaining free to walk away at any moment.

Larry grabs the back of Kirby's head and puts his sloppy mouth on hers like she's a Big Mac. She pushes him off again. "Whoa, buddy, let's slow things down a little." In an attempt to be tender, she reaches up to touch his long, feathered hair. It's soft and silky between her fingers. Larry Winter has good hair—like David Cassidy—and hasn't Kirby always wanted to have sex with David Cassidy? She moves her hands so that she's stroking Larry's long mustache. He used to be so clean-cut—he was an Exeter squash player when he dated goody two-shoes Blair—that Kirby can't help but be delighted by his transformation into a modern man. He isn't stuck in Camelot like everyone else on this Land-That-Time-Forgot island.

They start kissing again but it isn't any better and Larry's hands are sliding down her back toward her . . .

She pulls away. "Larry."

He says, "You are so . . . *cool*, Kirby. You give off this incredible vibe—sexy, fun, *fascinating*. I can't believe I spent so many summers mooning over Blair. I should have been with you."

The music from the bonfire floats down the beach. "Rebel, Rebel" by David Bowie. This is Kirby's song. *You tore your dress! Your face is a mess!* Who is Kirby if not the rebel of her family? She was the one who protested the war, swore at the cops, got arrested, got pregnant out of wedlock, and dated a rainbow of men, including the "one who got away," Darren Frazier. Darren ended up marrying Kirby's best friend, Rajani, and they now have four beautiful children, which was what motivated Kirby to leave Boston and move to New York—where she has managed to push herself even closer to the edge. Misbehaving is the only way Kirby has ever been able to steal the spotlight from perfect achiever Blair, only golden son Tiger, and Jessie, the precious baby.

But now, here is Larry Winter telling Kirby that he prefers her to her older sister. All of the longing and jealousy that fourteen-year-old Kirby with her braces and her acne felt are vanquished—poof!—in that moment. Her attraction to Larry Winter was never about Larry Winter, she realizes. It was about how she felt about herself. The satisfaction at being acknowledged as a sexy, fun, *fascinating* (this adjective gives Kirby a particular thrill) woman is more powerful than any drug.

"Hey, thanks, Larry," she says. "Now, if you'll excuse me, it's time I got back to the party."

8

Looks Like We Made It

Tiger can't believe it when Magee asks him to bring her a cold beer from the keg and he's even more surprised when she chugs the entire thing without stopping. Who is this woman and what has she done with his wife?

She emits a ladylike burp and hands him the empty plastic cup. "Another."

"Another?" Tiger says. "Seriously?"

"Please?" she says. "I want to get drunk."

"You . . . ?" Tiger can't believe this. "Are you sure?"

"Your grandmother is dead," Magee says. "And do you know what advice she gave me?"

Tiger is afraid to ask. "What?"

She said, "When you don't know what else to do, have a good, stiff drink."

Yes, Tiger thinks, that does sound like Exalta.

"And I don't know what else to do," Magee says. "We've tried everything."

"But you've been so careful with your health . . ."

"It's not working!" Magee says. "So I'm going to try the opposite."

"Okay?" Tiger says. He's skeptical but he fetches Magee another cold beer and when she finishes that, another. That's three beers, but Magee isn't finished. She wants something more, something stronger.

"Something *stronger*?" Tiger says. "There isn't anything stronger at this party."

"The flask," she says. "In your glove compartment."

"Ha!" Tiger says. Guess he should have known he couldn't keep a secret from his wife. There's a flask of Wild Turkey that Tiger keeps in the glove box of the Trans Am. Tiger offers the flask to any Vietnam Vet he happens to meet.

Magee is a veteran of sorts, he supposes. She put in all those hours of service to Exalta.

"All right," Tiger says. "I'll get the flask." He grabs it from the car and he and Magee both take a pull. Magee doesn't cough or sputter; she doesn't even grimace. She is tougher than half the guys in the Fourth Infantry.

LATER, TIGER AND MAGEE dance in the sand. The song is the Bee Gees, "Tragedy." But instead of a tragedy, the night feels like a miracle. Magee is joyfully, ecstatically blotto. She raises her hands in the air, she twirls around, sings along. It takes no convincing for Tiger to lead Magee down the beach with one of the kilim rugs rolled under his arm. They lay the rug out in a secluded spot in the dunes and they make love in a way that they never have before. Magee is uninhibited, carefree, wild. She leaves scratch marks down his back, bites his ear, thrusts right along with him until she screams. Screams!

Tiger falls back on the rug, breathless.

Best of my life, he thinks.

"Did that feel . . . different to you?" he asks.

"Oh, yes," she says. She props herself up on her elbow and grins at him. "Mark my words, Tiger Foley: nine months from now, you're going to be a father."

9

Reunited

Jessie didn't learn what she knows about love from being with Theo Feigelbaum. No—Jessie's first teacher in lessons of the heart is the man with the shorn head who is now sitting next to her: Pickford Crimmins. Pick.

Jessie jumps to her feet. "Pick?" she says. "I thought you were in . . . Africa?"

"I was," Pick says. "I got home to Cali last week. And then I called Bill and he told me about Exalta, so I hitched a ride with a buddy who was going to Philadelphia and I took a bus the rest of the way."

"I can't . . . I don't . . . wow." Jessie needs to get a grip. "So . . . how was the Peace Corps? You were in . . . ?"

"Kenya," he says. "I worked in Nairobi for a while, digging wells. Then I was sent out to the Mara, the Kenyan savannah. It was incredible, Jess. It was like an episode of *Wild Kingdom* every day. We saw a giraffe give birth, a cheetah kill, prides of lions, baby elephants, the black rhino. For six weeks, I lived with the Maasai villagers. I learned how to shoot a bow and arrow, I drank cow's blood, I learned the tribal dances."

Jessie nods dumbly. She thought it was amazing that she got an A in her Torts class and managed to successfully transport two pastrami sandwiches on the subway.

"I'm sorry I didn't have any time to write letters home," Pick says. "I'm sure Bill thought I dropped off the face of the earth."

"He's proud of you," Jessie says, which she's sure is true though Mr. Crimmins never says much about his own family—probably because his daughter, Lorraine, who lives on a commune in California, has caused so much anxiety and confusion to the Foley-Levins. Jessie knew Pick went to Africa with the Peace Corps and she'd been glad to hear that, hadn't she? Partly because she liked knowing that Pick was contributing in a positive way to the world and partly because Africa was so remote that Jessie's lingering feelings for Pick became a moot point.

Pick settles back in the sand and Jessie follows suit. The party rages behind them but Jessie doesn't care. Pick is here.

"So," he says. "Tell me about everyone. Actually, forget everyone. Tell me about you."

"I live in Greenwich Village," Jessie says. "I'm a second-year law student at NYU."

"Law school," Pick says. "Like your dad."

"I guess," Jessie says. The law that David practices—corporate litigation—is last on Jessie's list of interests. "I want to practice immigration law. Or maybe work for the ACLU. I want to help people."

"That's my girl," Pick says.

Jessie wonders if she's trying to make herself sound altruistic in order to impress Pick. She has never before mentioned immigration or civil rights law out loud. If she'd said this to Theo, he would have gone on a diatribe about Jessie's "privilege." She could *afford* to practice immigration law, hell, she could become a public *defender*—because she had a trust fund. But as for Theo, he was looking at a big firm, big money future. He wanted to be in-house counsel at a Wall Street bank.

"I made Bill promise to tell me if you got married," Pick says, "so I could come home and disrupt the wedding like Benjamin in *The Graduate*."

Jessie smiles. "You did not."

"I did."

"Well, I'm not married."

"Boyfriend?"

"Theo," she says, and even though Pick is sitting a foot away from her, she can feel him tense up. "But we broke up. He cheated on me."

"What an idiot," Pick says.

Jessie nudges him with her elbow. "You're one to talk."

"What?"

"That summer you lived with us, you left me in the dust for Sabrina."

"Sabrina who?"

"Sabrina was . . . the girl you worked with at the North Shore restaurant. You started dating her."

"Oh," Pick says. "I don't remember Sabrina."

"You *don't?*" Jessie says. She finds this unfair. Jessie had been crushed when Pick introduced her to Sabrina one fateful day at Surfside Beach; it was a moment that has both haunted her and served as a cautionary tale. When you fall in love, your heart opens in a burst of flower petals and gossamer streamers. But beware— because that same heart can just as quickly be cored like an apple, the most tender piece of you extracted and thrown onto the compost pile of the unrequited. For the past ten years, "Sabrina"—not the girl herself but the specter of someone prettier and more desirable— has haunted Jessie, inspired her even.

"You kissed me," Jessie says. "Twice. You really kissed me."

"Yes," Pick says. "That I do remember. Upstairs, in the cottage."

"And then a couple of days later, you were dating Sabrina."

"*I'm* the idiot, then," Pick says. "All I remember is that you were young—too young. I thought I'd get in trouble if anything else happened. The dynamic between me and your family was weird. I didn't know why at the time, but I know now. And I'm assuming you know?"

"That Wilder Foley was your father?" Jessie says. "Yes." Wilder Foley was Kate's first husband, the father of Blair, Kirby and Tiger, who had an affair with Lorraine Crimmins and got her pregnant. So Pick is a half sibling to Blair, Kirby, and Tiger, just like Jessie.

"When my mother and I left Woodstock that summer, I told her I wanted to go back to Nantucket to live with my grandfather. And she said we had burned that bridge forever."

Jessie takes a breath. Conversations like this happen all the time at funerals and weddings and baptisms, she knows. Secrets are revealed; there are reckonings.

"How *is* your mother?" Jessie asks, desperate to change the subject.

"Oh, fine," Pick says. "Busy with her organic farming, which is actually starting to make her some money. She fully believes organic produce is the future."

Jessie hasn't the foggiest idea what "organic" produce is, but she doesn't admit that.

"Now tell me about everyone else," Pick says. "Blair, Kirby, Tiger." He laughs. "Our siblings."

The phrase is so surreal that Jessie is stymied for a moment. But then she laughs along and starts to talk. *Blair and Angus divorced . . . Angus in Houston, Blair and the twins in a suburb of Boston . . . Kirby writes for* Cosmo, *if you pick up any issue at the grocery store checkout line, you'll see her byline, she lives in Soho, housesitting for this famous artist, Willie Eight, yeah, I'd never heard of him either, the only artists I know are dead except for Andy Warhol, who Kirby has met, she has a Polaroid of them together, she hangs out at Studio 54 and Limelight, dancing the night away . . . Tiger is married to Magee, they don't have kids yet, Tiger owns five bowling alleys and he drives that Trans Am you probably saw . . . He's a good person, my brother, I just want him to be happy*. Jessie finds her eyes are burning with tears as she says this. *I want them all to be happy, and if I had a magic wand, that would be my first and only wish—for Blair, Kirby, and Tiger to be happy.*

"What about you?" Pick says. "Don't you want to be happy?"

Jessie isn't sure how to explain it. She knows, somehow, that she is stronger than her three siblings. This is a bold statement because the three of them are big personalities; her sisters are beautiful and smart, and her brother is a war hero. But Jessie worries about the three of them in a way that she doesn't worry about herself.

"I am happy," she says. "Though I could use another beer. And you should mingle. I don't want to monopolize you."

"I have to tell you something," Pick says. He gets to his feet and offers Jessie a hand to pull her up. "I'm moving to New York."

"You are?" Jessie says.

"I was offered a job with the Economic and Social Council at the UN," Pick says. "Which probably sounds fancier than it is. The pay is peanuts. I'm going to have to live in Brooklyn."

Brooklyn? Jessie tries not to cringe.

"That's great!" she says. "We'll be neighbors."

Pick is still holding onto Jessie's hand. "Hopefully more than just neighbors," he says. "You know, when I was in Kenya, I had this recurring fantasy." He pauses. "Want to hear it?"

Fantasy? Jessie panics, thinking of the one awkward evening when Theo insisted on reading *Penthouse* "Forum" letters aloud to her. "Sure?" she says.

"My buddy, Tremaine, who I shared a tent with out in the Mara, had this tape recorder and three cassette tapes, one of which was *The Stranger* by Billy Joel. He played it *all* the time and do you know that song, 'Scenes from an Italian Restaurant'?"

"'Bottle of red'?" Jessie sings.

"'Bottle of white'!" Pick cries out. "Yes! So I always thought of you when I heard that song and I dreamed about meeting you in

New York City at a restaurant like that. Red-checkered tablecloths, a single candle dripping down the Chianti bottle, the whole deal." He shrugs. "I thought it would be romantic."

Me, Jessie thinks. *He dreamed about meeting* me.

"So when I get to New York, can we do that?" Pick asks. "Can we meet at a place like that?"

"Of course," Jessie says. She doesn't eat out at restaurants; she has no money. But the instant she gets back to the city, she's going to find the best Italian place in all of New York. Oh, man, you'd better believe it.

10

We Are Family

The kids are all at the bonfire, which leaves Kate and David at home alone. They watch the sunset and David opens a bottle of Pol Roger champagne. When Kate raises an eyebrow at the significance—is David *celebrating* Exalta's death? They did always have an uneasy relationship—he says, "Something to cheer you up."

He's right, as always: the bubbles cheer her. It's an unusually warm evening, so they drink with their feet dangling in the pool, the bottle in an ice bucket between them.

Kate's thoughts wander. Where is Exalta now? Anywhere? It seems impossible that she's gone and yet, that's what happens to all of us, eventually. It's a reminder to live while we can and take care with the legacy we're leaving behind. Kate feels proud of this house, this property, the decision she made ten years ago to move out here to the wilds of Madaket, to build a summer retreat where she can shelter her entire family. It had seemed radical at the time, Kate remembers.

"Do you want to go out to dinner?" David asks. "The Mad Hatter? DeMarco's?"

"It's too late," Kate says. "Everyone stops serving at nine."

"We could still order a pizza from Vincent's," David says. "Or skip dinner and get ice cream."

Kate says, "Let's do something crazy."

She can tell from the way his face brightens that he thinks she means sex there in the pool—or scouring Kirby's bedroom for a joint to smoke.

"I'm game," he says.

"Let's crash the party," Kate says. "We'll pick up Bill and take him with us."

It feels like a joy ride, even in David's staid lawyer car, the Cadillac. They have the windows down, Elvis on the radio, and Bill Crimmins—who Kate thought might be hesitant to join them—relaxing in the backseat, enjoying the fine leather.

"I'm so glad you called," Bill says. "The house feels too big now that she's gone."

"But now Pick is staying with you," Kate says. She finds she's relieved that Pick has shown up—as long as Lorraine is safely on the West Coast—so that there's someone to keep an eye on Bill.

They rumble down Barrett Farm Road through the open landscape until they come upon a line of parked cars and Kate hears music. She climbs out of the Cadillac in her bare feet. She's wearing a paisley beach cover-up, which is the only thing in her closet that looks even vaguely exotic. If Kate travels back a hundred years—okay, forty—she's a teenager being naughty, sneaking out of All's Fair while her parents sleep and hopping in the back of Trip Belknap's Studebaker, heading to a fire just like this one, populated with boys who do not yet know they'll soon be heading off to war.

Tonight, instead of defying her parents, Kate is defying her children.

Young people only. Bah!

KATE IS NEARLY TO the beach when she sees a young couple huddled together, obviously trying to make a clandestine escape.

"Blair?" Kate says. Blair is with . . . Joey Whalen. Surprise, surprise.

"Mom?" Blair says. Her face has always been easy to read and her expression now is one of sheer horror. She's been caught. With Joey.

Joey doesn't look caught, however. Joey is too smooth to ever look caught. "Hey Mrs. Levin, Mr. Levin, Mr. Crimmins," he says. He spins around and flings his arm open like a game-show host, as though the beach and the fire and the assembled crowd and even the ocean beyond are their grand prize. "Welcome!"

Blair and Joey, together—is that such a bad thing? Kate wonders. Joey Whalen is much better suited to Blair's temperament than Angus ever was.

Joey and Blair dutifully escort the old people with their brittle bones down onto the sand.

Blair takes Kate's elbow. "What are you doing here, Mom?"

Kate wants to say, *You are hardly one to be asking questions.* But instead, she smiles. "I came to party," she says, and this sounds so absurd, they both laugh. "Would you fetch me a drink, please, dear, and let your brother and sisters know I'm here."

"There's nothing to drink except keg beer," Blair says.

"That's fine," Kate says. "I'll have a beer."

"You will?"

"I will."

Blair returns with a foamy beer in a plastic cup and clearly she has also made the announcement because soon, Kate is surrounded by her children—Tiger and Magee, who look happier and more relaxed than Kate has seen them in years; Kirby, who Kate expects to be angry but who instead, throws her arms around her mother in what appears to be glee; Jessie and an incredibly handsome, upright young man whom Kate recognizes as Pick Crimmins.

The song changes and a cry goes up. The kids form a circle and start dancing. This, Kate knows, is her cue to exit, but suddenly David is on one side of her and Bill Crimmins is on the other and they, too, are part of the circle.

The lyrics announce the obvious: *We are family!*

Kirby dances in the middle of the circle and everyone cheers her on. She is replaced by Jessie and Jessie is replaced by Magee.

Magee can really dance. How did Kate not know this?

Magee heads straight for Kate with her arms outstretched.

"Your turn, darling," David says, placing an encouraging hand on her back.

My turn? Kate thinks. Surely not. Exalta would never in a million years have been caught in the middle of a circle dancing to a disco song.

It takes only a second for Kate to realize that she isn't Exalta. She is Kate Nichols Foley Levin, the new matriarch of this gathered family. She is in charge now and she will make her own decisions.

Kate passes off her cup to David and dances through the sand to the center of the circle. Her family cheers.

That's right, she thinks. She may be old, but she still has some surprises left.

About Elin Hilderbrand

Elin Hilderbrand lives on Nantucket, has three children, and is the author of twenty-seven novels, including *Summer of '69*.

Elin met Dottie in the spring of 2017 at the annual *Post and Courier* luncheon in Charleston and Elin says, "It was love at first sight." The two authors proceeded to meet on Nantucket every chance they got and they texted and emailed nonstop. They dreamed of doing a joint cooking show called "Cook the Books," where they would invite a third author on to make a signature dish for each episode. They also talked about a cookbook called "The Southern Belle and the Gray Lady." Elin's summer of 2020 novel, *28 Summers,* is dedicated to Dottie and Dottie makes a cameo appearance in Elin's summer of 2021 novel, *Golden Girl.* "I will never again have a writer friend like Dottie," Elin says. "Those of you who knew her understand what I mean, and those of you who didn't will just have to trust me. After Dottie, God broke the mold."

ALSO BY ELIN HILDERBRAND

Stand-Alone Novels

Golden Girl

28 Summers

Summer of '69

The Perfect Couple

The Identicals

Here's to Us

The Rumor

The Matchmaker

Beautiful Day

Summerland

Silver Girl

The Island

The Castaway

A Summer Affair

Barefoot

The Love Season

The Blue Bistro

Summer People

Nantucket Nights

The Beach Club

Paradise Series

Trouble in Paradise

What Happens in Paradise

Winters in Paradise

Winter Series

Winter Solstice

Winter Storms

Winter Stroll

Winter Street

Postcards from
Heaven

ADRIANA TRIGIANI

When you love a friend, you can't imagine your life without him. He's the person you call when something makes you laugh, or something awful just ruined your day. If you're lucky, that friend understands the complexities and challenges of what you do for a living. He can relate to the frustrations and setbacks that go with the job. He will celebrate with you when things go well. He will be the one to gently suggest that in success, it's important to keep your wits about you, and in failure, to do the same because both extremes have their traps. The loneliness of solitude, pressure of deadlines, and the fear dance at four a.m. that the words won't come in time are a few of the pitfalls of the writing life.

When we're talking about two friends who write for a living, mutual support and understanding are important while availability is essential. The daily conversation on the phone can be a lifeline. It seems only a writer can shore another writer.

Pat Conroy was that friend for Dorothea Benton Frank, and she for him. They talked an awful lot in their years of friendship before he died on March 4, 2016. He did not leave her behind though; the bond remained strong even after his death because in his fashion, in his own particular and original way, he kept in touch. He sent postcards from heaven.

To: Dorothea Benton Frank
From: Pat Conroy

Hey Dot. Settling in here. Good thing I like wide open spaces with
plenty of sky. Bliss is everything they said it was and more. I used
to believe serenity was for monks but turns out it's for everybody,
including writers. I like the zen. No characters roiling around in
my head. No sitting at a desk with my body in a chair for hours
on end, every muscle tensed like a freaked-out Halloween cat,
no book tour hoopla, and zero exhaustion from distant cousins
guessing who they might be in my latest novel. Just peace. Serenity
is completely satisfying.

How are you holding up? You're in that frenzy before pub, right?
To be fair, it seemed you were always in a frenzy before pub. Give
it a rest if you can. Books have a way of finding themselves in the
hands of the right readers. Don't push. We are not Fuller Brush
salesmen. Everybody needs a brush, but not everyone will like our
books.

I've been visiting Cassandra in her dreams. It's almost as good as
being there. I could visit you in your dreams but you scare too easy.

Love ya, Pat

To: DBF
From: PC

It's true that your grief and my absence from your life keeps the
connection between us intact. I believe I can alleviate some of the
pain and confusion on your end with these postcards. I know what
you're thinking, *postcards, not great*. Instagram is the new postcard

I guess: messages from people you know having fun in places
without you.

I wish I could come up with a better way to communicate. I
miss our long phone chats, especially the ones after dinner. Our
emailing was fun, too. This reaching out to the living by the dead
resembles a bad Wi-Fi connection. There are moments of perfect
reception followed by nothing. Intermittent communication, they
call it. You sure do seem a long way away from your old friend.

Love ya, Pat

To: DBF
From: PC

Dot, you called my name. The message got through!

I'd like to help.

I see the problem. Full disclosure: I can't render an opinion about
your latest book jacket because I am no longer there, and on this
side, cover art doesn't come up for discussion. I caught a brief
glimmer of you shuffling through the art boards opining, "Oh Pat,"
followed by your head hitting your writing desk like an anvil, which
led to a lot of weeping. Yours. Thanks for taking my name in vain.

There's only one thing to do since histrionics do not become you.
Call your agent and tell her, in your sweetest drawl, that you can't
possibly approve the cover art. Tell her nicely that your opus is
more complicated than a photograph of a woman with her back to
the reader, sitting on the beach wearing a one-piece bathing suit,
gripping a sun hat by the brim with one hand and clutching a mai
tai with the other. Tell them to lose the cocktail. You can live with

the rest. Say it casually, as though you're checking on the royalty rate in Bulgaria. No screaming, no crying, and do not attempt rage. If you do, I guarantee that you won't get what you want. The trick is: when they remove the mai tai from the cover art, suddenly the artist will not like it. He or she will create anew. New lady. New beach. New hat. You'll love the new approach. But if you want a new cover, keep your cool. Stay in the lane marked reasonable because you're a terrible actress. Really. No acting. Don't go into that field.

Love ya, Pat

To: DBF
From: PC

I feel like shit about that last postcard. You would have been a fine actress. You have the portraiture of, I don't know, Greer Garson by way of Margot Kidder. Hard to think of great actresses from the 1970s unless you get into Goldie Hawn and Liza Minnelli territory. Nothing wrong with either, very talented, but when I think of you, I go back to Hollywood's Golden Age and, no, I don't mean Shelley Winters in *The Poseidon Adventure*.

I gotta tell you I'm still laughing at when you said you woke up on the morning of your 57th birthday and looked in the mirror and screamed *Shelley!* Now, that was funny. You don't look like Shelley Winters, nothing wrong with her, by the way, you look like *you*, which is fine by me. Cassandra and I always said you were an Irish beauty. Fresh faced. Blue-eyed. Pie-eyed.

Love ya, Pat

To: DBF
From: PC

I stepped in it again with that last postcard. I did not mean
to disparage the great Irish, including you and me, with the
offhanded drinking comment. Pie-eyed, you know what I mean.
More to the point, and a better description of you: you're wide-
eyed, eager, curious, and adventurous. But let's face it, we know a
lad and a lass or two from the Emerald Isle who enjoy their spirits.
Anyhow, I meant no offense.

My initials are PC, which is everybody's shorthand for *politically
correct*, which I almost never am, even though I wish I were, or had
been, when I was alive if only to flaunt my moral superiority, which,
by admission, would mean I never had it in the first place. *Moral
superiority*, that is. I should have done the right thing more often,
but who knew at the time that slights and hurts are racked up over
a lifetime like parking tickets?

Would like to know what you made for dinner. Something tells me
pork chops. Is Peter home or is he off on a business trip? The kids?
I am sure they are thriving. They could care less about your old pal
Conroy. Who could blame them? If they did, they'd be living in the
past. Don't live in the past.

Love ya, Pat

To: DBF
From: PC

I didn't mean to tell you how to raise your children or give you
spiritual advice in general, including the ancient *don't live in the*

past nonsense. Live however the hell you want, because the truth is, eternity is just more of the same with one caveat. Nothing hurts. Not even my feelings, which is slightly odd because I have empathy for you; it remains on this side, but I don't need it for myself from you, or any of my friends or family. How bizarre is *that*? They say that's what it means to be divine—to shore up others, without regard to self. That's saintly, don't you think? It's either saintly, or just the surrender of will by a person who has learned to get along in a big family.

I've met a couple of saints but they are deadly dull. They parse their words as if each one had a calorie count and they were permanent residents at a Fat Farm. When they're not talking, they just sort of stare at you with big eyes. The statues of their visages in cathedrals look much better than the real thing. They don't seem too interested in leading our group forward, or even pulling us together in a common cause. They are of zero help when it comes to finding out what's in store for us here. I don't expect you to unpack their behavior (even though you were raised Catholic, as was I). They are aloof, which is as they were on earth. They were comfortable on pedestals.

I can't explain this place with any specificity. Life is confusing on earth, whereas on this side, there is a constant flow of understanding. It's like a river, but that's bad writing. It's not like I'm swept away here, or pulled under, we just *are*. We accept everything in the name of adaptation and transfiguration (a fancy word for mystical glow) whether the saints fraternize with us or not. Knowing you, there will be some fraternizing.

Love ya, Pat

To: DBF
From: PC

I have been thinking about the American South and the things I miss about it. After my wife, children, the marshes, and blue herons of South Carolina's Lowcountry, I rank covered dish suppers high on the list. There was nothing like them. I used to help roll the brown butcher paper on the tables in the church basement before the ladies set out the buffet. The covered dish suppers were fairly similar across the various denominations, the only difference: the Catholics always put candles on the tables whereas the Methodists placed flowers.

I liked the parade of the platters. The ladies of the congregation would arrive with their casseroles with a look of superiority tinged with the smug afterglow of daytime sex. (I didn't recognize it then but could easily spot it now.) The point is this. You've never seen such self-confidence. The women carried their Tupperware and 8 x 10 sheet pans down the steps into the church basement as if they were the crown jewels. Each woman believed her offering for the buffet was the best. There was a sense of self-confidence on the part of these gals that you could cut with a knife. Or was it arrogance? Who knows, until they place the pans on the table, and in short order, the ladies realize that most of the women didn't follow the sign-up sheet.

So, there are eight chop suey casseroles, several platters of deviled eggs, and way too many Texas sheet cakes. There's nothing green, no one made a salad, so the buffet looks autumnal brown and yellow, but who cares, everybody's hungry and nobody is interested in the loaves of cornbread or the fishes. (Who's the cheater who brought a bucket of Long John Silver fish instead of cooking?) Nobody's telling and nobody cares. Every dish that was placed on the buffet was made and served with love (except for the bucket from the drive-thru, and you could argue, even that was given with a generous heart).

Love everybody was the lesson, *no matter what they brung.*

That's what I miss the most about life back home. You can get along without the ocean, sand, and sun, but you would be hard-pressed to thrive without people who love you. In the South, they build people who know how to love. You get it, Dot. You always do.

Love ya, Pat

———————————————

To: DBF
From: PC

Forgive me for the last couple of postcards. I imagine I'm trying to explain the place I am so you might feel better about dying someday. You always said you never wanted to die, and I didn't either, but it's what comes eventually to anyone that is born, so it's wise to get used to the concept sooner than later. Some things about death as perceived by the living remain true. You hear about death mostly at funerals, and I know you heard these comments at mine, so I'll run a few by you in the hopes that the truth from me will give you some comfort.

He's in a better place.

That's partly true. Better in many ways, okay. But the place part, let me explain. This is not so much a place as it is a state. It's an ongoing feeling of peace, the same feeling you get when you've turned a book in on time and you know it's pretty good, maybe great, and the relief washes over you, after which comes the pride, in a job well done. You know the book is good and you're not even slightly tempted to call every snob you know and let them know that you hit your deadline and they can kiss your ass. There's none of that here. You finally know what it feels like not to care what anyone thinks. The afterlife is satisfaction followed by a nap. A soothing nap.

He didn't want to die.

No, he did not. But he did. And it was not a bit frightening. It was confusing until I figured out what happened and accepted the new state I was in. Yes, it was chaotic. It might have something to do with the fact that I was shouting, "Am I dead? Will somebody answer me? Am I dead?"

He saw the light at the end of the tunnel.

Not exactly. I saw nothing but haze. It was then that I tried to remember every book or television show on the subject of near-death experiences. I remembered a long interview on *The Sally Jessy Raphael Show* that featured a psychic who wrote books, can't remember her name but you will. She wore a wig. You said her hairdo, an explosion of weird wiglets, looked like the ones you wore to your senior prom. She came on the show and admitted that she had been dead several times. That could not have possibly been true! *Say No to Tarot!* Remember this lady? She spoke of voices and her mother and all that, and at the time I said to myself, I hope that's how dying goes! Wouldn't that be nice? But it turns out that there isn't a band to greet you—you sort of join the souls, and everyone is everyone, all one, if I may be so blunt.

I recall that book by the surgeon who fell off a moped, then into a coma, and when he emerged from it, wrote a book about it. You know who I mean. Remember you gave me that book as a gag gift one Christmas? You know, it was written by the brilliant surgeon who crossed over and saw goo and then a beautiful garden? I'm here now, and I still have no idea what he was talking about. There's no goo. There's no garden. Maybe the hospital put something in his IV and he had hallucinations. I've yet to see a butterfly here. Let's get back to what people said when I died.

He was too young.

Maybe. Seventy years doesn't seem old when you're 68. Or even 65. In some ways it felt very old to me. But here's the thing about age. Any age at time of death is too young unless you're 115 years old. And even then . . .

He had so much left to do.

Not really. I pretty much said what I needed to say and tried to write what I wanted to read. In that regard, I was blessed. I made a living doing what I loved the most, and here and there, folks loved what I wrote, which was heavenly. That's all I could do, Dot. Tell it like I saw it. And when a reader took my work into his heart, I knew it. Every single time. They were moved and their emotional reaction moved me. It was the perfect exchange. A tale well told in exchange for loyalty and affection. I would say that was close to divine.

Love ya, Pat

To: DBF
From: PC

Why was my funeral a circus? From my point of view, it looked like the aerial shot of the Homecoming halftime show of a Clemson football game. I swore they even spelled PAT in formation on the

church steps. Did they? Maybe it was your idea. You can be grand,
in the best of ways. You are also a good friend. You showed up.
You were there at the service. I got that one glimpse and that was
enough for me. For a man who hated to put on a necktie or shoes
that squeaked or, God forbid, a suit, it was something to behold.
I guess all the folderol was to let people know I was important.
But I never was, even on my best day, anything that bordered on
important. Maybe I was slightly interesting. That's a different kind
of important, at least to the person living the life. But there you
were, Dot, crying like you were at the front of the line at Lohman's,
certain they were never going to unlock the front doors to let you
in for the Midnight Madness sale. You took it hard, Dot, and that
got to me. I was there, now I'm here. It's nothing to cry about.

Love ya, Pat

To: DBF
From: PC

You wrote another novel and turned it in on time? What are you,
Dottie, a literary machine? You are a summer read wind machine!
You write of Lowcountry beaches and shrimp boils and cocktails on
the sand—soothing beauty and Southern lady hijinks. And there's
nobody like you. I wonder if you will get to 50 books before you
take the flight home. To here. I bet you've got a hundred more
ideas for novels. My mind did not work that way. I'd think about a
story for years and it would chug around inside of me like waves of
dyspepsia, followed by a bout of gas that kept me pacing the floor
until I passed it, after which I would sit down and write *I never
saw you chug* but I know you did. You worked hard. You tried to
make it look easy because that's what you wanted for your reader.

Profound thoughts, sure. Family dynamics, what else is there? Food, absolutely. Your love of Sullivan's Island and the Lowcountry? You were the ambassador of soul for those tufts of land you call home that floated on the ocean off the coast of South Carolina like a discarded wedding gown tossed off the side of a cruiser. You are the queen of all that, so I'm not surprised. *Queen Bee?* Do I have it right?

I heard you ripping the box open and you were shouting at Victoria to *get a video for Instagram.* In that moment, I was happy to be dead. Social and media are two words that should never meet, like child and actor or freak and accident. You should stop encouraging all that intrusion into your life by way of devices and get back to the basics. Everything we do is not interesting. Well, let me speak for myself. You are fascinating in your love of living and gracious dining and strong friendships. I know because I was the beneficiary of all three. Cassandra is still crying most nights. Give her a call. Will ya?

Love ya, Pat

To: DBF
From: PC

I have recognized no one, not a single person in the incoming area. I scan the crowd, thinking, there's gotta be *someone* I know coming through, which makes me wonder in a serious way if publishers, editors, publicists, and morning-show bookers go somewhere else instead of here? I hope not. I've heard enough stories to know that you don't want to go *there.* Are you laughing now, Dot? How many times did you say *Don't go there, Pat,* and I had no idea where you didn't want me to go. We'd go round and round about the meanings of phrases and words, as though we were the experts.

Maybe we were. About some things. Here's a list. You can add to it if you wish.

Pat and Dottie's Areas of Expertise

The American South

Hush puppies

Whiskey

Peanut butter balls and divinity candy

Candy apples

Vodka

Boiled peanuts

Po boy sandwiches

Hash brown potatoes

Gingham fabric, Florsheim shoes, and the *Atlanta Journal Constitution.*

(Well, for you, *the Charleston Post and Courier.* Beyond newspapers, you fancied *McCall's* magazine and *Life.* You remember *Life.* The big magazine when we were kids. The one the size of a turkey platter? I don't know how it fit in the mailman's bag. Did it? Did he carry it separately? Must have. Remember the pictures? You'd open those big, lush pages and find photographs so huge you could walk into them. You remember.) Back to the list.

Chryslers and Oldsmobiles and Fords

Cornbread

When men wore hats and women wore them, too. Hell, when everybody wore a hat when they left the house, including the children.

Gardenias

Magnolia leaves at Christmas (the dried ones)

I don't know if I ever told you, my mother made her own marshmallows. Who does that? Why do that? Only Southern women would figure out how to make a marshmallow and then spend the rest of their lives making a better one than the woman down the street. I don't know why it surprises me. They are crafty. They knit everything from bikinis to toilet paper holders shaped like mint green top hats.

It's like the Sicilians down our way. They put up thousands of jars of tomatoes every August, even though a can of crushed and peeled tomatoes is cheap. Is the labor involved in crushing fifty bushels and cooking them on a hot stove and pouring them into mason jars that you've spent hours sterilizing commensurate to the low cost of a single can? Don't know. Sometimes I get to thinking here.

Love ya, Pat

To: DBF
From: PC

Dot, heard you banging your head against the wall in your house in New Jersey. Enough with that. Getting a movie adaptation of your book is not the little piece of heaven you hope it will be. Sometimes they make bad movies of good books, and sometimes they make great movies of crap books, and sometimes they just steal your title and make a Porno. So, go figure and don't get yourself wrapped up in Hollywood.

Take your head off that vintage Schumacher wallpaper, because if you keep banging your head, you will ruin the rose trellis design and then you'll really hate yourself, more than you would if you never see a film adaptation of your books. Sit down. Listen to your old friend.

Art is not what it used to be, and it never is what it can be.

You are living in the world that produces too much of everything. There is too much to read, see, and do. The current state of art down below is a lot like the Mighty Cuyahoga in 1910 when they were dumping all manner of industrial waste into the river from the factory that made snow tires. The river became so infested with junk that it began to look like a burial ground instead of a waterway. They cleaned it up. They knew that beauty cannot thrive in clutter.

Clear your head.

Fight for your stories, but don't expect anything beyond that feeling you get when you hold that book in your hands for the first time. You know what I'm talking about. You lift your latest novel out of the box and you can smell the ink and the glue. A sense of accomplishment washes over you, and you take it in, only to have that pleasure killed off when some jackal on Amazon gives it a one-star review. A year of work reduced to one star by a person who cannot spell your name or confuses you with another author with three names and reviews *her* title and not yours. But don't fret about that either. Whether you're getting a lousy review, or assigned one accidentally, they don't really matter. Besides, there are many more readers who love you and your books than don't.

Be grateful.

There will always be a place for you on the shelf called *New Releases*. It's an honor to be there, and you know that. That will have to be enough, because, old friend, it *is* enough. You loved every book you wrote, whether it did well or not. Don't live in the light of past glory. We can't go back, and there's a good reason for that. We shouldn't go back. We have to work with what we have in the moment that it lives.

The present is always better than the past.

You can count on the present because you're living in it, while the past is always under rewrite, and therefore open to re-interpretation, which isn't good for anybody.

Trust your librarian and your local bookseller.

There was a time when there was a library where you borrowed books and a bookstore where you purchased books and that was that. The bookstore curated the new releases and the librarians chose from a catalog and bought the books they believed their patrons would read and enjoy. Curation is gone, replaced with online stores where you can buy anything you want, any hour of the day, and have it delivered. Deliveries include chili dogs, a sack of kitty litter, or the latest novel.

I wondered what would happen to art when it was available 24/7, and now you know.

Love ya, Pat

To: DBF
From: PC

Hey, Dot. I heard you calling. What are you doing in the hospital? I just saw a tube and figured you were in for something. I hope you didn't go to all that trouble for a facelift. You don't need one! Not yet. That was a joke, sister. Men don't notice them by the way. We are missing the gene that identifies the results of plastic surgery. Don't know why that is true. Cassandra will see a woman walking toward us, back when I was there and could walk, and she'd say under her breath: *new lips* or *forehead like an ice rink* or *Law me, she's so pulled she'll have to change her name to Taffy*. But I never saw any of that.

When a woman walked by, I only saw the pluses and never the minuses. I saw something flutter, something move, heard a laugh, a light womanly laugh, watch her hand move like a feather through the air, saw a dainty foot, a pretty leg, a big smile, small ears. I don't know what all I saw, but it thrilled me. I saw everything when I looked at a woman. Everything good. Everything beautiful, I hate that word, it's so worn out with meaning from being used to describe rugs, flowers, women, and whatever else goes by that people don't seem to have a word for.

How is it we don't create new words when we see something that astonishes us? Why don't we make up new words for the things that make us feel new? I would call my wife in the morning . . . well, I would say she looks *Sharoshola*. She looks *Sharoshola*—a new English word that means tousled and down-right gorgeous. I'll tell you what they don't have a new word for, old friend. They don't have a new word for *dead*. Dead is gone, over, finished, done. Gone and done do not rhyme so don't write a poem with them. Dead is final. But it doesn't feel it. Don't know how to tell you that there's no bad news from here. But whatever you're doing, for whatever reason you're in the hospital, get the hell out of there as soon as you can. If you've got a vein, they've got a tube for it. And they will insert that tube. So get the hell out of there. Take it from me. You can skip that step called pain in the life journey. Everyone should. Getting sick is not worth the time, keeps you from doing the things you want to do or should be doing.

Love ya, Pat

To: DBF
From: PC

I haven't heard from you, Dot. Where are you? I understand you're busy. You probably got out of the hospital and took that new face and went to a Writer's Conference somewhere fancy. Beware of those conferences, getting drunk with other authors will only lead to their shame and your blame. Always leave the party early, otherwise you'll end up with the bill. Are you laughing now? You never cared about the bill, hell, neither did I. I always wondered about people who dodged the tab, how much are they saving? The cost of a Diet Coke and a highball? Everybody knows they don't want to pay the bill when they don't pick up a check, which makes them ungenerous, and who wants to be that at three a.m. when the bar is closing? *Not a good look* as you used to say. I am listening for you, expecting some little shimmer of your good self, my friend, wondering if you and Peter and the kids are all right—and wondering, too, if you've heard from Cassandra? She was always a toughie, even though she was born in a peppermint wrapper—but I know things are not easy for her on that side, and I'm wondering if you know something? Well, I'll just wait to hear from you.

Love ya, Pat

———————————————

To: DBF
From: PC

I still haven't heard from you, Dot. I see your world changing from summer to fall, but you're not in it. This can only mean one thing. Something went wrong with the facelift. That's a joke. You must have been sick. I wanted to explain a couple of things to you before you get here. You may have wondered about the postcards. You may be curious how I got through to you.

You know those wet squares of paper you see on the sidewalk, the ones where the words are blurry from the rain? That's a postcard from me. The book you pick up off the shelf and there's a paragraph underlined, something about Anacondas in the wild? That, too, is me. The receipt you saved from a store you don't remember going into that has a note scrawled on the backside that says *soft shell crabs*? That's also me. I won't leave them around for you any longer. You must be en route on your new journey. I am here as it unrolls before you in whatever form it takes. Trust you are not alone. Take it from someone who has settled into his knowingness as you are about to settle into yours.

There's a dive bar in heaven called *Halo* where writers go. You'd think that it was called *Halo* in honor of the angels that fly overhead in flocks of such congestion that it reminds some of us souls of the old flight pattern over La Guardia Airport. Actually, the bar was named by Somerset Maugham, who frequented the joint and would say *Hello* (*Halo* in his British accent) to the new arrivals.

The name stuck even after Somerset moved on to another realm. I've already spent a chunk of my initial eternity in the bar. I'm comfortable enough to remain here awhile longer until I figure out my next step. Besides, it's such an interesting collection of souls, I find the clientele irresistible. All the questions that had dogged me for my entire working life have been answered one by one in the ebb and flow of the conversation as souls come and go. I have met my idols, most of them, and a few authors I liked in passing back on earth, I have learned to love full out and let go of all prejudices and judgments I might have had against our fellow writers. I have learned to expand my thoughts and open myself up to ideas I refused to entertain in your realm. To that end, I am embracing poetry. I am holding out to meet the poets, because I've always admired them.

Poets don't live on advances, nor do their poetry collections sell as briskly as a hot novel might. I've learned that I have a deep admiration and affection for those who created art for art's sake. Wasn't that the point of creativity? To insist, despite all obstacles, to proceed with the words, evocative and emotional, despite impediments? To write the poem knowing it may never be read? To hide the poems in the wall knowing they will never be found, but feeling that sense of fulfillment from writing it anyhow?

I'm hoping to chat with Emily Dickinson. There's a rumor that Emily will eventually show her soul, but so far she hasn't made it to Halo. The bartender keeps Miss Dickinson's favorite blackberry brandy on the shelf just in case. Even though you will never receive this postcard, I will sign off and wait for you.

Love ya, Pat

———————————————

Pat put down his pen. He tore the final postcard he had written to Dottie on earth in two, and then into little bits and pieces. He threw the confetti into the air. The tiny bits of paper dissipated like a vapor.

"Pat Conroy!" Dorothea Benton Frank stood in the entrance of the bar. "There you are!"

"Dottie?" Pat got off the bar stool and turned to face his friend. "Dottie, is that you?"

"Hell, yes. I've not entirely evaporated. Can you see my pearls through the ectoplasm?"

Pat squints. "Just barely, but, yes. What are you doing here? I saw you in a hospital."

"Well, I wasn't there for a facelift, you old coot. I got sick. I got worse and then I got a feeling that I should leave the hospital and find you."

"Why would you do that?"

"I don't know. I just did it. I was *compelled*. You know I don't make long-range plans. Takes the starch out of life."

"So, you knew you'd end up here?'

"Of course not. I had no plan to die. I'm one of those lovers of life. Couldn't get enough of it. I had so much going on. The kids. Peter. My grandson Teddy. Another grandbaby on the way. Don't make me talk about it. Well, maybe I should. I'm not sad when I talk about it. Why is that?"

Pat nods.

"You'll have to do better than that, old friend. You can't just nod like one of those bobbleheads."

"I'm acknowledging that you've arrived, that you were there and now you are here. You can do a lot of good for them from this side. When you're at peace, you see everything differently."

"Isn't it true? I feel great. What a year. And work, too. You won't believe it. *Queen Bee* went to number two."

"Get out."

"No, I mean it. Number *two*. Two as in second place, also known as the booby prize at the white elephant sale. Two as in the second, you know, the second twin, less pretty but still in the family and allowed to join the rest of the good lookers at the dinner table despite her homely self. I'm glad to leave all that behind. Number two, Pat. Second place. I'm like friggin' Avis, always trying harder." Dottie laughed, and soon Pat laughed with her. "Do you want to know who's Hertz?"

"Not really."

"Doesn't matter. I'm happy for everybody and for everything wonderful that happens to the everybodies of that weary world because whatever little taste of sugar they get, they *need* it. And yet,

I'm a bit mystified, in light of my own death, that I still have a wee bit of that old hungry feeling. You know the feeling. The *almosts*. You almost grabbed that brass ring, but for whatever reason, it was just out of reach. I left the earth without knowing what number one felt like."

"I'm sorry, Dot. That's a damn shame."

"Isn't it?"

"In a little bit, it won't matter anymore. You'll see. Is it important to you now?"

"Not so much." Dottie sat on the bar stool next to Pat. "Huh. You're right. All that tumult, really, truly is for nothing. I did all right. Right? Could not matter less. I just had to tell you, because I know you'd see the irony."

"I see it."

"I had to get out of there before the funeral. I waited until the dog days of summer to make my exit. You know I can't take the swampy heat."

"You lived on the beach."

"It doesn't matter. I sweat regardless. Kept the air-conditioning on 65 degrees right up until Christmas Eve. I left a carbon footprint the size of Wrigley Field behind because I used so much electricity. I was hot all the time. It was so awful I would've paid somebody to follow me around with an electric fan in full glacial air-conditioning if I could. I'm hot no matter what! It was hot at your funeral."

"How?"

"Global warming."

"It was March."

"Pat. Yes, you died in March, but it was hotter than a ski mask on a camel in Beaufort. If you would have died on New Year's Eve it would've been hot in Beaufort. Beaufort's an oven. An oven with peach pies baking inside, but an oven nonetheless. But I forgive you for leaving and for dying. All is well. The slate is clean."

"I remember slates," Pat chuckled.

"You bet. Blackboards and chalk and that filthy dirty eraser! How could they let children handle that dirty thing?"

"You're so demure."

"I know! But in the heat, we're all the same. A pack of blobs that melt. How's the weather here?"

"Nice."

Dottie leaned forward and looked closely at her old friend. "You're so serene, Pat."

"You're getting there."

"I am, aren't I? Is there any ruckus here at all?"

"Not that I've seen."

"Just peaceful?"

"Yeah."

"Even when you meet relatives?"

"Even when you meet them."

"How could that be true?"

"You've got nothing to prove here. You can't disappoint anyone. You can't please them either because everything is lovely."

"I doubt that."

"I promise you. You'll see for yourself. And then we'll talk about it."

"I miss my things. Is that normal?"

"It's part of the transition. You don't need all that stuff here. Let it go, Dot. I know it's hard. But you enjoyed your things and now you don't need them. You lived life to the hilt. Parties and overnights and guests and brunches. Your home looked like *Architectural Digest*."

"Didn't it? The '*Best Of*' issue."

"You like beautiful things for sure."

"Well, I tried to create an ambience. I didn't want my home to look like Scully & Scully was having a going-out-of-business sale, but you know, it might've from time to time because I like the look of proper English furniture, a high-polished walnut finish, but I also like Chinoiserie and jabots, and silk damask. But things have to make sense. You can't have just one cachepot over the bookshelves when you have two bookshelves. You need that extra cachepot. So that's how the accumulation of stuff in pairs led to Peter almost having a nervous breakdown over a pair of foo dogs I found on eBay. Poor Peter. The day those turquoise blue foo dogs arrived you would've thought we had to feed them for all the carrying on he did. My long-suffering husband. Full head of hair. And a great lover. Thank goodness he liked my taste, appreciated it. I had seven full sets of china. Herend, Limoge, and Lenox even."

"Seven sets of china? They didn't have that much dinnerware on the *Queen Mary*."

"You never know who will drop in." She shrugged. "But all that stuff? They're just things."

"Yep."

"I don't need them anymore."

"You don't."

"I think I might *like* not needing anything. Anything you have to dust turns to dust someday, so what's the point?"

"There isn't one."

"After all that and there's no point. Huh."

"You're already in the groove here."

"Am I?"

"Yep. You already seem calmer."

"Than what? Than what I was on earth? If you were sucked through the solar system in a hospital gown and not your best pearls and Chanel mules, you'd have to find a way to accept it. To be polite about a quick exit and why it happened so fast. To understand that you were never in control. At a certain point, you just let go and ride the ride. When I let go, my pearls returned." Dottie pats her pearls. "But not for long."

"Nope, not for long. You did just fine, Dot."

"Did I? I'm not so sure. I tried to create my version of order on earth. You know I was a long-term planner. Had my datebooks picked out through 2026. Had the blueprints on the beach house done and expanded the back porch so I could see more of the water. I surrounded myself with pretty things, good friends, and wore the clothes that pleased me with a purse to match. I wanted very much to teach my children about the good things. I wanted them to recognize them, but how silly. Really. My son, like all boys since the dawn of time, are raised to be clueless to the age of forty by their mothers, though my boy was sharp as a tack, despite my control. My daughter was raised in my image, and hers was such an improvement over mine, it's not even funny. She lives so much more to the point. She is funny and wise and such a good mother. Does it really matter if she knows the exact origins of pebble leather?"

"I don't know."

"Tuscany to be exact. Pebble leather doesn't matter now. I hope the important truths got through."

"I am certain that they did."

"I tried to be steady. Of course, I had my husband for that. I could always count on him. To love me or push me, either/or. I wonder if I came across as someone who could be counted on, because, Lord knows, I counted on him."

"You could be counted on. After all, love pulls all the threads together, and evidently always will. I'm sure your daughter believed she could count on you."

"She did. And there were times she thought I was nuts."

"Nah."

"Here and there. Not every day. But here and there I could go a little crazy. I loved the word 'ballistic,' because it was how it felt inside to be me, firing on all pistons. Whatever a piston is."

"It doesn't matter now."

"No, it doesn't. I hope my children go ballistic once in a while. After all, it's in the family."

"Nothing wrong with that."

Dottie picks up a tumbler of vodka on the rocks. "Is this mine?"

"Yep."

Dottie sips. "It's delish. I had to give up Dewar's, it made me puffy. Vodka is a streamliner. Thank you."

"I've been thinking, Dot." Pat studied his tumbler of whiskey as though it were a chalice. "There's no comparison. Skillet cornbread is preferable to pan."

"I am not going to pick up this argument on this side of heaven. Listen to me. Once and for all. Pan cornbread."

"Skillet."

"Pat, use your head. Pan is cake-like whereas the skillet cornbread is dense. Skillet style gets hard like quick-dry cement if you don't eat it right away."

"You're supposed to eat it hot, that's the point."

"But you can't always eat it hot. I'll give you this: I do like the crust on skillet baked. But that's all I like. You get crust with the pan, too, but it's thinner, like the top of a pancake."

"Not the same. Skillet baked gives you a thicker kind of carpet-like finish."

"Carpet? What are you talking about? Aubusson? Wall to wall? What? I hate comparisons of objects to food. Food is food. Besides, it's the lard that makes a golden crust."

"I've had yours."

"And?" Dottie asked and waited.

"It's pretty spectacular."

"So why argue with me?"

"What else have we got to do for all eternity?" Pat laughs. Soon, Dottie is laughing with him until she isn't.

"Pat, follow my logic. If you studied cornbread south of the Mason-Dixon Line, the baking style is a matter of geography and genealogy. Our recipes define our regions. Would you agree? We're South Carolinians. Okay, we make cornbread in a skillet or a pan. But traditional Tennessee skillet cornbread does not go down the same way that Georgia skillet cornbread might. You've got the Alabama version. And the Virginia style. Hell, we could go all night with the variations, but the truth is, in my opinion and experience, the pan is the key to the best cornbread."

"Dottie, I respectfully disagree. You need a seasoned skillet. One that is used for the sole purpose of making cornbread."

"But if we're going to have this discussion for the millionth time, you will just have to trust that I know best because I make the best cornbread."

"Trust mine. Skillet. Skillet style cornbread is popular in every region of the South," Pat insisted.

"Popular does not mean better."

"It can."

"Not always," Dottie countered. "We could argue that every region has a pan and skillet recipe. It's cornmeal based, Pat. And think about it. The variations. You have the Italians with the polenta. That's just moist cornbread stirred wet for hours until your arm almost falls off into the bowl, and instead of reattaching it, you just throw some tomato sauce on it and call it a day. Did you know I'm one eighth Italian?"

"You remind me every chance you get."

"Well I am. So that'll tell you that the Italian and South Carolinian, the Lowcountry South Carolinian in me, knows her way around a bowl of cornmeal."

"No doubt. But there's always something new to learn."

"You said my cornbread was excellent."

"It is. But I don't know how we choose the best cornbread if we don't include the variations. Think about it. There's the bayou. Louisiana, the Mississippi Delta. You've got coastal, inland, and New Orleans proper, which is actually its own country as far as I'm concerned. They do a crumble version of the old skillet standard."

"You can't count them. Cajun is a separate palate."

"Completely. But I would argue that Virginia, Tennessee, and

North Carolina are similar—at least when it comes to cornbread. And they make it like me, Lowcountry style. It involves a can of creamed corn. Keep the secret."

"What about firecracker cornbread?" Pat asked.

"Never heard of it. I think you made it up."

"I most certainly did not. Hot chilis and niblets stirred in. Fresh niblets right off the cob. Boil them until soft and into the batter."

"A fad for sure. I don't think I ever had it."

"You wouldn't. You never went to a dive bar."

"Only when there was no alternative. I can think of a couple of book tours in Florida when I could barely find my way out of the everglades. I think I stopped at a dive bar somewhere in there. With Nita Leftwich. Do you know her?"

"I never had the pleasure. The best food is in dives, Dottie. They use lard. Butter. Fat. You know, the essentials in your kitchen."

"They were. It's so funny to me now. I worried my whole life about calories. Now I wish I'd just had the butter every time instead of those margarines with the dumb names. You know, like that landfill-friendly *I Can't Believe It Ain't Butter*. Why don't they just call it whipped car wax because you can't digest it. Take it off the market. I'd call my butter I *Can* Believe It's Butter because it is authentic butter from the cream of a cow and it actually tastes like real butter because it is what it says it is in the first place."

"No false advertising."

"Nope."

"You worried about your figure?"

"Until the end. Old habits die hard, Pat. Remember, I once won a can of paint at the Charleston Jamboree when I was twelve years old and guessed the weight of a flatbed truck. It's my superpower. I can tell what things weigh from fifty feet."

"You'd better get a new superpower. We are weightless here."

"Isn't that wonderful? How exciting. Well, then I will not try to slim down my cornbread recipe."

"There's only one way to settle this."

"We can settle it?"

"You bake. I bake. Then we round up some judges." Pat looks around. "I'm not asking Kurt Vonnegut to judge our cornbread."

"He wouldn't anyway. Looks like he's still annoyed from this angle."

"He's actually a lot of fun."

"How about Tennessee Williams? I've been dying to talk New Orleans with him."

"But you're from Charleston."

"I can talk New Orleans when forced. And I can force him to talk Charleston." Dottie waves at Tennessee Williams. "Cajun this and that. I'm good at it."

"I can talk New Orleans, too."

"So go over and ask him to judge."

"I can't."

"Why?"

"I get nervous around souls I admire."

"You're never nervous around me."

"Exactly."

"Don't test me, Pat. What about Ada Boni? The famous cook—Italian chef—she wrote *The Talisman*."

"I know who she is. She's been dead so long it would take us an eternity to find her. Did you use her cookbook?"

"Only an eighth of it."

"You're not your genetics any longer."

"But I just found out that I'm part Italian."

"Doesn't matter. We're air and sky now."

"And memory." Dottie turned to Pat. "Which is why we must bake."

"Bliss needs no sustenance."

"I don't know about that. There's more to baking cornbread than eating it."

"Is there?"

"There's the whisking, and the greasing of the pan . . ."

"The skillet."

"Your skillet. There's the pleasure of pouring the batter. The scent of the house when it's baking. It's that clean scent of a summer field right before harvest. We bake to remember."

"Dot," Pat said impatiently.

"All right, all right. I bake to *win*. I'm new here. I flew in on the wings of Number Two. Okay? I promise to let go of my life when I'm ready to let go. I mean it. Truly."

"We need a chef to judge."

"Who's the cat who ran Cordon Bleu?"

"There are thousands of those high-end chefs. And none of them are interested in cornbread."

"We need someone who knows cornbread."

"Not many of those here."

"Oh, come on. Southern writers are a genre. Like ripped from the headlines movies on Lifetime—too many to count and not enough years to watch them all. I bet if we name the writers, they'll show up. The Southern chefs! Mama Dips! Miss Peacock from De-catur! What about the fiction types?"

"Who? Do you mean William Faulkner, Katherine Anne Por-ter, Reynolds Price, and Eudora Welty? Haven't seen any of them around."

"They're not social, that's why."

"Even if they were, they wouldn't come here."

"This is a very prestigious establishment. Look around, Pat. You can't do better than this."

"So choose your judge."

Dottie waved her arms from left to right, including the tables and the length of the bar. "You take that half. I'll take this half."

"Fine," Pat said.

Pat and Dottie split up to find the best judge. Soon, the clouds shifted and a new soul appeared in the entrance.

"Where am I? Look at this place." An attractive soul entered the bar. It was apparent she was pretty even though her ectoplasm was fading. A black chemise, pearls, and high heels were almost all that was left of her. She shoved her black horn-rimmed glasses up her nose and squinted. "Is this the writer's bar?" she asked as she sat down. "Doesn't matter. I'll have a Pimm's cup."

"A girl that orders a Pimm's Cup is a true girl raised in the South. Is that you, Julia Evans Reed?"

Julia spun around on her bar stool. "Dottie Frank?"

"What are you doing here?"

"What do you think? I'm writing an article for *Garden & Gun*."

"I have a subscription! Everything that's important or anything interesting that happens in the American South is in *Garden & Gun* these days. So what are you writing about?"

"That's a joke, Dottie. There are no more articles to write. No more books. This is the end of the line."

"Oh, right." Dottie sat down on the stool next to Julia.

"This is sort of a forced retirement deal."

"It's so final." Dottie sighed.

"Yes, it is."

Dottie turned to face Julia. "I didn't know you were sick."

"You didn't? There was a post on Instagram. But evidently no one read it. Not one person. That just proves nobody reads the copy on social media. They go straight for the videos of double-jointed me doing the shimmy at a Boxing Day lunch at the River Road Country Club in Greenville. Nobody ever reads the captions even after you spend an hour and a half trying to come up with something pithy for the post. If you want to keep a secret, just put it in the captions on IGTV. I actually wrote exactly what was wrong with me, but I might as well have written, *Help, I'm being robbed. I don't know these people and they're draining the liquor*, because no one ever mentioned the post to me, but of course thousands *liked it*. Ugh. *Like this* is what I would like to say to them."

"I would have told everyone I was sick had I the opportunity. I appreciate sympathy. Pity should be an expensive perfume and it should have the scent of my neck," Dottie said.

"What are you drinking?"

"Vodka because I don't swell."

"You won't feel anything going forward. I'm here ten minutes and know that for certain."

Pat joined the ladies. "Hello, Julia."

"Aren't you shocked she's here?"

"Nothing surprises me, Dottie."

"Any luck finding a judge?"

"Nope."

"Judge for what?" Julia asked.

"A cornbread competition."

"I know more about cornbread than I do about any other subject. I mean it. I'll be the judge."

"Pat, Julia said she'd judge. Where do we get the stuff? I need ingredients."

"The ingredients are in the kitchen."

Julia followed Pat and Dottie into the bar's kitchen. Two long aluminum tables, one marked PAT and the other DOTTIE, were filled with the ingredients to make cornbread.

Dottie clapped her hands together. "I like this already. Somebody already did the shopping. What fun!"

"I'm getting to work," Pat said seriously.

Julia took a seat and watched the writers sift, pour, and stir. "Dottie, what's in that recipe?"

"Okay, start with an 8 x 11 pan. Grease it. Put your stove on 425 degrees. I'm taking ½ cup of cornmeal, 11/2 cups of all-purpose flour, 1 tablespoon of baking powder, ¼ cup powdered milk, 1 cup of sugar. Sift all that and set it aside. Whisk ¼ cup warm water with 1 large egg, ½ stick of butter melted, and a pinch of salt. Pour that mixture over the dry ingredients and whisk until lumpy. Add in a can of creamed corn and whisk it in until all the lumps disappear. Now, I'm pouring it into the pan. And now, into the oven."

"Interesting. Creamed corn?" Julia asked.

"Do you have another use for it?"

"Not really," Julia laughed. "I guess creamed corn is to your cornbread what a can of onion soup is to every casserole my mother ever made since 1958."

"I'd say that's accurate."

"Pat, how are you doing?"

"I'm using a seasoned skillet. Throwing it into the oven at 375 to heat to temperature. I'm mixing 1 cup of all-purpose flour, 1 cup of cornmeal, ¼ teaspoon of salt, 4 teaspoons of baking powder, 2 sticks of softened butter, 1 cup of sugar, 4 large eggs. Altogether, beat it well. Then, you add a can of creamed corn."

"Hmm. Now you like the creamed corn where before you were turning your nose up at it. Suddenly everyone is on the creamed corn bandwagon." Dottie sniffed.

"Gonna try it," Pat said as he stirred the ingredients. "Can't hurt. Then add 1 cup of cheddar cheese, 1 cup of Monterey Jack cheese, 1 cup of smashed sweet mini tomatoes, 1 cup of diced green chilis, a shot of chili powder, you know a slight sprinkle. Pull the hot pan out of the oven. Throw in the mixture and back into the oven for an hour. Firecracker cornbread skillet style."

"I have a question for you all. In a place without time, how do you know how long to bake it?"

"It's done," Dottie and Pat said in unison, lifting their cornbread out of the oven.

"I think I'm gonna like it here. Instant Southern classics." Julia smiled. "I have a lot of questions about this place."

"Ask Pat. He's the old pro."

"Thanks, Dot."

"What happens when we fade away up here?"

"Don't know, Julia." Pat smiled.

"You're getting awfully transparent." Julia carefully cut Pat's cornbread into triangles.

"I have no plan," Pat admitted.

"No plan?"

"None."

"Okay. Starting to understand what is going on here. Just need to develop some sort of philosophy to get through it." Julia tasted Pat's cornbread. "I loved life because I lived it with one goal, one purpose: to have fun. Fun is vastly underrated. It ought to be one of the beatitudes. Blessed be the funny because without fun, what's the point?"

"You'll come to appreciate bliss," Pat said. "It's a deeper form of fun."

"Bliss. Well, you'll have to convince me. I feel I know bliss. How do you top that first bite of a Delta-style lobster roll or the opening drumbeat of the Martin Luther King Day Parade in New Orleans followed by a beignet and chicory coffee? Or the way a pair of Manolos feel out of the box when you slip them on for the first time and it's like they were made for you? I really liked living."

"So did I," Dottie said softly. "And dinner parties and cookouts and new shoes and jewelry. Sorry folks. I did."

"Won't matter after a while."

"Pat, keep saying it, maybe it will come true."

"You just have to be patient. Pretty soon, everybody you loved will find their way to you here."

"How do you know for sure?" Julia asked.

"Because it's already happened to me," Pat said.

"It has?" Julia sampled Dottie's cornbread. She chews slowly.

"It takes a while to find people," Pat said. "There's no rush. Eventually you will bump into every person you ever knew. And some you didn't, people you wanted to meet, but never had the chance."

"I've been very social since I arrived, and I think it's made all the difference in my transition. I mean, I just got here, or it feels like it, and who's the first person I find? My bestie Pat. How crazy is that?" Dottie said optimistically.

"There's no adjustment, Julia," Pat reminded her. "You will let go and when you do, everything will settle. Your troubles have no place to rest here. They're just gone. It is a resplendent thing to be whole and healthy again. You won't ever be sick again. That just wears you out. It wore me out anyway," Pat admitted.

"How was your passing?" Julia asked.

"Mine was fast." Dottie shrugged.

"Mine was slow," Pat admitted.

"Mine was slow, too," Julia said.

"Neither choices are good," Dottie said. "But both tracks get you here. I suppose that's the point, isn't it? To land where you're supposed to be after you've lived. I was so frightened about all of it. And there was no need to be. When I was on earth, I'd have a come-apart thinking about dying and the afterlife. It seemed so frightening. In retrospect, I was trying to hold it all together so I wouldn't frighten the people I loved."

"You seem to hold it together nicely," Julia said.

"That's an illusion. Determination and a good girdle kept me upright."

"And straight-backed chairs. You told me they helped your posture."

"That's true, Pat. My love of good furniture was a positive. I liked furniture so much I collected it even when I didn't have a place to put it."

"What did you do with it?" Julia asked.

"I hid it. Attics, basements, friends' houses. Their attics. Their basements. I loaned out antiques like I was Mario Buatta, half in the bag at the Armory Antiques sale on closing day hoarding genuine ottomans from the Ottoman Empire. Do you have children, Julia?"

"Thousands."

"You're an Auntie Mame?"

"Auntie Mirth." Julia grinned.

"I had a son and a daughter. Loved them both dearly. Did you have a best friend?"

"I did."

"That's what it's like to have a daughter. In case you ever wonder."

"I'm traditional, Dottie. But I never wanted traditional things."

"Well, I wasn't traditional so I surrounded myself with all manner of tradition. I thought it meant things mattered. Now I know they don't. Not even the bestseller list."

"Dottie arrived here shortly after she found out she was number two on the *Times* bestseller list."

"Well that sucks." Julia cut another square of Dottie's cornbread and ate it.

"I knew you'd understand. Number two! After all that! I mean I'm happy for the Crawdad lady, it was her first number one, you know, so I'd like to think I'm generous about it and happy for a fellow author."

"Only she had been number one for weeks. Months. Maybe a couple years."

"I *know*! Couldn't she just move aside for ten minutes and let me be number one? I mean, if she knew that I was coming here, I bet she would've called the warehouses and said, 'Hold the crates!'"

"Would you have called the warehouse if you were in her position?" Pat asked Dottie.

"Never."

"So there's your answer. What's so great about being number one?" Julia asked.

"I wouldn't know." Dottie laughed.

"You're about to find out. Dottie, you win. Your cornbread is the best," Julia announced. "It's number one."

"It is?"

"Simple. Tasty. Not too dry. Not too sweet. The can of creamed corn is blended just right."

"Thank you. You know, cornbread was a staple in my home and I got a lot of practice. And to be honest, if you add a can of creamed corn to the Jiffy box mix, it's mighty close to scratch."

"How was mine?" Pat asked.

"The creamed corn killed it. Too much going on and that's from a girl who likes too much going on."

"Creamed corn doesn't work with every recipe," Dottie said breezily. "I'm sorry, Pat."

"I'm sure Kurt Vonnegut would like a piece. Take him a square of your number one cornbread. Congratulations, Dot. You deserve it."

"On my way." Dottie picked up the platter and went back into the bar.

Julia leaned across the worktable. "There was no cream corn in your original recipe, was there?"

"Nope."

"You wanted her to win."

"Yep."

"You're a good friend."

"No, Julia. I just didn't want to hear Dottie carp about being Avis and trying harder for the rest of my eternal life."

Pat and Julia laughed.

"Buy you a drink?"

"Why Julia Reed, did you hear me talking about cheap writers who never buy a round?"

"I might have, Pat Conroy."

"So you know about the postcards?"

"What postcards?"

"The ones from heaven."

"Oh, *those*," Julia said and smiled. "You mean I have to write in this realm?"

"Yep. But here's the good news."

"I'm waiting," Julia said.

"No deadlines."

To: KSM
From: Julia

Listen here, baby sister friend, I don't have any idea how much, or if any of this will get through, but eventually you will know it's me, reaching out. I'm here. I made it. I'm on the other side. It is really pretty doggone fabulous here, even though I was skeptical at first, of course, because that's just the way I am about anything that supposedly is built to last, including eternity. I had gotten to the place in my life where I wanted peace, and peace I got, with no concept of time. When I looked back over my life, the only time I ever cared about were those minutes between dressing up and waiting for the company to arrive.

Sometimes I see shimmers of things. Shiny stamps. Or the red circle on a packing box from the mail machine over at *The Reed Smythe Company.* I miss our elegant little endeavor, but not because of the tables, glassware, and bits and bobs we sold. I miss hunting down the treasures we would sell and wondering if anyone else in the world would see the beauty in a medieval shaving cup. The shop was just another excuse to hang out, spend time together and laugh.

Sometimes I hear things. Your children. My mother's voice. My father's laugh. Don't look for me in sound. I never could sing very well and speaking from the great beyond always ends up sounding like Margaret Rutherford ordering a pizza during the reign of Queen Victoria.

To that end—

I will leave you messages in things. Okay, specifically books. If you pick up Dorothy Draper's *Decorating Is Fun*, I have underlined a few good passages which I believe are essential to decoration and entertaining. Not that you need it. Not that you'd believe it. You are no more likely to wallpaper a room on your own than you are to give yourself a haircut. You're a joy, all sunshine, promise and belief, which is what I loved about you. You could even be practical occasionally, which I never could be, not even once.

You may recall a few years back when I left that rental car on the side of the road with the keys in it when I was on book tour. I was in Tennessee, not Nashville. Knoxville. I did a charity gig there under a tent. It's all coming back to me. There was an auction of interesting items. Mint julep cups, rattan suitcases, and a painting of the United States flag on a handbag. I didn't buy anything. I did my speech and encouraged the women under the tent to buy up all the stuff on the tables.

The event was over. It turned dark and I was driving to the airport when the rental car filled with smoke. I couldn't get the heater to turn off, so I jumped out because I was afraid the dang car would combust with me in it. I walked away from the smoldering car. I thumbed a ride to the airport lickety-split and the driver turned out to be a lovely man who got his start in coal, then coached high school football, and now was on his way to his mother-in-law's for her birthday dinner. Great conversation about high school football and concussions.

About the car.

I forgot to tell the publisher that I abandoned that heap on the side of the road. And then, around three weeks later, evidently the dang car had been sitting there that long, was stolen, yes, *stolen* by a gang of teenage boys, the Tennessee four I called them, who drove my rental car all the way to Mequon, Wisconsin, which was their second mistake (the first being grand theft auto). Anyhow, the poor boys decided Wisconsin was way too cold once they arrived, geography being a foreign concept to them they failed to realize that north means frigid, so they abandoned the jalopy in the return lot at the airport and took a bus back to wherever they came from, somewhere outside of Knoxville, Tennessee. But leaving the car did not atone for stealing the car in the first place until it *did*. Well, it all worked out when the rental car company admitted that the origin of the rental car was Hertz in Mequon. I cannot make this stuff up, and the little criminals had actually done them a ding dang favor after all. That's a sidebar. Even the things we steal belonged to us in the first place.

Love ya, Julia

To: Victoria Benton Frank Peluso
From: Mom

Honey, I see her. The baby. You named her after me? Are you out of your mind? What happened to Anastasia? Aurora? What happened to all those names of all those Disney princesses that you liked a lot and said they worked with Peluso? Italian queen Yolanda, and Italian movie queens, Sophia, Claudia, and Monica. They were stunning names. I do like Thea as a nickname. Don't ever let them call the baby Dottie. It was a curse to have a nickname that came from the South and meant *crazy*.

I always liked when Daddy called me Doe, like a deer. I thought it was romantic and autumnal and slightly musical as every song has that introduction, doe/doe/doe. You know what I mean. I loved deer, except that time I hit one on Pawleys Island. I didn't even know they *had* deer on Pawleys Island. Trust me, they do. So, please drive slowly with high beams on when you're over there. The story ended well-ish. The deer lived, fled the scene without a scratch, but the car looked like King Kong had wadded it up like a gum wrapper and threw it down on River Road. That's when Daddy insisted that I drive an SUV or is it SVU, I can never keep that show with Mariska Hargitay and the style of that vehicle Daddy bought me straight. Well, Victoria, it's one or the other. Figure it out. And when you do, lemme know.

I see you're writing. I am so glad. It was my salvation. It's only right that your own mother gave you the keys to your own version of salvation. Keep at it. You're so talented, Victoria, much more than me. You're more beautiful, funny, and stylish than I ever was. That's as it should be. A mother pours herself into her children and hopes for the best. You'll see how you feel about Thea when she grows up and becomes a young woman that astonishes and amazes you, in the same way you astonished and amazed me. You were your own person, and you were mine.

I loved your brother equally, but you know boys. Thank goodness you had our Teddy first, because that makes little Thea seem like an angel by comparison. Teddy is your firstborn, but he's also Italian, which makes him an instant prince with or without title. (Add my one-eighth Italian genes and you have a future king on your hands!)

Every mother should have at least one daughter, and now you do! Don't share this with your friends who have boys. God bless those mothers of sons—they have to pretend to love sports. I would send your father with your brother. I can't think of a worse way to spend an afternoon even if the hotdogs are delish and the beer is cold.

Mind numbing boredom! Those poor girls will never have the joy of ransacking a mall with their daughters. How sad! Don't forget those daughter-deprived women. Be sure and bring them along whenever you go ransacking with Thea.

I left you some recipes in the old card box.

Don't forget your Charleston roots. You're married to a wonderful Italian chef, and that's all well and good, but sometimes, the only cuisine that can fill you up *proper* is from the American South. By the way, if you see JL written in the corner of the recipe card, it means *Junior League*, which means you can take that recipe to the bank. Those ladies play to win.

Make my cornbread recipe. Serve it hot out of the oven slathered in butter or crumble it into a bowl and pour milk over it. Serve those babies that South Carolina Lowcountry mush and one day Teddy and Thea will thank you. They don't know it yet, and maybe you don't either, but trust your mother: that which sustains you, binds you together. And yes, that includes cornbread. And if you're too busy, and there will be times you *are*, just get that box of Jiffy cornbread, follow the instructions on the box and stir in a can of creamed corn, and you'll be home again.

Love you for all time, Momma

In Memoriam

Pat Conroy

October 26, 1945—March 4, 2016

Dorothea Olivia Benton Frank

September 12, 1951—September 2, 2019

Julia Evans Reed

September 11, 1960—August 28, 2020

About Adriana Trigiani

Adriana Trigiani is the *New York Times* bestselling author of eighteen books in fiction and nonfiction, published in thirty-eight languages, making her one of the most sought-after speakers in the world of books today. Adriana is also an award-winning film director and screenwriter, playwright, and television writer and producer. Adriana co-founded The Origin Project, an in-school writing program that serves over seventeen hundred students in the Appalachian Mountains of Virginia. She lives in New York City with her family.

Adriana Trigiani met Dorothea Benton Frank at the Book Expo of America ten, twelve, or fifteen years ago and had been dear friends ever since. It turns out that hilarity is the gift of friendship that lasts. Adriana remembers Dottie with joy.

ALSO BY ADRIANA TRIGIANI

Stand-Alone Novels
Tony's Wife
Kiss Carlo
All the Stars in the Heavens
The Shoemaker's Wife
Lucia, Lucia
The Queen of the Big Time
Rococo

Big Stone Gap Series
Home to Big Stone Gap
Milk Glass Moon
Big Cherry Holler
Big Stone Gap

Valentine Series
The Supreme Macaroni Company
Brava, Valentine
Very Valentine

Viola Series for Young Adults
Viola in the Spotlight
Viola in Reel Life

Nonfiction
Don't Sing at the Table
Cooking with My Sisters (co-author)

Screenplays
Big Stone Gap
Very Valentine

Mother and Child Reunion

MARY ALICE MONROE

This story is dedicated to

Dorothea Benton Frank

beloved author, wife, mother, friend
and to

Christiana Harsch

dearest cousin, friend, and brave soul

CHAPTER ONE

Mother

A lazy sun rose reluctantly over the horizon. Elinor Earnhardt stood on the precipice of a sand dune overlooking the great breadth of beach, ocean, and sky. She crossed her arms, giving herself a hug, as a winsome smile crossed her face. The first rays of pink light brought a faint blush to the sand. Dawn was her favorite time of day. No matter how sad or lonely she might have felt the night before, standing on the beach when a new day began always had the power to fill her with renewed hope.

Especially today. For on this long-awaited day, not only a new day was dawning, but perhaps a new beginning. After today, her life would never be the same. Today, she would be reunited with the child she had released for adoption forty years earlier.

The thought made her heart beat faster. She deeply inhaled the morning air, still moist from the night rain. The lemony scent of primrose clung to the scant breeze. The sun yawned broadly, releasing more pink and yellow color into the shimmering haze that broke the darkness of the horizon. This morning's dawn was neither bright nor quick. Rather, the sun rose slowly, like a recalcitrant child, not quite ready to push back the warm blanket and rise.

Her smile slipped. Silly woman, she chided herself. What did she know about sleepy children? Or any child, for that matter?

Elinor bent to pick up her backpack and the red plastic bucket, her tools for turtle duty. No time for wool gathering. The Isle of

Palms/Sullivan's Island sea turtle team was expected to assemble at the nest at six a.m. sharp for a nest inventory. If you were late, they started without you. Well, she thought as her heels dug into the soft sand of the high-tide line, everyone but *her*. Elinor was the team leader and they couldn't start without her. But she was never late. What made her a good project leader was her need to dot every *i* and cross every *t* on her reports. Elinor played by the rules.

In the distance she spied the familiar orange tape and wooden stakes that marked the sea turtle nest. It was barely visible high on the dunes amid the thick crop of sea oats. It was August, and they were ripe with golden panicles. This summer marked her twentieth summer on the team, and even after all these years, working with sea turtles never got old. She used to rush to the beach at dawn before her classes. She'd taught biology at the College of Charleston. But when she retired after twenty years, she'd taken over as the turtle team project leader. Truth be told, the sea turtles—and the women on the team—were her life.

Elinor was the first person to reach the nest, which suited her. It gave her time to survey the nest without interruption. Her gaze swept the worn, two-foot-high stakes tilting in the sand; the raggedy orange tape that had survived fifty-three days of wind, rain, and salt air.

The hatchlings had emerged from the nest three nights prior. A healthy group that had scrambled in their comical Keystone Cops manner all the way to the ocean. The moon had been bright, the night clear, and there were no obstacles to their journey home. She'd counted at least seventy-five hatchlings as they raced past. A good boil. All that was left to do now was open the nest and count the hatched and unhatched eggs to track the season's nest success rate.

Suddenly her breath hitched. She caught sight of two tiny trails of turtle tracks leading from the nest. *Well, what do you know?* she thought with amazement. Two more hatchlings had sneaked out. *Good for you.*

She glanced at her watch: five minutes till six. She set her red plastic bucket filled with a spade, small towel to kneel on, plastic gloves, and her clipboard onto the sand, then dropped her backpack beside it. Rolling her shoulders, she thought again how she really had to begin an exercise plan. She'd gone up another dress size this year and she could actually *feel* her body begin to sag. Other than walk the beach in the morning and maybe a bit of gardening, she pretty much just sat and read books. Especially on days like today. She wiped a sheen of perspiration from her brow. It was going to be a hot one.

"Elinor!"

She turned at the sound of her name. A group of women were trudging through the sand toward the nest. She grinned and waved back at her teammates Maeve, Betts, and Ting. They carpooled to the beach in the morning from points on Isle of Palms. Maeve led the troop, her green backpack burgeoning. She and Maeve were peas and carrots on the team. They were close in age, both of average height and weight, even their mousy brown hair color was similar. Maeve wore hers in a blunt cut to the chin. Elinor's shoulder-length hair was usually bound back in a ponytail or a clip. Neither of them gave their hair much mind. What bound them from the moment they'd met twenty years earlier was their love of sea turtles.

Unlike Elinor, however, Maeve took care to exercise in a class at the rec center three times a week and ate healthily. She was always scolding Elinor for not joining her class, for drinking too much wine, and her love of chocolate. Nonetheless it was Maeve who was struck by a minor heart attack at sixty years of age. It had shaken her, deeply, and she'd given up any duties that might cause stress, including relinquishing the task of project leader to Elinor.

Maeve's voice was filled with excitement. "What've we got?"

"Tracks," Elinor replied, making a small gesture toward the two sets of hatchling tracks. She smiled seeing Maeve make a beeline for the tracks.

Betts overheard and without a word, bent over the two-inch tracks, pulling her camera to her face. Betts was tall with grayish hair cut short because, as she claimed, short hair didn't get in the way of her camera lens. She'd been the first female photographer on the storied *Chicago Tribune* newspaper, and she applied that same tenacity to getting a good shot of the turtles and documenting the action of the team. One never saw Betts without a camera in tow.

Ting released her easy smile at seeing Elinor. She made it easy to smile back. Her long black hair was braided under her team ballcap and her eyes were covered with aviator sunglasses. There was never any drama with Ting. She came for the turtles and let the question of who got to do what on which morning slide from her like water off a shell. Ting was the turtle whisperer. She could find eggs in the sand when no one else could. Elinor thought it was because turtles had always been a part of her life. Born and raised in Thailand, she'd worked with more species of turtles than anyone else on the team. In South Carolina, loggerheads were the only turtles that nested regularly on these beaches. In Thailand they had the whole gamut: loggerheads, greens, leatherbacks, hawksbills, and olive ridleys.

"Why don't you start?" Elinor said, giving Ting the nod to begin the inventory.

"Okay, boss," Ting replied, slipping off her sunglasses with a satisfied grin.

Elinor looked past Ting to see Caroline approach. She strode along the beach path with a youthful swing in her hips, her long legs in shaggy-edged jean shorts. Unlike the rest of them who wore the team T-shirt loose and baggy over tired nylon pants, Caroline's T-shirt was cropped short around a lean thirty-year-old body. Her spiky blond hair was too bright for natural and faux lashes fluttered like butterflies at her eyes. It was Caroline's power of observation and cheerful enthusiasm that had singled her out to Elinor from the one hundred plus volunteers who walked the beaches every morning in search of turtle tracks.

And her youth. Elinor felt some young blood was needed to begin building the next generation of team members. They needed that sense of wonder that came at first blush. Elinor was nearing sixty and didn't allow herself to be sentimental about the fact that she'd be leaving the team. Living on the beach made one attuned to the cycle of life, the repetition of seasons, the passing of years. Her mind trailed off, thinking again of another young woman, her hair blond but worn long. This woman was older than Caroline. Forty years old. Today.

She felt a quick ping in her heart. A few more hours. That was all . . .

"It's six o'clock. We should start," Maeve said, sidling close to the nest where Ting was already kneeling on her towel and putting on plastic gloves.

Elinor walked to her backpack and pulled out a notebook. She rifled through the pages, ragged from moisture, sand, and wind, and checked the schedule of nest duties. She looked at Maeve, lifted her brows in commiseration, then said, "Caroline, you're up."

Maeve set her lips but stepped back to allow room for Caroline to join Ting at the nest. Elinor's word was law on the team, and everyone knew her to be fair. Still, she knew it sometimes came hard on Maeve to have lost her role as team leader, waiting on Elinor to call the shots. There were mornings when the team gathered, pawing at the ground like horses at the gate.

As the two women began digging into the sand, Elinor turned and followed the barely visible trail of two tiny turtle tracks. The morning's light breeze scattered sand, almost camouflaging tracks, another reason why the volunteers walked the beaches at first light. As suspected, there was a meeting of turtle and ghost crab tracks, which ended poorly for the hatchling. She felt a stab to the heart. It was common enough. Nature wasn't always kind, but she always felt the loss personally. *Poor baby . . .*

Biologists hated it when anyone called a hatchling a baby. What did they know about the time and care and love that went into the tending of turtle nests? She'd sat on the other side of that desk and understood the science. But being present on the beach, sitting night after night like midwives, waiting and watching for the nest to heave and release an abundance of tiny, helpless hatchlings, well, it did something to your heart. You couldn't help but love them in a maternal way. And for her, hatchlings were the only babies she had. Her thoughts kept returning to that theme today. So she called them babies and didn't care one whit who heard her. Because in her mind, that's what they were. A bunch of motherless babies scrambling for home.

"We've got one!"

All heads turned to Ting, who held up a hatchling in her gloved hand. The tiny brown carapace was caked with sand and its flippers waved wildly in the air. Every woman's face burst into a grin of delight. *A baby.*

Elinor hurried to grab hold of the red bucket and delivered it to Ting. She gently placed the hatchling into it. Beside the nest, Caroline lay flat on the sand, her long arm scooping out handfuls of sand and empty eggshells. Ting and Maeve counted them, and all the while, Betts photographed the hatchling running in continuous circles around the bottom of the bucket.

"Eighty-one eggs," Ting called out.

"Five eggs did not develop." Maeve rested back on her heels.

The team looked at her expectantly.

Elinor checked her records. "We know there were eighty-six eggs in the nest because we relocated it due to it being below the high-tide line. Minus the five." She scribbled on her report then looked at the team with pleasure. "That gives us a very respectable ninety-four percent rate for this nest. That's a good one. Now, let's release this baby." She turned to Maeve. "Do you want to do the honors?"

"Why don't you do it?" Maeve offered. "It's your turn."

Elinor met Maeve's eyes and saw the commiseration shining there. Maeve was the only one on the team who knew how important today was. How she could use a little bolstering of spirit. She nodded gratefully and bent to pick up the red bucket.

"Come on, little one. Let's set you on your journey."

It was a perfect morning for a release. The waves lapped the shoreline serenely and the outgoing tide would help pull the young hatchling into the welcoming sea. She waited until the team gathered near, along with a lucky couple who just happened to be walking by. They were positively giddy, their phones out taking pictures. *Timing was everything*, Elinor thought with a smile.

And now, it was time for this hatchling to take its chances with fate. The team gathered near the water's edge. The rising sun cast a rosy gleam across the sea. With the dawn came the seagulls, calling out their raucous laugh. Elinor searched the sky to make certain none of those marauders were near to scoop up her one precious hatchling.

Elinore crouched low onto the sand and looked down into the red bucket. The lone hatchling scrambled around the rim, unceasingly following its instinct to move forward in search of the sea. So small. So helpless.

She heard the cry of a seagull and in her mind, she heard again the wail of a newborn.

Maeve bent close and asked quietly, "You okay?"

Elinor blinked then gave a shaky smile and nodded. "I was just giving this turtle a chance to exercise its limbs a bit."

"Everyone's waiting."

"Yes, good," Elinor replied, her focus returning. "Save your energy," she told the turtle. "You're going to need it. You have a long swim ahead of you to reach the Gulf."

Looking up she saw the team fanned out across the beach, all eyes on her. Elinor slowly tilted the bucket and watched the hatchling scramble out to the sand. Once on terra firma, the hatchling's flippers madly propelled the tiny turtle forward, across the uneven sand, around footprints, shells, and bits of sea grass. At last it reached the shoreline and got its first taste of salt water. A gentle wave swept up and washed over the hatchling, sending it tumbling back with the force of it. Elinor watched the beauty of instinct at play as the turtle's flippers switched from crawl to swim, and in that precious instant, the turtle was at home in the sea. It had found its home.

Elinor stepped closer, following the wave as it carried the tiny hatchling back into its embrace. She could barely see the three-inch turtle in the shallow water. She felt an inexpressible connection to this hatchling, this newborn that she had released from the womb of sand. She thought again of the child she'd released to the world, hoping—believing—that she would find the right home. She didn't want to lose sight of it and followed the hatchling deeper into the warm late-summer waters of the Atlantic. The waves pushed against her, caressing her ankles, then her calves, soaking her pants. She kept her eyes peeled on the tiny turtle swimming madly—seemingly joyously—on its way.

Elinor could go no further. She stood, arms limp at her sides, her gaze locked on the little brown speck in the sea. The moment a sea turtle dove deep and disappeared was emotional for her. Of course, she wanted the turtle to swim off, as nature intended. Yet today, the slender bond she felt with this hatchling tugged hard, drawing her with it to a time and place she had not traveled to in many years.

"Good-bye, sweet baby," she whispered as tears slid down her cheek.

Elinor heard again the piercing cry of the seagull. Instinctively she looked up, directly into the fiery ball of the sun. She closed her eyes and she was back in the hospital, forty years earlier, staring up at the white glare of a metal hospital lamp.

"One more push," the doctor had ordered.

Elinor's legs were up in the brutally cold metal stirrups. Her body was doubled up and sweat dripped down her face.

"I . . . I can't. . . ." she cried.

A nurse, large and full breasted, quickly stepped behind her and slipped strong arms around her, hoisting her up in support.

"You can do this, Missy. Just one more good one. You've done a real good job. We're almost there. Ready? On the count of three. One, two, three!"

Elinor felt another wave of a contraction building and an overpowering urge to push welling up. On the count she tightened her eyes, grit her teeth, and bore down. It felt like her body was being torn open, but she kept pushing. A guttural sound came from her that she didn't recognize.

"I've got the head. Keep going." The doctor's urging spurred her on.

She bore down again, straining and screaming with abandon. She felt her legs shake and dots swim before her eyes when, almost as a surprise, there was a sudden gush of release. She fell back against the nurse, panting yet feeling oddly glorious.

Then she heard a lusty cry. Instinct rallied and she found the energy to lift her head in time to see a pair of nurses bent over a small bloody bundle of flesh at the foot of her bed. Then they hurried to a large metal scale. Elinor craned her neck to see her baby, but her view was blocked by their bodies. She heard her infant cry and reached out. The need to hold her baby came from deep within, from a place she didn't know existed inside of herself.

"Give me my baby," she called out.

The nurse holding the baby turned to look at her, confusion

etched across her face. In her arms, Elinor saw the tiny pink legs kicking as the baby howled. She saw toes. Real toes of a real baby. *Her* baby. Instinct roared in her heart. She could make her baby stop crying. The baby wanted *her.*

She felt as fearless as a lioness. "Bring the baby here." She gathered her strength and dragged herself up to her elbows. Perched on the side of the narrow bed she reached out her arm. "Please!"

The doctor turned his head toward the nurse and over his shoulder gave a barely perceptible shake of his head, then with a quick jerk, indicated the door. Elinor saw with horror that the nurse was hustling her baby away.

"Wait!" she cried. "No, stop! I want to see my baby. Please!"

"Settle down," the doctor ordered with little sympathy. "We're not done here yet."

Elinor looked wildly around the room, panic stirring. She began to cry out, "I don't want to keep the baby. I know I can't. But please, just let me see it!"

It. The word felt wrong on her lips. "What did I have? Is it a boy or a girl?"

She was ignored. The doctor and nurse went about their work complacently, as though her anguish was standard procedure. No one would meet her gaze. No words of comfort were offered.

Elinor felt her uterus contract. Dazed and desperate in defeat, she fell back again on the bed, shaking her head from side to side, crying incessantly, "Please . . . please . . . please. . . ."

When the doctor was done, he left without a word. What could he say? Congratulations? The room was cold and empty. Elinor had never felt so alone. Not that she'd expected anyone to be in the waiting room for the happy news—not her parents, not her boyfriend. Not her sisters nor a friend. No one had come to visit her in the six months she'd been at the Home.

She put her hand over her belly, still full and flaccid. But inside, she knew her baby was gone. And with it, a part of her was gone forever. This loneliness was deeper and more devastating than she had been warned about in all the classes she had taken at the Home for Unwed Mothers. This was a dark, bottomless well, and she was sliding into it.

Elinor lay limp and stared up at the metal lamp, silent as tears rolled down her cheeks. The nurse with the full breasts was cleaning her up but Elinor knew nothing would ever wash away the pain.

The nurse came to stand beside her. She wiped her forehead with a cool cloth. "Now, now, it's all right," the woman crooned in a gentle voice. "You'll be fine. You'll see. It's all for the best."

Elinor just closed her eyes and shook her head. There were no words.

The nurse withdrew her hand. "I'm not supposed to say anything," she said in a low voice close to her ear. "But if it were me lying there, I'd want to know this much. Your baby is fine, too. A healthy seven pounds, two ounces."

Elinor opened her eyes and turned to look at the woman's face. Her eyes were large and dark and full of sympathy. This woman had children; she could tell. She was a mother. She'd nursed her babies, watched them grow. She'd recognized the desperation in Elinor's eyes.

Elinor didn't have to ask.

The nurse took a breath, then said, "You had a girl."

The cry of a seagull sounded again. Elinor blinked and once again saw the broad expanse of the ocean as it met the horizon in a line of infinity. She exhaled. The memory had been so real, she had water in her eyes.

"Elinor?"

She turned to see Maeve at her side. Then looked behind her. The beach was empty.

"Everyone is gone." Her voice was dull.

Maeve nodded. She searched her face then asked, "Are you nervous? About today?"

Elinor didn't reply. Feelings from her memory lingered, making her heart heavy. She merely nodded her head and looked again out at the sea. There had been a few times she'd stared out at the dark ocean water, feeling its pull, and considered following the turtle to its depths. To shed her earthly burdens, her myriad sadness and grief, and simply float cross the invisible barrier into another world. It would be easy. Stones in the pocket, like Virginia Woolf. One step too far, and she'd be released, too.

The hand on her arm tugged harder.

"Elinor, what's the matter?"

"I'm not so much nervous, as afraid. Maybe it's too late."

"It's never too late. You've been trying to find her all these years. You had to wait until she was ready. And now, it's finally happening." Maeve's voice was encouraging. "She wants to see you. Tell you what. I'll stay with you, if you like. You won't have to be alone."

Maeve felt an easing of tension at her friend's words. *You won't have to be alone.* She looked into Maeve's brown eyes and her smile was watery. "Thanks. I'd like that."

"Okay, then. What time is she expected?"

Elinor took a deep breath, bringing herself to the present fully. "She's driving from Atlanta. She said she'd arrive around four, give or take traffic."

"Are you making dinner?"

Elinor shook her head. "We decided we'd go to a restaurant, so there'd be no additional stress. I made reservations at the Long Island Cafe."

"Perfect spot."

"You'll join us?"

Maeve shook her head. "I'll be there for the meet and greet. But I think the two of you have a lot to say to each other without anyone else around." She paused then asked, "Is she bringing anyone?"

"She said this was a journey she wanted to take alone." She released a short laugh. "Rather like that hatchling."

"I was watching you. You were thinking of her, weren't you?"

"Seeing that turtle go off alone, it all came back. The hospital. The delivery. Maeve . . ." Elinor's voice hitched. "Watching my baby being carried off . . . It was the hardest thing I ever had to do. I never really got over it."

Maeve's face went still, her eyes laden with sympathy. Then in a swift move she turned toward the beach and, in a change of tone, declared, "I'm turning into a prune. Let's go home."

Elinor scoffed and joined her on the trek back. "Just my luck I'll be bitten by a shark before I meet my daughter." As they walked side by side out of the sea, Elinor added, "Thanks."

"What for?"

"For being my friend. For keeping my secrets. For understanding."

Maeve slipped an arm around her friend's shoulders, comrades in arms. "I've been thinking . . ."

"Yeah?"

"About the hatchling this morning. The one you were fixated on. I get why. Your little girl was your hatchling, and you had to watch her swim off on her own. But here's the thing to remember. When a hatchling matures at twenty-nine years, she swims back to the beach she came from." She stopped and faced Elinor. "So think . . ."

Elinor shuddered and released a long sigh. "My hatchling is returning home."

"Right." Maeve spread her arms wide. "The cycle of life continues."

CHAPTER TWO

Daughter

A journey of a thousand miles begins with a single step.

Kristina Hurst repeated this quote from Lao Tzu for the hundredth time that morning. It was her mantra to calm her nerves and to battle the urge to call her birth mother and cancel the trip.

This was what she wanted, right? She was the one to go to the adoption registrar and search. No one went for her. The response had come back in twenty-four hours. Her birth mother had long been registered, searching for her for many years. A small smile lifted her frown. She was searching . . . Didn't she always know that in her heart?

The first phone call was nerve shattering, nonetheless. Kristina's stomach still clenched just remembering hearing the phone ring, knowing it was her. Then the sound of her voice . . . *her mother's* voice. She'd been as nervous as her. Yet there was a gentleness in the tone, a determination to make Kristina feel at ease.

"Hello?"

"This is Elinor Earnhardt. Is . . . Is this Kristina Hurst?"

"Yes."

There was a long pause. "Oh, my dear girl. You can't know how wonderful it is to hear your voice."

Kristina heard her voice catch. The emotion flooding out washed away some of her own fears.

"Me, too."

"First, let me say thank you for going to the registrar. I've been searching for you for most of your life."

Kristina cringed. "I . . . I'm sorry. My mother, my adopted mother, didn't want me to. She . . . got terribly upset." The terms "birth mother" and "adopted mother" were awkward and felt odd on her tongue.

"Don't apologize! I didn't tell you that to make you feel bad. Just to let you know how incredibly happy I am to be talking to you now."

Kristina took a deep breath. She was not accustomed to a mother not blaming her, accusing her of making a mistake. She wasn't sure how to react. Elinor didn't let the silence linger, which Kristina was grateful for. She wasn't good at conversations. Her tongue got tied up with her nerves, leaving her mute.

They hadn't talked long. Just enough to share basic information and agree to meet at the beach across from Elinor's beach house on Isle of Palms, South Carolina, in August. It had been weeks away when they set it up, but now it was here, and Kristina wasn't sure she had the courage to go through with it. Did she really want to meet another mother? She was just feeling free for the first time in her life.

Kristina took a deep breath and repeated the mantra. *One step.* She only needed to be brave enough for this first step. Whatever happened after that, well, they'd wait and see.

Brave. What a complicated word. Like the word "courage," it brought up images of warriors on the battlefield, fierce, racing toward an enemy. She smirked. Hardly an image of herself. Her nickname had been *Mouse.* Sometimes, being brave meant simply having the courage to face one's own fears. To her mind, that's what made a hero. Action. In the novels she loved, the hero was boxed into a corner and forced to make a decision. Once made, she was compelled to act. This defined who she was—coward or courageous. Villain or hero.

She looked down at her suitcase lying open on her bed. She did a last-minute check: pajamas, toiletries, a day's clothing, a beach book because she was going to the beach, a small photo album. With tightened lips of resolve, she tucked her shoulder-length blond hair behind her ears and, in a swift movement, closed the suitcase, ran the zipper, and set the bag on the floor.

Immediately her cat drew near to sniff it. Kristina smiled as her heart pumped with love for her roommate. Minnie was her first pet and her closest confidante. Kristina didn't have many friends. She'd been a sickly child and grew up to be a shy adult, one accustomed to staying home. Few people knew how much courage it took for her just to leave her apartment each morning to go to her job at the library. Or to make this first step to meet her birth mother.

Kristina bent to pick up her suitcase before she slipped into another bout of self-doubt. "Okay, Minnie," she said to the calico. "Time for action."

Minnie followed her into the living room at a leisurely pace. It was a small, tidy room on the eighth floor of a nondescript apartment building in Atlanta. One of several similar buildings grouped in a cluster around a smallish park. Void of any architectural charm, she'd rented it seven years ago because of the wall of bookcases the previous tenant had installed. That and its proximity to public transportation and the view of a park rather than a highway. A librarian, Kristina's life revolved around books. In childhood, books had been her only friends.

She felt herself lucky to have one friend now, seeing Ann leaning against the kitchen counter reading the newspaper. Ann was a fellow librarian at the DeKalb Public Library. She was short like Kristina, but unlike her own painfully thin frame, Ann had a full figure to match her big heart.

"Ready to go?" Ann asked, straightening.

"I'm as ready as I'll ever be. Thanks so much for taking care of

Minnie for me. I've never left her before," she added, turning to glance again at her beloved cat.

"That's because you never go anywhere," Ann said with a grin. "Don't you worry one bit about Minnie. We're fast friends already, aren't we, precious?" Ann bent to put her hand out to the cat. Minnie immediately sat where she was and haughtily turned her head away. Ann chuckled and, rising, said, "We'll be fine. Don't give us a thought. You have enough on your mind." She shook her head with wonder. "Meeting your birth mother. That's big. Huge. So," she asked, stepping closer. "What are you feeling? I'd be a nervous wreck."

"I am," Kristina admitted. "But it's what I wanted, so . . ."

"Why did you wait so long to look for her? You weren't curious?"

"Of course, I was. But . . ." Kristina shrugged. The memory of her mother raging, forbidding her to search for her birth mother, flashed in her mind.

"Your mother," Ann finished for her.

Kristina paused then nodded. Ann knew the story.

It was only a year ago that she'd received word that her mother had been diagnosed with pancreatic cancer and only had a few months to live. Deborah wanted to see her. It felt like her own death sentence when Kristina had agreed to pay a visit. She still felt as though lice were crawling up her spine when she recalled once again walking into the small brick house in Gwinnett that she'd been raised in. Her wheelchair ramp still led to the front door.

When her mother had opened the door, Kristina had hardly recognized her. Deborah Hurst peered from a dark vestibule, gazing at Kristina through sunken eyes. She'd grown so thin and her hair, once dyed a vibrant red, was all white and so wispy her scalp was visible.

"Well, here you are. My sweet little adopted daughter." Deborah turned and said over her shoulder, "I didn't think you'd come."

When she opened the door wide to let her in, Kristina brought her hand to her nose. The scent of stale food, must, and mildew made her gag. She followed her mother into a house crammed full of tilting boxes, piled up junk, and broken furniture. There was no discernible distinction between the living room and bedroom. Blankets were strewn over both couches and bed. The entire place was a mishmash of rubbish.

Kristina brought her fingers to her eyes, feeling the onslaught to all her senses. She hadn't had contact with her mother since she'd escaped her clutches at eighteen. Not because she didn't try, but because her mother had been so furious, so outraged, that Kristina had dared to leave the house, she'd broken all contact with her. Kristina had known her mother was an obsessive compulsive. It appeared once she didn't have Kristina to fixate on, she'd transferred her sick, singular focus on hoarding.

Kristina had spent weeks emptying out garbage, getting servicemen in to fix the broken appliances, and scrubbing dirt, grime, and mildew from almost every surface. Her mother had never been a good housekeeper. Kristina had been her live-in maid most of her life. From the looks of the house, it didn't appear anyone had cleaned since she'd left. Everything was a mess—except for the hall closet. Opening it, Kristina found it just as pristine as it had always been. All the shelves were chock-full of neatly stacked and labeled medicines.

"God rest her soul," Kristina said, succinctly closing that memory. She looked at Ann's face, finding comfort in the compassion she found there.

"And now you're free to find your birth mother."

"Right. And here I go," Kristina said, mustering enthusiasm. "I left you a list of instructions for the cat," she told Ann, walking to the long granite kitchen counter that was open to the living room. The large window over the sink overlooked the small park and allowed sunlight to flow into the cramped space. "And here's the vet's phone number."

"I'm sure we won't need it. I'm all set. How about you? Do you have everything? They say you should bring pictures of you growing up."

"I have a few baby pictures. That's enough, I think." She huffed. "I don't want to show the others . . . with me so sick. I don't think I'm ready to go into all that just yet."

"I get that. It'd have to be hard for the birth mother to realize you were placed in such an abusive home. You want this to be a joyous reunion," Ann said, throwing her hands up in party mode. "And you'll be at the beach! Isle of Palms. Lucky you. Sure you don't want me to come along?"

Kristina laughed and shook her head, sending her hair falling forward. She promptly tucked it back. "I'm sure. You have to watch Minnie. Besides, it could be a nightmare. You know my luck with mothers. Don't be surprised if you see me back tomorrow night."

"Don't be negative. It'll be nice." Ann smirked. "I mean, your birth mother can't be worse than your adopted mother."

Kristina made a face. "Who could?" She put out her hands in a calming motion. "She's nice," she declared. Then let her hands drop. "From what I could tell on the phone, anyway."

"What's she like?"

Kristina's eyebrows rose. "Gee, I don't know much. She's retired. She was a teacher. Of biology. Oh, she loves books, too," she said with pleasure. "You know how I'm drawn to books about water. I was a mermaid fanatic when I was young. I found out we have that in common."

"Does she have any other children? Like, will you have half brothers and sisters?"

"No. She said she never married."

Ann lifted a finger to her brain in a gesture of *Aha*! "So that's where you get it from." Ann laughed. "Genetics will out."

Kristina blushed. "I don't think being single is on anyone's DNA."

"I wonder if she looks like you."

Kristina's eyes widened. That was what she most wanted to know. "I know, right? All my life I wondered who I looked like. I hear people say they have their dad's chin, or they look just like their grandmother. I never knew my adopted father, but from photos he didn't look at all like me. Deborah was a redhead with brown eyes. When I looked in the mirror, I saw this blond hair and blue eyes."

"You have beautiful eyes."

Kristina smiled, grateful for the compliment. "And Deborah's a husky woman. Me? I'm skinny with as much shape as a toothpick."

"Stop. You're not. I'd kill to be as thin as you."

Kristina rolled her eyes. She knew her kind of thin was never photographed in fashion magazines. "Be careful what you wish for. And by the way," she made a face. "I've heard the whispers that some people think I have an eating disorder."

"Not from me!" Ann said, aghast.

"Not from you. But still. You can tell them from me that no matter how much I eat—and I eat a very healthy diet—I never can gain the weight."

"Fast metabolism?"

She shook her head. "I'm a librarian. I spend my days reading. Maybe I take a walk a few times a week but that's it. No, I believe it's because of the many years of near starvation I had to live through at the hands of my mother. She wanted me to look thin and ill," she explained, then released a short laugh of scorn. "Not a diet I'd recommend to anyone."

"I'm so sorry."

Kristina shrugged it off. "It's all history now. You know, I used to like to watch television as a kid," Kristina added. "I was obsessed with family shows, comedies and dramas, I loved them all. I'd watch and critique the casting based on whether family members looked alike." She crossed her arms, remembering. "It was my pet peeve if they didn't. Silly, I know, but I was always looking for those family-inherited qualities."

"I'm looking more and more like my grandmother. The way she looks *now*! She's seventy-two."

Kristina laughed, grateful for Ann's sense of humor.

"Seriously," Ann said with concern. "Do you know what you're going to ask her? Like . . . why she gave you up? Don't you wonder?"

"Of course I wonder. What child wouldn't?" She puffed out a plume of air. "Truth be told, I already did ask her. When we talked on the phone," she explained, seeing the surprise on Ann's face. "Elinor, that's her name, told me that she was young when she found out she was pregnant. Still in high school. It happened with her boyfriend. Back then, girls didn't have as many choices as they do now. Her parents sent her away to have the baby"—she spread out her hands—"me. They didn't want any gossip."

"Aren't you just a little bit angry that she gave you up?"

"Angry?" Kristina shook her head in wonder. "No, not at all. It's funny, but I always knew she loved me. That she was looking for me. Even when I was very young, I never doubted it. Don't ask me how. I just . . . felt it."

"But to give you up."

"She did the only thing she could," Kristina said, feeling the need to defend her birth mother. "Think about it. She went through nine months of pregnancy, alone and far away from home. Then labor and delivery. Who does that unless there's love? She told me that placing me for adoption was the most selfless act of love she'd ever done. Because she wanted me to have a better life."

Ann snorted. "But look where you ended up."

Kristina's lips tightened and she shook her head. "She couldn't have known that. She thought I'd been given to a good family. That I'd been happy. And besides, I didn't realize how horrible my life was when I was little. It was all I knew." She shrugged in a *that's life* kind of way.

"You can't be so nice all the time. So forgiving," cried Ann. "Deborah was nuts! She gave you pills to make you sick. There's a name for what she did to you. Munchausen by Proxy."

Kristina held up her hand, feeling herself shut down. "Stop. Please, Ann. I can't go through all this now. That's my past. I survived. It's over and buried. Right now, I'm trying to garner up the courage to meet my birth mother. My future. I have to believe it's going to be better."

Ann rushed over to put her arms around Kristina, engulfing her frail frame. "It will be. I'm sorry. I'm an idiot. I shouldn't have dug into all that. I just care about you so much. I want to protect you from ever getting hurt again."

Kristina sniffed and said with exaggeration, "You can't."

"I can try." Ann released her and stepped back a bit self-consciously. "But hey, you're right," she said, striving for levity. "This will be a wonderful day. You deserve this to be the happiest day of your life."

Kristina spoke in a choked voice. "I just want the chance to tell her that I've loved her all my life. And maybe, just maybe, hear that she loved me."

"From your lips to God's ear." Ann pulled back her hair into her hands, her smile ripe with encouragement. "Now you'd better go. You know how Atlanta traffic can get. You don't want to be late."

Kristina sniffed and wiped her eyes. "Yeah." She grabbed her snack bag from the counter, walked a straight path to her suitcase, then took a final sweep of the room. She was struck with the sudden realization that her life would be changed when she returned to her apartment. For a moment she couldn't move.

Then she felt the soft fur of Minnie's coat rubbing against her bare leg, heard the gentle, reassuring purr. She bent and gave her cat a gentle pat. Then straightening, Kristina took her first step.

• • •

Kristina counted the miles as knots of tension formed in her shoulders. The past three hours felt like thirty and there were two more hours to go. She shifted her weight in the seat of the cheap rental car and reached for her water bottle. This journey had turned out to be a test of her endurance. The highway was one long stretch of cement road bordered by acres of sunburned grass, scrubby trees, and countless billboards. The August sun was relentless and no matter how cold she set the air conditioner, the car couldn't stay cool. She'd tried listening to one of the many audiobooks she'd downloaded, but the onslaught of memories was so unrelenting she couldn't follow the storylines. She gave up and turned on the radio. Why did Ann have to bring up her childhood? It was like opening Pandora's box. She couldn't keep the memories away.

She drove past one of several small Southern towns in the middle of nowhere down on its luck. A few red-bricked buildings sat boarded up, a derelict train station with no passengers. A water tower with chipping paint.

The sight brought to mind the water tower that was visible from her bedroom window in the Gwinnett house she grew up in. She used to sit and stare out at it and wonder what kind of courage it would take to climb up to the very top and holler at the top of her lungs. What would that kind of freedom feel like?

Kristina was near thirteen when new neighbors moved in next door. That summer her attention had shifted from the water tower to the new kid who shot baskets in the hoop set over the garage door. He was thin, like her. His bony knees were prominent under his khaki shorts. He usually wore a ball cap with the Georgia Bulldogs logo on it, but he'd take if off from time to time to wipe the sweat from his brow, revealing dark brown hair cut so short he looked like one of those Holocaust survivors she'd read about. But he sure had energy. He practiced for hours on end, shooting one basket after another. Her mother complained that the constant thumping of the ball was driving her crazy. Kristina grew to love the sound. Whenever she heard it, she'd smile, knowing the boy was just outside. She'd go to the window, set her chin in her palm, and watch and wonder why he didn't have friends play the game with him. Wondered, too, if he was as lonely as she.

The Hurston backyard was a postcard-size patch of mowed weeds surrounded by a rusting chain-link fence. Not a single tree or bush prettied up the plot. Neighbors had complained about how Mrs. Hurston didn't paint the chipping house trim or fix up the yard a bit to make it more respectable. They declared the Hurst house was an eyesore in the neighborhood. When a group from the neighborhood Woman's Club came calling to discuss the matter with Mrs. Hurst, her mother had gone on a cleaning frenzy with Kristina. They scrubbed the living room and her mother made a fresh pot of coffee. After the women arrived, Deborah rolled Kristina out into the living room in her wheelchair.

Kristina laughed to herself at the memory. Boy did their tunes change. Once they saw the "poor, crippled adopted girl," all thin and pale with that pitiful Buster Brown haircut, they crooned their apologies and praised Deborah Hurst for being a saint, taking care of an invalid child all on her own. From that day forward they showered them with Christian kindness by sending casseroles, boxes of homemade cookies, holiday gifts, and their husbands with paintbrushes and mowers in tow.

Except, Kristina could walk. Her mother told her she needed to stay in her wheelchair to save her strength on account she might collapse. She'd insisted Kristina use the wheelchair whenever she was in public. One never knew when one of her "bouts" might strike. And Kristina did feel poorly much of the time.

She'd grown up believing she had the best mother in the world. What other mother would selflessly dote on her, fix her special diets, take her to endless doctor appointments, and carefully dole out the many medicines she was given daily? Her mother told her that because she had an immune disease, she couldn't go to school, or have friends, or even go out in public often. Germs were everywhere and they could kill her. Kristina believed her implicitly and stayed indoors.

The summer she turned thirteen, watching the boy next door play basketball sent her thoughts spinning. If she had been four years old when she spied the neighbor boy, or even eight, Kristina might've stayed at that window and kept wondering about him. But Kristina was thirteen and her hormones were coursing through her body, giving her the courage to brush her hair, put on her best dress, and walk out to the backyard to say hello.

His name was Joe. He was so thin she could see the veins protruding in his arms. And bruises. He said any bump caused one. She liked the way his dark brown hair had a cowlick where he parted it, and the dreamy way he blinked his eyes. At first, Joe was as shy as she was. But being neighbors somehow removed the veil of unfamiliarity and they struck up a conversation. He asked her why she was not in her wheelchair. She told him she guessed she was getting better. She asked him why he was alone so much. He told her he had leukemia. He couldn't go to school any longer for fear of infection.

"Why, we're alike," she had told him with awe mixed with wonder. She quickly went on to explain about her own immune disease. Instantly, they'd shared a bond.

It wasn't long before Kristina was utterly and completely in love for the first time. She bloomed with color and felt so much better. She started to pretend to dutifully take the medicine her mother offered, then spit it out and flushed the pills down the toilet. The medicine made her feel sleepy and she wanted to be awake in the afternoons to talk with Joe.

Joe liked her, too. He told her so on their fourth meeting at the fence. Her heart thumped so fast she was sure she was having one of her bouts. But she wasn't. In fact, the bouts had stopped completely.

She didn't feel sick at all. Joe told her sometimes a child could grow out of an immune disease.

"You might be one of the lucky ones," he told her.

"Maybe you'll get lucky, too."

A sad smile crossed his face, one without malice or regret. "No, that card's not in my deck. But you? Why not?"

Kristina listened, and pondered his words. Imagine, no longer being sick and isolated. Living a normal life. Could that be possible? Hope filled her like a balloon with helium. She felt she was floating up the stairs to the back door. She rushed inside and followed the sound of the television to the living room, where Deborah was reclined in an easy chair, eating popcorn.

"Mother," Kristina began, near breathless with the excitement. She always called Deborah *mother*. Not mom, mommy, or mama. "I just heard the most exciting news."

Her mother kept her eyes glued to the television. "Oh yeah? Now what's that?"

"That sometimes, a child can outgrow an immune disease. Do you think that could happen to me? I mean, I'm feeling so much better. Really, I am. Maybe we could go to the doctor and ask him. Maybe I could even go to school."

Kristina felt the grin that stretched across her face freeze as she watched her mother's reaction. Rather than joy, Deborah stared back at Kristina, dazed, slack jawed. Then her face began to flush and contort into a macabre mask of fury. She leaped from her chair, upsetting the bowl, and sending popcorn flying.

"You ungrateful child!" she screamed with rage, pointing her finger accusingly. "Horrible girl. I wish I'd never adopted you. From the moment I took you home you've been nothing but a disappointment and hardship. All your life. Where would you be if not for me? Your mother didn't want you. I took you in. I made you my daughter. Don't you care how you hurt me?"

Kristina took a step back, confused. "I never meant . . ."

"I've slaved for you. Spent every penny I have on your medicine. I save nothing for myself. Look at this dress! It's five years old. I had a good figure, once. Good hair. I was quite a catch." She speared Kristina with a sharp look. "I gave up everything for you. Even my husband. He never wanted *you*," she said accusingly, pushing her digit out toward her. "You're the reason he left me."

Kristina shrank back, stung by this new accusation.

"But did I hold it against you?" She shook her head so hard she lost her balance. "No! You were my sweet, adopted baby girl. I swore I'd take care of you. And I did. Didn't I?" she cried. "Didn't I take good care of you? Better than anyone else could." She sideswiped her nose then added with derision, "Better than you deserved."

"I'm sorry. I didn't mean to upset you. I thought you'd be happy I'm feeling better."

Deborah frowned and patted the pockets of her housedress. Finding them empty, she turned heel and paced the room in search of her cigarettes. Kristina crossed her arms tightly across her chest, warily watching her, waiting for the next outburst.

At last she found them, lit one, took a deep drag. Then, exhaling, she turned her head and eyed Kristina with undisguised suspicion.

"Who told you that crap about growing out of your immune disease?"

Kristina's throat tightened around her lie. "No one. I read it."

"Where?"

"Uh, maybe it was on the news. Or on the television." She rubbed her arm. "I . . . I don't remember."

"Hmmm." Her mother took another drag from her cigarette.

In the deathly silence, Kristina heard the thud of a basketball hitting the net. She closed her eyes tight, groaning inwardly. Deborah sauntered closer to the back window, and with one finger, lifted a slat of the blinds to stare out. After a minute she let the blind snap back and spun around to face Kristina, her dark eyes blazing.

"You've been talking to that boy."

"No. Well, maybe a little, but not, you know, talking."

"How dare you! You broke my strictest rule," her mother shouted. Her face had once again taken on the crimson hue of fury as she pointed her digit and pounded out the words inches from her face. "You are not allowed to talk to strangers."

"He's *not* a stranger!" Kristina shouted back, feeling her backbone straighten. "He's a neighbor. And he's nice. He doesn't have germs because he doesn't go anywhere. Like me. I don't see why I can't talk to him."

"Because I forbid it!" Her mother slashed her arm in the air with finality.

"No!" Kristina shouted back, feeling the flame on her own face burn. "You can't make me stop. I want a friend, Mother!" Kristina felt her bravado crumble as the child she still was emerged in defeat. Tears rushed to her eyes. She covered her face with her hands and slid to the floor on watery legs. "I'm so lonely."

Her mother was all sweetness then, wrapping her arms around her, rocking her like a babe.

"Shhhh," she crooned. "I'm here. Your mother is here. I will always be your best friend. Isn't that what we promised each other? To be best friends forever? You'll never need anyone else. Not while I'm alive."

Not while I'm alive.

Kristina heard the words echo in her mind even as the rumble of thunder sounded in the distance. She shook the memory away and peered into the sky. A line of thick, black storm clouds was moving in from the west. The wind was picking up, too. Kristina was not a skilled driver and the thought of driving through a storm had her gripping the steering wheel tighter. She reached over to turn the dial of the radio stations to find the local weather. She paused when she heard a weatherman reporting a fast-moving storm front heading toward the Augusta/Aiken area. Flash flood warnings were issued.

Kristina felt a flicker of fear and pressed the gas pedal harder in hopes of getting out of the path of the storm. Within minutes, fat raindrops splattered across her windshield. Feeling her heart quicken, Kristina flicked on the windshield wipers and turned on the headlights. She wished the wipers could sweep away the memories flooding her brain, too.

Kristina and her mother had lived in a state of war since that first big argument about Joe. Despite Deborah's ceaseless haranguing, berating, and even the occasional beating, Kristina had refused to stop seeing Joe. What could Deborah do to stop her? Especially once Kristina discovered that Deborah had been collecting disability payments for her sick child. Things in the small brick house went from bad to worse. Word got out that Kristina could walk, and the neighborly charity dried up. As the house fell into disrepair, Deborah turned to drinking, blaming Kristina, of course, for being such a horrid daughter and driving her to it. Deborah would pass out when drunk, which was frequent, giving Kristina the chance to sneak out and visit with Joe.

Their love was the purest thing Kristina had ever known. Joe was kind and patient. They were each other's best friend. They spent every free quiet hour together, lying side by side on his bed in his room, talking, watching TV, listening to music or reading books. Or outdoors on his soft grass at night studying the stars. He taught her how to throw a basketball. She taught him how to knit. He gave her chocolates, which she adored. She wrote him love letters that she'd leave in the fork of the tree that stood beside the chain-link fence.

And they kissed. They touched. Curious, but innocent. Once Joe began chemotherapy, he was uninterested, or unable, to pursue sex. She didn't care. She was content loving him.

Their favorite thing was to lie in each other's arms and make up stories about their love and how it would go on and on and they'd live happily ever after. Knowing it would—could—not happen made them all the more desperate to play the game. He called her his *Cinderella* because of the way the wicked "step" mother made her do all the chores and kept her hidden from the outside world. Which she'd thought was pretty spot-on. She called him her *knight in shining armor* because he had rescued a damsel in distress. Again, she nailed it.

Outside the little car, the rain became torrential. Kristina flicked the windshield wipers to a higher speed as the rain pummeled the roof and thunder roared around her. Kristina clenched her teeth as she turned on the emergency blinkers and slowed the car to a crawl in a long line of red lights barely visible in the thick fog. Over and over she had to reach up to the windshield in a desperate attempt to wipe away the mist. She leaned far over the wheel, trying to see more than ten feet ahead of the car.

From the distance she heard the wail of an ambulance then saw the blinking red lights approach. "Oh God Oh God," she murmured as she wildly wondered what to do. There was no place to pull over and the ambulance was on her tail. Squinting, clutching the wheel, she spied a large green exit sign and, not caring where it led, she flicked the turn signal and took the exit. As the ambulance siren faded into the distance, Kristina inched her way off the ramp and to her eternal relief, spotted a gas station just ahead. Terrified she'd be hit by some oncoming car or truck she couldn't see in the fog, she rolled down her window to better hear the traffic. Rain gusted in, drenching her. She quickly rolled the window back up, wiping her face with her hand. Throwing her fate into God's hands, she drove across the street, breathing again when she made it safely to the entrance of the gas station. She parked beside a gas pump under the wide awning. The sudden silence was deafening. With a shaky hand, she turned off the ignition.

She was safe. For the moment. Her world was trapped inside

this tin box. She felt wet and the humidity was building with the air-conditioning turned off. For no reason, and for a thousand reasons buried deep inside of herself, Kristina unbuckled her seat belt, brought her legs up to her chest, and burst into great heaving sobs.

Maybe she wasn't brave enough for this journey. She didn't think she could go any farther. She just wanted to return to her apartment, to Minnie and her books, where she felt warm and safe. Why had she started this quest? She'd finally created a life for herself that was predictable. Normal. Sustainable. Wasn't that enough?

"Joe," she called out into the vacuum. "I need you. I miss you so much."

She cried for a long time. At last the heat and humidity overtook her and she fell into a deep sleep. The sound of an ambulance was the last thing she heard.

• • •

The flashing red lights in the driveway next door awakened Kristina from her sleep. She leaped from her bed and raced to the window to peer out. *Joe . . .*

To her horror she saw a stretcher being wheeled from the house to the open doors of the ambulance. Joe was lying on it and his parents were trailing behind in their pajamas. Mr. Cohen's arm supported his wife.

Kristina grabbed her bathrobe and raced out the front door. The ambulance was pulling away by the time she'd arrived.

"Joe!" she cried after it.

Mrs. Cohen came closer to put her arms around her. Both women were crying openly, fear trailing down their faces.

"We're going to the hospital," she told Kristina. "Would you like to come with us?"

Kristina didn't give a thought to what her mother would say or do when she found out. She jumped into the Cohens' car, barefoot, and sat in stoic silence, praying all the way to the hospital.

The blackness filled the car, though dawn was but an hour off. The hospital waiting room was air-conditioned and clean, that much could be said for it. But the pale green and white paint, the bad art, and the uncomfortable wood and polyester chairs were dismal. She imagined Joe leaning close to her and saying in a low voice, "It's the definition of institutional décor."

How long she sat waiting for the chance to see him, she couldn't remember. But the sun was high in the sky by the time Mr. and Mrs. Cohen returned to the waiting room, their faces haggard and shoulders drooping.

"He's asking for you," Mrs. Cohen said gently.

Kristina looked into her red-rimmed eyes and saw the unspoken message. This would be her good-bye.

She gingerly pushed open the door to his room and peered inside. More institutional décor. Her eyes went directly to the slender form lying in the metal hospital bed, hooked up to an IV. His eyes were closed. He lay so still, and his skin was so white she sucked in her breath, wondering in a panic if she was too late. But then his eyes fluttered open, and seeing her, he smiled weakly.

Her heart leaped to her throat. "Joe!"

She hurried to his side and clasped his hand. Tears began to flow uncontrollably. "Don't go," she begged him. "Fight this. You can. You're the strongest, bravest person I know."

The shake of his head was barely perceptible. "It's my time."

The words struck her to the core. He meant to leave her. Here. Alone in this horrible, lonely world. It was inconceivable.

"Then I'm coming with you," she said, squeezing his hand.

A teasing smile crossed his face. "A suicide pact?"

"Yes."

He made a mild, mocking face. "Please . . ."

"I mean it," she said fervently.

"Kristina . . ." His expression shifted to sympathy.

Imagine, she thought with shame, *he* was offering *her* consolation.

"That's not one of our stories," he said. When she frowned, his smile slipped away, and he spoke earnestly.

"Listen to me. This is *my* time. My destiny. Not yours."

"How do you know? Maybe it's my destiny to go with you."

His laugh was soft and weary. "What's your hurry?"

"You're all I care about on this earth."

"Not true. You love your mother."

"No, I don't," she fired back with more vehemence than she'd intended. "I hate her."

"You don't," he said with conviction. "But I'm not talking about Deborah. You have two mothers."

Kristina's mind spun. "*Her?* My birth mother? I don't even know her."

"But you do. Somewhere, somehow you do. And you love her."

He took her breath away. He knew her better than she knew herself. "I don't even know where she is."

"Then find her."

"You know I can't," she said pulling back her hair from her face in a gesture of frustration. "I promised Deborah I wouldn't."

"And you keep your promises."

"Yes," she said, feeling the truth of it. "I know it doesn't make sense. But Deborah, for all that she's bat-shit crazy, is still the only mother I've ever known. She's her own worst enemy. She's unstable." Kristina looked at her hand over his. "I won't add to her misery. She is still my mother."

"You're a good person."

She sniffed and wiped her nose. "I'm not. Any goodness you see in me is because of you." She leaned closer so her face was inches from his. She stared into his dark brown eyes, the color of chocolate, and still saw the inner light shining in them.

"Please, help me come with you," she said in a pleading voice. "It hurts too much to stay in this world if you're not in it."

Sadness flickered in his eyes. Joe patted the mattress. There wasn't much space on the narrow hospital bed, but both Joe and Kristina were pencil thin and she managed to settle in the small bit of mattress. His body was all bones and flesh, but it was all Joe. She curled up on her side and rested her head in the crook of his arm. She smelled medicine and starch, but not Joe. His scent was already lost to her.

"See, here's the thing about dying," he told her in an even voice that, against his chest, sounded to her like a lullaby. "It's like graduating. If you live a good life, you'll be rewarded and get to go on. How . . ." She felt the slight lift of a shoulder. "I'm not so sure."

"I thought you didn't believe in heaven or hell."

"I never told you that," he replied. "I said I don't know what heaven is. In Judaism, the afterlife is not as well defined as in Christianity."

"You mean the pearly gates?" She heard his laughter rumble in his chest.

"There are lots of theories," he continued, speaking softly. She heard the weariness and worried if speaking was taking too much of his energy. Too much of his precious time.

"Maybe you shouldn't talk."

"I want to," he replied. "I don't know if I'll have another chance. And don't you know? Talking with you was what I've lived for these past years. You kept me alive."

She felt herself come undone. "Joe . . ." she cried, clutching him tightly.

He patted her hand and kissed her forehead. "Let me finish," he chided. "So, this heaven thing . . . I think I finally figured it out. For me, anyway. I've read a lot of opinions. Some of them were wise. Some . . . not so much. Me, I'm more logical. I believe in a God who is all-powerful and all-just. So, it makes sense, to me, that God will not allow evil to triumph. God rewards good people. He's the final judge."

Kristina listened to every word. "Okay. By that theory, Hitler doesn't go to the same place as his victims."

"Right," he said with a short laugh.

"Then you're saying you believe in heaven?"

"I believe in eternity. A place with no beginning and no end. It's infinite. Like love," he said, gently stroking her arm. "I'll be there waiting for you, whenever you arrive."

She clung to him. "I want to go there with you."

"No. Not yet."

"But why?"

"You have to find your purpose. I believe each of us was given a purpose to fulfill in our life. It's tied in with our destiny. Kind of like a test we must pass or fail to reach heaven, or whatever you call it." He paused. "Kristina, I believe you have yet to discover your purpose."

"How will I know if I've achieved it?"

He lowered his head and she felt his kiss on the soft hairs of the top of her head. "You'll know."

She lifted her gaze to meet his, so dark and unfathomable. "You found your purpose?"

"I did."

"What was it?"

His gaze kindled. "Not what. Who. *You*, Kristina. Loving you was my purpose."

This broke her. Kristina buried her face in his chest and wept, telling him over and over that she loved him, soaking his shirt with her tears, as he gently stroked her hair. When at last she quieted, the room was quiet. The gentle rise and fall of his chest reassured her that Joe was still with her.

"Kristina?"

"Yes?"

"I have something important I want to say to you."

She felt her breath still and whispered, "Okay."

His voice was soft, but deliberate. "I've talked this over with my parents. They're in agreement. I don't have much, but what money I have I'm leaving to you. It's just under ten thousand dollars."

"What? How did you get so much money?"

"It's money I've received from gifts over the years. My bar mitzvah. I saved it, knowing I'd find a good use for it one day." He paused, letting that sink in. "You have to leave your house. Your mother. Right away. It's not good for you to stay there. My parents will help you in any way they can. Use the money to go to school. Start your life. And when you're ready, find your mother."

It was all overwhelming. She clung to him tighter. "But Joe, how do I do all that? You can't give me all your money. It's too much."

He smiled. *"A journey of a thousand miles begins with a single step. I'm just giving you a first step."*

CHAPTER THREE

Reunion

MOTHER

Elinor put the final touches on the bouquet of flowers she'd arranged especially for Kristina's visit. White roses and lilies with blue hydrangeas. Her favorites. Only the best for today, she thought with a final adjustment.

Stepping back, she perused the dining table. It sat in the middle of the brilliant turquoise-colored room enclosed on three sides with white plantation shutters. The epitome of a beach room, she thought with pleasure. The flowers were a counterpoint to the large coconut cake with the words *"Happy Birthday Kristina, 40!"* encircled in roses made of blue and white icing.

She glanced at her watch. Dinner reservations were for six-thirty. Her plan was for them to meet on neutral territory, on the beach. Then they could walk back here, have a bit of cake and champagne, then go out to the Long Island Cafe for a leisurely dinner. This would be followed by bedtime. "Keep moving," Maeve had advised. "You don't want to get stuck in the mud."

Elinor smoothed out her white linen tunic top, thinking what a shame how linen wrinkled up so quickly. She spread out her blue silk scarf across her chest. She paused to look at her hands. They were shaking!

She shook them and puffed out a plume of air. She was being

silly. This wasn't like her. She could face down a classroom full of students, speak to a large group without skipping a beat. Today she only had to meet one woman. What was there to be nervous about? She'd been waiting for this day for forty years. To the very day. She inhaled and blew out slowly, calming herself. She chose to meet at four o'clock today because forty years ago, that was the time Kristina was born—4:18 p.m. to be exact. Elinor hoped Kristina would be pleased to learn that. It was one of a series of little surprises she had planned for Kristina.

Including her birthday gift.

She picked up the small, wrapped package from the side table and carried it to the Sheraton dining table, setting the box beside the cake. She pinched the white bow to perk it up a bit. Elinor had thought long and hard about what might make a suitable birthday gift for Kristina's fortieth birthday. It was the first time they'd be celebrating her birth together.

She didn't want Kristina to think she was taking her adopted mother's place. She would never do that. Yet she wanted her daughter to know that she was loved and cherished by another woman . . . another mother, as well. Elinor agonized over the decision, plaguing Maeve with a series of texts listing possibilities. She kept coming back to her original idea like a broken record. Maeve finally texted back in capital letters: JUST GO WITH YOUR HEART!

So, she did. Elinor moved her hand over her bare neckline. She was giving Kristina a gold turtle necklace. It had been her favorite for years, a rare extravagant purchase when she'd traveled to Hawaii. She rarely took it off. The turtle had always symbolized her belief in feminine independence and resilience. And yes, motherhood. She wanted to give her daughter something meaningful. She wrung her hands looking at the wrapped box. She hoped it wasn't too much too soon.

She'd been warned by articles she'd read not to have too many expectations for the meeting. To act naturally, to let her daughter guide the conversation, and to have photos to share. Her gaze moved to the two photo albums neatly stacked on the dining table. One was a smaller collection of photos of the Earnhardt family, labeled with births and deaths. She had made copies of the originals so she could present the album to Kristina to keep.

The other was quite old and ratty-looking, with worn, bent corners and coffee stains. She smiled, thinking how this album held the heart of this cottage. It had been the guestbook of the Earnhardt beach house for more than half a century. It was chock-full of photos of family holidays and reunions held in this very house—many of them in black-and-white—including several of herself as a child, a leggy teen, and later, the maiden aunt.

She cast her gaze around the tidy 1940s beach cottage that once upon a time was oceanfront but after Hurricane Hugo devastated the island in 1989, the local powers-that-be cut through the dunes and built a road and lots that were situated even closer to the sea. She shook her head at the shortsightedness of greed. This beach house was one of the few that remained intact after that storm. Pure luck. Others, including the one next door, were destroyed by tidal surge, fallen trees, or boats in their living room. People were still digging up silver spoons in their gardens.

Her parents hung on to the beach house when everyone else was selling. It was more than a summer home to them. It was a way of life. How many times had she heard them say that they were waiting for the day they could play with their grandchildren in the cottage? Even after she had found a different family for her baby. Elinor never heard that comment without a stab of pain and resentment. It still hurt how they didn't have a clue how scarred she'd been by the experience of being ripped apart from her family, her friends, her boyfriend and sent to a Home for Unwed Mothers without once visiting her.

When she'd returned from the Home, Elinor shut herself off from the world. Her parents had told everyone she'd spent a year studying in London. But the truth has a way of leaking out. Whispers about where she'd really been had circulated the halls of high school. She was unceremoniously dropped by her so-called friends. The sad truth was, she didn't care. Her personal loss felt so much greater than those friendships. She'd felt numb and, in hindsight, had few memories of that time in her life. Yet the memories of the Home and her baby were as fresh today as they were forty years earlier.

Elinor walked past her own bedroom with its white matelassé coverlet and Oriental carpet. Her gaze fell to the doll that sat in a place of honor on a blue velvet side chair. A soft smile of affection flickered across her face. She went to pick up the baby doll and held it out to study its face. It was a sweet, chubby-cheeked baby doll with blond curly hair and wide blue eyes. The doll's pink lips were open in an *O* for feeding.

"Hello, Baby," she said, smoothing the wiry curls. When she'd returned from the Home, her nights were filled with nightmares of the birth, and when she awoke in the morning she was depressed. Her parents, worried, sent her to a therapist in Charleston. He was freshly shaven and seemed not much older than she was in his new suit and wire-rimmed glasses. She'd sat with her arms crossed and glared at the man as he gave her advice on how to deal with being a mother who gave away her child.

In the end, the therapist gave her two things, both of which proved helpful. First, a prescription for an antidepressant. Her father was appalled that a child of his needed any mental drugs, but her mother hushed him up and encouraged her to take the pills.

The second thing he recommended was a baby doll.

Eighteen-year-old Elinor had howled with laughter at that one. "How about a teddy bear?" she'd sneered as she walked out of his office. She never returned.

Then her mother brought a baby doll home from a shopping trip in Charleston. Elinor was furious.

"It's just to help you sleep," her mother had said.

"I'm not going to sleep with a baby doll!" she'd shouted, throwing the doll to the floor. "I told you I didn't want one."

Her mother, crestfallen, bent to pick up the doll, dusted it off, and then cradled it in her arms. Elinor saw her face relax into a sad smile as she looked into the doll's human-like pink-cheeked face and it felt like a smack in the face. She ran to her room and slammed the door. Later, as she lay alone in the dark, she realized that her mother might also have regrets and long for the baby she never saw.

Not another word was spoken about the doll. It had just disappeared. Until one night a few weeks later. Elinor was trapped in another horrible dream, sobbing, and calling out, "Please! Let me see my baby."

All she remembered was feeling her mother wiping the hair from her face, a kiss on her forehead. When she woke up the following morning, the baby doll was cuddled in her arms. She'd named the doll *Baby*, not daring to give it a proper name, and the doll had stayed in her bed.

"Hello, Baby," Elinor said, stroking the wiry blond, synthetic hair. She had a true fondness for the doll. Dare she call it a love? Baby had spared her many hard nights over the years. As she lay the doll on the bed, the doll cried out *Mama* in its mechanical wail. Elinor paused. After all these years, that mournful cry still had the power to elicit a sigh from her. She used to lie in the dark, flipping the doll over and over, listening to the wail and never believing she'd ever hear that word from her daughter.

She could have had more children. She'd had many boyfriends over the years. Lovers. Proposals, even. Yet Elinor had never wanted to marry. She used to tell herself if her parents had really wanted a grandchild, why had they forced her to give away the only child she'd ever have? Was her decision not to marry subconscious punishment for her parents? Time had softened the edges of her pain and Elinor honestly didn't believe it was. If that painful experience had changed anything about her, it was simply that she preferred making decisions for herself rather than have them made for her.

For there was love between her and her parents, and when they'd given up hope that their only child would ever marry, they were determined to give her a financial leg up in life. On her fortieth birthday, they handed her the deed to the beach house with great ceremony.

And someday, Elinor thought with more pleasure than she felt she deserved, she'd leave the house to her only daughter. That was another of the surprises she'd hoped to share today.

She strolled aimlessly through the house, looking at each room with what she thought might be Kristina's eyes. It was a charming place with the charm from a time long gone. The rooms were small, but Elinor had an eye for color and design. The walls were refreshed with crisp whites, pale blues, and spots of color. She'd replaced dated Formica counters with marble; added large, potted plants and circulating fans. The house was a far cry from the worn plaids, rattan, and lime greens of her parents' décor.

She entered the guestroom where Kristina would sleep. Fresh summer flowers from the farmer's market sat in a vase by the bed, along with Evian water, a dark chocolate bar, a scented candle, and a *Charleston Magazine*. She knew it was the little things that made one feel welcome. Elinor bent to smooth the blush-colored duvet. A memory flashed, eliciting a crooked smile. This was the room in which Kristina was conceived. It was prom night. She snorted a self-deprecating laugh. Of course it was. In fact, the deed happened in this very bed. Elinor straightened and headed to the door. She didn't plan on sharing *that* secret with Kristina.

Her phone pinged and Elinor rushed back into the living room to grab it. It was Kristina. She took a deep breath, praying she didn't have a change of heart.

Storms hit. I had to pull off the road. I'll be late. Maybe five?

Elinor slowly lowered the phone. Disappointing, yes . . . but not devastating. She was still on her way. She took a breath of relief. Lord help her, what was she going to do to while away another hour? She already was on pins and needles.

The doorbell rang, startling her. *That must be Maeve*, she thought and hurried across the living room to answer the door. "Coming!" Opening the door, she saw her friend standing on the freshly painted, covered front porch changed from her Turtle Team T-shirt to a crisply ironed pink blouse. In her arms she carried a wrapped gift and a large pink balloon that said *It's a Girl!*

"I heard it was someone's birthday," Maeve said cheerily, stepping into the cool of the house. "Lord, it's hotter than Hades out there. Hurry and shut the door."

"You sure can be bossy," Elinor chided. "Anyone ever tell you that?"

"Every day," she sang out as she walked toward the dining room. "My, isn't this festive," she exclaimed. Then, pointing to the cake she asked, "Caroline's Cakes?"

"Of course."

Maeve set her gift on the table. "Yum."

Elinor walked closer to the large balloon in Maeve's hand and gave her friend the stink eye. "A balloon? Really? You know we're trying to outlaw them here on the island. Just sayin' . . ."

"I know, I know," Maeve muttered with a wave of her hand. "No one is going to release it. I promise you I will personally deflate it and toss it into the trash after our little party, okay?"

"It's very nice," Elinor conceded.

Maeve stood in front of the table with her hands on her hips and surveyed the party décor. "You done good," she said. Then turning she asked, "When does the birthday girl get here?"

"Not till five. There were storms on the way down."

Maeve lifted her wrist and looked at her watch. "Well, phooey. I'm ready for a glass of champagne."

"Will white wine hold you over?"

"Sounds dreamy."

"You spruced things up a bit," she said when Elinor returned with the wine. "Very nice."

Elinor was pleased with the compliment. "Just a coat of fresh paint. The house was looking a little tired. It was overdue."

"How'd you get it done so fast? I can't get Ben to change a light bulb."

"Ever try doing it yourself?"

Maeve cast her a sidelong glance. "No." Then looking around she added teasingly, "Trying to set a good impression?"

Elinor blushed at the truth of it. "I wanted the cottage to look its best. So she'd like it, and"—she walked over to fluff up a pillow—"maybe return for a visit."

"Don't get your hopes up too high."

Elinor frowned. "I've been warned, thank you very much."

Maeve took a sip of her wine.

Elinor felt badly she had spoken so sharply. She knew Maeve was only trying to be supportive. "I'm sorry if I'm a bit short," she said after a beat. "I'm anxious."

"It's okay. I figured."

"I really am glad you're here."

"Of course," Maeve replied. She was sincere. "You've always been there for me."

Elinor didn't know what to say. When Maeve's grandchild died from cystic fibrosis, she'd had a hard time. It was one thing for someone older to die. One could rationalize that the person lived a long life. But a child . . . there was no getting past that. Elinor, having lost a child, understood and never left Maeve's side.

"You know," Elinor said in an upbeat tone, striving for a change of mood, "I got a birthday card for Kristina every year of her life."

"You're kidding?" Maeve tilted her head, perplexed. "But, you didn't know where to send them."

"No." She pointed to a sweetgrass basket on the coffee table. It was filled with envelopes. "There they are. I didn't have her name, so I couldn't address them." She smiled. "Now I have a name to add."

Maeve's expression softened. "You're giving them all to her today."

"It's one of my surprises." She glanced at the pile of sealed envelopes. "I wrote something to her each year. I can't remember all that I said. I hope it's not too maudlin."

"Confession time," Maeve said, raising her palms. "I went to her Facebook page this morning and put a Happy Birthday notice up."

Elinor was shocked. She wasn't sure how she felt about that. "But . . . she doesn't know who you are."

"I figured I'd explain all today." Then, seeing Elinor's face she blurted, "Why? Was that wrong? I just wanted to let her know how excited we all were."

"No, of course not," Elinor said in a rush. "She has to be happy about a birthday greeting, right?" She chewed her lips. At least Elinor hoped she would be. This was all still so new. She wasn't sure what did or didn't cross the line into *too much*.

Her phone pinged. She met Maeve's eyes, startled, then rushed to her phone on the table.

"It says she's on Isle of Palms," Elinor announced. She felt her heart rate accelerate. "She'll be here any moment." Elinor looked out the front window and brought her fingers to her lips, tapping them. "I told her to park in my driveway." She moved her arms to wrap around herself, suddenly awash in self-doubt. "Was it silly of me to suggest we meet on the beach? Maybe I should text her to come to the front door. I should just stay here."

Maeve rallied, nudging her friend toward the door. "Stick to the plan. It's showtime. Just go!"

• • •

DAUGHTER

Kristina left the mainland via a long stretch of road called The Connector. It carried her over vast acres of cord grass, dark green and vibrant. The marsh spread out around her like a velvety carpet, dotted here and there with white egrets standing in exposed mud. The tide must be going out, she thought, and wondered what it might be like to live in an area dictated by the tides.

The Connector arched over a long ribbon of water she knew was the Intracoastal Waterway. A motorboat was racing below, sending a long stream of wake behind it. Then, without warning, there was the Atlantic Ocean. Her breath caught in surprise at seeing the ocean looming before her, so broad and majestic, cloaked in a brilliant blue hue that reflected the cloudless sky. The sight filled her with hope.

She drove on, leaving The Connector and crossing onto Isle of Palms. The first thing she spotted was the water tower. It stood starkly against the horizon, like an omen.

"I'm here, Joe," she said aloud, feeling sure she was heard. "I couldn't have made it without you."

She felt his presence, as she often did throughout the years. Joe had given her a start with his gift of money, true. However, it was as though he'd always been by her side, holding her hand, each step of the journey, ever since that first step leaving the hospital after his death.

At the stoplight, she reached for her phone and texted Elinor that she'd arrived on the island. The thought struck that she'd see her mother soon. In minutes. The light changed and she pressed the gas, moving forward across Palm Boulevard straight toward the sea. When she turned right onto Ocean Boulevard, her stomach tightened, and her fingers began to dance in anticipation on the wheel. This was really happening. There was no turning back now.

She craned her neck from side to side, gaping at the mansions that bordered Ocean Boulevard. Peppered here and there on across the street were quaint cottages. Elinor's house would be one of those. Oddly, that pleased her. It felt less daunting to go to a more normal-size house than some grand mansion. Still, she was relieved Elinor had suggested that they meet on the beach. She'd explained why on their phone call.

"The beach has always been my sanctuary. My church. Most mornings I stand at the shoreline and say a prayer for your health, your happiness. A prayer that someday I would meet you. And at last, my prayer has been answered. So it seems only fitting that we meet in God's church, don't you think?"

At last Kristina found Elinor's address. She was here. She swallowed hard and pulled into the driveway beside a tidy white beach cottage with a large, covered porch fronted by giant hydrangeas. A small blue flag hung over the entrance with wording in sunshine yellow: *Welcome Kristina*.

Stepping out from the car, she felt as though someone was watching her. She glanced up at the row of front windows. Was her mother in the house? Should she knock on the door first? She stood on rubbery legs that still thrummed with the five-hour journey. Turning her head, she spied a bit of blue water between the houses.

The ocean called her home. She closed the car door, adjusted her purse on her shoulder, and began to walk toward the designated Fifth Avenue beach path. Her flat heels dug into the soft sand as she made her way in the shade of two large houses. The narrow path led over the dunes, cloaked with small yellow flowers and tall, drooping sea oats. She paused at the top, feeling the salty breeze of the sea caress her cheeks. Elinor was right, she thought. Being by the water had a way of calming the nerves. Staring out at the breadth of sea and sky, she felt on common ground.

Her gaze scanned the beach. She saw a blue umbrella and two matching chairs. A dog running joyfully along the shoreline. Two women jogging. Then she froze. One woman, not twenty feet away, stood alone near the dune. She was older. Kristina zeroed in on details. Her hair was a wispy, light brown, like her own. She was of average height and weight and wore a white linen shirt with a bright blue scarf. The woman stood motionless, staring back at her with wide eyes the same blue color as her own. This woman looked like her. Kristina would have known her in a crowded room.

Recognition washed over her like a wave, sweeping away hesitation and fear.

The woman lifted her hand in a wave. "Kristina!"

Kristina's breath caught in her throat and she rushed forward. Step by step, she was at last going home.

• • •

MOTHER

The sun glared bright and hot, even at five p.m. Still, Elinor resisted putting on her sunglasses. She wanted Kristina to be able to recognize her. If there were any similarities in appearance, at least. There was no way to know. They'd not exchanged photographs. Perhaps they should have, she worried. What if she didn't recognize her? Oh Lord, she should have suggested they carry roses, or some such marker.

She felt her heart beating erratically again and turned toward the siren call of the sea. She stared out at the vista and felt the familiar pull. She closed her eyes and heard the sea whisper in the waves, *There, there. You know where you are. Who you are.*

When she opened her eyes again, she breathed deep and felt as serene as the gentle waves lapping the shore. She was ready. Turning back toward the beach path, she saw a young woman step out from it. She stood at the top of the dune. The breeze lifted the ends of her shoulder-length hair, the same thin, wispy brown as her own. She was quite thin, almost shapeless in the pale blue shift she wore. The brown leather purse hanging from her shoulder seemed too big for her frail body.

Elinor stood motionless as the young woman's gaze scanned the beach. She wanted to call out, but her voice wouldn't come. She felt time stand still. Then the young woman turned her way and she knew the moment she spotted her. Her thin shoulders went back and slowly, deliberately, she removed her large sunglasses, revealing impossibly large blue eyes.

It was like looking in a mirror. Elinor's hand darted up and she found her voice. "Kristina!"

Her child, her baby, was moving now, toward her. The tug of the umbilical cord was a force of nature. Elinor couldn't take her eyes off Kristina's face. She saw tears glistening in her daughter's eyes, as they did in hers. She opened her arms.

Elinor closed her eyes as her daughter stepped into her outstretched arms. Once empty, now filled. She embraced her child, rocking side to side, feeling Kristina's arms tighten around her. She smelled her scent, inhaled it, knowing it. Her reaction was visceral.

The gulls cried overhead. Yet over their taunting, raucous laughter Elinor heard one word cried close to her ear. Two small syllables, a child's alliteration, that she'd waited a lifetime to hear.

"Mama."

About Mary Alice Monroe

Mary Alice Monroe is the *New York Times* bestselling author of twenty-seven books including her latest novel *The Summer of Lost and Found* (May 2021, Gallery Books), and her first middle-grade book *The Islanders* (June 2021, Aladdin Books).

Monroe's books have been published worldwide. She's earned numerous accolades and awards, including: induction into the South Carolina Academy of Authors' Hall of Fame; Southwest Florida Author of Distinction Award; South Carolina Award for Literary Excellence; RT Lifetime Achievement Award; the International Book Award for Green Fiction; and the prestigious Southern Book Prize for Fiction. Her bestselling novel *The Beach House* is a Hallmark Hall of Fame movie.

Mary Alice Monroe is also the co-creator and co-host of the weekly web show and podcast *Friends and Fiction.*

Monroe found her true calling in environmental fiction when she moved to the Isle of Palms, South Carolina. Captivated by the beauty and fragility of her new home in the Lowcountry, Monroe's experiences gave her a strong and important focus for her novels.

Monroe and Dorothea Benton Frank were Lowcountry neighbors. Dottie—as she was called among friends—lived across the inlet from Isle of Palms on the neighboring Sullivan's Island. Together they became part of a small tribe of Lowcountry writers who gathered together over the years for meals and conversation supporting each other's careers and personal lives. Dottie's energy and spirit will be forever missed.

ALSO BY MARY ALICE MONROE

Stand-Alone Novels

The Summer Guests

A Lowcountry Christmas

The Butterfly's Daughter

Last Light over Carolina

Time Is a River

Sweetgrass

Skyward

The Book Club

The Four Seasons

The Long Road Home

Girl in the Mirror

Beach House Series

The Summer of Lost and Found

On Ocean Boulevard

Beach House Reunion

Beach House for Rent

Beach House Memories

Swimming Lessons

The Beach House

Lowcountry Summer Series

A Lowcountry Wedding

The Summer's End

The Summer Wind

The Summer Girls

Children's Books

The Islanders

A Butterfly Called Hope

Turtle Summer

Lowcountry Stew

CASSANDRA KING CONROY

Before Nellie Bee gets here, I look again to make sure every little thing is lined up exactly as we like it. When she and I first met, we'd bonded over the similarities of our detail-obsessed personalities—which our husbands call neurotic, of course. Low-slung canvas chairs positioned exactly so? Check. Icy pitcher of mojitos? Check. Two silver julep mugs? Check. Both of us like our mojitas strong, with extra lime, and we like our chairs placed right where the waves recede so the hot foamy water washes over our feet without splashing us.

The beach is perfect today—or as perfect as the Atlantic Ocean gets. Before moving to the Lowcountry, I'd swum in the Gulf of Mexico on frequent family vacations to Corpus Christi, but not the Atlantic. Being in the Atlantic is such a different experience. There's even a different texture to the water. Bram looked skeptical when I observed that gulf water feels silkier on your skin, like someone's added bath oil. And he calls my notion absurd that the water here feels and tastes saltier than the Gulf. But he does agree about the color difference. The Gulf of Mexico looks like emeralds left to melt in the sun, while the Atlantic's the grayish-green of a swamp. At first I wasn't keen on the daily swims my new husband insisted on, but I, too, have come to love them.

Nellie Bee and I won't be swimming here, though. We seldom do, unless it's in the pool. Our beach visits are always at water's edge and fortified with strong drink. When I hear a stroller on the beach call out "Hi, Nell!" at my sister-in-law's approach, I turn my head to watch her trudge across the sand, trailing the towel she brings for wiping her feet. Even though I know Nellie Bee's here to "talk some sense into her idiot sister-in-law" (or so she said on the phone), I grin and wave to her. She sees me, but she's paused to look out over the ocean and doesn't return my wave. I think she's more exasperated with me than angry—or at least I hope so. In the five years we've known each other, we've never had a cross word and I don't want to start now.

Toting her shoes in one hand, Nellie Bee's still dressed for golf in jaunty little skorts and a blue polo with the Fripp Island logo. That woman and her golf! It's another of her obsessions, she says, but at least healthier than mojitos. She stands motionless for a long moment to breathe in the brisk salt breeze, and behind the sunglasses, I imagine she's closed her eyes. It's late afternoon, and the sun still hangs high above the horizon, its blinding glare obscured by wispy streaks of clouds. Low tide, and the waves lap against the shoreline with a soft swishing sound. I watch sandpipers retreating from them, spindly-legged, then I turn my gaze back to Nellie Bee, trying to gauge her mood before she joins me. We usually get together once a week after one of her golf games. But today she'd called to convene what she referred to as an emergency meeting, and had asked me to make our drinks extra strong. I took that as a bad sign.

My sister-in-law and dear friend, Nell O'Connor (called Nellie Bee by the family), bears such a strong resemblance to my husband Bram that they're sometimes mistaken for twins. Twenty months apart, they're Irish twins, but Nellie Bee's quick to remind everyone that she's younger. Plus, she was the one born in South Carolina; since her "twin" was born in Ireland, he's more Irish than Southern, she says. It's the distinctive coloring that makes them so much alike, what Bram calls the black Irish: the dark hair, bright green eyes, and milky skin. In the past few years his hair's become heavily threaded with silver, but Nellie Bee's only slightly streaked, like pricey highlights. Nellie Bee gripes, saying she looks older, but to me it makes her even more striking. The resemblance between her and Bram has more to do with their strong personalities than with physical appearance: Bram's a force of nature, one of those dynamic people who lights up a room when he enters it and turns heads wherever he goes. His sister's the same, though she pooh-poohs the idea that she has anything like his charisma. Squaring her shoulders, Nellie Bee turns abruptly from her reverie and heads my way, a scowl on her face.

"Sister-woman!" I call out when she plops down in the chair next to mine, trying to lighten her mood. She's not having it.

"Don't you be sister-womaning me," she says, tossing her golf shoes on the sand. "Not till I have a cold one in my hand, anyway."

I pour mojito into one of the engraved silver mugs Bram gave me for a wedding gift (at her suggestion) and pass it to her. She has a set of them, which I'd admired. Presenting his gift, my new husband announced his sister ordered him to marry me, or else. Even if his twinkling eyes hadn't betrayed him, I would've known he was joking. No one tells Bram O'Connor what to do. Nellie Bee had hooted when I repeated what he'd said. "He's so full of it" was her response. "I told him the opposite. I wouldn't wish him on anybody, let alone a sweetheart like you." Unlike her brother, she was only halfway joking. She adores her brother but claims I'm a saint for putting up with him.

I remind her of that after she clicks her mug against mine and we chant our favorite toast: "'Balls,' said the Queen. 'If I had 'em, I'd be King.'" After taking a long, thirsty drink, I say, "You can save your speech, sistah. You were the one who warned me not to hook up with your brother."

Nellie Bee gulps her drink then sighs in satisfaction. "God, that's so good. And yes, I did. Though it shouldn't have been necessary. I figured no woman in her right mind would marry a man named Bram Stoker." She and Bram have told me how shamelessly their mother, a Stoker from Dublin, had played up her kinship with the infamous author of *Dracula*.

"Wife number one did," I say with a sly smile.

"I said in her right mind." To my surprise Nellie Bee drains her glass and holds it out for a refill. We always limit ourselves to two drinks that we sip slowly to make them last. "You'd better refill yours, too. You're going to need it."

"So you're upset with me then?" I say it lightly but with a rush of anxiety. I treasure her friendship and hate to think of us at odds.

"Oh, honey." She pushes her sunglasses to the top of her head and turns her gaze on me. The blue shirt turns her darkly fringed eyes to aquamarine, a lovely contrast to her pale skin. Anyone else who spent so much time on the golf course would be deeply tanned; she freckles instead—arms, legs, and across the bridge of her nose. Her expression's troubled. "You know how much I adore you, Chris. But you're a damn fool for agreeing to this reunion. And my brother's a bigger one for putting you in such a position."

"He didn't pressure me, sweetie. I agreed willingly."

While true, it lacks conviction. If I know one thing about my husband of five years, it's his power of persuasion. It's one of the ways he reached the top of his game—and TV ratings—before age thirty and stayed there for twenty years. Now, despite his retirement a few years ago, reruns of his cooking show, *Southern Heritage*, are still much in demand. As are pleas for him to film a new series. We both know that's behind this *Return to the Lowcountry* special the food network has talked him into doing. One reason I agreed to be a part of it—even after hearing the details—was curiosity. When we married, Bram retired from the show, tired of all the traveling involved. Plus he wanted time to write a food memoir, which he'd been hard at work on ever since. Does he want to do the show again, despite his swearing otherwise? If not, then why the enthusiasm for this special? Nellie Bee and I have different answers to that, and she's here to argue hers.

"Bram didn't pressure me, either," Nellie Bee admits, rattling the ice in her glass. We've had this discussion before. Nellie Bee and her husband will be part of the special, too, since the show will feature Bram hosting a family get-together. The thing is, it not only includes Bram's son, wife, and new baby, but also Bram's ex-wife, whom Nellie Bee detests.

"I was all for it until I heard she'd be here," she tells me. "Therein lies the problem. The return of the spider woman."

I lean back on the canvas chair and sigh. The sun's not unbearably hot yet, early June. Matter of fact, it feels good, warm and nourishing on my face. I'm slathered with sunblock but still shouldn't be sunbathing, I know. I push my sunglasses up on my head, then squint against the glare. "Well, you know Michael won't participate unless the mama bear's included."

Nellie Bee snorts. "That's an insult to bears the world over. That woman doesn't have a mama bone in her body. And Michael's a fool." I feel her eyes on me but don't turn to meet her gaze, knowing what I'll see. Her tone tells me that she's more upset than I realized. She goes on with a litany against her nephew that I've heard before, though not quite so fiercely. "Michael's a sweet boy but too easily influenced. Always has been," his aunt declares. "Especially by the fair sex. First it was his mama and now his prissy wife, the princess. Obviously he inherited his daddy's taste in women."

As soon as I let out a hoot of laughter, she realizes what she said. When I tease, "Oh, thanks a lot," she tries unsuccessfully to suppress a giggle. It's the opening I've been waiting for, and I press on. "Listen, I know you're just trying to protect me, and I appreciate it. More than that, I love you for it. But the whole thing will only take a few days. And trust me, I intend to avoid the dragon lady while she's here. Doing this will be good for all of us. It'll give me a chance to meet the baby and get to know Michael better. Bram needs to spend time with his first grandchild. How can that not be a good thing? Bram's finally on good terms with his son, and now this chance to solidify their relationship has come up—"

"Or have it blow up in his face." Nellie Bee snorts. "Which is what I've tried to tell Bram. Despite having to tolerate Her Highness, his daughter-in-law, filming the special would be a perfect chance for him to be with Michael and the baby. But once I heard that Jocasta was coming, that soured the whole thing for me. You don't know that woman like I do."

"I don't know her at all." I'd met Bram's ex-wife, Jocasta, at Michael and Missy's wedding in Atlanta, three years ago. Aside from forced pleasantries, Jocasta and I'd had little interaction, but my impression of her lingered like cloying perfume. It wasn't her stunning blond beauty; I'd seen pictures and expected that. Nor was it the charm; Bram'd told me that his ex could be quite bewitching. What surprised me about Jocasta was the extent of her flattery and fawning, as if she set out to lure everyone she met into her silken web. How could a man as astute as Bram not have seen through such artifice? After her initial curiosity about me, she turned her full attention to captivating Missy's high-society parents. Every time I caught a glimpse of her, she was either posing for pictures with them or hanging raptly on their every word. They appeared equally enamored with her, but why wouldn't they be? Jocasta Wainwright's from the cream of Charleston society, making her their social equal. All of them, cut out of the same gold-threaded cloth.

Nellie Bee peers in her empty cup with a frown. "God, I want another one bad. But, gotta resist. I'm driving home. Matter of fact, I need to get on back now."

"Why don't you stay over, have dinner with us? Call Charlie to come out. You know Bram will fix enough to feed half of Fripp Island."

She's shaking her head before I finish. "If I do, we'll just keep fussing about this TV thing. I don't want to get my brother riled up, and I don't want to be at odds with you. I just want you not to do this. It's not going to turn out like you expect."

I eye her with amusement. "And what do you think I expect?"

"You know damn well," she says with a snort. "The saintly, widowed therapist—who the jaded TV chef had the good fortune to marry—steps in to save the day and mend the well-publicized rifts of his screwed-up family."

"I'm not exactly a therapist," I correct her. "A child psychologist who works with migrant families doesn't get to do much therapy. I'm more of a social worker these days."

"That's therapy in my book," she says tartly. "The thing is, you might fool a lot of people, Christina O'Connor—"

"Murray." I correct her more playfully this time, but she ignores me.

"My point is, you don't fool me. You're a lot more vulnerable than you appear." Nellie Bee picks up her towel to wipe the sand off her feet, and I stare at her in surprise.

"What does that mean?" I demand. "When have I ever claimed not to be vulnerable? I've always been vulnerable and not afraid to show it."

She turns flashing green eyes on me. "Oh bull crap. You put up a good front, acting so calm and composed. But I know it's an act. I'm worried about you, Chris. Really worried."

"Worried about me? That's ridiculous." Like her brother, Nellie Bee's intensity can be a bit overwhelming. But you know where you stand with her. Then it hits me that something else is bothering her, something she's hesitant to say—which is not like her. "C'mon, Nellie Bee; spit it out. What's this really about?"

We stare at each other until she throws her hands up in the air, flapping the towel dramatically. "Okay, okay. I didn't want to say anything but—"

"I knew it! What?"

"I think this reunion thing's an elaborate ploy to get Bram back—"

"Is that what's bothering you? I've known that all along. No reason for you to worry, though. If he decides he wants to return to the show, I'll play the good wife and be supportive of his decision."

"Not the freaking show!" Nellie Bee screeches it so loud that a couple of seagulls standing near us lift their wings and take off, squawking in protest. Looking around to make sure no one hears her, Nellie Bee leans toward me and lowers her voice. "I'm talking about Jocasta. She's the one who wants him back."

I blink at her, baffled. "You mean she got the food network to film a special so she'd have a reason to see him again?"

"Of course not, idiot. Jesus! Use that brilliant mind of yours here. She merely seized the opportunity the network offered. They proposed a big special, Bram Stoker O'Connor on the twenty-fifth anniversary of the launch of his show. It'll be modeled after the original special they did on him—the young O'Connor family at home on Fripp Island. Then they'll show viewers where he is now—divorced but remarried, his son grown up with his own family, and everyone—including the ex-wife—getting along beautifully. It'll be a family reunion to end all family reunions."

"I still don't get why you think Jocasta orchestrated it."

"She didn't! What she orchestrated was Michael's insistence that either she be a part of it or he wouldn't come. And I know that because Michael told me himself. His mother begged to be included."

"That doesn't mean she wants to get back with Bram, Nellie Bee. Or that Michael's complicit. He just wants the grandparents of his daughter to be on good terms. That's what he told Bram, and Bram agrees."

"Bram doesn't know pea-turkey. Of course he doesn't see through her scheme. He's never seen through her."

"But . . ." My head's spinning, either from the mojitos or the craziness of such an idea. "He must've eventually come to see her for what she really is. I mean, Jocasta left him for another man and took Michael with her. Losing both his wife and son almost destroyed him."

"I hope he told you that he tried to get her back, even after she broke his heart?" When I acknowledge that he did, Nellie Bee goes on. "I'm not sure what his version is, Chris, but I can tell you what I saw. He'd been a fool for that woman, and I've never seen anyone so devastated as he was by her betrayal. When she filed for divorce and was awarded full custody of Michael—by claiming, rightfully, I must concede, that Bram traveled too much to take care of a child—my brother fell apart. Then Jocasta remarried and he plunged into despair. That's when he tried to drown his sorrows with booze. He was barely able to go on with the show."

I nod and look out over the ocean, remembering Bram telling me this before we married and observing the pain it still caused him. I'd insisted on complete honesty about our pasts. Both of us had loved before and had our lives shattered by loss, me by the unexpected death of my husband, whom I'd loved dearly, and Bram's by divorce and estrangement. Bram swore he was over his ex-wife, but hearing the story from Nellie Bee's point of view makes me wonder. Did he ever truly get over her? "Go on," I say, bracing myself.

Nellie Bee's gaze holds mine. "Here's the thing, Chris. Because Bram was so well-known by then, their private life became public. You might've seen the article *People* did. Their angle was the one that hurt Bram most, how Michael turned against his dad. He bought his mother's lie that she only left his father because he ran around with other women and neglected her and their son. Jocasta played Michael's disillusionment with his dad for all it was worth."

"Why do you think that her second marriage didn't work out?" I ask, though I figure her response will be the same as Bram's: husband number two wised up quicker than he did.

Nellie Bee refutes that. "It didn't work out because the new guy wasn't Bram. Bram'd become a celebrity chef with a hit TV show, and surprise—Jocasta drops husband number two and decides she wants number one back. Even during her marriage, she wanted him back. He didn't tell me that—I found the emails she wrote him. I wasn't snooping; I used Bram's computer one day when he was gone and I checked on the house. In the emails Jocasta swore she'd never loved anyone else and wouldn't give up until they were together again. Did he tell you that she turned to him for comfort after her divorce?"

My look of surprise reveals the answer, and she sighs before saying, "No, I didn't think he had, or you'd understand why I'm worried. Bram, being a typical man, let himself be taken in again by a damsel in distress—which Jocasta played to the hilt. She claimed the man she'd left Bram for cheated on her. Ha! I'd call that poetic justice. But not Bram. He said the experience had changed her, and made her realize how her leaving had hurt him. He was thinking of giving her another chance. I'm convinced that if my brother hadn't met you then, he'd be back with that woman now."

I try not to let her see how this affects me. Bram had sworn he'd told me everything about his stormy relationship with his ex. But he left out the part of the story where she'd tried to get him back, and he'd considered it. The sin of omission. Or maybe worse, I think with a jolt, remembering. Because he'd asked me, I'd told him that he'd been the only man I'd been with since my husband's death. It was then he'd admitted to having had a few "flings" since his divorce but nothing serious. He hadn't been honest with me. He wouldn't have confided in his sister if he hadn't been serious about a reconciliation.

Stunned, I probe Nellie Bee for more. "So that's why you're worried." My voice sounds shaky and confused. "You think Bram's having second thoughts about our marriage."

Nellie Bee's eyes widen in dismay. "Oh, Chris, no! Of course I don't think that, honey." She reaches out to grab my hand and squeezes hard. "Bram loves you, I have no doubt. He's a different person since you came into his life. I've never seen him so content, especially after the hell that woman put him through. It's her manipulations that worries me, and how cunning she is. Remember, she had Bram under her spell for years. That he finally married someone else is a mere inconvenience to a woman like her. I think you should tell Bram that she can't come here. Tell him it's either you or her, but not both." Seeing my reluctance, she presses on. "I know it's not your style. You're the least controlling person I've ever met."

"But what about Michael?"

"I'll make my nephew see reason. He has a wife now, and I can promise you that girl wouldn't allow an ex of his anywhere near him."

"The special's only a week away," I cry. "I can't change things now. The production crew will be here—"

Nellie Bee flaps her towel as if to swat away my protests. "You can't stop the special but you can stop her from being a part of it. Trust me, Chris, giving that woman a way back into your husband's life is a huge mistake, one that you'll come to regret. Promise me that you'll tell Bram no way in hell, okay? Please. Before it's too late."

• • •

It ends with me promising Nellie Bee that I'll give it a lot of thought. After our good-bye hugs, she heads back to her house in Beaufort and her sweet, amiable husband, while I lug my stuff back to the golf cart. I wish I could as easily pack up my troubled thoughts, tote them somewhere else. The sun's now low in the sky with the promise of a spectacular sunset, so I pause before backing out of my parking space by the beachfront villas. (One of the villas Jocasta has booked for the filming, I recall.) Maybe I should go back to the beach to quiet my inner turmoil before facing my husband. A sunset walk always calms me. I discovered its healing balm when I moved here right after our marriage. At our house the sunset view's limited because the house is hidden in the midst of dense foliage: live oaks, palmettos, and oleander bushes. Bram and I have our cocktails on the upstairs porch to watch the sky above the treetops turn pink, then the pink glow deepens and spreads through the leafy branches below. Other people watch the sunset, he and I like to say, while we prefer the sun-glow. But some evenings I go to the beach alone, seeking the setting sun. Occasionally Bram joins me, coming downstairs to find me gone, and we stroll hand-in-hand, bare feet in the rolling waves. Wordless, we stop and stand in reverence as the sun lowers itself into the ocean, turning everything—water, sky, sand—into a magic world of red and gold.

The golf cart ride home serves the same purpose, and I feel myself relaxing. I take deep gulps of the brisk salt air and it fortifies me. It's the time of day I love most, when Fripp Island's at its loveliest. A nature preserve, Fripp, named after a hero of the Revolutionary War, is to me a celebration of the wild beauty of the Lowcountry, and I fell in love with it the first time I came here. Funny; what little I, a native Texan, knew of the Lowcountry before then came from Bram's TV show. I love to cook and was a devoted viewer of *Southern Heritage* until I was widowed, when food lost its appeal.

That was before Bram came into my life and everything changed, in a heady rush of excitement and passion unlike anything I'd ever experienced. Although I'd loved my husband Joe Perez dearly, and with great devotion, our love was more like a calm pool of still waters. With Bram, it's been a roaring waterfall tumbling me from unseen heights. And that feeling hasn't changed. For Joe, several years gone now, I still feel a deep love and grief. For Bram, my love is fiercer, and I realize that I can't bear the thought of losing him.

I met Bram three years after my husband's death, when I traveled from my home in Houston to attend a conference in New Orleans. In the lobby of the historic hotel where the organization I worked for had booked me, I saw a notice that Bram Stoker O'Connor was filming one of his shows on the patio that evening. Hotel guests could sign up to be a member of a small, select audience. Recalling how much I'd once liked his show, I signed up.

The show was not only entertaining, but afterward the famed

chef invited his audience to enjoy the dishes he'd prepared. I'd been utterly enchanted by Bram and his colorful showmanship—mesmerized, even. He was much better-looking than he appeared on TV, broad-shouldered and muscular with piercing green eyes and soot-black hair streaked silver at the temples. He drew in the audience with the amusing stories he related as he worked, told with the charming lilt of an Irish accent. Since I'd read that his Irish parents had come to South Carolina when he was a toddler, I suspected the accent was a bit of an affectation. Even so, I swooned along with the rest of the women when he came around to see what we thought of the food. For some reason, he singled me out to tell me about the origins of the Lowcountry shrimp dish I tasted. Dazzled, I nodded and smiled and complimented the dish before someone dragged him away. To my surprise, he asked me to wait so we could continue our conversation after he'd made nice with the other guests.

I was surprised when the crowd began to clear out and Bram showed up with a glass of wine and an invitation to join him at a corner table. "Your observation about the shrimp seasoning was so astute," he said in a low, confidential voice, "that I'm dying to hear more." It was something we'd laugh about later, the worst pickup line ever. But at the time he seemed so earnest that I had no reason to think he was coming on to me. And truthfully, it wasn't just his earnestness. A widow in my mid-forties, I was hardly a femme fatale, certainly not in a city swarming with them. I was a professional woman who looked the part: fit and trim, with light-brown hair pulled back and secured with a barrette at the nape of my neck. I'd been told that my best feature was my sherry-colored eyes that lit up when I smiled, but other than that, I considered myself rather plain.

At the secluded table Bram selected, partially hidden by a sweet-smelling wisteria vine, he and I shared a bottle of wine and a plate of incredible food as we talked about everything under the sun—except shrimp seasoning. (A ploy, he'd admit, to get to know me.) When he found out that I was in New Orleans for a conference on immigration issues, he wanted to hear about my job. Because he himself was an immigrant, he always sought out the origins of the dishes he prepared and told his listeners their stories, one of the reasons his show was so popular. "We're all immigrants, aren't we?" he said, his intense eyes holding mine. "And every family story is also about its food."

I hadn't thought of it that way, and grew animated telling him how I could use that idea in my work with my clients. "You've inspired me," I told him with so much excitement that I blushed. He leaned forward and placed a hand on my arm. "No, no. It's your work that inspires me," he said softly.

Looking back, I think I was a goner from that moment on. We stayed until the bar closed around us, which in the Big Easy isn't till the wee hours. And I had an early-morning meeting. I couldn't make the breakfast he invited me to, nor lunch either, but we had dinner together. After that we were inseparable the rest of my stay. He even attended the requisite conference get-togethers with me, dazzling the overly serious psychologists with his gregarious magnetism. During my breaks, we took in the sights. He'd been given the hotel's presidential suite, where we had some of our meals. And our last night together, I stayed with him. I'd never done anything so brazen before, but I was in Sin City, and falling hard for the most fascinating man I'd ever met. The next day, I told myself, I'd be back to my grief-dulled life in Houston. Why not take an erotic memory home with me?

It'd be a few months before I visited Bram at his home in the South Carolina Lowcountry, though he came to Houston the weekend following my return from New Orleans. After that, I joined him in each of the coastal cities where he was filming: Biloxi, Mobile, Tampa, Miami, Palm Beach. Ours was a heady courtship, exhilarating and exhausting. I'd fallen hard for Bram, and he appeared to feel the same. We'd only been together three months when we confessed our love. There were several organizations in the Lowcountry like the one I worked for in Houston, Bram said. Could I leave Texas to work for one of them? Just in case, he'd made inquiries and found they needed qualified staff. When I'd said maybe one day, Bram pulled me into an intense embrace. His gestures were always like that: dramatic and over the top, but he surprised me by what he said next. "Not one day, Chris—now! I want you to marry me. And I don't want to wait another minute." He took my face in his hands and kissed me so intently that it literally took my breath away.

My deceased husband, Joe Perez, had been a soft-spoken man of Hispanic descent, an immigration lawyer who was the polar opposite of Bram Stoker O'Connor. I had two adult children, a daughter in Manhattan and a son in San Diego, and I had to tell them that their mother had taken leave of her senses and decided to marry someone I'd only known a few months. They handled it better than I dared hope, having seen me submerged in grief for so long. My son, William, so like his father, asked only if I was sure. But my daughter, Victoria, said, "Go for it, Mama!" So I did.

• • •

By the time I turn into the partially hidden driveway of our house, I've managed to quiet the turmoil that my talk with Nellie Bee stirred. Bless her heart; she only wants what's best for me and her brother, but I've decided that her fears are unwarranted. Bram's obsession with his former wife is over and has been for several years. I know now what I didn't know before, that he was on the verge of taking her back when he met me. And knowing something of the pain she's caused him, I believe his turning to me was an act of self-preservation, whether consciously or not. Something was telling him that he had to move on from the toxic relationship he and his ex had been bogged down in for way too long. So many of his friends have told him that marrying me was the best thing he ever did for himself, which of course I modestly denied. But now I'm thinking they might be right. I love him enough to do anything to keep him from being hurt like that again. I don't know Michael well, having only been around him a couple of times, but maybe he'll come to see that, too, being here with us. Now that he has his own child, he's more likely to understand what his conflict with his father has cost both of them.

As I steer through the gates to the house, the scent of gardenias is intense. Besides oleander, gardenia is the only flowering plant to grow successfully on Fripp without being consumed by the deer who roam the island like skittish dogs. I close the gates behind me then drive the golf cart along the pebbled driveway to the parking area underneath the raised house. The house faces a mysterious, murky lagoon, where gators sun on the grassy banks. Snowy egrets nest in the trees surrounding the lagoon, festooning the branches like feathery blossoms. The house is the only truly isolated one on Fripp, situated on a little inlet of land far from the maddening crowd. Once the gates close behind you, you might as well be on your own island. It's the reason Bram settled here, for the solitude he needs to work. He likes to think of the lagoon as his moat, with the gators standing guard to keep his too-zealous fans at bay.

The house itself is what's known as Lowcountry style, two-storied and elevated high off the ground, with double piazzas (we call them porches in Texas), set off by a semi-circular brick stairway in front. Painted a dull gray green, the house blends perfectly into the leafy foliage enclosing it. Carrying the beach tote, my steps are light as I climb the stairway and enter the house. I'm grateful that the leisurely, gardenia-scented drive from the beach gave me time to compose myself. I didn't relish a showdown with Bram about Jocasta. Nellie Bee was right in what she'd said earlier; my training provided me with conflict-management skills, but that doesn't mean I relish using them with family. By nature (and ethnicity, I tease) Bram has a fiery, confrontational temperament. Joe had been so even-tempered that I rather enjoy the novelty of my and Bram's infrequent skirmishes. Even better is the way we make up, when one of us reaches out to the other in the dark of night. A bit of anger can ignite the passion in lovemaking, and in turn, lovemaking can dispel anger. It doesn't work like that with seething rage or deep-seated resentment, but it can be a healthy way of dissipating the little day-to-day rifts of marriage.

For the five years we've been together, Bram and I have faced only a few of those. He tells me he's just too damn tired and old to fight, which I laugh at. Neither is true. He has the energy and virility of a much younger man. Following his retirement, he started writing his food memoir, which he's calling *Lowcountry Stew*, and has worked tirelessly since. Or as far as I know, he has. When I get home from work, he's closed away in his office, the same as when I'm home. Despite Bram's breezy assurances when we were courting, I could only get part-time work after moving here. Three days a week, I drive an hour to Bluffton as the consulting psychologist for a nonprofit that works with the area's large migrant population. In truth, it's such intense and challenging work that I'm not sure I could do it full-time. After a ten-hour workday, every time I drive over the bridge to Fripp Island I lower the windows of my car and let the bracing salt breeze carry the troubles of the day out with them, all the way across the Atlantic.

During each evening cocktail hour Bram dutifully reports how many pages he's written or tells me about some of his research. He's published cookbooks, but they're the coffee-table kind with photographs of lavish dishes and fancy dinner parties. For those he created and perfected the recipes while his editor wrote the headings. The memoir will have some recipes, but he's mainly telling the stories that go with them. He claims it's the hardest and most grueling work he's ever done, and he thinks that anyone who writes a book deserves a Nobel Prize just for finishing the damn thing. Based on the articles I've published in professional journals, I agree with him wholeheartedly. Writing isn't for the faint of heart.

Deep in thought as I rinse out the thermos, I don't hear Bram come up behind me, and I let out a startled yelp when he puts his hands on my waist and his lips to my neck. "You scared the devil out of me," I laugh, leaning into him.

"Umm. I love it when you talk dirty," Bram murmurs into my neck, in the melodious voice that always makes my knees go weak. I told him once that his voice melted my resolve like the hot wax dripping down a candle.

I turn to slip my arms around him, then peer up into the deep green of his eyes. "I just love it when you talk, period. You could read a phone book to me and it'd sound like the Song of Solomon."

He raises an eyebrow and grins a wicked grin. "Damn, baby. That might be the sexiest thing you've ever said to me."

"Then I need to work on my pillow talk," I say, returning his grin.

"Wanna start now?" He cups my face in his hands for a kiss. When we pull away, he takes my arm to lead me upstairs, but I hold back.

"Let's wait till we can fall asleep together. That's my favorite part."

"If that's the case, then I need to work on my technique." We laugh together, and his gaze falls on the thermos I dropped into the sink when he embraced me. "Wish I'd known you were seeing Nellie Bee today. I've got some papers to send Charlie."

"I wasn't planning on seeing her until later in the week, but she called an emergency sistah meeting."

"Emergency meeting? What's going on?"

"Why don't you open our wine, and I'll grab the glasses. I'll tell you while we catch the last of the sun-glow."

But when we settle into our favorite chairs on the piazza and clink our glasses together, I have second thoughts about sharing Nellie Bee's concerns. Not only are the treetops gilded in the pinkish-gold glow of the setting sun, so are Bram and I—as well as the porch chairs and hanging plants and even the wineglasses in our hands, and it's simply too beautiful to spoil. When he prods me about his sister's so-called emergency meeting, I shake my head and hold up a hand until the glow has faded into twilight, and the cicadas tune up for their nightly concert. As is his habit, Bram likes to have a couple glasses of wine before starting dinner. Because of the mojitos, I can only have half a glass, so I make it last as long as possible while basking in the warm glow of our contentment.

Bram breaks into my reverie. "Okay, Bride of Dracula. What aren't you telling me?"

That brings on a smile. "You haven't called me that in a long time."

"That was our first big fight, best I remember."

"Oh, yeah, and not long after we married. It was your fault, of course. You snapped at me about something and I snapped back. Somehow we ended up yelling at each other. I said your ancestor Bram Stoker would be proud of you because you suck, too. I thought it very clever of me."

"Not as clever as me calling you the Bride of Dracula."

"Was, too."

"Was not."

Again, we smile at each other, and I finish off my wine. When he holds up the bottle, I wave him off. Then, abruptly, as if to cover up his concern, he asks, "Is Nellie Bee sick? Or Charlie?"

"Oh, sweetheart—no," I say, chagrined. "Nothing like that. Nellie Bee's just worried about . . . ah . . . the special that the network's doing, and how it's going to work out."

Bram rolls his eyes. "That's ridiculous. It'll go smooth as clockwork, as Nellie Bee knows full well. She's been to enough of my shows."

"Well, she'll be in this one, which is quite different," I remind him. I feel guilty putting it that way since that's not Nellie Bee's concern, but I'm loathe to bring Jocasta into our lovely evening.

"That's even more ridiculous. Nellie Bee's far from camera shy. Matter of fact, she's as much of a showboat as I am. All she and Charlie have to do is the same as the original special—chat, eat, and have a jolly good time. Or at least, fake having one. I'm sure my big-mouth sister can handle that."

"I don't think that's all she's concerned about," I say hesitantly.

Bram rolls his eyes again. "Oh, I know what's bothering her, and I might've known she'd run to you about it. Which really annoys me, I have to say." He pours himself another glass of wine then slams the bottle down on the glass-topped table between us, causing me to startle. "Nellie Bee needs to chill out, and I plan to tell her so. I don't want her interfering in our marriage like she did my last one."

I blink at him in surprise. "What do you mean?"

Scowling, he turns his head to fix his dark gaze over the lagoon. The water's so murky that even the lingering pink glow fails to brighten its blackness. Count Dracula's beast-filled moat, I think, which usually amuses me. Today it feels ominous.

Bram rubs his face wearily. "I'm glad that you and Nellie Bee have bonded, Chris, I really am. At first I was a bit uneasy about the two of you getting so close because I know her so well. Too well. I adore my sister, but she can't seem to stop meddling in my life. She's always done it."

"I don't see it that way, Bram. She's overly protective of you, but—"

"Overprotective?" he groans. "C'mon, Chris. I'm almost sixty years old. What the hell does my sister need to protect me from?"

From yourself, I want to say—to shout, even—but don't. I see where he's going with this and don't like it. Taking a deep breath, I steady myself as I try to come up with the best approach to take. Bram pours himself another glass of wine, which I note with concern. I didn't need Nellie Bee to tell me that he drinks more when he's stressed; I've witnessed it. We all do at times, but his tendency to drown his sorrows has caused him too many problems not to be worrisome. "Bram . . ." I begin cautiously, but he stops me.

"Don't answer that. It was a rhetorical question." His tone raises my hackles, but he goes on. "Listen, Chris; you and I have been together over five years. We're doing fine without anyone's interference." Turning his laser-like eyes on me, he asks, "Don't you agree?"

I lean over to put a hand on his arm. "Sweetheart, of course we are. We get along beautifully."

He gives me a sideways glance. "I can be hard to live with, I know. I'm difficult and demanding and hot-headed—"

"As well as tender, loving, and thoughtful. We are all flawed, Bram. I can certainly be difficult, too."

"You're stubborn as hell," he says, and I smile.

"You weren't supposed to agree with me." When he smiles a bit ruefully, I press on. "But I don't agree that Nellie Bee's overprotectiveness will affect our marriage." Not above pulling the therapy card when need be, I add, "And you know I'm alert to such things in the families I work with. I'm very much aware how family interference can be a harmful factor in a marital relationship."

"Oh, God," he says. "How did I end up with someone who uses phrases like that?"

Grinning, I swat his arm. "Just your good fortune, I guess."

The mood lightens, and his shoulders relax as he sits back to sip his wine. As tempting as it is to let his accusation against Nellie Bee go, it's not wise to let it become a rift between us. Switching back to therapist mode, I echo what he said. "Am I hearing you correctly, that you feel Nellie Bee has a tendency to be overprotective and interfere in your life?"

He barks out a laugh. "Please tell me you didn't just say that."

"Bram!"

He looks at me with a mocking grin. "Yes, my dear Dr. Murray, you heard me correctly. My sister needs to give it a rest. I haven't said anything before because you're so fond of her, and . . . well . . .

it hasn't been necessary until now. But you need to know that Nellie Bee's interference was a factor in the breakup of my marriage to Jocasta."

"How so?"

Bram sighs, as if reluctant to say more. For a long minute I think he's not going to, then he explains. "Nellie Bee disliked Jocasta from day one. Like I've told you, I met her when I was working in Charleston as a chef. Long before I got my own show. Jocasta was way out of my league, but somehow we hit it off and started dating. Mom and Da were still teaching at USC then; Nellie Bee was living with them to finish her master's, so I took Jocasta to meet the family. I think Nellie Bee was intimidated by her, Jocasta coming from such a prominent old family. Whatever it was between them, it started then. Nellie Bee told our parents that Jocasta thought she was above our humble family. But Jocasta isn't like that. It was just my sister's insecurities coming out."

I long to argue that, au contraire, I'd seen his snobbish ex-wife in action, but I let him have his say. "And what was Jocasta's attitude toward Nellie Bee?"

"As you might imagine, she picked up on my sister's dislike of her. They never got along. Which was regrettable to me since I loved them both. When I got my big break with the show, we bought the place on Fripp, and Jocasta and I started our family. Then Nellie Bee married Charlie and moved to Beaufort, where he had his law practice. Mikey was about six when the first real problems between Jocasta and me started. He was twelve when we split."

He falls silent and I prod him to continue. "And you think Nellie Bee moving here gave her the opportunity to interfere in your marriage?"

"I know it did, Chris. Nothing my wife did found favor with my hyper-critical sister. But worse, she tried to turn me against Jocasta, too."

"Oh? Tell me how."

He fiddles with his wineglass, lost in thought. "I was traveling so much, and after we had Mikey, Jocasta no longer went along. Fripp can be a lonely place, and I understood when she and Mikey stayed with her parents in Charleston while I was away. Then Nellie Bee told me that Jocasta was seeing her old boyfriend—who her parents had wanted her to marry—when she was with them. Tongues were wagging all over South Carolina."

I can't let this go and say as gently as I can, knowing what a painful subject it is for him: "But sweetheart . . . you told me yourself that your marriage fell apart because your wife got involved with someone else. Surely you can't blame your sister for that."

"No. I blame myself. But Nellie Bee shares some blame, too. She set out to poison me against Jocasta by telling me about the old boyfriend, knowing I'd confront Jocasta about it. Which I did. I can be jealous, and we had frightful rows. Jocasta admitted seeing a lot of this guy when she was in Charleston, but swore it wasn't serious. She was just lonely. I believed her, and we smoothed things over. Until Nellie Bee told Jocasta that I was seeing other women when I traveled—which I wasn't, by the way—and Jocasta wasn't as forgiving as I'd been. She's jealous, too, and wouldn't accept my denials. That's when she took Michael, moved back in with her parents, and filed for divorce."

I jump on the obvious flaw in his reasoning. "If you weren't cheating on your wife, that means Nellie Bee lied, and for no reason except to cause trouble in your marriage. Do you really believe she'd do that to a beloved brother and nephew, even if she disliked her sister-in-law?"

Exasperated, he runs his hands through his hair. "No, of course not. But it didn't happen quite that way. Nellie Bee found what she thought was evidence of my affairs, which she shared with Jocasta. If only she'd come to me instead, I could've explained it."

"Evidence? What evidence?"

He glances at me, then sighs heavily. "I got fan mail, Chris.

Still do, but nothing like then. It's what happens in the business—male or female, you get propositioned. And some of the notes and letters were pretty graphic. Nellie Bee's always nosed through my stuff, and she found some of them that I'd hidden from Jocasta. I should've destroyed them, so it was my fault. Damn my male ego, hanging on to them! And look what it costs me."

It's a lot for me to take in, and finally I say, "But Bram—why didn't you tell me this? All you said was that your wife left you to marry a former boyfriend. And how much it hurt when she was awarded full custody, and you saw your son so infrequently."

"Well, I also told you about Michael blaming me for the breakup. His mother told him that I'd cheated on her and cared more about my sordid affairs than him. That part's entirely on Jocasta, so don't think I'm not holding her blameless in this."

"I know you're not. But you certainly didn't tell me that you blamed Nellie Bee for any of it."

He lowers his head. "I don't blame her, exactly. But I know what she's up to. My sister's having a shit fit about Jocasta's inclusion in the TV special. That's what her so-called emergency meeting was about, wasn't it? She's trying to enlist your support to stop it from happening."

"Frankly, her concern seems legitimate to me—considering you failed to tell me not only that you were seeing your ex-wife when you and I met, but that you were seriously considering taking her back."

Bram's face darkens. "I was afraid she'd tell you that. Did she tell you how she found out?"

"Yes. You told her."

"That's true, but only after she confronted me, claiming she'd heard rumors about me seeing Jocasta. I didn't buy it, because I knew she'd been snooping in my computer while I was gone. But I let it go."

"Bram, that's not the point. You should've been the one to tell me this, not your sister. I had to admit to her that it was news to me—despite you and I promising to be honest with each other about our past. That was extremely important to me."

To my surprise, he gets up so abruptly that his chair slams against the wall. "I've got to start dinner," he says.

"Oh no you don't!" I stand to face him, and when he won't meet my gaze, I move around my chair to stop him. "Don't do this, Bram. We need to talk about it—"

"No, what we need to do is eat." He looks down at me, but his expression's guarded. "I've been working all day and I'm famished. I'm going to fix dinner, and we'll talk later."

Reluctantly, I step aside. Without a backwards glance, he brushes past me to go inside, and the door swings closed behind him. I stand for a few minutes before turning back around, flummoxed. Bram's unexpected defense of his ex-wife shocks me more than his annoyance with his sister. I can't decide whether to follow him inside, play sous chef as I usually do, or just let it be. Automatically I pull his chair away from the wall and line it up with mine. My obsessive-compulsive need for order, I think ruefully. If only I could take the bits and pieces of my life and line them up as neatly. With a sigh, I begin to gather the empty glasses and wine bottle to take inside.

When I set them on the kitchen counter, Bram's at the stove with his back to me. As if nothing happened, he says over his shoulder, "I need your take on this mango sauce for the sea bass. Might have too much cilantro and serrano."

"No such thing," I say, forcing a light tone. "I'm a Texan, remember. To hear you tell it, I was wearing a sprig of cilantro behind my ear when we first met. Not true, but makes a good story." I decide not to say anything about our confrontation until after dinner. Maybe it's true, that he's just tired and hungry.

Later, I've dozed off in bed when I hear Bram slipping into the room. Although it's not unusual for him to come in after I've turned out the lamps and fallen asleep, I'm sure it's deliberate to-night. During dinner we talked about the food as he took notes, as he's apt to do when creating new recipes. I've grown used to hearing him mutter things like "Needs salt, don't you think?" as he takes a bite then scribbles away. He was so intent that I didn't bring up our previous discussion until after we'd finished dinner and cleaned the kitchen. Then he held up a finger and said, "You're right, sweet-heart; we should talk this out. But first I need to make some calls." After he'd scurried away to his office I went to mine for my own calls, catching both Victoria and William in, which rarely happens. Afterward I returned emails then went upstairs to read, waiting for Bram and our talk. He waited me out.

Annoyed as I am at his avoidance of me, I'm so groggy I can't rouse myself to have another go at it—or at least, not for another ar-gument. When Bram slips his arms around me, I turn to him, sleep-dazed, and his mouth covers mine. And with that, all thoughts of overprotective sisters and scheming ex-wives are pushed aside for less cerebral considerations. If his purpose was to put a stop to my questions, his method couldn't have been more effective.

. . .

As soon as I hear the spin of gravel on the driveway, I shut down my computer with a smile. I tease Bram that I'm as excited about see-ing his grandbaby as he is. My step-granddaughter! The way things look now with my kids, young professionals not ready to start a family, little Adeline O'Connor may be as close as I get. I stop by the bathroom to smooth down my hair and put on a touch of lip gloss. "They're here, Bram," I call out from the stairway leading up to his office. Because Michael and Missy have so much baby par-aphernalia, they rented a car at the airport. I hear car doors slam-ming but wait for Bram before going down to play hostess.

During the past week, Bram and I had declared a truce. He apologized for not being honest about his ex but clammed up on further discussion. Why couldn't I just be happy that he and I found each other when we did, he'd demanded? If he'd wanted to get back with his ex, he wouldn't have pursued me. Which was such a potent argument that I let it go. I was too busy for much else. In order to take a week off, I'd put in extra days at work, then got home exhausted. Bram put aside writing the memoir to plan for the filming. As in the original special, it'd start with an opening shot of the family playing on the beach, but the hour-long show would focus mostly on Bram in the kitchen preparing Lowcountry-themed dishes for the family dinner. The final scene would show everyone gathered around the dining room table. All the cast of characters had to do was as Bram said: stuff our faces and fake having a good time.

Bram and I stand helplessly aside as Michael and Missy haul baby Adeline and a mountain of baggage out of the car. When we try to help, Michael waves us off and loads himself down like a pack horse. Eight months ago, when Adeline was born, Bram flew to DC, where Michael works as a congressional aide, to meet her. After a brief visit he returned a bit despondent. He'd looked forward to preparing healthy meals for them to freeze for later, only to find her parents there with a private chef in tow. This time it's Jocasta who's playing fairy godmother, bringing with her a nanny from an exclusive service in Charleston. This we learned when I emailed Michael and offered to line up a sitter for the filming. Nellie Bee hooted at my assumption that three grandparents and a great-aunt would've been enough help. "Honey, you've got a lot to learn about how the other half lives," she teased.

Bram gives his son and daughter-in-law awkward half-hugs and offers to carry the baby, whom Missy's toting in a big car seat contraption. With a weary smile of gratitude, Missy hands the car seat over. After my welcome to the young couple, I stop Bram so I can see the sleeping baby. She's small and delicate, with a fuzz of pale hair and long lashes resting on pink cheeks. "Oh, look how precious she is!" I coo and gush like a pure fool until Bram shoulders past me in exasperation.

Chagrined, I hurry to hold the basement door open as everyone files in. Next to the golf cart parking is the newly renovated basement area. It'd been one large game room for TV viewing, a pool table, and bunk beds until recently, when I'd talked Bram into converting it into private quarters for guests and future grandchildren. Neither Michael nor Missy have seen the final results and I watch anxiously for their reaction.

"Wow. Nice," Michael says, looking around with a grin, and even Missy (who's obviously used to the best) seems pleased. She's a perky little thing with dimples and a beguiling smile. Nellie Bee dismisses her as an entitled princess, but she seems sweet enough to me. "Oh, Papa O'Connor—this is wonderful," she cries. "It was so dark and dreary before."

"You can thank Christina." Bram shrugs. "I thought it fine the way it was."

"You would, Dad," Michael says, but his tone's light. He's a preppy young man with his mother's blond coloring and slender build. The only thing he got from his father was Bram's rich, melodious voice, minus the hint of Irish brogue. Because they're so different, Bram seems baffled by his son, whose main interests are tennis and politics. When I asked Bram if Michael planned to run for office one day, he merely shrugged. The few times I've observed them together, they appear ill at ease. But so much better than Michael's teen years, Bram told me. He'd take awkwardness over anger any day.

Missy tucks the baby in the new crib to finish her nap, and I point out other additions to the refurbished rooms. I can't help but wink at Bram when Missy exclaims over the kitchenette area I'd pushed for. Bram had argued it was unnecessary with his enormous kitchen, while I'd countered that guests might prefer some private meals. When I show them how I've stocked the fridge and pantry, I'm inordinately pleased by their gratitude.

It's later before we have the first indication of how things could go wrong. After the baby wakes up and is playing on a quilt, I suggest to Missy that they take a dip in the ocean before dinner. Seeing Adeline at ease with Bram and me, off they go. When I get on the floor to join Adeline at play, Bram plops down beside me. "Look at Grandma," he teases, eyes twinkling. "Maybe I should have a talk with your kids. Doesn't look like they've figured out where babies come from."

I laugh as I roll a musical ball to Adeline, and she laughs with me, clapping her chubby little hands. "Aww . . . look, Bram! What a happy baby. Does she remind you of Michael at this age?" As soon as I say it, I cringe at my insensitivity. Bram doesn't respond, but he looks at his granddaughter with such longing it almost breaks my heart. I've seen him watching her, eyes aglow, but he's kept his distance. Finally he nods.

"Aye, she's a bonnie wee lass," he says, laying on the exaggerated brogue to hide the catch in his voice. Suddenly he stands and lays a hand on my shoulder. "Since Grandma's got this covered, I'll go do some prepping for dinner."

I start to protest but catch myself, thinking he needs some time to himself. He spent a lot of time and effort fussing over a meal of Michael's favorite dishes. I think back to what Nellie Bee said, that this reunion could either bring Bram and his son closer, or tear them apart again. I know he has to be anxious, though of course he'll act otherwise. And deny it vehemently if I prod. Or worse, sneer at my tactics. It's an occupational hazard; a simple inquiry on my part can put others on the defensive. Even Joe, mild-mannered as he was, would bristle if he thought I was analyzing him.

I hear the golf cart roll in, then the kids squealing in the outdoor shower, where the temperature fluctuates wildly. They come in wrapped in towels and looking sun-kissed and happy. Adeline regards her parents with interest but keeps playing. "Adeline's such a little angel," I tell Michael. Missy had announced she needed the bathroom first so she could feed the baby. Beaming, Michael kneels beside his daughter as she gnaws on a toy. "She's got my disposition," he says.

"So you were a good baby, huh?" I ask, studying him.

Without meeting my eye he says, "You're a child psychologist, right?" When I nod, somewhat wary, his mouth tightens. "You'll have a heyday in this family."

"Michael, if you ever need to talk—" I begin, but Missy appears, donned out in a bright sundress, to call, "Bathroom's ready!" Michael heads off and she scoops Adeline up, taking her to the kitchenette area. Without asking, I place the new high chair by the little pull-down table I'd designed, pull a chair around for Missy, then plop down in the other one. "Thanks, Christina," Missy chirps. A hand flying to her mouth in a childish gesture, she gasps, "Oh! Is it okay if I call you that?"

"Of course. Or Chris. Whatever you're comfortable with."

Brow furrowed, she microwaves a couple of little food pouches then squeezes the contents into a sectioned baby plate. Pulling herself closer to the high chair, she says, "My mom wants Adeline to call her Mimi, and Michael's mother likes Jo-Jo. But I haven't thought about you since you're not really her grandmother. Guess she can call you Christina, too." Like a hungry little bird, Adeline opens her mouth eagerly each time Missy brings the spoon her way.

I don't let Missy see how her remark stings. New to the role of stepmother, I've been foolish to assume I'd be treated otherwise, or that Adeline will think of me as anything except some old lady who lives with her grandfather. For the briefest of moments, I have an inkling of how Michael's rejection hurt Bram. It makes you feel devalued, I realize. Oblivious, Missy feeds the baby and chatters about how rough the waves were and how the undertow terrified her.

Michael, changed to shorts and a polo shirt, has just come to the kitchenette to grab a water bottle from the fridge when Bram comes in the door. He takes in the scene with a playful grin. "I trust that's gourmet food you're feeding my granddaughter, Missy."

Missy preens but before she can answer, Michael snorts. "It better be, considering what it costs."

His wife makes a face at him. "Oh, hush. You know it was one of Mommy and Daddy's gifts to us. The best present ever!"

Bram stands with his hands on his hips to watch Adeline finish her supper. "Glad to see she's got a healthy appetite."

"Tell Papa O'Connor that you're Mommy's little piggie," Missy coos as she wipes off the baby's face. Adeline's lower lip quivers and she lets out a wail when she realizes the meal's over. Missy wags a finger at her. "Now, now. That's all for tonight. You may eat like a little piggie but Mommy can't let you look like one." To Michael she says, "Daddy? Would you fix her bottle?"

I note Bram's frown but he keeps quiet. He's asked me if I think Missy's anorexic, as little as she eats. My reassurances that most young women her age are obsessed with their weight failed to satisfy him. A typical chef, Bram loves feeding people and doesn't take kindly to the unappreciative. If he'd been feeding Adeline, she'd still be eating. I dare not say so, but her portions seem pretty meager to me, too. Maybe I'll find a tactful way to suggest that an increase won't make her overweight, as tiny as she is.

"So," Bram says, turning his attention to Michael. "Chris and I have our wine about this time, then I finish fixing dinner. Sound good to you two? I'm making some of your favorites tonight."

Michael takes the baby's bottle from the microwave and looks at Missy expectantly. When she takes the baby out of the high chair, I blurt out, "May I feed her?" To my surprise, she hands her over. I take the baby and bottle to the rocker quickly before she changes her mind. When I position Adeline in the crook of my arm and hold the bottle for her, I see that it's less than half full.

Missy turns to Bram with a pleading look, her hands clasped in front of her. "Poor Papa O'Connor! I know you've worked hard on dinner, but Michael and I are going to pass tonight. We've had a long day and—"

"Pass on dinner?" Bram thunders, and Missy flinches. But with her chin held high, she doesn't waver.

"I'm sure it's wonderful, but please excuse us tonight. You and Christina enjoy a quiet dinner alone. It'll be your last one for the next few days."

"But—what the hell will you eat?" Bram sputters. His face is flushed and his eyes narrow in disapproval.

"Dad—" Michael begins, but his father holds up a hand. Before anything else can be said, Adeline finishes the bottle and lets out a wail even more indignant than her protest at the meager baby food.

Feigning innocence, I say to Missy, "If you'll show me how to mix it, I'll fix the rest of her bottle."

"Oh, she always cries like that," Missy says dismissively as she takes the baby from me. "Don't you, little miss piggie? Sometimes she'll cry herself to sleep, she gets so mad. Tries to make us feel guilty for putting her to bed hungry."

"Bram," I say quickly, noting his glowering look with alarm, "let's go upstairs and have our wine so they can get the baby down for the night." I turn to Michael with a forced smile. "Why don't you come upstairs with us, and your dad can fix a tray for your supper?" To Bram I say brightly, "You'll come up with the perfect thing, I know, for two weary travelers, and we can have your special dinner tomorrow evening."

I know he's not happy, but what else can we do? Reluctantly, Bram nods and Michael lets out a sigh of relief. Glancing at his wife, he assures her he'll be back in a few minutes to help with the baby. He leaves with us to go upstairs, but it's Bram who has the last word. As I'm closing the basement door, he sticks his head back in to say to Missy, "That baby's hungry. Fill up her bottle and she won't cry herself to sleep." Then he closes the door with a slam.

• • •

Since the production crew would be getting in later in the afternoon, I propose a picnic lunch on the beach before their arrival. Even as I make the suggestion, I'm not sure it's the right move. Bram's still fuming over the kids' rejection of his dinner last night. He might've been less touchy if it'd only been Missy, but when he'd suggested that Michael take the tray to his wife then join us for dinner, Michael balked. Missy wouldn't allow that, he'd said, then bristled when his father rolled his eyes in disdain. I'd been sitting close enough to give Bram a kick of warning, but he'd ignored me. "You mean she won't let you join your family for a dinner she wouldn't eat anyway?" he snapped. When I kicked him harder, he wisely shut his big mouth.

To my surprise, everyone thinks the picnic's a great idea, and off we go. The day's too perfect not to enjoy: not too hot for early June but still brightly crisp and sunny. We set everything out under beach umbrellas meant to keep us safely shaded. Bram channeled his disappointment over last night's dinner into preparing a feast: fried chicken, deviled eggs, marinated veggies, and mini fruit tarts. I'm delighted that Michael invited his aunt Nellie Bee to join us. She and I haven't had our beach time in over a week.

Even the ocean breeze is kind today, blowing in gently with a sharp salty tang. As we spread our blankets in the shade and unpack the picnic basket, the mood's jubilant. Missy brought a walker-looking seat to put Adeline in, and Nellie Bee plops down by her. Stroking Adeline's fuzzy head, Nellie Bee coos and carries on over her great-niece. With an indulgent grin, Bram says, "Between you and Grandma Chris, that little girl's going to be spoiled rotten."

"That's what grandparents—and great-aunts—are for," Nellie Bee responds tartly.

And that's when Michael puts a damper on our bright, cheery day. As he passes around icy bottles of Perrier, he says nonchalantly, "Mom's going to be even worse, I'm sure. She's here and will be joining us in a few."

I freeze over the paper plates I'm unwrapping, and Bram's head snaps up. "I thought your mom wasn't getting in until late this afternoon," he says to Michael, frowning. Over breakfast (with Michael but not Missy, who doesn't eat in the morning), Michael had once again squelched his father's dinner plans by saying they'd be with his mother.

Misinterpreting his father's frown, Michael peers into the basket. "No worries—you've got plenty. Even with the nanny coming."

"Oh, look," Missy squeals as she jumps to her feet to wave. "There they are!"

We turn our heads toward the wooden steps leading down from the villas to watch the two women approach. Even though she's wearing an enormous straw hat and big sunglasses, I would've recognized Jocasta anywhere. No one else could make an ankle-turning walk down steep beach steps look like a Parisian runway. The white caftan she wears billows out around her in the breeze, and she reaches up to hold her wide-brimmed sunhat. The young woman trailing behind her appears to be in a uniform, and Nellie Bee nudges me with her foot. I dare not look her way, especially now that Jocasta has appeared before us. Both Michael and Missy hurry out to hug her as Bram gets to his feet, ducking under the umbrella. Reluctantly I rise, too, as does Nellie Bee, though with a put-upon grunt. I note with satisfaction that when Jocasta reaches out to Bram, he offers his hand instead of a hug. Although it's been two years since I've seen her, she's as stunning as ever. She's older than me, almost Bram's age, but looks considerably younger. When I'd lamented that to Nellie Bee, she'd smirked and said thank the good Lord for collagen and Botox.

Just as she did at the wedding reception, Jocasta turns the fawning charm on each of us, even me. "Oh, Nellie Bee—I'm so delighted that you're here!" she cries, as if they were long-lost sisters. Her eyes sweep over me as she says, "And Christina, how lovely to see you again. You must share the secret of that gorgeous tan." Her gaze falls on Adeline and she gushes in delight. "My adorable little Adeline!" But when Michael takes the baby to hand over to his mother, Adeline puckers up, lets out a wail, and buries her face in her father's shirt.

"Adeline!" Missy gasps in dismay, but Michael laughs it off. "It's the hat, Mom," he says. "I'd forgotten that they scare her."

Or maybe it's dragon ladies that scare her, I think with unseemly glee, but Michael proves to be right. Jocasta removes the hat and her dark-blond hair tumbles over her shoulders. When she pushes the sunglasses on her head and reaches for Adeline, she relents and goes to her. Jocasta kisses her cheeks, and Adeline gives her a dimpled smile. "And aren't you a lucky little girl to have dimples exactly like your precious mommy's," Jocasta says with a glance at Missy, who beams in pleasure.

With a pretty tilt of her head, Jocasta beckons to the young woman who's been standing meekly aside. "Everyone, this is Nanny. She comes highly recommended by all of my friends." She runs through our names so quickly that the poor girl couldn't possibly remember them. Although Nanny nods shyly at each of us, she's dignified and poised for someone who appears so young. What looked from a distance like a white uniform is more subtle, designed to mimic a tennis outfit with its smart little skirt and crisp cotton shirt. Nanny's well-trained, I note; when she takes the baby from Jocasta, Adeline regards her curiously rather than wailing again. "Shall I feed her?" she asks Missy, with a musical lilt to her voice that suggests the Caribbean islands, and Missy eagerly agrees.

Finally we settle down on the blankets to enjoy the picnic, plates in our laps. I notice that after getting her plate, Jocasta manages to seat herself next to Bram. Nellie Bee relinquishes her spot by the baby to the nanny and seats herself by me, her plate piled high. A chicken leg in hand, she turns to the nanny and asks in a voice so loud that it's obvious she intends everyone to hear: "A nanny named Nanny? That's rather a coincidence, isn't it?"

Before the girl can respond, Jocasta answers for her, cloyingly sweet. "Monique prefers to be called Nanny when at work. Don't you, dear?"

"It's fine," Monique says obediently, without raising her eyes from the task of spooning baby food into Adeline's eager little mouth. There's no mistaking the gotcha! look Jocasta gives Nellie Bee, and I fear my sister-in-law has erred by poking a stick in the dragon's lair. My intention is to stay out of her way as much as possible.

As if to lighten the tension, Michael says to Bram, "It's like the folks you employ referring to you as Chef. Right, Dad?"

His point's well-taken, but Nellie Bee can't let it go. Turning her head to me, she says sarcastically, "And like your clients calling you Psychologist, Chris. Charlie always refers to himself as Lawyer. Why, most of them don't even know his real name."

She's gone too far, and Bram gives her a warning look. We're saved from having it go further when Adeline begins to cry. Holding up the empty bowl, Nanny turns to Missy and says, "Where is her food, please?"

"She's had plenty," Missy snaps. I dare to meet Bram's eyes, which flash with anger.

"Surely it wouldn't hurt for her to have a little more," Michael suggests to his wife, who gives him a dirty look.

"You know that specialist I consulted laid out exactly how much she could consume without putting on extra weight," she tells him haughtily, over the piteous wails of her daughter.

"And I agree with him," Jocasta says with a smile of approval for her daughter-in-law. "Adeline's too petite to overfeed. Remember that obesity starts in childhood."

"There's not a chance in hell that child will ever be obese," Bram says curtly as he wads up his napkin and throws it into the basket.

"Amen to that," Nellie Bee whispers to me. "Poor little thing's destined to be skinny as a rail and obsessed with her weight, just like her mama and grandmother."

Despite all Nanny does to distract her, Adeline keeps fretting. Finally Bram gives Missy his laser-sharp glare that I've seen frighten grown men into submission. "Either you feed that child or I will," he says between clenched teeth.

Her face flushed, Missy sighs mightily and motions Nanny toward the diaper bag. "There's a banana in there. You may give her some of it. But mash it up and don't give her but a little bit!"

During the awkward silence that follows, I glance down at my plate and blurt out the first thing that comes to mind. "Bram? Didn't you tell me that you added something new in the deviled eggs? I'm thinking tarragon. Right?"

He grins and stuffs one in his mouth, chewing happily. "You got it, sweetheart." Looking around, he asks the others, "What'd you think? Is it a keeper?"

I realize too late that my attempt to change the subject should've been about anything but food. While Michael, Nellie Bee, and I piled our plates high, Jocasta and Missy took only a few marinated veggies—very few. Michael helps out by gobbling down a couple of deviled eggs and giving his dad a thumbs-up. Nellie Bee agrees, and we finish eating in silence. I glance over to see how the baby's doing, then hide a smile to see the whole banana gone. Nanny meets my eye and gives me a wink.

After the fruit tarts have disappeared—thanks to me, Michael, and Nellie Bee—we put away the picnic stuff with sighs of contentment. Even better, Nanny's taken Adeline into her arms and rocked her until she dozed off. Adeline smiles in her sleep, dreaming of banana.

I suggest that Bram give us a run-through of what to expect

when the production crew arrives. With a nod, he begins to walk us through the procedure. Fortunately the others quickly become engrossed in the details of the filming, and the tension over the baby is gone. At one point during Bram's narrative Jocasta interrupts with a joyful clap of her hands. "Oh, Bram—you didn't tell me that Steve will be directing! Nothing could please me more. I always loved watching him at work. Such a dedicated professional."

Bram agrees. "Yeah, I insisted on Steve. You remember his partner Rick?"

"Of course I do." Jocasta smiles up at him, eyes shining. "Who could forget Rick, the best-looking man I've ever seen."

"Oh, thanks a lot, Mom," Michael jokes, and Jocasta throws her head back to laugh.

"Except for you and your father, of course." She turns her adoring gaze to Bram, and Nellie Bee again nudges me with her foot. "I hope Rick's coming, too?" Jocasta says.

"I forgot to ask," Bram admits, and Jocasta lays a hand on his arm with a groan.

"Some things never change," she purrs. "Remember the time you forgot Michael and left him at the studio?"

"No way, Dad!" Michael cries, laughing. "Did you hear that, Missy? Bet your parents never forgot you."

"Of course not," Missy giggles. Evidently she's forgiven her father-in-law for embarrassing her, and she joins in their reminiscences. Nellie Bee leans toward me to whisper, "If they keep this up much longer, I'll puke." Oblivious, the four of them—Bram, Jocasta, Michael, and Missy—laugh and talk together, seeming to forget everything else: not just the other picnickers but also the sea, the sand, and the sun hanging high overhead. Finally Nellie Bee can take no more, and she stands abruptly to say, "I hate to break up this happy family reunion, but I've got to go."

Bram flushes as he stumbles to his feet to bid his sister goodbye. He glances at me apologetically, and I give back a look of reassurance. I expected some reminiscing and had braced myself for it. But I hope my look also conveys another message: I'll tolerate a little, but don't push your luck, buster.

• • •

The big day of filming is on us, and I find myself surprisingly nervous. I'm anxious about being on TV, too, after assuring Bram I wouldn't be. But that was before the lights and cameras were set up in our house, and before the production crew arrived. What had been an upcoming event is suddenly *real* in a way it hasn't been before. As we dress for breakfast, I sink down on the bed, clad in my bra and panties, and tell Bram I don't think I can do this.

Frowning, he comes out of the bathroom smelling of aftershave and looking spiffier than usual, his wet hair slicked back. He sits beside me on the bed and takes my hand. "Sweetheart, listen to me, I'm an old hand at this, and I can help you."

I look up at him expectantly and he says, "It's only natural to be scared your first time on camera. But this surefire tip works like a charm." Leaning close, he whispers, "Put some clothes on."

I punch his arm, smiling, and realize that his joking around is just what I need to get through this. It's been lacking these past few days. Instead we've all been on edge. Tempers have flared and harsh words spoken. I adored the producer Steve on sight, but he's a tough taskmaster. Although he's walked us through everything several times, the show will be filmed live, he tells us. An audience doesn't respond as well to a staged performance. Although Steve makes sure we know what's going to happen when, he refuses to allow any rehearsing of the scenes, saying it kills the spontaneity. Hearing this yesterday, I'd gone to Bram in a panic. Although I knew his shows were filmed live, it hadn't occurred to me this one would be. I'd assumed we'd be put in place and told what to say. If we messed up, they'd film it over until we got it right. Bram laughed at my naivety.

What we've done the past two days has been more tedious than

nerve-racking. The crew had to determine what time of day the
light's right for the beach walk. The biggest scene, which would
be filmed in the house, isn't as crucial, lighting-wise. As if we were
mannikins, they put us in place then peered through the cameras at
us. After this went on for hours, I realized why Jocasta had brought
Nanny, and felt guilty (though only a tad) for assuming it'd been to
show off. After much conferring, Steve decided to include Adeline
on the beach walk but not the dinner. Too risky that she'd be sleepy
and cranky. I'd breathed a sigh of relief. Tension was again running
high between Bram and Missy, with Michael torn between them.
Another fight could be a disaster.

To avoid so much running back and forth, a shifting of quarters
took place that I didn't know about until afterward. Nanny moved
into the bunkbed room next to Michael and Missy. No problem
there; what takes me by surprise is finding Jocasta in the guest room
across from Bram's office. After taking his advice and putting my
clothes on, I'm heading to breakfast when I hear a noise in the guest
room. Curious, I stick my head in. To my surprise, Jocasta sits at the
vanity applying makeup. I see her suitcase open and clothes strewn
across the bed. Turning her head, she eyes me smugly. "Bram
thought it'd be easier for me to be here," she purrs. "Surely he told
you." I mutter something inane and scurry out.

Midday, cast and crew gather in the dining room before the
filming of the beach walk. Bram has laid out sandwiches and various finger food, but everyone's too geared up to eat much. Thankfully there's a kitchen crew, who'll clean up and prep for the evening
meal. Between bites of a fish sandwich, Steve gathers us together
and goes through everything once again. Late afternoon, we'll all
head to the beach for the sunset walk, where Nellie Bee and Charlie
will meet us. Then we'll return here to change clothes. After they
film Bram in the kitchen, we'll get into place for dinner. Piece of
cake, he assures us. But for now, the cast should go to our rooms and
rest. He wants us bright-eyed and bushy-tailed for our big moment.

In our bedroom, I'm too wound up to rest. And it's not just the "big moment." Although I saw Bram after lunch, long enough to tell him I was heading up for a nap, we haven't had a chance to talk. I can't pretend that Jocasta staying here—in our *house*—doesn't bother me. He's got a good excuse for forgetting to tell me, granted, but that's not what troubles me. It's Jocasta's too-obvious pleasure that I didn't know. It feels underhanded on Bram's part, somehow, as if he sneaked her in and figured I wouldn't notice. I'd love to talk to Nellie Bee, who'd understand my turmoil, but I dare not. I can't risk her confronting Bram. Not today.

Nellie Bee! I'd forgotten that after the beach walk, she and Charlie are coming here to change, and I'd planned on putting them in the guest room. She'll find out about Jocasta then, and all hell's liable to break loose. Unless . . . It hits me that I have no choice. Nellie Bee and Charlie will have to use my office, and I'll pretend it was my idea to put Jocasta in the guest room. Nellie Bee won't be happy with me, but I'll explain later. Just getting through this day is the only thing now.

There's a daybed in my office where Nellie Bee and Charlie can lay out their clothes, so I start downstairs to clear it off. Mainly I pile papers on it. Just like earlier, I've reached the stairs when I hear sounds from the guest room. But this time, it's voices I hear. And one of them is Bram's.

Standing outside the guest room door, I hesitate, wondering what to say to him. *I heard you and want to know what the hell you're doing in there?* I can only imagine how Jocasta would love that. But nothing could be going on, could it, with me right down the hall? Or does Bram think because I'm resting, with the shades pulled and the fan going, it'd be the perfect chance to sneak into her room? It's so preposterous that I shake it off and raise my hand to knock. And that's when I hear him. "Don't worry," he says in the melodious voice that I love so much, the one that weakens my knees. "She doesn't know I'm here. She's napping."

I freeze, stunned, before lowering my clenched hand. I can hear Jocasta's soft murmurs but not what she says—except for the one word that might as well be a shout: "Bram." It's spoken with so much longing that I want to run back to the safety of my room. But I'm unable to move—especially after I hear Bram's low chuckle, a sound that tears me apart. Jocasta's soft, seductive laugh in response is a further stab to my heart. Whatever he says to her next is so low and muffled I can't tell what it is, which is a blessing. How could I bear to hear my husband saying the sweet words of love he'd whispered to me only a few nights ago, before *she* came here and changed everything? Stifling a sob, I turn away. But I don't go back down the hall to the room I share with Bram. Instead I continue down the stairs to my office. My movements are robotic. Unblinking, I clear papers from the daybed and file them methodically away.

The obsessive-compulsive nature that drives me crazy at times serves me well now, carrying me through the rest of the afternoon. Finished in my office, I go back upstairs to dress for the beach walk. Wear something fun, Steve'd said, and I pull on white shorts and a bright aqua tee with a dolphin on it. On the bed I lay out Bram's choice, khaki shorts and denim shirt. I'm tying my hair back when he comes in, careful to close the door quietly. "Oh!" he says with a start, seeing me at the dresser. "I thought you were asleep."

You sure did, I think, but say nothing. I'm not sure I can without bursting into tears. But I won't cry. I won't give her the satisfaction of seeing my pain—Jocasta or Bram, either one. Seeing his clothes on the bed, Bram says, "Thanks, sweetheart," before coming over to give me a kiss on the cheek. I flinch but he doesn't notice. Her perfume is faint on the collar of his shirt, and when he pulls it over his head, I clear my throat and say, "You might want to shower."

Frowning, he tosses his shirt aside. "Not till after the beach. But don't worry, I'll be quick because I gotta get to the kitchen. Then you'll have plenty of time to primp."

I can't get to the door without walking past him, and he takes my arm to smile down at me. "Relax, baby. It'll be over before you know it. I promise."

"Yeah," I say as I pull away and walk out the door. *That's what I'm afraid of.*

The filming of the beach walk goes so smoothly that everyone's jubilant afterward. The crew applauds us, and Steve swears that we're a bunch of pros. I went through the motions, smiling and chatting just like Steve'd told us to do. They're using a voice-over for this part, so it didn't matter what we said. With the camera crew walking backwards several steps in front of us, Bram and I lead off, hands clasped. If he noticed my trembling hands, my halting steps, he gave no sign. Michael and Missy were behind us, with Adeline in her father's arms. Behind them came Nellie Bee, Charlie, and Jocasta. Nellie Bee had refused to stand beside Jocasta and made Charlie walk between them.

Holding his hands up like Moses on the mountain, Steve gathers us around for a final pep talk. It's a family dinner, he says, not red carpet night at the Oscars. No posing and posturing; just relax and enjoy a great meal with our dearly beloved. "And for God's sake," he bellows, "make a big deal over the food. Some of you eat like little birds but not tonight. Tonight, you're ravenous wolves!"

• • •

I'm seated at one end of the table with Bram at the other, so we have to face each other the entire time. As hard as I've tried to hide my distress, I can tell that he's picked up on it. I catch him eyeing me in concern, his eyes troubled. *Just get through this*, I tell myself. As I'd feared, Nellie Bee was furious to find Jocasta in the guest room I'd promised them. Thankfully, she blamed Jocasta instead of me, assuming she'd invited herself and I'd allowed it rather than cause a ruckus. Having Nellie Bee turn on me now would've been more than I could take. But she, too, has picked up on the pain beneath my fake smiles. Just nervous, I told her when she demanded to know what the *hell* was wrong with me. I could tell she didn't buy it. Like her brother, she watches me warily.

Steve's noted the animosity between Bram's ex-wife and his sister and wisely placed poor Charlie between them again. Across from them, Michael's seated next to me with Missy closer to Bram. In stark contrast to me and Nellie Bee, Missy and Jocasta are dressed to the hilt. Wanting color, Steve had insisted on approving our outfits, even Bram and Charlie's shirts. I chose a simple linen top of sage-green with cropped pants, and Nellie Bee a similar outfit in bright blue. Missy's stylish dress is patterned with sunflowers, but Jocasta steals the show in a stunning coral sheath with a plunging neckline. Despite my despondency, I hide a smile every time Charlie peers over his glasses to steal a glance at his dinner partner's décolletage.

Once the first course is on the table, Steve gives the go-ahead and the filming begins. We've been warned not to look at the cameras or the high-reaching lights around the table, which are hot and blinding. Bram begins with a blessing, asking us to join hands as he offers thanks. Jocasta's on one side of me and Michael the other; I give Michael's hand a squeeze but barely touch his mother's cool, slender fingers, yanking my own away as soon as the amens are said. She throws me a knowing smirk.

Bram introduces the crab bisque by describing how he dropped a crab trap into a nearby deep-water creek to gather the crab. Everyone oohs and ahhs while we try to muffle our slurps. The sous chef removes our bowls and serves shrimp salad as the next course. For the benefit of the unseen audience, Bram explains how to cast a shrimp net, even getting to his feet to demonstrate the dance-like motions. I try not to glance his way but can't help myself; his showmanship draws me in as it did the first time we met. And why had I insisted he wear the dark-green shirt that makes his eyes like emeralds? As he takes his seat, he gives me a smile, but I quickly look down.

The presentation and discussion of each of the courses carries us through the meal. As our main dish of grilled flounder served with tomato gratin is brought out, Bram goes around to pour the special wine he's selected to complement it, a lovely Sancerre. We've had a different wine with each course, and I've already had way more than I usually drink with dinner. Not to mention the cocktails we'd had beforehand. To calm our nerves, all of us are drinking a lot. Everyone keeps gulping it down and holding up their glasses for more.

When Bram gets to my chair, he lays his hand on my shoulder and leans in close to pour the wine. "It's not nerves that's bothering you, is it?" he says quietly. It's that deadly beautiful voice of his that gets me, and I swallow painfully. "Christina?" he says. If I didn't know better, I'd swear it was genuine concern. Afraid the cameras might catch our exchange, I force a smile. "I'm fine," I murmur back.

He pours my wine, swirls the bottle, and leans close again. "Bullshit," he whispers in my ear, then moves on to fill Michael's glass. It's then I notice Missy glaring at her husband, her lips in a tight line of anger. So Bram and I aren't the only ones, I think, which makes me even sadder. Why are relationships so hard to get right? My gaze travels unwillingly to Jocasta, who's sipping her wine as she cuts her dark eyes around the table, coming to rest on Bram. I try to look away before she catches me staring at her, but I'm not quick enough. She raises her glass of wine to me, and I resist an overwhelming urge to throw mine in her face.

With fresh strawberries in season, Bram presents a spectacular sponge cake piled high with berries and whipped cream as the grand finale. As the wineglasses are replaced with coffee cups, we dutifully exclaim over the dessert. Even though their praise for the cake is profuse, Jocasta and Missy try to pick out a couple of strawberries without getting a smidgen of cream. With a wicked gleam in her eyes, Nellie Bee says, "You've outdone yourself, Bram! Can we have seconds?"

"Oh, I insist," he replies with a wink. Nellie Bee motions for the sous chef and tells him to bring everyone a second helping.

"I couldn't possibly!" Missy gasps in horror, then catches herself. "But it's so good, Papa O'Connor."

"How would you know?" Nellie Bee says with a snort. "You haven't touched it."

Michael lets out a guffaw of laughter; Missy throws him a poisonous look, and Jocasta leans toward Nellie Bee to say in a cloying tone, "Now, Nellie Bee. You know how the young girls watch their figures."

"No, but I know how my husband watches *yours*," Nellie Bee says tartly. Red-faced, Charlie chokes on a mouthful of cake and coughs into his napkin, and Michael lets out another guffaw. Seeing the goofy look on his face, it dawns on me that he's drunk as a skunk.

Missy grabs the carafe of coffee and says pointedly to Michael, "You haven't had your coffee yet, darling."

Michael grins at her. "Don't want coffee. I'm having another drink instead." Seeing his wineglass gone, he calls out to the sous chef, "Hey! Bring me another glass, my good man."

"I've got a really nice dessert wine," Bram offers, and I realize he's unaware of how much his son—and everyone else—has already consumed.

"Hot damn!" Michael cries, waving widely to the sous chef. "Bring everyone a glass. Put it on my tab." When he laughs uproariously at his joke, Nellie Bee joins in, clapping her hands and laughing in glee, and Bram turns to me in alarm.

Thinking quickly, I motion for Missy to pass the coffee carafe, then I get up to take it around the table with a smile plastered on my face. "Who'd like coffee instead?" I say brightly. My attempt to sober up the culprits fails; no one but Jocasta and Missy hold their cups up. Even worse, Missy tries to push hers off on Michael. "Here you are, my darling," she says through gritted teeth as she thrusts the cup under his nose.

Michael's goofy look turns belligerent and he swats at it, sloshing coffee across the table, which brings on another drunken peal of laughter from Nellie Bee. When Charlie, sweating profusely under the lights, lays a restraining hand on her arm, she shakes him off. "Leave me alone, Charlie. I've waited twenty-six years for my nephew to wake up and smell the coffee." Poking her husband with her elbow, she giggles. "Get it? Smell the coffee? Ha!"

"What does that mean?" Jocasta snaps, and Nellie Bee gives her a feline smile.

"You're a smart cookie, Toots. You figure it out."

Bram's look of alarm has increased, so I cast around wildly for another angle. The perfect distraction hits me and I blurt out, "Bram! Why don't you tell everyone about *Lowcountry Stew*?"

"Another course?" Michael groans. "Sorry, Dad, but I'm stuffed."

Bram shoots me a look of relief then announces: "I'm finishing up a memoir I'm calling *Lowcountry Stew*, which is coming out next year, God willing."

"I'll drink to that," Michael declares as he salutes his father with his glass. Nellie Bee and Charlie applaud, but Missy's too focused on glaring at Michael to notice.

Jocasta raises her blond head sharply. "A *memoir*? You didn't tell me it was a memoir, Bram. I thought you were working on a cookbook."

Shooting her a disdainful look, Nellie Bee says, "Why would he tell you anything, Jocasta? Best I recall, you dumped my brother years ago."

Jocasta's face flushes, and the cameraman behind me snickers. With rising panic, I look around for Steve but can't see anything in the blinding lights. Where is he, and why isn't he stopping this?

"Oh, Papa O'Connor, how exciting!" Missy cries with an eager smile. "Will all of us be in your book?"

"Sure will," Nellie Bee says. "And you get to be the princess. A role you were born to play."

When Missy squeals in delight, Michael snorts. "That wasn't a compliment, your highness." When he hiccups and giggles, Missy gives him a shove and a look of disgust.

"Bram?" Jocasta drawls as she flutters her lashes at him. "Surely your book won't include any . . . ah . . . family secrets, will it? I mean, that could be embarrassing to some of your family members."

"Not me," Nellie Bee says pointedly. "Won't embarrass me a bit. But *I* wasn't the one who ran off with my boyfriend."

"Who did that?" Missy gasps, wide-eyed.

"No one!" Jocasta hisses. "Nellie Bee's nothing but a trouble-maker."

"Hey, wait a minute," Charlie says, turning to glare at her. "I don't appreciate that, Jocasta."

She gives him a pitying look. "Poor old Charlie. Surely you've noticed that nobody in this family gives a jolly damn what you think."

Snarling, Nellie Bee leans toward her. "You say one more thing, Jocasta, and you'll wish you'd kept your skinny ass in Charleston."

With a smirk, Jocasta says, "Oh, my. Looks like some of us have had too much to drink."

"Including you," Nellie Bee counters. "Trying to drown your sorrows. But guess what? When you sober up, you'll still be making a fool of yourself mooning over my brother. And he'll still be in love with Chris, not you."

Jocasta's face flares red and she glances furtively at the cameras before turning back to Nellie Bee. "I wouldn't be so sure of that," she hisses under her breath.

"Why don't you ask him?" Nellie Bee's voice is loud, not caring who hears her. "I dare you."

Jocasta's so furious that her hand's shaking as she raises the delicate glass of dessert wine to her mouth. The sticky red liquid sloshes out and splashes the front of her dress. "Now look what you've made me do," she screeches, grabbing for her napkin. "The whole family, nothing but a bunch of drunken Irish slobs."

"You talking about me, Mom?" Michael says with another hiccup. "Or do you mean Princess Leah? No, wait—she's high society, like you."

"Okay, that's enough," Bram says, but his voice is drowned out by Missy's, who turns to Michael furiously.

"Don't you dare take that tone with me, Michael O'Connor," she spits out. "I know what you did this afternoon when you thought I was asleep."

"*What?*" Nellie Bee asks, leaning forward in breathless excitement.

Missy whirls her head to Jocasta. "After our fight, you ran to Mommie Dearest, knowing she'd take your side like she always does. You probably told her what a terrible wife and mother I am, and how you regret marrying me."

Michael's face reddens and he grabs for Missy's arm. "Now, honey, that's not true. You were napping, so I went for a little visit with my mom, true. But we didn't talk about you."

"Yes you did!" she screeches. "When I woke up I went looking for you. I was about to open the door of your mom's room when I heard y'all laughing and talking about me."

It hits me so hard that I push back from the table with a loud gasp. I stare from Michael to Jocasta in disbelief. "This afternoon? That was *you*, Michael? You were in your mother's room this afternoon?"

Michael looks at me as if I've lost my mind. "I was just visiting with Mom, Chris. Okay, Missy's right. We did talk about everybody, like we always do." He glances over at his wife apologetically, suddenly sober. "But I swear, Missy. We didn't say anything bad about you. I'm sorry if you thought otherwise."

She looks baffled, then says, "Well, I couldn't really hear that well—"

With dawning understanding of what I heard, and how mistaken I was about it, I let out a peal of laughter that startles everyone at the table. Nellie Bee stares at me then joins in, though she has no idea what I'm laughing at. Neither do I, but I can't seem to stop myself. All the pent-up emotion I've suppressed in order to get through the evening comes pouring out. Heard through a closed door, a son's voice sounded like his father's, and I jumped to the worst possible conclusion. I laugh so hard that my shoulders shake and tears roll down my cheeks. When I hear Steve bellow out, "Okay, that's a take!" I force myself to take deep breaths and try to pull myself together. Suddenly Bram's there, and when he pulls me to my feet I throw my arms around him, holding on so tight I'm afraid I'll squeeze the life out of him.

"It's okay, sweetheart," Bram says as he cups my face in his hands. "I was so nervous after my first show I puked for days. It could be worse."

I look up at him through my tears. "You have no idea how much worse it could be," I tell him with a laugh, but this time, it's a laugh of such joy and relief that I feel light-headed, and cling to Bram even harder. He has no idea what happened this afternoon or what I foolishly thought of him, and I might never tell him. Maybe, just maybe, even the best of marriages needs some secrets.

When Steve appears with a bottle of champagne, Bram, still holding me close, waves him off. "You'd better let the crew enjoy that, Steve. This bunch's had all they need tonight." He leans down to kiss me lightly on the lips. "Even my bride, it appears."

Steve chuckles. "Yeah, I noticed. I was getting worried toward the end."

"*You* were?" Bram says with a snort. "You're cutting out the last part, I hope?"

Steve blinks at him in disbelief. "Are you insane? The audience will eat that up. Wait till Rick sees it. We argue all the time about who has the most screwed-up family." Popping the champagne cork, he grins at Bram. "Yours might win the prize."

At Steve's signal, the crew cuts off the overhanging lights and the room plunges into darkness. The only light comes from the flickering candles on the table, but it's just enough. In the soft glow, I see a tipsy Nellie Bee lean into Charlie, who kisses the top of her head, and Missy takes a drunken Michael in her arms in forgiveness. Although she's slumped in her chair, Jocasta's forlorn gaze is fastened on Bram, as it has been since she arrived. But I know now that she'll go back alone, while Bram and I will remain in the home we've created together.

I reach for Bram's hand. "Come on, sweetheart. It's been a long day. Let's help this crazy family of ours get themselves to bed."

With an exhausted smile, he raises my hand to his lips. "I cannot wait."

About *Cassandra King Conroy*

Cassandra King Conroy is an award-winning author of five best-selling novels and two nonfiction books in addition to numerous short stories, essays, and magazine articles. Her latest book, *Tell Me a Story*, a memoir about life with her late husband, Pat Conroy, was named SIBA's 2020 nonfiction Book of the Year.

When Pat gave Dottie Frank a blurb for her first book, *Sullivan's Island*, Cassandra invited Dottie for a visit to Fripp Island, and the Conroys and Franks became fast friends.

A native of LA (Lower Alabama), Cassandra resides in Beaufort, South Carolina, where she is honorary chair of the Pat Conroy Literary Center.

Dottie and Me

MARY NORRIS

At an authors' lunch outside Detroit in May 2016, a brunette in a bold red-and-white-print dress made a beeline for me. She was Dorothea Benton Frank, known to her friends as Dottie, the author of bestselling books set in the Lowcountry of South Carolina, and she was eager to talk about grammar, of all things. We were in a clubby room with a bar and retractable walls, enjoying a cocktail or something milder, before appearing on a program that featured Steve Hamilton, a curly-haired, prolific author of mysteries, and Lesley Stahl, the *60 Minutes* correspondent. We watched Stahl make her entrance, impeccably coiffed, a loose coat thrown over a slim dress. Her book about being a grandmother had just been published, and Dottie and I had a strong suspicion that the big turnout for this event—more than a thousand tickets had been sold—was for her.

The authors sat at a long table on a platform at the front of the room and were given five or ten minutes apiece to pitch their books while the audience, mostly book-club ladies seated at big round tables in a banqueting hall, consumed a three-course lunch. Dottie didn't touch her food, except to push it away; she never ate at these affairs, she explained. We were there to sell and sign books. Dottie's talk was fluid and practiced, with many wisecracks. She told the story of how, when her beloved mother died, her grief was compounded by learning that her four siblings intended to sell the family home on Sullivan's Island, near Charleston, where she grew up. She couldn't bear it—to lose both her mother and her childhood home in one blow? By now she was living in Montclair, New Jersey, where she and her husband, Peter Frank, raised two children, although she frequently returned home to South Carolina. She asked her husband, an investment banker, if he would buy the house. (*Suspense*) "And he said no." So Dottie determined that although she had never written a book before, she would churn out a bestseller and make enough money to buy the house herself. And she did. (*Applause*)

The bestseller was *Sullivan's Island*, the story of a woman betrayed by her husband who returns with her teenage daughter to the place where she grew up and rebuilds her life. Steeped in memories of the Lowcountry, it came out in 1999 and sold more than a million copies. That I had never heard of this or any of Dottie's other books did not surprise or perturb her one bit. They were beach reads, so-called domestic fiction, a genre that she was well aware did not get reviewed in publications like the *New York Times* or *The New Yorker*. Anyway, Dottie didn't need me. She had a devoted following. Her books were so popular that you couldn't just show up at her signings: you had to buy a ticket. There was even a Dorothea Benton Frank Fan Fest in Charleston. Dot Frank was an industry.

After the signing, Dottie was going straight to the airport for her next gig. But she gave me her business card and told me that an event similar to the one we'd just done would be held in Charleston in November, and she'd get me invited. I emailed her the next day, before I could lose her contact information. "Tickled pink to hear from you!" she wrote back. "Send me your address and I'll send you a copy of my funniest book!" She sent two, with inscriptions, *Sullivan's Island* ("It all started here") and *The Last Original Wife* ("For Mary Norris—My new BF!"), and added, "I can keep you in beach books forever!" Later that year, I was invited to an authors' luncheon hosted by the *Post and Courier* in Charleston. The first night, the organizers put me up in a serviceable hotel, with the usual hideous hallway carpeting, on the outskirts of town. My room overlooked the football stadium of the Citadel, the famous military academy. That weekend, there was a big game as well as a reunion, so the hotel was fully booked, and after the luncheon I would have to move across the river to a different hotel, even more remote. When I told

Dottie this, she asked, "Are you packed?" I was. "Come home with me," she said.

Suddenly there I was, driving to Sullivan's Island with Dorothea Benton Frank. Her fans would be pea green with envy! In the car, she gossiped about her children, just as the women in her books do. Her daughter, Victoria, she told me in confidence, was pregnant. (Victoria's son, Teddy, would be born the following year, in 2017, and turn Dottie into a fan of Lesley Stahl's grandmother book.) She had encouraged her son, William, to try online dating and threatened to write his profile herself. (He has since married.) That day was Victoria's birthday, and Dottie was throwing a dinner party for her, so on the way home we stopped at the grocery store to pick up a few loaves of Victoria's favorite frozen garlic bread.

The house wasn't the one Dottie had grown up in. It wasn't even the one that she had bought with the bestseller money. She had traded up to a mansion by the sea. The street was lined with palmetto trees—pronounced pal-metto, not palm-etto, she told me—and alongside the house was a pristine white cottage to which she gave me the key. But instead of retiring to the cottage I hung out in the kitchen while Dottie bustled around, whipping up dinner for twenty. I also admired the many ship models in glass cases in the hallway and living room—Peter collected them. Then I settled in a rocking chair on the back porch and tried to read. But I couldn't concentrate. I couldn't get over how I had scored. I had been delivered from a hotel in suburbia to this magnificent historic property with a view of Fort Sumter. For dinner, Dottie seated me with her on the porch while her daughter and friends took over the dining room. The climax of the evening was when Peter fired a blank from a small cannon, of the type used to signal the start for yacht races, off the back-porch steps.

The next morning, Dottie came to the cottage to invite me for coffee and show me a note from a reader, who loved her work but felt compelled to write, "I shuddered each time I read 'was' when it should be 'were'! My Mom taught me (and she was a grammar fanatic!) when it comes to using 'was' or 'were' you use 'were' when it is contrary to fact." The fan had cited a line of dialogue from *Lowcountry Summer*: "None that I know of, honey. I wish there was a pill." Dottie wanted my professional opinion: How should she answer? Was she obliged to use the subjunctive? "Tell her this is fiction and this is how people talk," I said. She was pleased to be able to quote a copy editor in her reply, adding that, for her own part, she believed that "it's more important for dialogue to ring true than it is for it to be grammatically correct."

We stayed in touch via email and Facebook. When Dottie learned that I was working on a book about Greek, she told me that the protagonist of her latest book was from Corfu. At a book festival in Savannah, she met Colson Whitehead and Jay McInerney, who she thought might be a cousin. She was a big fan of other writers. Her twelfth Lowcountry tale, *Queen Bee*, came out a few years later, in May of 2019, and Dottie was all over Facebook and Twitter promoting it. That August, I saw a note on her Facebook page from her family, stating that she was in the hospital. Less than three weeks later, on September 2, 2019, came the announcement that she had died, of myelodysplastic syndrome (MDS), a bone-marrow condition, at the age of sixty-seven. Tens of thousands of people expressed their sadness on her Facebook page; the memorial service, at Grace Church Cathedral in Charleston, was sure to be mobbed. Luckily, those of us who could not make it to Charleston had only to open a book to be with Dottie. In her breakthrough novel, *Sullivan's Island*, the plucky narrator, Susan, gets a job as a columnist for the *Post and Courier*, and when her teenage daughter—impressed, for a change—asks her what she'll do if she ever has to write about death, she replies, "That may possibly be the toughest question I've had to answer all day, but even death has humor, wakes and funerals especially. I guess I'd advise people not to take hams to the bereaved."

About Mary Norris

Mary Norris joined the editorial staff of *The New Yorker* in 1978 and was a copy editor and proofreader there for more than thirty years. Originally from Cleveland, Ohio, she lives in New York and Rockaway.

ALSO BY MARY NORRIS

Greek to Me

Between You & Me

Making of a
Friendship

JACQUELINE BOUVIER LEE

I remember the first time I saw Dorothea Benton Frank, I thought I had won the grand prize by being able to attend one of the biggest book events in the United States. Little did I know the real gift was about to come into my life dressed in pearls and a crisp white shirt.

The size of the Jacob Javits Convention Center in New York City is overwhelming, and this Southern girl was just excited to be at a book event in the middle of Manhattan. Book Expo America is the largest annual book trade fair in the United States and many up-and-coming authors as well as established authors are seated at booths to showcase upcoming titles.

I was new to the book business and I needed authors. I knew that event was the place to find them. I walked the aisles scouting authors and handing out cards trying to make deals with writers who I thought would be a good fit for my South Carolina store. Later I would find out how author tours actually worked; to say I was "green" was an understatement.

I had been told I needed some strong authors if I wanted to jump-start my career as a community relations manager. Not one soul was interested in coming to the Carolinas to do an author signing. I decided to take a break, grab some lunch, and regroup. Fully nourished I said a little prayer that maybe the afternoon would be kinder to my pursuit.

I continued my trek among the hundreds of bibliophiles, some carrying suitcases to take home all of their treasures. I make a right turn and hear a woman talking to an eager reader about peaches and using the word "ya'll." When I saw the large pearls around her neck I knew we would be friends forever.

I listened as her fans regurgitated different stories word for word from her books. They knew her characters, they knew the different islands Dottie so vividly described in her books, and they all seemed to know about the infamous toothbrush scene from her first book. That toothbrush came up several times, as it would throughout the many years we spent together.

Finally it was my turn to meet this vision of Southern loveliness. I explained who I was and which big box book company I worked for. I explained what I was trying to do and gave her my card.

The first words out of her mouth were I would be glad to come to your stores, she promptly gave me her email address and phone number, and the rest as they say is book history.

That first signing was a doozy! We held it in Florence, South Carolina, a store that I later found out was much too small of a venue for Dorothea Benton Frank. There were so many people in that store that I am sure we were breaking the fire code. She never flinched or said anything to me about not having enough chairs. Instead she regaled the audience with stories of how she would accompany different members of her family from Sullivan's Island to Florence to buy false teeth. The audience loved it and roared with laughter, and each one had to tell her their favorite story about false teeth as they came through the line. One lady even took hers out of her mouth to show Dorothea what a good job they had done.

That was one of many of Dorothea's superpowers: she was relatable and her fans loved that about her.

Dorothea was always there to help you if you needed something (superpower number two). I can't tell you how many times her fans would come through the line and say they needed help with a charity event, or that a local library might be closing. She always asked what could she do to help?

I loved how warm and funny Dorothea was, she was that way to each and every person she ran into. A lot of people I have worked with over the years are one way to the fans and a completely different unlikable person once the camera's stopped rolling, but not Dorothea. To this day I have never met any other celebrity that has invited hundreds of their fans to their home. She was not fussy as people made their way upstairs to the guest rooms or opened the door to her refrigerator to see what she had inside. She wanted them there and they were her friends. She would give you the shirt off her back and ask for nothing in return. That beach house felt like "our" house. I remember saying I was so exhausted after a couple of surgeries and she offered her guest house to me. When I asked her when she would be arriving she said the house is yours, and gave me the code to the gate (superpower number three).

Dottie was a wonderful human being, kind and helpful, and if she dreamed it, she found a way to bring it to fruition (superpower number four), and if you dreamed it, and were willing to put in the work, she helped make your dreams come true as well. She is responsible for my book career being so successful—once she came to my stores other publishers started calling me and sometimes the authors themselves reached out to me. When I left the book business and decided to go work at a country club, she told me point-blank you will not like it. And she was right. It was not for me.

Her family was very important to her (superpower number five); our daughters are around the same age and we often shared stories over dinner of how we were raising our girls. She loved fiercely and cared for my child as well. I will never forget how she called me twice a day until my daughter came through a very difficult surgery.

We have been through good times and bad, she has given so much advice, helped so many people, to say I miss her is an understatement.

Queen, you came and did your thing, you have left us with the tools we need to get through this thing called life, rest well; we got it from here.

Dottie:
The Sparkling
Comet

GERVAIS HAGERTY

There is a tribe of women writers in Charleston. They are bound together like chapters in a hardback. When a tribe member releases a book, Nathalie Dupree throws a party.

My mother, a poet, had been taking me to these celebrations long before I understood how lucky I was to be included. My most salient first memory of speaking with Dottie occurred in Nathalie's lemon yellow dining room, where guests smeared homemade pimento cheese dip on crumbly made-from-scratch biscuits. I was a teenager; Dottie spoke to me as though I was an adult. "Either your face can look good, or your ass can look good, but you can't have both."

Ha!

I knew Dottie was a bestseller, but I was confused because from what I learned in high school English, writers weren't happy. They hid in the corners of their rickety homes, tied to their typewriters by cobwebs. They chewed their fingernails to nubs agonizing over metaphors and forgot to check for boogers before speaking engagements.

And here was Dottie, this sparkling comet whizzing around the party, laughing and cracking jokes. Wasn't the writing life a slog? Dottie looked like she was having fun. That left an impression on me.

The last time I spoke with Dottie was also at Nathalie's. We were in the front parlor, a quieter room separated from the food and drink by the blockade of newcomers in the foyer. Dottie was with her daughter, Victoria. They sat side-by-side, shoulder to shoulder, their arms bent in perfect parallel. I remember thinking how close they seemed.

I had finished a draft of my first novel—written from the point of view of one person—and was planning my second book. I had a question; I might as well ask a master storyteller. "Should I write from multiple points of view?"

Dottie smiled a big, red-lipsticked smile. The diamonds on her ears winked like stars. "Oh, yes. That way they can keep secrets from each other."

I have the privilege and honor to work with Dottie's longtime editor, Carrie Feron. On our phone calls, we often end up talking about Dottie, and when we do, the energy changes. Even with hundreds of miles between us, I can feel a celestial shift, like I've floated into the wake of their deep and enduring kinship. Carrie adored Dottie. I think for many people, it was impossible not to.

After I submit my copyedits for my first novel, I'll get back to working on book number two, which, of course, has multiple points of view. Thanks to Dottie's advice, there are constellations of secrets. And, following her example, I'm having a whole lot of fun.

About Gervais Hagerty

Gervais Hagerty grew up in Charleston, South Carolina. After reporting and producing the news for both radio and television, she taught communications at The Citadel. When not writing, she works on local environmental and transportation issues. She lives in Charleston with her husband and two daughters.

ALSO BY GERVAIS HAGERTY

In Polite Company

Essay and Poetry by Marjory Wentworth

MARJORY WENTWORTH

I met Dottie in the early 2000s at a party on a Saturday evening. I was first introduced to her husband, Peter. He told me that he traveled a lot for work and that he likes to read poetry on airplanes, because he could read in bits and pieces when it was quiet, and it really gave him something to think about. He seemed interested in my work, and I told him that it was part of the wall text at the Gibbes Museum of Art in an exhibition on the ACE Basin. He flipped when I told him that and he said that his wife, Dottie, had just finished a novel called *Plantation* set in the ACE Basin. He ran off to find her; she was talking to my husband, who is also named Peter! We spoke briefly, and I must have given her my card. She was so excited to hear about the ACE Basin Exhibition, which was closing the next day.

Sure enough, Dottie went to see/read my poems at the Gibbes Museum, bought my first book, and showed up at my door on Sullivan's Island with the book and a bottle of wine and she asked me if she could include one of my poems in the front of her forthcoming novel, *Plantation*. It was as if we had both been writing about the same place at the same time. Dottie said that I could say everything she wanted to say in just a handful of words. So, my poem "River" appeared in the front of Dottie's novel *Plantation*. The first print run was 800,000 copies. That's a lot of eyes on a poem!

We became fast friends, and after that I was sent galleys and wrote the poem after reading the draft of Dottie's novels: *Shem Creek, Isle of Palms, Pawley's Island*, etc. It was such an honor to be included in her books, and I am forever grateful. I used to tell people that Dottie was my biggest fan, and she was. When I was appointed Poet Laureate of South Carolina in 2003 she sent me a case of wine and a set of wineglasses engraved with the words "Sullivan's

Island"; she framed and proudly displayed the broadside of the first inaugural poem I wrote, "Rivers of Wind."

Our children became friends and remain friends today. Victoria's first prom date was with my son Hunter, and my son Taylor was an usher in Liam's wedding. Dottie and Peter folded us into family gatherings and other occasions. The love and generosity were boundless. A couple of years after we met, my husband and I had serious pneumonia at Thanksgiving. Not only did Dottie drop everything and make homemade chicken soup to "cure" me, she and her sister Lynn made an entire Thanksgiving dinner for our family and brought it over to our house. I can still remember listening to Dottie on the phone telling our son Hunter how to baste a turkey.

My heart is filled with memories of my dear friend. I miss her so much, and I still pick up my phone to call or text her and then I remember that she's gone. I open one of her books; I hear her husky voice reading the passage. I see her beautiful smile, and she is with me, and we are laughing like we always did.

"REUNION BEACH"

The sea is calling us
home. There is nothing
stronger than that
pull; each wave dispelling
the patient passage
of time. No
beginning, no end
in the horizon's blur,
where gull feathers
and stars are caught
in wind, swirling
above miles of sand
holding a crush
of memories.

Sandpipers scattered
at the edges
of low tide; green
ribboned steams
of seaweed
sliding
beneath your feet
as you took your first
stumbling steps
toward the sweep
of sea. Your mothers'
hands on either side
holding you up
like warm wings.

So many hours
lost in the long
sun, dribbling
watery sand
onto castle walls
gathering shells in buckets.
A red sneakerful carried
home, where bleached star-
fish lined windowsills
and brown conches circled
the garden like guards.
Your favorite grey whelk
held to your ear
before you could sleep.

You learned patience, walking
slowly through shallow water
until you found the row
of sand dollars, cold
beneath your feet,
picking one up with your toes
holding it like a prize.
Summer days spinning
cartwheels in one direction,
body surfing until the sun
dissolved over the city
and shrimp boats
lit up in a line like
a string of low-lying stars.

Carving the name
of your first crush
into the hard sand

far from the tide line,
you smoked your first Marlboro
on the overgrown path
through wondering dunes.
Standing at water's edge
with your school friends,
you watched blue and rust
cargo ships slide by the island,
wondering what lay below,
dreaming of wherever
they came from.

You brought us
the world
of this island,
its wax myrtles
and palmettos,
pelicans
flying low
along the shoreline—
each beloved object
of your home place
lining the pages
of your stories
like sand scattered
between sentences.

We will return
in September,
the month of your birth,
the month
of your death.
We will retrace your

footsteps, watch
dolphins dip in
and out of waves, as if
they are following us,
hear your laughter as gulls
call back and forth
beneath wisps
of clouds, where we
will see you
in the radiant light.

"RIVER" FROM **PLANTATION**

The river is a woman who is never idle.
Into her feathering water
fall petals and bones

of earth's shed skins.
While all around her edges
men are carving altars,

the river gathers flotsam,
branches of time, and clouds
loosening the robes of their reflections.

Her dress is decoupage—
yellow clustering leaves,
ashes, paper, tin, and dung.

Wine dark honey for the world,
sweet blood of seeping magma
pulsing above the carbon starred

sediment. Striped with settled skulls,
wing, and leaf spine: the river
is an open-minded graveyard.

Listen to the music
of sunlight spreading
inside her crystal cells.

Magnet, clock, cradle
for the wind, the river holds a cup
filling with miles of rain.

But when the river sleeps,
her celestial children
break the sticks of gravity,

grab fistfuls of fish
scented amber clotted with diamonds,
ferns, and petalling clouds;

adorn bracelets of woven rain,
rise with islands of sweet grass
and stars strung to their backs

to wander over the scarred surface
of the earth, like their mothers
simply searching for the sea.

"TOWARD THE SEA" FROM **BULL'S ISLAND**

The wind is an empty place. You enter
expecting something softened by the sea.

A piece of cedar shaped into a body
you once loved. Perhaps the hand that held you
from a distance or the face that simply
held you here. Still moving in and out of time
during the hour when night meets day,
you try to find your bearings.
You pick up objects. You want to remember.
Jagged edged rocks in the palm of your hand.
You hold them up in the moonlight.
They are earthbound, filling with sky.
You walk on further, pause to scoop tiny iridescent
shells, the colors of cream and roses.
Little by little the air brightens into hours,
which are either empty or full of all the things
you love and remember, depending
on which direction the wind is coming from.

"IN THE DREAM OF THE SEA" FROM
THE LAND OF MANGO SUNSETS

I call you from the open water
surrounding us, speaking
across divided lives.

I call you
from the waves
that always have direction.

Where strings of morning glory
hold the dunes in place,
I call. In winter,

when wind pours
through cracks in the walls.
Inside, I call

although my voice
has been silent
and dissolving.

In sand
pulled back
into the body

of the sea,
from the blue
house built on sand

balanced at the edge
of the world
I call you.

Drowning stars,
shipwrecks, and broken voices
move beneath the waves.

Here, at the open
center
of my ordinary heart

filling with sounds
of the resurrected,
in the dream

of the sea,
I call you
home.

"TANGLED" FROM **PAWLEY'S ISLAND**

We return to hear the waves returning
to the beach, one after the other, connecting

us like blood. Long before we came
here, we were listening, remembering

wind, spinning salt, uninterrupted
sunlight. This is a place where dreams

return, fish bones tangled in seaweed.
Rinsed clean and kept, whatever sorrows

come are folded into the sea's
unbearable secrets.

"SHEM CREEK" FROM **SHEM CREEK**

I
The swollen earth splits its skin
into waterways, scattered
and winding in every
direction, releasing winds
that carve the land to shreds. Where
sun-filled clumps of spartina,
smoothed into supplicating

rows of heavy bent heads, crowd
the edges of Shem Creek;
marsh wrens build their tiny nests.
As if they are playing hide
and seek, porpoises appear
then disappear below the sea.
Fish birds littering the sky:
egrets, gray herons, and terns,
oyster catchers, pelicans,
gulls diving and turning through
the thick pink tinted air.

II

Weaving through miles of treeless
Subdivisions and strip malls,
the creek gathers everything
from oil, soap, and gasoline
to tires and refrigerators.
After the rain, run-off fills
the oyster beds with dioxins.
Arsenic and mercury
drift through the water in clumps
of invisible clouds
as if no one will notice.

III

Beyond the clutter of traffic,
tourist shops, seafood restaurants,
hotels, bars, and parking lots;
docked shrimp boats bob up and down
beside the docks, where the creek
pours silently into the sea.

"BARRIER ISLAND" FROM ISLE OF PALMS

Where nothing is certain, we awaken
to another night of delicate rain
falling as if it didn't want to
disturb anyone. On and off
foghorns groan. The lighthouse beacon
circles the island. For hours, melancholy
waves tear whatever land we're standing on.
Listen to the sea-rain dripping
through fog, suspended at the edge of earth
on a circle of sand where we are always
moving slowly toward land.

A STANZA FROM "THE SOUND OF YOUR OWN VOICE SINGING" FROM FULL OF GRACE

The weight of love is the heaviest burden
you have learned to carry.
In the silence of the heavens,
it's a dream that wakes you
with the sound of your own voice singing.

About Marjory Wentworth

Marjory Wentworth is the *New York Times* bestselling author of *Out of Wonder, Poems Celebrating Poets* (with Kwame Alexander and Chris Colderley). She is the co-writer of *We Are Charleston, Tragedy and Triumph at Mother Emanuel*, with Herb Frazier and Dr. Bernard Powers; and *Taking a Stand: The Evolution of Human Rights*, with Juan E. Mendez. She is co-editor with Kwame Dawes of *Seeking, Poetry and Prose Inspired by the Art of Jonathan Green*, and the author of the prizewinning children's story *Shackles*. Her books of poetry include *Noticing Eden, Despite Gravity, The Endless Repetition of an Ordinary Miracle*, and *New and Selected Poems*. Her poems have been nominated for the Pushcart Prize six times. She was the poet laureate of South Carolina from 2003 to 2020.

Wentworth serves on the board of advisors at the Global Social Justice Practice Academy, and she is a 2020 National Coalition Against Censorship Free Speech Is for Me Advocate. She teaches courses in writing, poetry, social justice, and banned books at the College of Charleston.

Marjory first met Dottie in the early 2000s at a party; the next evening Dottie showed up at her door with a bottle of wine and

Marjory's first book of poems and asked her if she could include one of her poems in the front of her forthcoming novel, *Plantation*. Their mutual love of the South Carolina Lowcountry bonded them, and their friendship was immediate. Both women were married to men named Peter; even their children were the same ages, and they remain friends to this day. Sometimes friends become family, and it doesn't get better than that.

For further information, see marjorytwentworth.net.

ALSO BY MARJORY WENTWORTH

Out of Wonder

We Are Charleston

New and Selected Poems

Taking a Stand

The Endless Repetition of an Ordinary Miracle

Shackles

Despite Gravity

Noticing Eden

Essays and Recipes

NATHALIE DUPREE

Snails

All I wanted for my thirteenth birthday was to dine at the nearby French restaurant like a grown-up. After much parental negotiations, Juli, my best friend since first grade, and I arrived on the local AB&W bus at Longchamps just as it opened for dinner.

Dressed in our Sunday best, we were greeted by the tuxedoed maître d' as if we were royalty as he led us to our candle-lit white-clad table. Holding out my chair, a waiter whisked a huge napkin onto my lap and a menu nearly as large as I into my hands. After a few moments of being dumbfounded by the multiplicity of choices we asked for help and left ourselves in their capable hands.

And so I began my romance with fresh parsley, garlic, escargots, and French food, a strange and exotic land to a Southern girl. Before they arrived, we could smell them, the garlic and butter also providing a welcome sizzle. "Escargots," the waiter said, are very special in France.

The fat escargots, served on a scorching hot round tin plate with indentations for the delicate pale shells, seduced us with their aroma before we saw them. The waiter, delighted by our unabashed enthusiasm, taught us how to hold the snails with a special implement, as well how to pull the snails out of their shells with a tiny fork. We sopped the bread in the indentations holding the buttery remains, sated only when every last bit was gone.

Finally, we were presented with little bowls with rose petals floating in them and told to lightly run our fingers in these finger bowls to clean them from our excesses. From then on, I have always relished dipping bread in the garlic butter sauce, even preparing it when there are no escargots. Sometimes I use this sauce with fresh clams; other times mushroom caps; but have been known to eat just fresh home-baked bread, garlic, parsley from my garden, and good butter.

Juli and I had just become of the age to wear stockings and garter belts—long before panty hose. When we left the restaurant it began to rain. We huddled against the wall and hid each other while removing our stockings, one by one, so we wouldn't get them wet in the torrent that followed while we waited for our bus in the dark. We stood barefoot, against the wall, until finally the child in each of us broke loose, and we danced around, not caring about anything but being grown-up enough to eat out in a restaurant where waiters hovered over us and we could eat anything we liked. The garlic memories danced in our mouths until long after we got home. When I arrived home and Mother asked me about the evening I described it all, especially the escargot and their sauce. "Oh, my," she said, "I'm surprised you would eat snails." I didn't say a word, although it was the first I had realized escargot meant snails in French.

By sophomore year in college, Juli (now called Juliette) and her much older, sophisticated beau (also her boss) took me to dinner in a real candle-lit restaurant, with obsequious waiters and an extensive menu. Iceberg lettuce was the only lettuce I had ever eaten before. That night we had romaine lettuce in our Caesar salad, crisp and cooling, coddled egg sauce (which the waiter prepared at the table for the salad, mashing in the delicate anchovies) and crispy croutons fried in butter. I do not understand how anyone who has had a proper Caesar salad can desecrate it with chicken or other additions.

I ate my second escargots that night, drenched in a thick butter and garlic sauce, each plump snail in its own hollow in the circular plate topped with the sauce and fresh garlic. Juliette's beau showed us again how to use the escargot tongs and gave us permission to dip our bread into the left-over sauce. As if he could have stopped me.

• • •

The snails I ate in Paris, with real French bread, were better than the ones that I cooked. Or maybe it was being in France for the first time, or just France. Although one can walk through the huge Parisian Chefs Market, Rungis, and see tin plate after tin plate with stuffed snails, ready to be popped in the oven, it is possible to see, even in the modest "Super U's" of France, five or six kinds of fresh snails on ice, ready to be cooked by the enterprising chef or house-wife.

By then I had been eating and cooking snails for years. Not fresh ones, of course, but the kind in a can tucked into a hearty plastic sleeve with delicately striped taupe and white shells piled on top. Fresh parsley was available in grocery stores when no other herbs were, or, alternately, there was dried parsley and butter along with freshly chopped garlic.

How I Got to France

After my annulment at age twenty-five from my first husband, Walter, I decided it was time to go to France. I contacted my old beau, Chester, who was working for a law firm in France, and was promised a place to stay in Paris as well as in Cap d'Antibes in the South of France.

I had never dreamed I would have enough money to go to Europe. I thought it was for other people, and that it would take thousands of dollars. But a girl I had worked with had told me she had traveled to Europe for very little money. There was enough in the settlement from Walter for the trip, barely.

My stepfather, John Cook, retired from the White House Travel Office, but, working at a travel agency, booked this trip. I decided to go to London first, made arrangements to stay at the YWCA, and then fly to see Chester in Cap d'Antibes, traveling on by myself to Paris, where I would stay in Chester's apartment. All I had to do was provide the airfare and a little more money. It was mid-June in Washington and I dressed in a shocking yellow—near chartreuse—sleeveless summer dress. It was my first international trip and I was late to the gate where Mother and John were anxiously and angrily awaiting to see me off. I was the last one on the plane. The stewardess (as they were then called) huffed at me for being late and told me where to sit. I sat down in the front of the plane, second seat back, next to an Englishman.

We were asked if we wanted anything to drink and I said "No," quite firmly.

After I had turned down escargots, foie gras, lobster, and other grand foods, the Englishman could stand it no longer.

"Why aren't you eating and drinking?" he asked. "Are you sick? It's a long flight."

"I'm on a very tight budget and I don't want to spend money on the airplane. I want to save it to spend when we arrive!"

He was a very attractive man, much older than I, but not overwhelming in any way. "But everything in First Class is free," he said.

"But I'm not in First Class. I have the cheapest seat you can get."

"No," he said, "you are in First Class. I am in First Class, so you must be, too."

I was furious. I had told John to get me the cheapest tickets possible, and now I was in First Class. How could that be? I could see dollars floating out the window and I called the stewardess over.

"Am I in First Class?" My tone was belligerent.

She looked a bit stunned.

"Yes," she said. "Can I get you something?"

"Yes. I don't want to be in First Class. Could I get a seat in back and get some money returned?"

"Well, no, once you are ticketed you are ticketed."

"Look at my ticket, then. Surely I'm not in First Class!"

She perused my ticket and my boarding card. "Your Boarding Card has you seated in First Class, although your ticket is for coach."

"But am I paying more? I didn't want to pay more!"

We wrangled about for a while, and finally the Englishman said, "Look here, why don't you settle down, sit back, and enjoy it. If you were seated here by mistake, or someone arranged it, it is still where you are sitting." He turned to the stewardess, who was a bit flummoxed by my anger. "Would you please bring champagne and escargots for the lady? She has a little time to make up for!" That was that. I flew First Class to Europe, probably bounced up either because someone knew my stepfather, or because I was late and they had given my seat away.

I ate escargots, caviar, and lobster and even drank a bit. The Englishman told me everything I was to see and do in London, enjoying introducing me to the world. I was deliriously happy. I didn't even have to pay for dinner, which was delicious.

When we arrived, he insisted on my sharing his taxi, and took me on a tour of London before shaking my hand and dropping me off at the YWCA, where I had a clean and bright sunny room with a thick and puffy quilt to tuck me in. I went to Harrod's Department Store, with its incredible food hall. I was freezing in my sleeveless dress, realizing that June in England was not necessarily hot as it was in DC, and purchased a pink wool dress and jacket on the fifth floor. I then went down to the Food Hall, where I shopped and ate. I've never lost my love for England and Englishmen, returning in a few years to live happily for two years and study at the London Cordon Bleu.

But France, ah, France. France enveloped me with passion for food and romance. Never had I been so overcome with either. I was captivated by the country's sensuality by the end of my first day there.

Chester and a couple of his other houseguests met me at the airport in Nice. We drove up to lunch at La Colombe d'Or in Saint-Paul de Vence. I was enchanted and overwhelmed. Saint-Paul de Vence has a breathless view of a valley that plummets down through thickets of trees and wildlife. The Colombe d'Or's vast collection of paintings on its walls were by some of the most famous of the Impressionists who had lived nearby, eaten there, and traded their paintings for meals. Small wonder, a meal there was the cost of an oil painting.

My first meal in France consisted of crudités (my first experience with fresh French produce, lovingly picked and presented), grebe (a tiny bird) pâté, and crusty French bread. We asked for butter, and it was sweeter than cream.

It was from Chester's cook in his Cap d'Antibes home that I learned the marvels of French home cooking. After I ate my first omelet I rushed into the kitchen to learn how to make one. I pestered the cook until she showed me, breaking the fresh eggs into a bowl, whisking them with drops of water and pouring them into sizzling butter in an omelet pan. She poured it around the pan, made a little motion to move the runny part under the cooked part, seasoned it with salt and pepper, and within minutes it was done and flipped, folded, into the dish. I ate it, too, just to taste it again.

Following the second omelet, I sat down to meet French lettuce, tender, leafy, with no crunch but enormous flavor, each leaf barely coated with vinaigrette, for the first time, sitting outside under a grape arbor, a few blocks from the Riviera. I was in heaven, not France. Every pore in my tongue seemed alive, ready to savor every taste of food.

When we went to the beach club we were served another astounding combination, tiny grape-size tomatoes mixed with tiny black Niçoise olives. Who knew that tomatoes and olives could be like that, the saltiness better than Cheese-Its. And so it went, every day a revelation. We went to see Giacomettis and Chagalls, in museums small and large. When it came time for me to leave for Paris, Chester told me he had arranged a hotel room for me rather than my staying in his apartment. I was a little uncomfortable with that and couldn't figure out why the plans had changed. It was years later that I found out he was living with a good friend of mine from San Francisco, Judy, and didn't want me to see her picture and things in his apartment. (He always was a charming cad, as you will see.)

I arrived in Paris midday, in June 1966, tanned and happy after a week in Juan-les-Pins, sunning, eating, and learning to make my first omelet. My hotel was a shock. Its tiny entrance was manned by an aging woman behind a scarred wooden counter. The hallway was darkened. There was no one to help me lug my suitcases up the narrow twisting stairs with faded fleur-de-lis patterns on the wallpaper. I was sure I had wound up in a dump.

When I opened the door to my room I gave myself over to Paris, as if to a new lover. It was large and airy, the view, of a park with a few beautiful old homes overlooking it, enhanced by the geraniums on the balcony.

The wallpaper, too, was faded, but of flowers and birds. When the window was opened, the light curtains ruffled. I hardly spent any time in that room, but it was, and is, part of Paris to me. Charming, old, graceful, clean, tastefully furnished, and mine. Looking back, I wonder if I had ever stayed in a hotel room by myself before, in any country, before that trip.

There was a giant bathtub and a bidet in the bathroom. The only time I'd heard about bidets was from a friend who had soaked his socks in one, stopped up the bidet, and the resulting water on the floor had caused such a problem his parents had wound up paying a huge bill to the hotel. I hadn't quite understood what the use of the bidet was, but I gathered French women were fastidious about their parts and it made good sense to me.

I called a girl I knew who was now working for the American embassy, and we made plans to meet when her workday was done. I was tremulous as I went up to the guards, who instead nodded me in with no concern. My friend was waiting for me and took me down to a dining room with softly padded furniture, muted lighting, and a bar. We settled in a sitting area of our own to catch up on our lives.

Within a few minutes, two glasses of champagne showed up on the waiter's tray, and with a flourish he said, "The gentlemen over there were concerned that you were only drinking Coke, and sent these to you." Of course, then, as now, Coke is infinitely more expensive in France than wine. One of the men came over to my friend and spoke to her. He worked in the embassy, too, and they knew each other by sight. With that introduction, we became an ever-expanding party of Americans in Paris. A six-foot-tall American was particularly charming, slightly older than I, perhaps in his mid-thirties to my late twenties. He was trim but not skinny, fair-haired, blue-eyed, well dressed, and articulate. Neil Kirkpatrick frequently did business in Paris.

I can only wish for every young woman that she meet a lover with a huge expense account her first day in Paris and be taken to a three-star restaurant for lunch. My first lunch in Paris, the next day, was with Neil, at Laurent off the Champs-Élysées. It was bright and sunny inside and Neil spoke French well enough to be treated with deference by the maître d'. Of course it might have helped that price was no object those days with Neil, who was a vice president of Max Factor and had a generous expense account.

For dessert we had a soufflé omelet. Since I had just had my first omelet a week before, I hardly knew what to expect. I certainly had no idea what wild strawberries were. This omelet soufflé was a creation of beaten eggs and their whites, nestling red berries smaller than raspberries inside. The soufflé was a puff of delight. It was the first time I had met wild strawberries, whose fleeting season cannot be forced or extended. Ripened in the sun, tenderly picked, worshipfully prepared, they were as akin to the strawberries of my life as sugar is to rock salt. They were these God-given packages of taste, delicate to swallow, exquisite to savor.

Soufflé Omelet with Fraises des Bois

Serves 2

Roughly translated into berries of the forest, these grow wild in many European places. I first met them in the book *Heidi* when I was a young girl. Heidi went strawberry picking with some other young people. Grandfather sat home waiting and dreaming about these incredible berries, with their deep red and full flavor, both sweet and rich. They are unlike any modern strawberry in the US. When the young people had filled their containers with the wild berries, they sold them rather than bring them home. Grandfather, furious, made Heidi taste a coin and bemoaned the berries it replaced. Which was better, he demanded? When I met those berries again at Laurent, I knew they were better than any berry I had ever met. I remember them still. Cosseted in a soufflé as light as air this dish is my favorite way of serving them.

3 large eggs, separated
1–3 tablespoons granulated sugar
⅓ teaspoon vanilla extract
2–3 tablespoons butter
Confectioners' sugar as needed
Crème fraîche (optional)
1½ cup fraises des bois

1. Beat the egg yolks with a tablespoon of the granulated sugar and the vanilla extract in a medium bowl until well combined and slightly thickened.
2. Using an electric mixer, beat the egg whites until they form soft peaks.
3. Fold the egg whites into the egg yolk mixture, using a rubber spatula until most of the egg white can't be seen.
4. Heat a heavy nonstick or omelet pan with the butter until it is foaming.
5. Meanwhile taste the strawberries and add any of the extra granulated sugar if needed.
6. Quickly add the egg mixture to the heavy pan and spread out evenly in the pan. Cover pan and reduce the heat to low. Cook 3 to 4 minutes or until the egg is lightly set on top and the bottom is golden brown. If necessary run the spatula around the pan to release the eggs.
7. Slide the omelet onto a serving dish. Spread the strawberries down the center of the omelet. Fold the omelet in half over the filling. Dust the top with confectioners' sugar.

Divide into two plates if desired. Serve with crème fraîche or other heavy cream, sweetened.

It was not long before I found myself sharing Neil's hotel room, with the approval of the French hotel staff who had been concerned about such a handsome man being alone for so long. When Neil invited me to stay with him at his hotel, I was concerned about what the hotel staff would think about my having a key, coming and going. I imagined that like American motels and hotels, the management were disapproving. He laughed. "They have been worried that I have been here several weeks, alone, and will be delighted. They are French, after all."

It was the first time I saw terry-cloth robes made available to each guest and understood the French love of lovers, cosseting and encouraging them. My time in Paris was glorious, and I left reluctantly. It was a good time for Neil and me to meet. I was already planning to move to New York as soon as I returned from my trip. My annulment was final, my settlement was the money I was traveling on, but I was still wounded from all that had gone before. Neil's divorce was pending and had been equally acrimonious. We were both ready for someone that liked us, if not love. Maybe we didn't even want love from each other. What we had was sufficient.

We cried on each other's shoulders about lost loves, bad marriages, mistakes we had made. We relished our meals in Paris, as well as a good sex life without tensions and complications.

Shortly after I returned to the States, I moved to New York City and a new job and new roommates. I cooked a few days a week at Neil's, simple suppers we both enjoyed, and on occasion cooked for his mother Corrine and stepfather Sol. One day Neil asked me to cook a birthday dinner for Corrine. I dearly loved her, with her perfectly made-up plump face, long acrylic painted nails (the first I'd ever seen), and tastefully chic clothes. Like my mother, she was a Christian Scientist, in large part responsible for my return to Christian Science at that time. We went to church together every Wednesday and Saturday, so we were very close. It was easier to accept her love than Neil's.

His mother had a favorite dish she hadn't been able to get in New York—mountain oysters. As I told Neil, I had a real appreciation for oysters and other seafood, and presumed that mountain oysters were, like mountain trout, a fresh-water variant of some sort. There were a lot of foods I'd never eaten. After all, I had just had my first fresh omelet and first loose leaf lettuce in France the previous summer. Neil picked me up the morning of Corrine's birthday and said we were heading downtown, I assumed to the fish market. But no, we wound up in the slaughterhouse district. That's when I found out we were—I was—cooking not oysters at all, but an oddly oyster-shaped meat, also called lamb fries, which was—were— testicles. I was a bit stunned, but game. I was also a bit stunned to find out that so many animals had testicles. How could I forget the blue balls of my youth, I wondered, where the boys ran around the outside of the car so I could protect and preserve my virtue? Well, I mean I knew all mammals had testicles, I suppose, or something like testicles, but who knew that ducks had them? And veal? And pigs, large and small? And who knew they were so cheap? They were about twenty-five cents a pair, no matter the size. We figured a pair per person would do, but we couldn't figure out what kind Corrine liked, or which were the best, or even what size. I also felt that we needed some for me to practice on.

The butchers, who found it humorous, no doubt, to tell me how to cook them, told me I could slice them in half and sauté them like scaloppini, or batter and deep fry, or roll in crumbs and pan fry, and on and on. They could hardly contain themselves with the debates—whether to peel them or not to peel them, and which kind were best. I soaked it all in and wound up thoroughly confused. We left with nearly thirty dollars' worth of testicles, each carrying two bags full.

Walking down the street, we passed a Chinese man selling snails. They were in tin cans that were about two cups in size. Their price? One dollar. Having previously spent up to ten dollars for the kind that came in the tiny can with the shells piled in a plastic sleeve on top, I was thrilled! What a bargain! We got them whole-sale. We purchased two cans and happily set off for Neil's high-rise on East Eighty-Sixth Street.

Neil dropped me, the snails, and the mountain oysters off. I read one of the cookbooks I had brought with me—which one I cannot remember—and it said to soak the snails in a barrel of water sprin-kled with oatmeal, the barrel covered with a cement block. I was on the eighteenth floor of an apartment on East Eighty-Sixth Street, and there was no barrel and no cement block. I put the snails, still in their shells, in the sink with the oatmeal and water.

Neil's apartment was a typical New York one-bedroom apartment. The dining room table was immediately inside the entrance, to be pulled out during dining. The kitchen was adjacent. The living room formed an *L* with a balcony just outside the sliding glass doors. I covered the table with newspapers and then plates to hold the various types and sizes of mountain oysters. Neil's large butcher's knife in hand, I practiced on the mountain oysters. I peeled some. I cut some in half. I fried some. I marinated some. Testicles piled high on the table, divided by size, I went to the balcony with the cookbooks, sat in the sun and mulled over the dinner.

I dozed, perhaps, in the warm sun. As I stood and walked back to the kitchen, I thought I heard a sound. A little clicking. Standing at the kitchen door, I realized it was the snails, clicking around the kitchen as they hauled their shells.

These were very tiny snails, not French snails at all. They were no bigger than my fingernail. And there were hundreds of them, roaming around Neil's immaculate kitchen, having been rejuvenated by their snack of oatmeal and water, and eager to explore their surroundings. They were between the stove and the refrigerator. On the walls. On the ceilings. On the floor. On the cabinets. And they were alive. All of them. Leaving a trail of snail residue behind them.

I suppose it had been self-evident that they were alive when I put them to soak in the water. But it wasn't, not to me. Now I realized that they were alive, I became squeamish at the idea of picking them up.

I ran next door. There were two men living there together. I hadn't really met them, but I had seen them when I came and went to Neil's. I knocked frantically on the door, and when they came to the door I was too speechless to articulate the problem. They came rushing back into the apartment with me, responding to an unknown emergency.

There, some peeled, some not, some sliced, some not, piled high, all sizes and shapes, were the mountain oysters, testicles with the knife resting on the cutting board. The men took one look at me and turned on their heels. This was a long time before Jeffrey Dahmer, the serial killer of young men who kept some of his victim's parts in a freezer, but it was clear they had an instantaneous impression of a mass murderer or at least a mass castrator. "No," I said, "you don't understand." They kept running, to the elevator. I ran after them.

When I caught up with them, sans knife, I must have looked easy to overcome by force, so they listened. They started laughing in disbelief and followed me to the apartment. Bless their hearts, they helped get all those snails up while I put the mountain oysters in the refrigerator.

Neil returned with the rest of the food when the job was half done, and helped with the rest, laughing as hard as the rest of us. I proceeded to boil the snails in their shells, then remove them from the shells and bake the shells to sterilize them, like the book said. And then it hit me. These were New York City snails. They had been roaming around, God knew where, eating whatever. The oatmeal was to clean out their digestive tract, and I didn't believe it had been cleaned in the short time it had taken them to pep up and jump out of the sink.

I threw them all away and sent Neil out for more snails. The kind that came with a sleeve of shells. And the mountain oysters? The best kinds are duck and veal, fried. But Corrine wanted the lamb ones, and of those we had plenty. I'm a specialist in them now.

I have long given up remembering Neil as I lie in bed some nights, but I often remember my first Parisian dessert and the wild strawberries. I was not prepared for their exquisiteness, the sumptuousness of the cream enveloping them, or the weightlessness of the omelet soufflé into which they were tucked. I frequently make soufflé omelets at home, usually limited to using raspberries or strawberries, but these days we can find crème fraîche or mascarpone to accompany this soufflé. And I've been known to wake up laughing about testicles, large and small. I even have some quail ones, the size of small pearls, in my freezer, sent by the owner of South Carolina's quail farm. She doesn't expect me to reorder them, she said, as no one thinks they are delicious, but she wanted me to know their size.

Majorcan Snails

When I was thirty I found myself chef of a restaurant in rural Majorca—one hour's drive from the major city, Palma. I neither spoke the language nor had worked in a restaurant (except a coffee shop in Cambridge) before. I could hardly believe I had been hired.

My then-husband, David, whom I had married after Neil and I had broken up, was the bookkeeper. I was chef. Neither of us spoke Catalan—the patois of French and Spanish that is spoken in Majorca. I had barely scraped by college Spanish, confident I would never need it. Wrong again. The maître d' and one of the waiters spoke English, but the maids who doubled as prep cooks did not. The restaurant was in an old finca, or farmhouse, built around an olive press with an extensive garden. There was a massive olive tree just outside of the door of our bedroom and I could pick figs and roses during the short walk up to the restaurant.

A few evenings later, it rained just as we closed the restaurant for the evening. We hadn't seen much rain. We welcomed it and that particular, fresh smell rain has after a long dry spell. Taking a drive down the dark and winding country roads, we started seeing little lights dotting the fields. We were bemused—even, perhaps, a little alarmed. Could it be poachers? If so, what on earth were they poaching, and why were they using flashlights to do so?

The next morning, we were eager to share our observations and went up to the restaurant together quite early, finding all the staff—waiters, gardeners, and kitchen staff alike—already there and prepared to solve the mystery. All around the kitchen were buckets of snails. Alive. I eyed them warily, having familiarity with live snails. The lights we had seen were all the local people out with lanterns and flashlights, looking for snails. In fact, the staff viewed us with a bit of derision for not having a few kilos of our own to add to the stash.

There was a great deal of joking about how many snails everyone could eat, most people claiming a hundred each, and a long discussion about the preparation. The upshot was that the snails were washed and placed back in the buckets. The tops of the buckets were covered with a wire mesh to prevent their wiggling out. The snails were to be fed cornmeal, rosemary, and/or fennel until Sunday, which was several days away, and a day when we didn't serve lunch.

After church on Sunday the kitchen, normally empty, was full of rapidly talking people. The maids, their husbands, the wife of the arrogant maître d', all moving around, hands in sinks, scrubbing snails, rinsing ducks, separating eggs, or chopping herbs.

I joined the maître d' in moving several tall stockpots to the back of the stove. To each we added a dead and cleaned duck, a dead and cleaned chicken, handfuls of thyme and fennel from the garden, dozens of peeled garlic cloves, cut-up onions, and, finally, the clean snails. We opened several bottles of a favorite Spanish white wine and poured them atop the snails, then added water to fill the stockpots three-quarters of the way to their brims, and covered them with lids.

Turning the gas on high under the pots, we waited until bubbles appeared and then turned the heat down to a simmer. The aroma was torturous, for we were all ravenous. Meanwhile, we whisked eggs with oil to make the aioli, the local farm-raised eggs mounting easily. We pulled down the ripe red Majorcan tomatoes from the white-tiled arched hallway where they were strung together, separated by knots, to semi-dry. One group chopped the tomatoes until, after what seemed to be a very long time to me and my stomach, the pot was deemed "done." Pulling out the chicken and duck with tongs, we cooled them until we could remove the flesh from the bones and discard the skin. We scooped up the snails and put them in another pot while we boiled the strained stock down to a rich, full-flavored broth, as sumptuous as any eaten in a three-star restaurant.

Finally, duck, chicken, and snails were stirred into the thick broth and we ladled the mixture into bowls, adding dollops of the aioli. I headed to the terrace, where I could look at the acres of fig and olive trees and the rosebushes lining the walks, and eat my snails slowly, wondering at the magic of the midnight rain.

How I Got Started

On my first day in 1959 as emergency substitute cook of the Harvard Coop, I reached with confidence into the oven to retrieve the tuna fish casserole. It smelled like it should, I knew, for my mother had made it repeatedly for the family, although with cream of mushroom soup and American cheese rather than sautéed onions and a cheese sauce like the newspaper recipe I had followed. I could hear a little gurgle from the oven, which meant all was going well, I thought; when I last peeked in, there had been little bubbles on the surface, looking like it was cooking as it should. But I couldn't see the breadcrumbs, which in the recipe picture were on the top, and had been sprinkled over my casseroles as well.

When the first long Pyrex dish emerged from the huge oven, grasped by my thick cotton hot pads, I saw a bubbling cauldron of grease and gray rather than tinges of light brown crumbs dappling the cheese sauce that was to hold the conglomeration together.

Panic rose in my throat as I experienced every cook's nightmare—the inability to feed waiting mouths. At nineteen, I was ill prepared to cook dinner for the twenty ravenous young men and women milling around the dining room of this international student house in Cambridge, Massachusetts. I had desperately wanted to succeed at this meal. Now it looked like I might fail. Again.

The members of the co-op in 1959 had been reluctant to let me take on this task. Like my father, they wanted their dinner on time. Each resident paid fifteen dollars a month for dinners, and ate, boardinghouse-style, at six o'clock each night. My rent was thirty-five dollars a month for a room I shared with three other girls. I had already shown my incompetence at my first agreed-upon chore.

The Harvard Coop had no resident manager. It was as close as I ever came to a commune, but it was a far cry from that. Still, it was daring, as I was sharing quarters with both men and women, or, as I called them, boys and girls. We were a diverse lot—some MIT students, some Harvard, others who were researchers and/or graduate students, and me. None of us had any money. There were four girls in my room, and even at that the rent seemed high.

We each had an assigned task. Mine had been forwarding the mail to residents who had moved away. I rarely did it, putting the mail in the top drawer of the hall chest up with my good intentions. Two of the Mormon students, who had left to go on a Mission, came back to the house to visit, but also to see what happened to their mail. The mail included draft notices advising them to show up on what turned out to be the next day, for active duty in the Army. Everyone, including myself, was pretty disgusted with my disorganized indolence.

Simultaneously, the cook, a heavyset woman with massive arms and a tendency to sing spirituals with a thick Boston accent as she cooked, got sick. Her husband called us to say she would be out for a few weeks for an operation. In order to get myself in the good graces of my housemates, I volunteered on the spot to take over the cook's job since I kept my own hours at my paying job, coming and going as I pleased. I knew I liked cooking, had spent some time in the kitchen visiting with the cook, and thought I could do it. I didn't really feel there was an option—I was never good at chores, per se, and couldn't see myself doing anything else. I had started the day of the tuna fish casserole.

Maybe it felt a little like a hair shirt, this idea of cooking every day, but I thought I could do it. Until my greasy tuna fish casserole stared me in the face. Now it looked like I was going to sink deeper into failure and shame. I had moved to Cambridge to become a new person, and found I still was not the woman I wanted to be.

I had multiplied the entire recipe by three in order to have enough food, and miscalculated, hence the resulting disaster, a layer of grease topping a gloppy lumpy slosh of milk, flour, and cheese, sprinkled throughout with breadcrumbs and clumps of tuna fish on the bottom. I felt a burning in my throat—a familiar feeling when I thought all was lost and I would flop and did not want to, did not want to, did not want to, fail. I needed to fix this, to find a way to turn the disaster into a modicum of success, or at least something edible.

In desperation, I improvised. Turning the oven up to Broil, I opened a commercial sack of the pale white bread common to the times—pre-sliced, white, soft, and squishy. Spreading the bread onto a metal cookie sheet, I ran the pan under the broiler, praying I would remember to remove it before the toast burned.

After skimming the excess grease the dishes' contents looked a lot better. Pouring everything left in the dish into a huge dented pot with a long handle, I turned the heat underneath the pot on high and kept stirring until the whole mess inside it came to a boil and the ingredients combined to appear to be a sauce holding tuna fish. I poured in frozen English peas from the freezer, stirring until I smelled the toast browning.

I reached in, just in time to prevent burning, and pulled out the pan. I slid the toast onto oval serving dishes rescued from one of the cupboards and turned the toast over to reveal the white un-toasted side. Now was not the time for such niceties as toasting on both sides. I took the pot of sauce, tuna, and peas and poured it over the slices of half-done toast. I stuck my finger into the near-empty pan and scraped around the sides before putting my finger in my mouth. Yum. I had succeeded!!!

Walking into the dining room, my bounty on the platter, I looked at the waiting faces. "Tuna fish à la king," I said, renaming the meal I was presenting so proudly. My heart was beating with excitement, and my throat had eased up enough for me to speak.

They dug in, and that was that. No one complained, as they sometimes did for the regular cook, and I scuttled away to finish the brownies that would cap my meal. Suddenly I felt victorious and happy. They had liked it! Or, at least, hadn't disliked it enough to tell me. That moment of holding my success aloft was my gold Oscar. I had won.

Within the first few days I understood the difficulty of multiplying a recipe by more than two, because it is not easy to get the ingredients measured accurately—particularly when using an uneven number—and because food changes as it "grows." Three times as much fat is not needed to cook three times as many onions, for instance. I learned how important good smells were to appetite and cooking onions permeated the house with an aroma of well-being. I learned not to change a recipe drastically when I had hungry mouths to feed.

The expectant look on the faces of the diners—a captive audience, in a way—was important to me, just as it had been important to me as student director of *Our Town* to hear the applause when the play was over. I wanted that look to change into one of satisfaction and elation. And I learned I loved cooking. I was happier in the kitchen than I was anywhere else. Along with that happiness came what I call the triumph of taste—that moment when one knows one's food is good, just before sending it out to be consumed.

My second night as cook the Israeli boy, Uri, an exacting scientist, helped me fix spaghetti and meatballs. The recipe called for twenty meatballs. I again multiplied the ingredients in the recipe, but this time by an even number, and used some judgment rather than following illegible jotted numbers. I pulled all the ingredients together with my hands and arms, as I had seen the cook do, combining them as I moved, kneading them into one. I took a taste and liked what I had done, albeit raw. I passed the cookbook to Uri, who had no frame of reference, to follow. When Uri read to make twenty meatballs, he did just that, as unquestioningly as he would add two ingredients together in a chemistry class. He shaped them carefully and methodically into twenty balls the size of softballs before slipping them into the oven. I wasn't watching, and he didn't question his assumptions.

It was nearly time to serve before I saw what he had done and realized I had another calamity. Not only were his softballs too big to be called meatballs, they were still red and raw in the middle. Inedible in their present state, I dropped them in a couple of large frying pans, poked and tore them apart, sautéing them as fast as I could before topping the sauce and spaghetti with them. Platter once again held high, I announced the name of the dish—spaghetti and meat sauce. From this I learned to read the body of the recipe and make changes in the body as well as in the ingredient list, adapting what I had to the number of people I had to serve. I learned that a recipe is only as good as the interpreter, that it was not as inviolate as a chemistry formula, requiring all the senses, including a sixth sense, a hunch about the way a recipe should go.

My mother always said I was mean when I was hungry. Not only was (and am) I, but all the inhabitants of our house seemed to be. A late meal or an inadequate meal caused ill-will and crossness. Whoever was in control of the food was in control of the mood of the co-op. Later I was to understand this had been true in my family as well as in the world. Food is the most powerful control issue in a home, nation, the world. Without it, little runs right.

I also learned never to tell anyone what you are cooking until you know what it will be, particularly if you have never cooked it before. There is a fine line between anticipation and disappointment, and the inexperienced cook is better served seducing with mystery and aroma.

Each day brought new lessons, going from fear to a growing feeling of satisfaction. I basked in the approval of the diners, feeling a fulfillment and contentment mixed with joy that was new to me. The rest of my weeks of cooking went so well I couldn't wait to get to the co-op after my job at Massachusetts General.

When the cook returned to work at the co-op, I was bereft. I didn't do anything else as well as I had cooking for the co-op, nor did I enjoy any other work I did, certainly not my paying job, as much. To find something I loved, like cooking, that I was good at, was a gift of enormous proportions. On the phone my mother begged me not to become a cook, rattling off a list in opposition to the idea—I would have to work at night with men, the work would be too hard for such a skinny girl since I couldn't lift those heavy pots, and, the clincher, Southern ladies didn't cook. Cooks were hired help and treated as such. They were not part of the party, or embraced enthusiastically for their successes, as I was at the co-op.

Mother wanted to believe she had brought me up to be a lady. In short, would I be marriageable if I was a cook, a hired person who had no stature? (I wonder if she ever thought she had succeeded in making me a lady, a person who did not swear, and would have worn white gloves if they were still in fashion; a woman who was gentle and prayerful, always followed the correct form outlined for wives in the Officers Manual of the US Army.) She had loved being a colonel's wife, the power and respectability it gave her, and grieved when it was gone. She wanted that for me, even while knowing I was not the kind of person who could ever deal with the restrictions. Mother would always just shake her head when people complimented her about me, as if she were surprised that I had accomplished anything, because she was not sure I was a lady.

I knew no lady who worked in a kitchen, although I knew there were a few that owned restaurants and were hostesses in their own restaurants. In 1959 there were hardly any female waitresses in fine-dining restaurants, much less female chefs. I figured I couldn't even get a job, which was probably true, and that my mother was right. I knew nothing about cooking schools, if there were any. When

Julia Child became a national figure on PBS a dozen years later, she made it possible; even though she never worked in a restaurant to my knowledge, she elevated females to a respectable level in the kitchen.

From the moment we met, Dorothea Benton Frank taught me. Though she never told me to lose weight, she shared a tip from her fashion days and told me emphatically to wear V-necked black T-shirts to look skinnier. One look at my arm flaps and she added I should always wear sleeves.

She shared that if one can write funny, one can write one's own ticket. For her, writing humor wasn't hard. According to her, she kept a pin in her Pucci pocket for pricking her own pomposity. Recently I reread all of the introductions to her books and laughed at each one, no matter how tragic, no matter the circumstances, and decided rather than a pomposity-pricking pin she used a pen she kept in her Gucci. The pen works better as it contains ink.

She had many virtues, including her love for her family, her generosity to charities, her leadership, and the fact she never wrote about me. When we met I had a certain leeriness of writers. Pat Conroy had written what my husband calls an affectionate carica-ture of me in *Pat Conroy's Cookbook*, "borrowing" parts of my own snail and mountain oyster story and embellishing it. Anne River Siddons had morphed me into a character composite with a friend's peccadilloes in *Hill Towns*, which had also hurt my feelings. It had taken me a while to challenge Anne's husband, Heyward, about it, as in the book "my" character had had some romantic sprees and included a pass at Heyward. Did Heyward really think I had made a pass at him? It was hard to believe. We had not one spark between us, much less a spark of lust on my part. Had he told Anne that to make her jealous, as some husbands do? Or did Anne make it up with delusions about Heyward's prowess? When I brought the book up, "Oh, no," he said, "it wasn't you. That incident was all about a mutual friend of ours I'll call Hortense. She got drunk and made a pass years ago." However, as an author Dottie was always direct and open with me, and I figured if she did write about me she would at least make me skinny, sober, and faithful.

We had more in common than wearing black V-necked T-shirts with sleeves. We loved food, cooking, reading, and shared a favorite Charleston dress shop, sometimes even finding out we had purchased the identical items. Cooking was important to both of us and I knew it from her first book, *Sullivan's Island*. One either wants to cook, eat something, or have sex as one reads her books. Eating is easiest. Her food is not pretentious, it is all eatable food, duplicable food, food that will make you hungry, even if you have just eaten a meal.

Her female characters are allowed to be titillated—horny even—when looking at a certain man. They are even allowed to sleep with men they wouldn't ever want to marry. Fortunately for her, Dottie started writing in an era when women could have sex in a book. I took a writing course in 1962 on how to write a romance novel, and it seared me through and through. The teacher said that books didn't sell when women had sex. To be a successful romance writer, he said, the women had to be virgins, and even their passions would stop short of fulfillment until marriage. I had taken the class to learn how to write, and so I wrote about the first time I had been raped. He told me in no uncertain terms that didn't happen to romance novel women. So I gave up.

Not Dottie. She never gave up. She was determined to write so she could earn enough money to buy her family home when her husband resisted.

Dottie's characters have a way of making readers laugh at how silly relationships are that bind sensible women to husbands and lovers with few redeeming qualities, a full measure of hot air and what we politely call Dick-Do in the South. (This rampant male disease is when one's stomach extends more than one's D . . . Do.) Often I wonder if she just took the things she loved about Peter, her husband, and reversed them in her cads.

Her love of food showed in her generosity of entertaining. No one went hungry at a party of Dottie's, no matter how many people showed up. The first party I attended at her family's Sullivan's Island home, the one she purchased from her siblings with money earned with that break-out novel, was a party for SEBA, the South Eastern Bookseller's Association. Famous writers lined the piazza with the swimming pool in the background, the buffet was plentiful and ongoing, and the caterer exceptional. If the piazza had caved in, as has happened at other parties for more foolish folk who overloaded them, every important Southern author would have been silenced. A clever way to get rid of competition, perhaps, but not Dottie's style.

The kitchen was the center of her parties and Dottie reigned there, cooking shrimp and grits with her daughter Victoria at her side. A college graduate working for her father, Peter, Victoria's true ambition was to cook. Whenever I went to New York, I would visit Victoria and we would eat out somewhere and talk about food. One day, Dottie told me Victoria wanted to attend cooking school. Dottie was dubious, perhaps for the same reason my mother was. And I think she wanted Victoria to be able to have her own earning ability, too, if she needed it. It didn't surprise me Victoria wanted to cook professionally so I made a list of all the jobs available where Victoria could earn her way in the world including personal chef, food writer, food stylist, and restaurant chef as well as many others. I wrote Dottie a letter and enclosed the list. The next thing I knew Victoria was enrolled in Culinary School. Oh, and she met a good guy there.

What surprised me about Dottie's response was how seriously she took Victoria's longing for a culinary education, how she considered her approach, the importance for Victoria to have a paying career, and later, her enthusiasm for her daughter's chosen path. It was perhaps the thing I admired most about her, that ability to reconsider, change one's mind and enthusiastically support that which she had opposed. Mind you, she kept her eye on the chefs whose kitchens hired Victoria. If a woman could have a character swing an andiron at a faithless husband, imagine what she would do with an iron skillet if someone harmed Victoria.

I encouraged Dottie to add recipes to her novels. I have never forgiven myself for not insisting she let me proofread any recipe she used. She put in her sister's pound cake. Recipes have a way of dropping ingredients, and slashes for fractions are the very worst, as I know all too well. The final instructions dropped an ingredient much to Dottie's chagrin and brought her countless reader letters. She never included a recipe in a book again. My hope then was for Victoria to write a cookbook with her mother. And Victoria may do that yet. I've included the corrected pound cake recipe here, with hopes her sister will forgive me for the earlier one and her readers will think of her when they bake it.

Lynn Benton Bagnal's Pound Cake

Dorothea adapted the pound cake recipe of her sister, Lynn, who lives on Edisto Island in South Carolina, for use in *Shem Creek*. Alas there was a technical glitch so something was not right. Dottie subsequently listed the correct recipe on her website, but not until she bemoaned the mistake to me. Southerners clarify the flour they are using as biscuits are so prevalent many bakers only keep self-rising flour on hand. Lynn, who makes four pound cakes a week, uses salted butter, but the recipe here uses salt and unsalted butter.

POUND CAKE

3 cups plain flour—not self-rising
1 teaspoon salt
2 sticks unsalted butter
3 cups sugar
5 large eggs
1 cup heavy whipping cream
2 tablespoons vanilla

1. Preheat oven to 325° F. Arrange racks to fit tube pan in center of oven.
2. Generously grease and lightly flour a tube pan.
3. Sift flour and salt together three times.
4. Beat butter with sugar until light and fluffy in the bowl of an electric mixer.

5. Add eggs, one at a time. Beat only until each disappears.

6. Blend in 1 cup flour followed by ½ cup heavy cream.

7. Repeat with another cup flour and the rest of the heavy cream. Add remaining flour to begin and end with flour.

8. Fold in vanilla.

9. Add batter to pan, level it and rap lightly on the counter to knock out the air bubbles. Place pan in center of the oven and bake for 1 hour and 15 minutes, or until it's browned on top and begins to pull away from the side of the pan. Remove from oven. Wait 10 minutes and invert on a cake plate. Do not cover until cool to touch.

LEMON GLAZE

2 tablespoons cornstarch

⅛ teaspoon salt

¾ cup sugar

⅔ cup water

3 tablespoons lemon juice

1 egg yolk

Lemon rind, finely grated

1 tablespoon butter

1. Stir cornstarch and salt into sugar.

2. In heavy pot or double boiler, add water, lemon juice, and egg yolk.

3. Put over high heat and stir in dry ingredients.

4. Cook until you see a bubble or it thickens.

5. Remove from heat, stir in finely grated lemon rind and butter.

6. Cool and pour over cake.

Dottie hosted sit-down dinners at her homes, particularly the final home they purchased on Sullivan's Island, with room for a catered sit-down dinner for Victoria's engagement and other special occasions. If the food was her forte, her seating was devilish. It takes a certain kind of humor to seat the town's matriarch with the town's rake.

The last time I saw Dottie was at a weekend book event for her readers, held in Charleston. Those weekends are grueling with events, signings, and late nights. Close to the last minute she asked if I could show up and make biscuits at the event hotel because she was exhausted. Already there when I showed up with my biscuit gear was Carrie Morey, who had cooked enough biscuits for the entire crowd at her restaurant, Hot Little Biscuit. Carrie and I are Pork Chop friends, as Dottie knew.

Pork Chop friends are friends who subscribe to the Pork Chop Theory, created by Shirley Corriher and me. She had been my student at Rich's Cooking School, but as so often happens, she was more gifted than I. We were members of the same culinary associations and competing for business opportunities. We had a choice. Our lives had been full of jobs where there was just one spot for a woman, and to get it you had to, as one woman cook said, "push everyone else out of the boat." It didn't suit us, so we decided we wouldn't do it that way. Somehow we developed the theory that if there is one pork chop in a pan it will go dry, but if there are two or more pork chops in a pan the fat from one will feed the other. We determined to make room for others in the pan and very shortly after were elected to be on the same board of directors of an international association.

Now there are many other Pork Chops in the culinary world. Carrie Morey is one. We've shared the stage, employees, steered each other to book contracts and helped each other whenever a leg up—or some fat in the pan—was needed. We each think our biscuits are better than the other's but eat each other's enthusiastically. A biscuit from one of us is a damn good biscuit. Now that I think about it, tired as she was when she arrived, Dottie was being a Pork

Chop again that day, making a spotlight for me and Carrie, and telling everyone to buy our books.

Dottie and I were always going to meet in New York and eat escargot and frogs legs together, enough garlic to distance ourselves from everyone around us. Her favorite story of mine was my snail and mountain oyster story, which Pat Conroy partially borrowed for his cookbook. No matter, I tell it better, but it's not the only time snails played a role in my life.

About Nathalie Dupree

Nathalie Dupree is the author of fourteen cookbooks. She is best known for her approachability and her understanding of Southern cooking, having started the New Southern Cooking movement now found in many restaurants throughout the United States, and co-authoring *Mastering the Art of Southern Cooking*.

Nathalie, as she is known to her fans, has won wide recognition for her work, including four James Beard Awards and numerous others. She was also founding chairman of the Charleston Wine and Food Festival and a founding member of many culinary organizations, including the prestigious Southern Foodways and the International Association of Culinary Professionals.

She is married to author Jack Bass and lives in Charleston, South Carolina. She travels extensively.

Essays by Dorothea Benton Frank

Back in 2018, Dottie, as I always called her, wrote three essays for her readers because carpal tunnel syndrome prevented her from signing tip-in sheets. (Tip-ins are what we call the pieces of paper with an author's actual signature that we bind into a book.)

Dottie actually wanted to buy a few tubes of bright red lipstick and kiss the pages, but I thought some essays would be less likely to smear.

Carrie Feron

Editor

Dorothea Benton Frank's Letter to Her Readers I

Dear Family,

I wanted to add something to the back of this book to pose a question to y'all. Is the world becoming meaner, crazier, and more unkind, or is it my imagination?

So last week I was watching the news on mute and trying to figure out how to use my new Instant Pot, when I thought I saw a peacock at an airport on the screen. I restored the sound and there was the story. A woman at Newark Airport was trying to board a United Airlines flight with a huge live peacock. She claimed it was her emotional support animal. I'm not kidding. Emotional. Support. Animal. It wasn't like you could put that bird in the overhead or in a little crate under the seat. This bird had a five-foot-long train. What if the little darling opened its feathers into a fan and decided to hop around, perhaps making a deposit here and there? The whole world would need emotional support animals. That's what.

Let's talk about social media. What about people posting their vacation pictures while they're still on vacation? Then they're surprised and upset to come home and find out their houses have been robbed. Seriously? Never mind naughty selfies going viral. Whose fault is that? Please! And please, before you take another selfie, check the background. Not that social media is all bad, because it isn't. In addition to hearing from readers I also get to visit with my family and old friends who live far away. I'm just saying, use your heads, people. As to snark? Could we please lighten up? Is it necessary to be so mean? You know, growing up in the South a girl could be as ugly as a mud fence, but if she had nice manners that was all that mattered. So what if the only guy who asked you to prom weighed three hundred pounds? He loves his momma and he has beautiful manners. That's what my momma would've said. My favorite character of all time is Miss Lavinia from *Plantation*. Her best quote? *Remember! Good manners are the moisturizer of life.*

Sometimes I don't know whether to laugh or cry. Mostly I laugh because there's no point wasting my tears on other people's lunacy. But it seems to me the state of the world has taken a dubious turn. Or maybe I'm just out of touch. It's possible.

Anyway, I could cite as many examples of this kind of behavior as I'm sure you could. The increasingly off-the-wall things people do is why I'll never run out of plot. Like we say up here in Yankee territory, I should only live long enough to use the material I have on my desk just today, y'all. (I hold dual citizenship.)

People ask me how I get the ideas for my books and where the characters come from. Maybe the more interesting point is, *How do you know when it's time to stop trying to change the world and to start writing?* Long before I published my first book my husband and I took a vacation. We were in Ravello, Italy, some twenty-five years ago coincidentally overimbibing with Gore Vidal and a bunch of his friends. (I've never had the right moment to use this story until now.) There must have been eight or ten of us gathered around the banquettes in the bar in the Hotel Palumbo. I swear, fate took us there. I knew Gore Vidal lived in Ravello and I held out a faint hope that he might appear in the restaurant that night. He did. So I asked the bartender to send him a message that some American fans would be delighted to buy him a drink in the bar after dinner. When he appeared, neck scarf tossed jauntily over his shoulder, I saw the bartender upturn a bottle of Johnnie Black and take a long chug. Back then Mr. Vidal had that kind of unnerving presence and effect on people.

We introduced ourselves, he and his friend were as charming as they could be, and we ordered several rounds of drinks, discussing life above the Amalfi Coast and what a dream it was to live in Italy. His friends continued to appear and join us. I'm sure he thought we were a couple of nincompoops, but I didn't care. I was working up the nerve to ask him a question.

"Mr. Vidal," I finally said, "how do you know when it's time to start writing?"

"Are you writing a book?" he asked.

"I'm thinking about it," I said.

He paused, leaned back, and looked at me quite seriously. After a few minutes he answered my question.

He said, "You'll write your book when you can't *not* write your book."

I knew it was true and I was almost to that point. Several months after we returned home I began to write *Sullivan's Island*. By the way, my husband, Peter, ever the gentleman, picked up the tab for Gore Vidal and his friends. Five hundred dollars. Peter teased me about it for years.

Anyway, the point of this little segue and the peacock story is that when the world has had enough nonsense the pendulum will start swinging the other way. And when you need to express yourself, you will. I owe Mr. Vidal a great debt and he owes my husband a retaliatory cocktail. No, he wouldn't owe us anything. I get to tell this story and to be fair, he gave me a lot of encouragement as the evening went on.

Writing is like that—your need to speak starts choking you and you write to be heard. And to make your point or points and to be understood. But you have to mold your story in such a way that people want to hear it. It's even better if people ask you to tell them a story.

I find that humor is one of the more powerful tools in my approach to fiction. We probably all need to learn to laugh at ourselves a bit. How about, we all need to laugh more. The world is a crazy place, especially lately.

In the pages of this book, *By Invitation Only,* I'm playing *what if* again. And I'm asking you to decide who are *the Haves* and who are the *Have Nots.* Perception is everything. But sometimes things aren't really what they seem to be. I hope you'll enjoy this, my nineteenth novel; I'd love to hear from you.

Wishing you every good thing,
Dorothea Benton Frank

Instant Pot Hoppin' John

Serves 4 to 6

It's good to remember a couple of things when the world seems to have gone completely nuts. First, in spite of everything, humans never lose their capacity to invent marvelous things, like the Instant Pot, my new favorite kitchen tool. And second, holding on to a few simple traditions can provide us ballast against the buffeting winds of craziness and remind us that everything is fleeting, and that includes the bad stuff. Eating Hoppin' John on New Year's Day to ensure good luck in the year ahead is just that sort of tradition. And cooking the black-eyed peas and rice in an Instant Pot means that the good luck can be on the table in a fraction of the time.

4 tablespoons (½ stick) unsalted butter

1 red bell pepper, seeded and cored, cut into ½-inch dice

1 green bell pepper, seeded and cored, cut into ½-inch dice

1 jalapeño, seeds and ribs removed if desired, finely chopped (optional)

2 celery stalks, cut into ¼-inch dice

1 yellow onion, cut into ¼-inch dice

4 garlic cloves, finely chopped

8 ounces (about 1¼ cups) dried black-eyed peas, picked over and rinsed

8 ounces smoked ham, cut into ½-inch dice (about 1½ cups)

4 cups low-sodium chicken broth

1 teaspoon dried thyme

1 teaspoon freshly ground black pepper

2 bay leaves

1½ cups long-grain white rice

½ teaspoon kosher salt

4 green onions (white and light green parts), thinly sliced

Hot sauce, for serving

Turn an Instant Pot to Sauté and melt the butter. Add the red and green bell peppers, jalapeño (if using), celery, onion, and garlic and cook, stirring occasionally, until the vegetables are slightly softened, about 4 minutes.

Stir in the black-eyed peas, ham, broth, thyme, black pepper, and bay leaves.

Close and lock the lid. Use the Manual button to set the Instant Pot to high pressure for 10 minutes. When the cooking time is complete, let the cooker go to Keep Warm mode for 10 minutes. Using a towel to protect your hand, twist the steam-release handle on the lid to Venting to release the remaining pressure.

Meanwhile, rinse the rice under cold water until the water runs clear. Drain thoroughly.

Open the lid. Gently stir in the rinsed rice and salt. Close the lid and twist the steam-release handle back to Steaming. Use the Manual button to set the Instant Pot to high pressure for 6 minutes.

When the cooking time is complete, let the cooker go to Keep Warm mode for 10 minutes. If the pressure has not yet released entirely, use a towel to protect your hand and twist the steam-release handle on the lid to Venting to release the remaining pressure.

Open the pot; the mixture should be moist but not soupy. Remove and discard the bay leaves. Scatter the green onions on top. Use a large fork to gently fluff the Hoppin' John and incorporate the green onions.

Serve in individual dishes, passing the hot sauce at the table.

Dorothea Benton Frank's Favorite Cocktails: Limoncello Spritz

With a nod to the town of Ravello, here's a perfect Italian-inspired sparkler: the classic Italian liqueur Limoncello, brought together with vodka, brightened up with fresh lemon juice, and fizzed up with a big pour of sparkling wine. Tart and lively, it's an excellent pairing for Hoppin' John, its bright acidity cutting right through the substantial, hearty dish.

¾ ounce vodka
¾ ounce Limoncello (Luxardo recommended)
½ ounce fresh lemon juice
¼ ounce simple syrup
Sparkling wine

Combine all ingredients except sparkling wine in cocktail shaker with ice. Shake vigorously, then strain into a wineglass with fresh ice. Top with 2 ounces of sparkling wine. Garnish with a thin lemon wheel and a sprig of lemon verbena.

By Carey Jones and John D. McCarthy, authors of *Be Your Own Bartender: A Sure-Fire Guide to Finding (and Making) the Perfect Drink for You*, published November 2018; johnandcarey.com

Dorothea Benton Frank's Letter to Her Readers II

Dear Readers,

When you announce to friends and family that you intend to earn your living as a professional writer, they look at you like you've got a loose screw. Maybe I do, but so far it's working out a lot better than either they or I could have predicted. So I thought I'd share with you what my writing life looks like and how it all began.

My father had been home from World War II for a decade before I came into the world in 1951. He served in Europe, where he followed Patton's army and taught and demonstrated bomb disposal, actually publishing a manual on the topic. Somewhere in this world there is a picture of my father, the major, sitting on a live bomb, a huge thing of probably ten or more feet in length with fins on one end. He's smoking a cigar and laughing. Figures.

As a child, I loved newspapers (the funnies, especially) and I loved books. So did my dad. I can remember every night when he came home from work, he would eat supper and then he would read the *Charleston Evening Post*, now the *Post and Courier*. When he was sufficiently caught up on the world, sometimes we would take a drive down to Mr. Louie Burmester's place of business, just a few blocks away on Sullivan's Island. It was just the two of us. He would shoot the breeze with Mr. Louie and I'd enjoy a small vanilla ice cream cone on the house. Then I was allowed to choose a Golden Book, which he would read to me later that evening at bedtime. I think they were twenty-five cents. Anyway, this little excursion didn't happen every night, but we made the trip together often enough for me to amass a small mountain of children's books. By chance, the night before he died, he read me every single one. He was just forty-two and I was only six months past my fourth birthday. My mother was devastated and never got over losing him. Well, to be honest, she recovered well enough to marry and sadly bury two more husbands. They were lovely men.

By the time I was seven, my older siblings were all out of the house. My sister married, and my brothers either joined the Coast Guard, went to boarding school in Texas, or moved to California seeking fame and fortune in the music business. I became sort of an only child. Basically, I had a childhood with enough drama that could turn anyone into a writer.

Stella Maris Grammar School in Mount Pleasant, South Carolina, was where I would receive my primary school education. We spent our days under the firm hand of the Sisters of Charity and the stalwart nuns of Our Lady of Mercy. They were dedicated to expanding our minds and saving our heathen souls while imbuing us with a love of God and a fear of the Devil. We were taught to understand our faith through the Baltimore Catechism. We learned that our purpose on this earth was to know God, to love God, and to serve Him in this world. We gave up candy for Lent, we said rosaries and other prayers called, believe it or not, "ejaculations" to work off time in Purgatory, and we did penance for sins yet to be committed. We won holy cards in spelling bees and threw overripe persimmons at each other during recess.

It was roughly 1959. I was a young girl of around eight years when I realized we didn't have a school newspaper. Working as a school journalist seemed to me to be a perfect extracurricular activity. We had one big campus that consisted of a kindergarten and grades one through eight. I thought, surely there must be enough going on to produce some kind of a newspaper. A monthly seemed appropriate. I pointed this out to Sister Miriam, our principal, and told her I had a plan.

She listened and smiled at me and said, "Well then, let's go start us a newspaper."

I was thrilled. It was my first publishing experience. My plan was to ask each class to submit one page of news and if they wanted to, they could include a cartoon. My secret was that I would write a Dear Abby–type column called Ask Stella. There was a box—probably an empty tissue box—where students could discreetly write out a question anonymously, drop it in, and Stella would answer. What made me think I could offer valuable advice to eighth graders is anyone's guess. I think we published three or four issues before the whole venture fizzled. Maybe the novelty had worn off. I remember being a little disappointed. But here's what I remember most—the smell of mimeograph ink. And what it felt like to organize a team and to put writing out there for others to read. There was criticism. There were kudos. It was worth it. It was also the beginning of coming to understand myself and of some deep-seated desire to be understood by others. To have a voice and have it heard seemed very important, even then.

The fifties and Catholic school did not really go hand in hand with self-expression. In fact, we were unquestioning, well-behaved, polite little lambs for the most part. We did our jobs by doing massive amounts of homework and projects, but we kept our opinions to ourselves.

Time marched on and soon the civil rights movement began. There was the Orangeburg Massacre, the bombing in Birmingham, and the marches on Selma and Washington, DC. Then came the Vietnam War and the women's rights movement. My teenage years were fueled by heated debates and massive change all around and in my world. And guess what? Suddenly, I had opinions. I wasn't afraid to voice them because if I hadn't learned anything up until then, I sure knew the difference between what was right and what was so terribly wrong.

Later, a job in Charleston took me to a job in San Francisco and then in 1973 to a job in New York. I became an importer of women's apparel and traveled all over Europe looking for inspiration and then all over Asia looking for production. I had a brief marriage of arrogance and then when that firestorm ended, I met Peter Frank. What a romance we had! Anyway, we married and three years later our daughter was born. Knowing I couldn't be much of a parent if I was out of the country or on the road somewhere domestically for almost half of the year, I retired. We left the city for the suburbs of New Jersey and our son was born. I was so bored I thought I would die, so I began to volunteer. I was class mom a number of times and still say that if I could get back the amount of time I spent in the car line waiting for one of my offspring to appear I'd be ten years younger. But life was good, almost idyllic.

Then the unthinkable happened. My mother was diagnosed with stage IV melanoma and she passed away quickly. Burying our parents is the natural order of life, but that doesn't mean it's easy. I was completely heartbroken. And then my siblings wanted to sell her house on Sullivan's Island to settle her estate. Now I was deeply depressed because I had lost my mother and was about to lose my sense of place in the world. How would I bring my children home to know their aunts and uncles and cousins if I didn't have a house? And I had given up my career and therefore my own income. Peter wasn't interested in stepping up for a second house, so I began scratching my head. What to do?

Well, given the fact that my children were in school, it had to be part-time work. But what could I do to earn enough money to cover a modest mortgage, taxes, and maintenance on that house?

Still an avid reader, I stumbled across a bestseller in paperback that I had not read. It was written by a wildly popular author at the time. After I finished I thought, *You know what? I can do this. I can write books!* It seemed like the perfect solution to my situation. I was so naïve I didn't know the odds were stacked against me of ever getting published. I didn't have an MFA, or even a BA. I just sat down and did it.

But how did I decide what to write about? Well, I already knew I wanted to write about the Lowcountry because I missed it so desperately. But something was bothering me and after a lot of thought I figured it out. My children were being raised in a bubble of peace and prosperity. I grew up with history happening all around me. They had no clue what my childhood had been. So I decided to tell a story that would show them the difference between the childhood they knew and mine. It took a while to get a manuscript together, but I finally did.

I used to believe that much of life was serendipitous. But now I suspect certain things are almost preordained. Call it fate, luck, or the hand of God, selling *Sullivan's Island* was just about the fastest thing that has ever happened in my entire professional life. It was published in January of 2000 and when I saw the first copy I was so overwhelmed, I wept. *Sullivan's Island* debuted on the *New York Times* list at number nine, which was pretty unheard of back in the day. The rest is history, thanks to a smart sales team, a talented marketing team, a great editor, and booksellers everywhere.

I'm always writing these days, or thinking about writing. How is my day structured? We rise early, have breakfast, read the newspapers, and dress for work. Then my husband drives to his office and I go to my office upstairs. I check my email, maybe make a phone call or two, and then settle down to write until noon. I have a small lunch, watch the news and the weather, and then I go back to my office, writing until three or four. It's not very glamorous but it sure is a lot of fun.

By Invitation Only is my nineteenth novel. It's a story of two families who are the Haves and the Have Nots. A wedding's being planned, things go haywire, and the proverbial tables are turned. One thing's certain: one side has terrible manners and could use a dose of Sister Miriam. I think it's surely one of my favorites and I hope it will be yours, too!

Wishing you all every good thing,
Dorothea Frank

Shrimp and Grits

Serves 2 to 4

For all those years when I was desperately missing the Lowcountry, one sure way to make myself feel a little better was to cook up a batch of shrimp and grits. For decades, before it became a trendy appetizer and dinner menu item in restaurants across the South and beyond, this simple, comforting dish was a Lowcountry breakfast staple. The truth is that no matter what time of day you serve them, shrimp and grits are always deeply satisfying. For best results, use coarse whole-grain grits or, even better, Anson Mills quick grits (www.ansonmills.com).

FOR THE SHRIMP

1 pound large shell-on shrimp
6 ounces thick-sliced applewood-smoked bacon (about 4 slices), chopped into ¼-inch pieces
¼ sweet onion, finely chopped
½ teaspoon sea salt
½ teaspoon freshly ground black pepper
¼ cup all-purpose flour
2 garlic cloves, minced
Juice of 1 lemon
2 green onions (white and light green parts), thinly sliced

FOR THE GRITS

2 cups milk
1 cup stone-ground grits

4 tablespoons unsalted butter

1 teaspoon sea salt

½ teaspoon freshly ground black pepper

To prepare the shrimp, peel and devein them, reserving the shells. Rinse the shrimp, drain thoroughly, and set aside.

Place the reserved shells in a medium saucepan and add 2 cups water. Bring to a gentle boil over medium heat (be careful not to let the liquid foam up and boil over). Reduce the heat and simmer, uncovered, until the liquid is reduced to 1 cup, about 30 minutes. Strain the shrimp stock into a glass measuring cup and set aside; discard the shells.

To make the grits, in a medium, heavy-bottomed saucepan, bring the milk and 2 cups water to a boil. Stir in the grits. Reduce the heat and simmer until cooked, about 30 minutes, stirring occasionally. Stir in the butter, salt, and pepper and keep warm on the side.

Meanwhile, to finish the shrimp, line a plate with paper towels. Place the chopped bacon in a large sauté pan and cook over medium heat, stirring occasionally, until the bacon is browned, about 10 minutes. Use a slotted spoon to transfer the bacon to the paper towels and set aside.

Pour off all but 2 tablespoons of the bacon fat and place the sauté pan over medium heat. Add the onion, salt, and pepper and sauté until lightly browned, 4 to 5 minutes.

Meanwhile, spread the flour in a shallow dish and dredge the reserved shrimp in it to coat thoroughly. Add the shrimp to the pan and sauté just until pink, about 4 minutes.

Stir in the garlic and cook until fragrant, about 30 seconds. Stir in the reserved shrimp stock and lemon juice and bring to a simmer, gently scraping up the browned bits from the bottom of the pan. Simmer until the gravy is heated through and slightly thickened, about 2 minutes.

Stir in the green onions and reserved bacon. Serve the shrimp over the hot grits.

Dorothea Benton Frank's Favorite Cocktails: Throwing Persimmons

When the trees burst with bright orange fruit, the kids might have their fun throwing persimmons during recess—but adults can make their own sort of fun. The mellow, distinctive flavor of the fruit is a beautiful pairing for bourbon. Infusing the spirit is simple—just cut up a persimmon, add a few black peppercorns for depth and a very faint spice, and let sit. From there, it's simple as can be to make a quick, refreshing drink with lemon and ginger ale. A light, refreshing pairing for any classic Southern dish; shrimp and grits, perhaps?

1½ ounces persimmon–black pepper bourbon (recipe below)
½ ounce fresh lemon juice
¼ ounce simple syrup
Ginger ale

Combine all ingredients except ginger ale in cocktail shaker with ice. Shake vigorously, then strain into a tall glass with fresh ice. Top with 2 ounces of ginger ale. Garnish with a thin slice of persimmon.

FOR THE PERSIMMON–BLACK PEPPER BOURBON
8 ounces bourbon
1 whole, ripe persimmon, top removed, cut into slices
¼ teaspoon whole black peppercorns

Combine bourbon, persimmon, and black peppercorns in a sealable container. Let steep for 24 hours. Strain, discarding solids, before using.

By Carey Jones and John D. McCarthy, authors of *Be Your Own Bartender: A Sure-Fire Guide to Finding (and Making) the Perfect Drink for You,* published November 2018; johnandcarey.com

Dorothea Benton Frank's
Letter to Her Readers III

Dear Readers,

I wanted to reach out to you all for a couple of reasons. One, to thank you for buying my books, for which I am seriously and eternally grateful, and two, to try and get to know y'all a little better. I'd love to hear from you to talk about *By Invitation Only* and others and I'd love to hear how you identify with the situations found in these pages.

Unlike the characters in *By Invitation Only*, my family does not now and never did own a farm, except my brother-in-law who grew cotton and soybeans and slaughtered the occasional hog. When I was about eight, visiting my oldest sibling, Lynn, and her husband, Scott, in Manning, South Carolina, during Thanksgiving week he would go out into the country to the farm with a whole host of men. They'd dig a pit, build a fire, put the hog on a spit, and commence drinking bourbon and basting the beast for the next twenty-four hours. On Wednesday or Thursday morning they'd reappear smelling like wood smoke and booze, looking like who did it and ran. We say when it comes to pig we eat everything but the oink. We did. They had pounds and pounds of pulled pork, but there was a small mountain of sausage and hash, too. I think we had turkey on Christmas but Thanksgiving was the other white meat. To this very day, I can still taste the pork, silky and smoky and melt-in-your-mouth tender.

There was always a football game on the television as Scott's brother-in-law was Alex Hawkins who played for the Baltimore Colts and who, by the way, helped me catch my first fish. A couple of years ago Alex turned up in Columbia, South Carolina, at a talk I was giving at the university. We marveled over how many years had passed and who knew then I'd be living a writer's life now?

If there was time to walk you through my childhood and later years, you'd probably say that I was destined to do something like this, given my history of 1950s and '60s classic Southern women's oppression. *We knew it! Sooner or later she was gonna blow!* But I think that maybe talking about the here and now is more interesting as it relates to this particular book.

In the last three years, both of my children have married. Our most recent wedding in October 2017 for our son, William, was a breeze. The groom's family gets off very easy. My husband and I threw a Lowcountry barbecue, including an oyster roast for the rehearsal dinner. The bride's family had never had the pleasure of wild, fresh-caught shrimp and grits with andouille sausage prepared by Lowcountry chefs or wild roasted oysters that came from the May River around Beaufort. We were blessed with a balmy night in October, so we decided to have it in our front yard, which looks at Charleston Harbor. It would have been more picturesque if it hadn't been pitch-black dark. Nonetheless, we hired a jazz trio to set the mood, put up a small tent, strung lights, and rented farm tables and chairs. There were lanterns and bales of hay topped with pumpkins and gourds everywhere. Our bride, Maddie Clark, is about the best thing to happen to our family in eons, so pretty and so smart. Except for my son-in-law, Carmine Peluso, who is handsome and wildly talented. And except for the child he and our daughter, Victoria, brought into this world last June. Ted. Ted is the true love of my life.

I had an occasion to serve on a panel with Lesley Stahl of *60*

Minutes in April last year, right before Ted was born. We were at the *Post and Courier* Book and Author Luncheon in Charleston along with several other authors, talking to eight hundred people, chatting them up and signing books. My daughter was there and she was heavy with child. Lesley took one look at her and then back to me and said that we were in for the greatest thrill of our lives. Lesley was there to promote her book *Becoming Grandma.* She began to tell us the story of her daughter's delivery of her grandchild and how we were going to love this child so much it would astound us. She was right.

I remember thinking, I have to be excited for my daughter's sake, that I was sure to love this child, but I'd keep my wits about me. I swore I'd never be one of those pathetic grandmothers with a thousand pictures on my phone, making everyone suffer them and stories about Little Johnny's tiny precious teeth.

So Ted came into the world last June and I lost my mind. I did. I have at least six hundred pictures of him on my phone and should we meet at a book signing or somewhere, please save a little time for Ted. And wait until you see the videos! And his precious tiny teeth. No, really! They're two little perfect pearls! Just yesterday he broke the skin of a clementine with them and sat there sucking the juice. At eight months! Einstein!

Lesley was right. I didn't even know there was this kind of happiness to be found on earth.

So many of the things I have just described to you can be found in this book but written in another way. Irma the sow of Diane's barbecue is reminiscent of the pork I ate on Thanksgiving and how it came to be on my plate. The decorations from Diane's barbecue look an awful lot like the decorations we had for Will and Maddie's rehearsal dinner, as do the tent, strung lights, and pumpkins. But praise the Lord, I don't have all of Diane's drama in my life. Otherwise, I'd go off the grid and live in a cave. On the page, it's hilarious. But in real life? Not so much. With the possible exception of Ramsey Lewis playing at a party. I'm such a fan of his!

This is how my books come to life. Current events make you remember your childhood. They make you muse and wonder how a singular event from your past would play out today. And what if you want to rewrite history? That, my friends, is one of the great joys of this work. You can make your enemies die from a wretched disease or you can humiliate them or you can just kill them. Or you can make your favorite characters good-looking and rich but super nice.

I love to help underdogs rise and help the hopeless find strength. And I love a little romance, but the unexpected kind where people get caught being naughty in the wrong place. I especially love to bring characters together to fall in love when they are older and not looking.

I hope there's always something in my books that maybe you didn't know before. For example, you might not have known that Edgar Allan Poe lived on Sullivan's Island before the Civil War (*Porch Lights*). Or maybe you didn't know about the summer when George Gershwin lived on Folly Beach and wrote the libretto for *Porgy and Bess* with Dorothy and DuBose Heyward (*Folly Beach*).

Mostly my stories take place in the Lowcountry of South Carolina. Sometimes they travel to other climes for a while. But to tell you the truth, there's so much wonderful history to discover in and around Charleston that I don't need to wander too far to bring you new and interesting fun facts. My job, as I see it, is to entertain and inform. I like to think of my readers laughing in the passages where I laugh. And maybe shedding a tear or two when I'm writing about something more emotional. And because I believe in the power of stories to bring people together to find common ground and understand each other more fully, my sincere hope is that my stories will deliver that satisfaction for you.

Please let me know if you've enjoyed this story and please come out to say hello if my summer tour is bringing me to somewhere nearby.

Wishing you all every good thing,
Dorothea Benton Frank

Smoked Pulled Pork Sandwiches with Slaw

Serves 12 to 16

In spite of my indelible memories of the incredible Thanksgiving pork we had at my sister and brother-in-law's place when I was a kid, I haven't ever found a good enough excuse to dig a pit and roast a whole hog myself. But that doesn't mean that I haven't prepared plenty of silky, smoky pulled pork in my suburban backyard. Far from it, thanks to my trusty charcoal grill and this method (with a tip of the hat to the wildly informative website www.amazingribs.com). For best results, season the pork shoulder with salt at least eight hours before smoking it.

One 5- to 7-pound bone-in pork shoulder
2½–3½ teaspoons kosher salt

FOR THE DRY RUB
2 tablespoons mild chili powder
2 tablespoons sweet paprika
2 tablespoons mustard powder
2 tablespoons ground cumin
2 tablespoons freshly ground black pepper
2 tablespoons light or dark brown sugar
2 tablespoons granulated sugar

FOR THE SLAW

1½ pounds red and/or green cabbage, shredded (about 12 cups)

2 large carrots, peeled and grated

½ cup mayonnaise

½ sweet onion, grated

2 tablespoons apple cider vinegar

1 teaspoon sugar

1 teaspoon kosher salt

1 teaspoon freshly ground black pepper

½ teaspoon celery seed

1 to 2 cups barbecue sauce, plus more for serving

Small slider or brioche buns, for serving

Special equipment: Charcoal grill; 1 to 1½ pounds smoking wood chunks or chips, such as hickory, oak, or pecan; leave-in meat thermometer

The day or night before smoking, sprinkle ½ teaspoon salt per pound of pork all over the shoulder and refrigerate it for at least 8 hours and up to 24 hours.

Meanwhile, make the rub: Mix together all the spices in a bowl or jar. Cover and set aside until needed. (You'll have about 1¼ cups spice rub and will use about half of it for the pork; store the remainder in a tightly closed jar in a cabinet for up to 2 months.)

Early the next morning, start a fire in a charcoal grill with a lid. When the coals are covered with gray ash, rake them to one side of the grill, creating a cooler zone on the other side to use for indirect cooking. Let the grill cool to 250°F. Scatter some wood over the coals. Place the cover on the grill until the wood begins to smoke. Adjust the vents on the bottom of the grill and in the lid so that there is sufficient airflow to keep the wood smoldering, but not so much that it ignites or flares.

Remove the meat from the refrigerator, brush it all over with water or apple juice (or bourbon—up to you!) and generously coat it all over with spice rub.

Place the shoulder fat side down on the grate on the cooler side of the grill, not directly over the coals. Insert a leave-in meat thermometer, ensuring that the probe is at least 1 inch from the bone and is hitting the middle of the meat. Cover the grill, arranging the lid so that the vent is directly over the meat. The temperature on the cooler side of the grill should stay between 225°F and 250°F while the meat cooks, so regulate the temperature by opening the vents wider to increase temperature and closing them slightly to reduce temperature; add more charcoal as necessary. For the first 2 to 3 hours, add more dry wood every 30 minutes, or as often as necessary to maintain the smoke. (The meat will only absorb the smoke during the first few hours of cooking, so you can stop adding the wood after that.)

Cook the meat until it reaches an internal temperature of 203°F, 8 to 12 hours. When it reaches about 150°F, it may stall there for a long time. At this point, you may either let it stay on the grill (it will eventually move up) or you can remove the shoulder from the grill, wrap it tightly in aluminum foil, and return it to the cooler side of the grill; this will speed up the cooking while still giving you excellent results—the outer "bark" may be somewhat softer than it would be otherwise, but the flavor and tenderness will be the same.

Meanwhile, prepare the slaw: In a large bowl, toss together the cabbage and carrots. In a small bowl, whisk together the mayonnaise, onion, vinegar, sugar, salt, pepper, and celery seed until well blended. Pour the dressing over the cabbage and stir until well coated and combined. Cover and refrigerate until needed.

When the pork is done, you can either pull it right away if it's close to serving time, or leave it on the cooled grill or in a 170°F oven for up to 2 hours (wrap it in foil if it's going to be sitting longer than that). About 30 minutes before serving, use two forks or your hands to pull the meat, discarding the bone and any big pieces of fat. Drizzle 1 to 2 cups barbecue sauce over the meat to keep it moist. Warm the remaining sauce in a small saucepan.

To serve, set out the pulled pork, warmed barbecue sauce, coleslaw, and buns, and let people assemble their own sandwiches.

Dorothea Benton Frank's Favorite Cocktails: Peach Season

While you fire up the grill for that pork shoulder, why not toss on some fruit for a cocktail as well? Fresh peaches take on great depth of flavor when grilled—their sugars caramelizing, the fruit taking on a bit of char. All that flavor translates into a lively summer cocktail when shaken with vodka, lemon, and mint, with a bit of club soda to lighten it all up. The fruit's natural sweetness and the bright burst of lemon are a perfect counterpart for rich, smoky pork.

½ peach, cut into three slices (plus additional for garnish)
Vegetable or canola oil
1½ ounces vodka
¾ ounce fresh lemon juice
¾ ounce simple syrup
8 mint leaves
Club soda

Lightly brush peach slices with vegetable or canola oil (to prevent sticking). Over high heat on a grill or grill pan, cook until well-charred on one side, then flip and repeat, approximately 2 minutes per side. Remove from heat and let rest until cool enough to handle.

In the bottom of a cocktail shaker, muddle the grilled peach until fully broken up. Add ice and all remaining ingredients other than club soda and shake vigorously, at least 15 seconds. Double-strain into a rocks glass with fresh ice. Top with one ounce of club soda. Garnish with a peach slice and three large sprigs of mint. (Tap the mint firmly against your hand before adding to the drink.)

By Carey Jones and John D. McCarthy, authors of *Be Your Own Bartender: A Sure-Fire Guide to Finding (and Making) the Perfect Drink for You*, published November 2018; johnandcarey.com

Understanding My Mom

William Frank

What can I say about my mom? At least what can I say that hasn't already been said? Mom was beyond measure. She was more than just a mother to me; she was my best friend. She taught me so much, not just the standard things but stuff like how to draw, how to sew on a button, and how to cook a steak. I got a lot of mileage out of that last one. Rather, the most important thing she taught me was how to laugh. I'll never figure out how she was able to make me crack up no matter how I was feeling. Mom turned humor into an art form and could wield it with surgical precision. I cannot stress enough how necessary this was to parent me. Every time I came home from school and told her about some drama that felt like the end of the world she would roll her eyes, give me a nudge, and make me laugh about how something virtually identical happened to her. This would pull me out of my head and back toward what mattered. Mom was at heart a teacher and a storyteller and perhaps the only way to convey what she meant to me is through stories of how she impacted me.

When I was six, I loved Transformers. Hasbro was in the process of reissuing some of their older stock and I wanted one called Silverbolt. Silverbolt was a robot that turned into a jet and could combine with four other robots into a bigger robot. It was all I wanted in the world ever since I saw it at FAO Schwarz. Furthermore, at the wise old age of six, I was becoming wary of Santa. I told Mom that I was testing to see if Santa was real. If I got Silverbolt then I would know for sure that he was real. This sent Mom on a mission. The only problem? Silverbolt wasn't for sale. It was a display model only and would never be released in stores. But that wasn't so much a problem for Mom as it was for Hasbro. First, she called FAO and they didn't have it. Then she called FAO's parent company until she finally got to Hasbro itself. The salesperson at Hasbro stated plainly that it was impossible to send one out as only a few were made. Mom's response was that then they had to tell me that Santa and Christmas weren't real. At that moment they suddenly found one for me and on Christmas there he was. I exploded. I had never been so happy in my life. I believed in Santa for way too long after that and I still have Silverbolt to this day.

Mom had a tenderness that was impossible to measure but she didn't have a tolerance for, let's call it nonsense. She suffered fools as well as ice cubes tolerated lava. She could always see right through me, which made it very hard to get away with anything. As a child I liked exactly three things: movies, comics, and action figures. Getting me to try anything new was akin to pulling teeth. When I had to try something new like football or soccer, I would usually respond with a halfhearted attempt. Followed by complaining that it was too hard, and it was like Sisyphus pushing a rock up the hill. Mom's response was that's nice, but the rock is going up the hill. I hate to admit it, but she was usually right. Mom was more than smart, she was wise.

She always had her eye on the big picture and wasn't afraid to do what it took to set me straight. The best example of this was when I was twenty-four. I was finishing law school and Mom noticed I wasn't very socially active but more importantly she could see how that was affecting me even if I couldn't. Mom suggested I try online dating. I responded with a litany of reasons why that wouldn't work for me. Mom looked me in the eyes and told me either I could make a profile, or she would do it for me. Mom did not make idle threats. I promptly made a Match profile, not a real one, just one to say I did it. Mom found the profile and told me to fix it or start thinking of ways to describe myself. Terrified, I brought it up to snuff and shortly thereafter met someone. We married three years later.

The only thing greater than Mom's mind was her heart. When Mom was in your corner you could not lose. I always wanted to be a lawyer, but I was never good at standardized tests. Mom never let me quit my dream and did everything in her power to help me pass the LSATs and even more to pass the bar. She was there each step of the way cheering louder and louder. When I graduated law school, she even gave me my diploma. It's one of my happiest memories not just because of that sweet moment, but seconds after she handed it to me, she came up behind me and hugged me right onstage. She was happier than I was when I got Silverbolt. Mom didn't just celebrate success, she magnified it and could make you feel like you had saved the world.

Perhaps most of all Mom loved a good time. She was a master of ceremonies bar none. She really shined when it came to birthdays. People who knew my mom knew that a Dot Party was an event not to be missed, but birthdays were on a whole other level. My favorite birthday story isn't mine but my dad's. When Dad turned sixty Mom was determined to give him the night of his life. She raised a tent on the tennis court, hired a DJ and invited everyone, and I do mean everyone, my dad ever knew. From Grandma and Grandpa to his college roommate and even childhood friends. She topped it off with his favorite food and speeches from all the special people in his life. It's the happiest I'd ever seen my dad. We carried on late into the night, until our neighbors called the cops. But Mom, ever the hostess, convinced them to join us.

Mom would do whatever it took to ensure people were happy and was not above acting silly or making a crude joke to make people laugh. She had a way of making people have fun no matter what they were doing. Always keeping the mood light and happy in the house and ensuring everyone kept smiling. For instance, during family game nights my dad would take the game, usually UNO, very seriously. Victoria and I would groan at this mandatory fun, so Mom's response was to pass me cards under the table to ensure Dad lost. I'd be mortified but take the cards. Dad would catch on and break out laughing. Then the game would really begin.

People mattered to Mom. She could take a random person, speak to them for thirty seconds, and be their best friend. I think that's why she was so successful as a writer. Fundamentally, she cared about people very deeply. I can't even count how many times I walked in on her late at night answering emails from fans. I'm so proud of Mom and all she accomplished and I'm thankful not just for everything she did for me but also how she touched so many people's lives. I hope you get that from reading this anthology and Mom becomes as great a friend to you as she is to me.

Photograph Credits

Unless otherwise noted, photographs are courtesy
of the respective author.